O9-AIC-518

"The only thing we have to fear is fear itself."

Say hello to fear. . . .

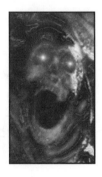

MORE ZOMBIE TERROR FROM EDEN STUDIOS

All Flesh Must Be Eaten™
ZOMBIE HORROR ROLEPLAYING GAME

Zombie Master Screen

FORTHCOMING

Enter the Zombie
(FALL 2001)

Pulp Zombies
(WINTER 2001)

A Fistful o' Zombies
(SPRING 2002)

All Flesh Must Be Eaten

The Book of All Flesh

EDITED BY JAMES LOWDER

EDEN
STUDIOS INC

The Book of All Flesh is published by Eden Studios, Inc.

This collection © 2001 by Eden Studios, Inc. and James Lowder; all rights reserved.

Cover art and interior art © 2001 by George Vasilakos; all rights reserved.

Similarities between characters in this book and persons living or dead are entirely coincidental.

ALL FLESH MUST BE EATEN is a trademark owned by Eden Studios, Inc.

Reproduction of material from within this book for any purposes, by photographic, digital, or other methods of electronic storage and retrieval, is prohibited.

Please address questions and comments concerning this book, as well as requests for notices of new publications, by mail to Eden Studios, 3426 Keystone Avenue #3, Los Angeles, CA 90034-4731.

Visit us at at www.edenstudios.net and www.allflesh.com.

FIRST PAPERBACK EDITION

10 9 8 7 6 5 4 3 2 1

Eden Studios publication EDN 8700, October 2001.

ISBN 1-891153-87-0

Printed in the United States.

ACKNOWLEDGMENTS

All works are original to this anthology, and are printed by permission of the author.

Introduction by James Lowder. © 2001 by James Lowder.

"Consumption" by Steve Eller. © 2001 by Steve Eller.

"Dust Bowl" by C. Dean Andersson. © 2001 by C. Dean Andersson.

"Susan" by Robin D. Laws. © 2001 by Robin D. Laws.

"Number of the Beast" by Kenneth Lightner. © 2001 by Kenneth Lightner.

"Dawn of the Living-Impaired" by Christine Morgan. © 2001 by Christine Morgan.

"Trinkets" by Tobias S. Buckell. © 2001 by Tobias S. Buckell.

"Murdermouth" by Scott Nicholson. © 2001 by Scott Nicholson.

"Calliope" by Aaron T. Solomon. © 2001 by Aaron T. Solomon.

"Prometheus Unwound" by Matt Forbeck. © 2001 by Matt Forbeck.

"Salvation" by L. H. Maynard and M. P. N. Sims. © 2001 by L. H. Maynard and M. P. N. Sims.

"Take, Eat" by John C. Hay. © 2001 by John C. Hay.

"Sifting Out the Hearts of Men" by Warren Brown and Lana Brown. © 2001 by Warren Brown and Lana Brown.

"The Other Side of Theory" by Daniel Ksenych. © 2001 by Daniel Ksenych.

"Inspecting the Workers" by Jim C. Hines. © 2001 by Jim C. Hines.

"Last Resort" by Michael Laimo. © 2001 by Michael Laimo.

"Same Night, Different Farmhouse" by Gregory G. Kurczynski. © 2001 by Gregory G. Kurczynski.

"Middles" by Robert E. Vardeman. © 2001 by Robert E. Vardeman.

"One Last, Little Revenge" by Ed Greenwood. © 2001 by Ed Greenwood.

"The Cold, Gray Fingers of My Love" by Pete D. Manison. © 2001 by Pete D. Manison.

"On-Line Zombies and Dry-Land Skates" by Scot Noel. © 2001 by Scot Noel.

"Hollywood Flesh" by L. J. Washburn.© 2001 by L. J. Washburn.

"Scenes from a Foreign Horror Video, with Zombies and Tasteful Nudity" by Mark McLaughlin. © 2001 by Mark McLaughlin.

"La Carrera de la Muerte" by Joe Murphy. © 2001 by Joe Murphy.

"Electric Jesus and the Living Dead" by Jeremy Zoss. © 2001 by Jeremy Zoss.

"Live People Don't Understand" by Scott Edelman. © 2001 by Scott Edelman.

TABLE OF CONTENTS

Introduction

Move to the edge of your seat.

Perch on the very brink of that couch or La-Z-Boy.

Are you uncomfortable? Good. If this book does its job, you'll stay that way for a while.

Horror stories are supposed to do that—cause unease, stir up unwelcome thoughts, make you distrust pat phrases like "everything will be fine." A well-crafted tale of terror should demolish those numbing self-deceptions and lulling luxuries in which we wrap ourselves. It should tear away, if only for a moment, the shield that separates us from the primal dark. Terrible, hunting things populate that darkness, and sometimes they have bigger fangs and bloodier claws than we can imagine. We all know the truth of that, if not from firsthand experience then from the parade of cannibal serial killers and vengeance-crazed terrorists trotted out nightly on the news.

Some monsters, as we all know in our hearts, are quite real.

Like zombies.

A foundation of fact underlies the popular concept of the living dead. Obscure? Yes. Misunderstood? Most certainly. For generations in Haiti, the Bizango secret societies have punished enemies of the social order through the use of zombification. Only in the last twenty years has the research of such scholars as ethnobiologist Wade Davis made it clear that organic toxins can be used to create a zombie—that is, someone who seems to die, only to be later extracted from the grave a drug-numbed, will-deprived slave.

The earliest published descriptions of the victims of zombification—such as those found in W. B. Seabrook's 1929 Haitian travelogue, *The Magic Island*—failed to convey the truth behind the sensational images of "dead men working in a cane field." Still, the notion that such monsters did exist swiftly and certainly fixed itself in the Western psyche. Shortly after its introduction by Seabrook, the zombie was snapped up by Hollywood as the ideal low budget movie menace. Initially at least, zombie characters required little in the way of make-up, just some tattered clothes and perhaps halved ping pong balls for eyes. Certainly, the role demanded little acting skill; anyone with the ability to move with Al Gore's grace and stare as if possessed of George W. Bush's IQ could make a go of it.

Though they surely raised the scare factor of such minor, but nevertheless classic films as *White Zombie* (1932) and *I Walked with a Zombie* (1943), the living dead tended to be featured players in less-inspired fare, like *Zombies on Broadway* (1945) and *Zombies of Mora Tau* (1957). They also shuffled ceaselessly through the pages of popular fiction magazines in the 1930s and 1940s. As with the cinema, the pulp magazines offered some interesting treatments of the zombie theme— Manley Wade Wellman's "The Song of the Slaves" in *Weird Tales*, or Theodore Roscoe's "A Grave Must Be Deep" in *Argosy*, for example. More often, though, the walking dead appeared as the bland and blundering minions of the criminal masterminds who foolishly set themselves against The Spider and the era's other pulp heroes.

For a time, the sheer repetition of this clumsy, uninspired depiction, in both films and fiction, muffled the "ring of truth" that had made the zombie such a compelling night-stalker in the first place. Not until *Night of the Living Dead* (1968) and its redefinition of the zombie as aggressive, self-motivated threat did the archetype regain its impact. To be sure, the zombies of George Romero's Living Dead trilogy diverge in many ways from the historically more accurate drug-dulled slaves. Yet Romero's films, particularly the second and third in the series, successfully encapsulate the central notion that makes the real-world zombie so chilling: as a monster, it is more like us than not. Everyone holds the potential creature within. All it takes is the right trigger, the momentary lapse, to step irrevocably from human to inhuman.

The Living Dead films, with their strong strain of social commentary, also suggested that the zombie could be a rich and endlessly malleable symbol for post-modern humankind. To be sure, the zombie, now caked in gore, remained a mainstay of low-budget horror films and slapdash modern pulp. But authors of considerable talent—represented in such noteworthy collections as *The Mammoth Book of Zombies*, *The Ultimate Zombie*, and the directly Romero-inspired *Book of the Dead* and *Book of the Dead 2*—helped secure the living dead a place in serious horror fiction. The nature of justice, the meaning of death, and the place of individual expression in a mass media-driven society are only some of the themes dealt with in the new breed of zombie fiction.

Wide and varied subject matter was a goal in putting together this collection as well, and the authors delivered, turning in stories that take on corporate culture, political correctness, and the nature of love. There are a variety of tones here, too, from the facetious to the lyrical, with content touching upon everything from TV talk shows to cutting edge scientific theory to such literary classics as Thorton Wilder's *Our Town*. The zombies in this collection stalk across Civil War battlefields, lunar mining colonies, and the carefully manicured lawns of suburbia.

This range of settings makes *The Book of All Flesh* particularly representative of *All Flesh Must Be Eaten*, the role-playing game with which it is linked. *AFMBE*, as the game is known to its dedicated fans, emphasizes the flexibility of the zombie theme, offering players the chance to face off against the living dead in the Old West, the far future, the world of the martial arts hero, and a dozen other places and eras. This anthology also offers up its share of tales of survival, the hallmark of the *AFMBE* gaming experience.

Which brings us back to the role of horror fiction. A good tale of terror causes unease, and it does so in the name of entertainment, in the name of art—and in the name of survival. Horror fiction does everything it can to remind the reader of the dangers of the dark. Perched on the edge of your chair, you are just a bit less of a target. If you question things actively, take less at face value, you are one more person who stands a chance of fighting off the lulling comfort that is our own society's formula for zombification.

—James Lowder
August 2001

CONSUMPTION

STEVE ELLER

At the end of the world, the angel sounds a trumpet. It drones like a car horn.

✣ ✣ ✣

The strange dream jars me awake. Slumped over the steering wheel, my chest throbs and it's hard to catch my breath. My spine is a running flame as I fall back into the driver's seat. The horn falls silent, but its ghost echoes in my ears.

How long was I sleeping on it?

I see nothing when I check the side mirrors, but my eyes aren't to be trusted anymore. Not after all they've seen. Such a loud noise, out in the middle of nowhere, might as well be a dinner-bell.

So I was wrong about the angel. But it's still the end of the world.

My journal rests open across my lap, one page half-covered with words I can't recall writing, the other as blank as the open sky in the windshield. The last sentence I'd scrawled before passing out flows down the page like cooling blood.

There's something you need to know, the sentence says. *The world is a different place now.*

"Amen to that," I say, shutting the book and sliding it into the glove compartment. "Amen to that."

The RV rests on the shoulder of the road, tail-end halfway blocking one lane. But getting hit isn't something I have to worry about. I haven't seen another car for days. Not one that was moving, anyway. Scratching my groggy head, I try to recall how I got here. I don't remember driving, let along stopping. The last thing I recall is the Tucson city limits in my rearview mirror.

The keys hang in the ignition, turned to Off. At least the battery won't be dead.

A clear plastic bottle leans in the dashboard cup-holder, and I take a long drink of tepid water. My throat is as parched as the landscape outside. Sand shimmers golden in the light of a half-risen sun, stretching unbroken to a horizon that seems to melt into the sky. Below cloudless azure, only a few scattered cacti dot the endless desert.

I turn the key and start the engine. The interior of the RV

is stiflingly warm, but I can't waste gas by running the air conditioner. And the only safe time to roll down a window is when I'm moving. Cranking my wheels, I bounce the RV back onto the road.

I grab a bag of potato chips from behind my seat and tear it open with my teeth. I munch as I drive, listening to the hot blacktop whining and popping beneath the tires. The speedometer touches sixty, and I lower my window. Breeze caressing my face, I open my mouth to taste the fresh air.

If it wasn't for gas, I'd have everything I need right here.

Well, almost everything.

✣   ✣   ✣

"If you want something bad enough," the angel whispers in my ear, "you'll find it. Whether it's there or not."

✣   ✣   ✣

My foot rises from the floorboard, hovering above the brake. I hadn't been sleeping this time, only drifting in some semi-alert state as mile after mile of Interstate 10 disappeared beneath me. I wonder how long I've been driving, mind wandering its own way, before the angel spoke to me.

This isn't the first time I've seen a mirage. The toe of my sneaker touches the gas pedal, just enough to kick off the cruise control. Squinting to knock my eyes back into alignment, I study the figure at the side of the road ahead. If a mirage, it's more tenacious than most. It grows more solid, more distinct as I near it. Just to be safe, I roll up my window.

The figure is small and slender. Dark tank-top against sunburned skin. Denim shirt tied like a belt above khaki hiking shorts. More reddish flesh between pant-leg and boot. Long brown ponytail beneath a wide-brimmed hat. No knapsack or gear.

I tap the brake, looking harder for the telltale signs. The more recently they've resurrected, the more difficult it is to distinguish them from living people. But I see no dried blood, no frayed wounds on the exposed skin.

The surest sign is always a vacant look in the eyes, like they use a sense other than sight to guide them. This one wears mirrored sunglasses, so I can't tell.

When I'm close enough to make out a hint of face, the figure raises a hailing left hand. A good sign. I've never seen one of the resurrected do more than wave its arms like tree branches in the wind as it hurries after a meal.

Its right hand slides behind its hips, as if hiding something. Probably a weapon. Another good sign.

Heart hammering, I floor the brake. Being still for more than a moment is unnerving, so I lean across the passenger seat and unlock the door quickly. Hot, dry air bursts into the RV as the door swings open. For a moment my heart stops, and I wait breathlessly.

Is this how it feels to be one of them? No heart thrumming in your chest? Breathless with excitement at the chance of finding a living person?

"Hey," the figure says.

Its head pokes into the vehicle. I see a jut of jaw, a wedge of peeling skin above a scooped neckline. The voice, the first I've heard in days, is wearily soft. It seems empty and dry, as if becoming part of the desert.

"Can I get in?"

The head tilts back and I see its face. Her face. A girl, maybe late teens or early twenties. But there is something old in her eyes. Something wounded or broken. Maybe she's not so much weary as wary.

Smart girl.

I hear a thud, like a stone falling to the sand. Her right hand, empty, touches the passenger seat.

"Are you alone?" she asks.

More than you'll even know.

"Yes," I say.

✜ ✜ ✜

The angel's voice is beautiful, as soothing as a child's bedtime song. Hair the color of gingerbread snares flecks of sunlight.

✜ ✜ ✜

"So that's when they all raped me. Can I have one of those chips?"

"Oh, I'm sorry," I say. "Here, just take the whole bag."

"You sure?"

"Yeah, I've got plenty. It's not as if I have to pay for anything anymore."

"I'm Amber, by the way. Did I already tell you that?"

The girl smiles, desiccated skin crinkling at the corners of her eyes. The dark stains on her teeth make me wonder what she's been eating to stay alive.

"Yes, you told me. But that's okay."

"So after all that, I guess I was a little bit leery of getting in with you. What did you say your name was again?"

"I didn't actually." I can't help returning her grin. "But it's Luther."

"Now that's a name you don't hear everyday."

"Most days, I don't hear anything."

I see the familiar sadness glistening in her eyes, always so close to the surface. It's an aspect common to everyone I've encountered since the resurrections began. My only wish is that I could take my thoughtless words back. There's enough misery nowadays, without creating our own.

"So did you know any of them?"

"No," she says.

I sense the relief in her voice, to be back on a tolerable subject. Better to talk about a gang-rape than a world where the dead resurrect and come after you, mouth open.

"I think I might be able to recognize some of them," Amber goes on, "but not all five. My eyes were closed sometimes, too."

"You can forget about the police, you know."

"I've forgotten about almost everything."

This time, it's her turn to regret the words. Amber winces, stares down at the silver foil inside the chip bag. Her sorrow radiates from her skin like heat. Her story is a poignant one, but we all have a story these days. The only ones who don't have a tale to tell aren't talking anymore. They're just shambling around city streets or wandering the countryside, looking for their next warm meal.

"Right there," Amber says, pointing through the windshield. "That's where it happened."

A hundred yards off the road, two stone hills rise from the desert, vivid red against the sand. It's the only spot of shade for miles around. No wonder Amber's attackers chose it. They could take their time there, out of the sun.

She'd walked quite a ways back toward Tucson. But she never would've made it all the way there. And even if she had, she wouldn't have liked what she found. I hadn't.

"Were they protesters, too?"

"Yeah," she says. "But I don't think any of them were PETA."

"I can't believe somebody actually tried such a crazy thing."

"It was supposed to be a demonstration rally." Amber shrugs. "You know, that we shouldn't just kill the resurrected. They might really be some new form of life that needs to be respected. It was supposed to raise awareness, but it turned bad."

"Jeez," I say, unable to suppress a laugh. "I'm sorry, but did anybody actually think offering a hungry zombie a veggie burger was a good idea?"

"Looking back, it wasn't too awful smart." Amber laughs too, in a nervous bark. Tears come, but they seem more from pent-up anguish than amusement. "So more resurrected start coming out of the woodwork, and we all have to take off. The rally turns into a huge riot scene. Somebody cops my bicycle, so I have no wheels. The guys in the Jeep motion me over, and I'm in no position to refuse a ride."

Unwinding the shirt from her waist, Amber buries her face in it. Her shoulders buck, but she is out of tears. Her breathing sounds labored through the thick cloth.

"I'm sorry," I say, for lack of any other words.

"They kept talking, all the time they were . . . you know. Saying they were going to eat me. Then laughing at the *oh-so-clever* double meaning. God, what a thing to say to somebody."

"I'm sorry," I say again, more at a loss than before.

Amber lifts her face, and I see tiny chip crumbs dotting her chin. She exhales deeply, as if it's all finished in her mind now.

"There's a cave back in there, you know. I found it after they put me out of the Jeep. There are markings all over the walls. Like cave-paintings."

"Who left them?"

"Who knows? Maybe someday someone will see our markings and wonder who we were."

"You think?"

"I don't know."

"Maybe we'll spot that Jeep pretty soon," I say, "flipped over on the side of the road. If any of them are resurrected, I'll let you run them over."

"Aw, now you're just trying to cheer me up," Amber says, crumpling the empty bag.

"Throw it on the floor. I'll dump the trash when I stop for gas. Las Cruces is east of here someplace."

"Okay." She rubs her eyes. "So what's your story?"

"Huh?"

"Come on, I've been rattling on and on since you picked me up. What about you? Is this your RV, or did you find it?"

"No, it's mine. I still owe the bank a year's worth of payments, but I don't think they'll be coming to repossess it anytime soon."

"I guess not."

"Me and my daughter used to like to take road trips. This is much better than traveling in a car."

"How old was she?"

Amber doesn't have to finish the question—how old was she *when she died.*

"Ten. Almost."

"How long ago?"

"Right after," I say. "Right after it started."

✛ ✛ ✛

"There's been a marked resurgence in certain diseases," the doctor says.

His eyes are huge and brown, brimming with sympathy. It almost seems genuine, rather than a trick he learned in med school. His labcoat is an immaculate white, bearing a namepin with a half-dozen syllables. But I've given up trying to pronounce his last name. His first name is Veejay. It sticks in my mind because it makes me think of MTV.

"Even before the resurrections began," he continues, "some newer versions of old illnesses had begun to surface."

"Just tell me," I say, trying to keep my voice even.

"Very well. Your daughter has tuberculosis. So far, her particular strain has proven resistant to established treatments."

Tuberculosis.

The name rings almost ridiculous in my head, conjuring images of florid turn of the century novels. Of men with waxed mustaches, and women in bustled skirts. Of gaslights, and blood spots on lace handkerchiefs.

Then an ironic thought hits me. Another name for tuberculosis is *consumption.* The world is tumbling down around us as the dead resurrect to consume the living, and my little daughter contracts consumption. I feel like laughing, but if I start, I might not be able to stop. I'll laugh until I swallow my tongue, or my heart bursts.

"So what do we do?"

"We pursue a more aggressive treatment," Doctor Veejay says. "But I must warn you, we are near the crisis point at this hospital. Staff is not reporting, medical shipments are not arriving. We are well past capacity with patients. And the morgue is working around the clock to make sure . . ."

He stops talking. I wonder what he sees in my eyes.

"I'm sorry," he says. "But you need to know the truth."

"So the outlook is. . . ?"

"Not good."

✛ ✛ ✛

"I'm so sorry, Luther."

"That was months ago. I've been on the move ever since."

Amber fidgets in her seat. I can tell she wants to ask me

more. Being silent is difficult these days. Our voices are all we have to bind us together now. Our voices, and the meat under our skin.

"Go ahead and ask," I say. "I don't mind."

"What was her name?"

"Alison. Alison Grace."

"That's pretty."

"I used to call her Al-G. You know, like algae."

"I hope she didn't suffer."

"No, she didn't. I wouldn't let her."

Dusk is already gathering at the horizon. Traveling east, the days always seem shorter. Or maybe I slept longer than I'd thought. I'll have to pull over soon, and wait for tomorrow to look for gas. It's not safe to drive at night. One piece of glass on a darkened road could be the difference between life and death.

Amber has been quiet a long time. Instead of her warm sorrow, I sense a coolness between us now. From the corner of my eye I notice the muscles in her face tightening. Her gaze is too focused straight ahead.

"What's the matter?" I ask her.

"What you just said—that you wouldn't let her suffer. What did you mean?"

"I couldn't watch her waste away in some hospital bed."

"Did you help her die?"

I can hear my knucklebones rattling softly against the steering wheel. There is indictment in Amber's voice, and I don't care for it. What does she know? A silly little girl who almost got herself killed in an animal rights rally. How could she understand?

"Letting go is hard," I tell Amber. "I did what I had to do."

"I'm sorry about your daughter, Luther. But I don't agree with mercy killing."

She doesn't understand. She can't understand.

"The world is a different place now."

"I know," she says, shaking her head. "But that doesn't change—"

My throat tightens, but I can't stop the words.

"I trapped one of them, with myself for bait. I tied it down in my garage and used a circular saw to cut off its arms and legs. But its mouth kept snapping."

"What?" Her gaze focuses on me. "What did you do that for?"

"My daughter was so sick, coughing up bloody spit onto her chin. She would've died. Nobody even cared that I took her out of the hospital. I guess it saved them the trouble of cremating her. I brought her home, and held her against its mouth. And let it bite."

"Oh my God, Luther. What are you saying?"

"Then I burned it."

Amber tries her best to hide her unease, but it breaks in tiny waves across her face. Her eyes study the darkening landscape outside the RV. I'm no mind reader, but she has to be wondering if she could survive a jump from a vehicle doing sixty. And how long she could survive outside.

"I don't want to hear any more, Luther."

"I couldn't let her go," I say, the world shimmering like a dream through my tears. "I couldn't let her die like that when there was another way."

"Luther, stop now."

"But I couldn't stand the thought of her out in the world, wandering around. She was so small. Someone could hurt her."

Amber falls silent. I don't even hear her breathing. When I look her way, she is gazing back into the RV. Toward the closed bedroom door.

When she glances back at me, her eyes don't have time to focus. I hit her with my fist, right below her cheekbone.

Jamming the brake, I steer onto the shoulder and kill the engine. Dust rises, yellow clouds filling my windows. For a moment, it seems there's no world outside. I grab Amber and haul her back into the RV. When I open the bedroom door, I hear tiny chains rasping against the vinyl floor on the other side. I pitch Amber's boneless body inside and close the door.

Staggering back to the driver's seat, I see Amber's shirt on the floor. I wipe the sweat from my face with it, then toss it over my shoulder onto a stack of empty food bags and discarded clothes. I'll clean it all up when I find some gas.

Settling into my seat, I fetch my journal from the glovebox. But I don't have anything to write tonight. I drop the book onto my lap and close my eyes.

Before sleep can carry me away, I remember to check the doorlocks.

✛ ✛ ✛

The angel looks at me, but she doesn't speak. I'm not sure if she even sees me anymore. Her little mouth is red.

Dust Bowl

C. DEAN ANDERSSON

"Sucks." Jimmy Veech spit between the iron bars he'd welded over the truck's open window on his side. The open window made it easy to poke a gun between the bars and shoot dead'uns, but it also let in cold air. Couldn't roll up the window either. Jimmy let a dead'un carrying a big rock get a little too close last month. Broke out the glass. Don't see that much, a dead'un lugging around a rock or stick, but it only takes once to lose a window or your life.

Jimmy had found a new window, but couldn't afford it. Every morning for almost the week since the big snow, we'd been coming up empty patrolling down slick Texas roads, over rolling hills and flat prairies. Roads usually had wide ditches on each side, fields beyond, not many trees. Not finding any dead'uns meant not getting extra money from state bounties. We were both running short of funds.

So I tried to cheer him up. "Hell, Jimmy, always going to be more dead'uns for us to kill, long as people keep dying out of town." In cities, when somebody died someone usually knew it and took care of them before they could wake up hungry. "Hunting will be better when it warms up some. Too cold for live ones or dead'uns."

Jimmy scratched the gray stubble on his bony chin. "Too cold and a half with a cherry on top."

"Cherry?" I laughed at that one. Most times Jimmy said "whipped cream on top."

"Never had you no cherry on top of nothin' I'll bet. 'Fore your time, 'fore the dead started in walkin' and messin' up the good times. I sure miss me little things like cherries on top, and cherry limeade. Never had you none of that neither, right, kid?"

I'd turned twenty-five last summer, but I was never going to be anything but a kid to Jimmy. He never called me by my name, which was Frank Culvert.

I was four when the dead started walking. Mom and Dad and Sis were in the first batch to get killed and gnawed on. Happened way north of Dallas, toward the Red River, on our farm. Me? I hid until my folks and sister woke up dead'uns and came after me.

I ran far and fast. Neighbors saved me, raised me, taught me to kill dead'uns. I still liked killing dead'uns, when I could find one.

The folks who saved me, Carl and Hanna Dalton and their kids, died later on of some kind of plague. I was around fifteen. Jimmy had worked with Carl one time, so he knew them and me, got me hired to drive patrol and kill dead'uns with him for the State of Texas, which kept me from being drafted onto a Fed work gang in some other state.

Dead'uns out of town usually ended up finding a highway to walk down. Don't know why. Maybe it was a familiar thing from when they'd been alive and driving cars, same as those dead'uns who'd crowded shopping malls the first months after the Dead Bug started them walking. But whatever the reason, road patrollers like Jimmy and me usually found dead'uns to kill along empty country roads and interstates most ever day.

Had a drink from the bottle Jimmy had brought along, made a face at the taste of his homemade hooch, handed it to him.

Jimmy took a pull from the bottle, capped it, put it on the seat between us. He straightened his faded orange Texas Longhorns football champions cap that he'd found on the side of the road one time. He thought it looked sharp on his bald head. He'd looked for another one for me. But I'd told him I would stick with my Stetson. It's a black one with a leather band and a silver buckle. Had it about a year. The dead'un that'd been wearing it also sported a wide leather belt with a champion rodeo buckle. That also looked good on me. But I sold the dead'un's boots—they were too small—and stuck with my tough lace-up, steel-toed, bullhide workboots.

Jimmy slapped his leg. "Cherry limeade be damned! Don't miss it like I miss me how it used to was, back when I started in workin' for the Texas Highways—"

"Oh, boy! Come on and tell me again how it used to be, Jimmy. Maybe I've forgotten some of it." The truck hit a deep rut hidden under snow. The old buggy bounced, rattled, shuddered, slid a little. Dust rose from the seat cushions.

I decided to try and get the jump on Jimmy this time. "Tell me how the worst you'd usually have to do on morning patrol was to maybe fill out a Texas Highway Fixit Request on something like a bridge guard rail."

Jimmy spit out the window.

"Or maybe you'd find a road sign like a curve warning or stop sign that'd been pulled down during the night by damned kids who thought it was funny."

"Damned kids is right."

"But mostly all you'd find was a critter or two that had been run over and stayed dead back then, to scrape off the blacktop with a shovel and toss in the ditch for the crows and turkey vultures and coyotes."

"Hey!" Jimmy pointed. "There's a big'un!"

I saw it. The dead'un was stumbling along through the snow a hundred feet or so out in the field that ran next to the road. "Money on the hoof!"

"Two hundred pounds easy!" He grabbed the high-powered rifle that had been leaning against the seat between his legs.

I speeded up to get closer quick, and slid a little sideways in the snow stopping. But I knew I wasn't going fast enough to end up in a ditch, and I didn't. "Wonder what happened to its pants?" The dead'un was naked below its dirty gray shirt-tail.

Jimmy chambered a cartridge. "Maybe died screwin' somethin' or was in the john when some dead'un got the jump."

"Shoot its ass."

"You think its brain's in its ass, kid?" Jimmy took aim out the bars over the window.

The dead'un got whirled 'round by Jimmy's bullet ripping through its left butt cheek. Bullet left a little hole going in and a big one going out on the other side, through its blue-gray dead belly. Both holes started oozing the thick black stuff dead'uns have for blood. But the dead'un didn't go down, and it didn't stop walking because of those holes. It started staggering toward us for a meal on wheels.

Jimmy lowered the rifle. "Nope, its brain weren't in its ass." Folks had discovered early on that the only way to stop a dead-'un was to kill the brains it had left, few as that might be.

Jimmy let it come near the truck to save us a walk in the snow. Got close enough I could see one of its eyes was missing and it had something orange sticking out of its left nostril.

Jimmy's next shot made the dead'un's head jerk and spurt some black ooze. Thing flopped down in the snow near the road and didn't move any more.

We left the motor running and the heater with it while we got out and threw that big dead'un in the back of the truck. Held our breath best we could. It'd been walking more than a few days. Decay was working on its face and hands and feet, but it hadn't been a dead'un so long it'd lost all its fat, and that was going to be good news for us when we put it on the scales at Highway HQ to get our state bounty figured.

I pulled the orange thing out of its nose. "Damned wood

pencil!" I cleaned it off in the snow. "Still got a point on it. Eraser, too." I slipped it in my coat pocket.

Jimmy was wearing his big green army coat and me my thick peacoat and both of us some good leather work gloves, but you better believe we were grateful to get back in the truck where the heater was still going strong. Jimmy jerked off his gloves and stuck his hands near the heater vents.

"You think somebody tried killing it with that pencil, Jimmy? Maybe thought they could reach its brain through that eye that was put out?"

"Might could be."

"Why don't you try it next time? Get some pencils and use them instead of your gun. Shooting's too easy."

Jimmy laughed and patted his rifle. "By damn if we didn't get us a big'un what's pretty fresh! Worth a couple or three rotten dead'uns like what we usually get. What say we go on home, get our bounty, and get us a head start spendin' it."

"Won't fight you." I turned the truck around and headed back to town. But about a mile later we saw another dead'un standing in the center of the road.

"Damn if this ain't our day, kid!"

It had on a yellow parka with the hood pulled up over its head, black gloves on its hands, and some kind of boots on its feet. Raised its hands like it wanted us to stop so it could have a tasty meal.

I stopped the truck slantwise about ten feet from the dead'un. Jimmy stuck the barrel of his rifle through the bars. He was raising the barrel to aim when the dead'un hollered, "Don't!" and pushed back the hood of its parka.

It was a living woman with big, frightened eyes. Red hair framed her face.

"Shitfire on a shingle." Jimmy lowered the gun. He had a scared expression on his face like the time a dead'un almost got him. He'd almost murdered a woman. "Where the hell'd she fetch herself from? Didn't see me no stranded car."

"Me neither. Come on." Jimmy pulled his gloves back on, grabbed his gun. We jumped out.

The woman put her hands together like she was praying and hurried to meet us. "Thank God! I need help!"

Jimmy squinted at her. "Wouldn't doubt it."

I looked up and down the road, still didn't see a stranded car. "What are you doing out here?"

She pulled her hood back over her head against the cold. "I thought I heard an engine a while ago, then I heard two gunshots and ran to the main road, hoping you'd come back."

"Didn't mean what are you doing out here in the road," I said. "Out here in the damned country is what I meant."

"Long story. No time to explain."

"Guess we ain't bein' too polite, ma'am." Jimmy touched the brim of his orange Longhorns cap. "I'm Jimmy and this here's Frank. We work for the Texas Highways, patrollin' for dead'uns. Sorry I almost shot you."

"Please, we have to hurry. I have a van full of kids stuck down the side road over there."

I looked where she pointed, saw the side road. "You brought kids out here?"

"I had to."

Jimmy shook his head. "Too bad, ain't it, kid? How some folks just ain't got no sense?"

"Are you going to let those kids freeze? Please, help us!"

Back in the truck, she sat between us with her knees near the heater vents. "That heat feels good. God, I hope the kids are all right. I waited in the road quite a while. Please, hurry?"

"Want us to get stuck, too?" I headed down the side road. "Easy does it is best in the snow."

"The road's been used and is in pretty good shape."

I could see she was right. "Wonder how come?"

Jimmy said, "Seem to recollect there's a farm down it a few miles. Didn't know no one lived there no more."

The woman nodded. "I was trying to get there. One of the kids distracted me. I got careless. Thank God we weren't farther from the main road."

Over the first rise, out of sight of the main highway, I saw a big white van stuck in the snow. But when we got there what came out of the van were not kids. Two men with guns. Other armed men popped into view all around us.

"Shit!" Jimmy started to raise his rifle, changed his mind. Too many of them with too many guns. "Shit!"

The woman chuckled. "Both of you, get out."

We'd heard talk about hijackers in the country. Hadn't thought much of it, since there wasn't much to hijack out there anymore except the occasional supply truck convoy, well protected by army men. "Guess them bandit stories were true, Jimmy. Should have shot her for a dead'un."

"If he'd tried, he'd have died. Someone was watching from the ditch. And if you'd kept going the other way, there was another woman and another watcher waiting there, too."

I tried to think of something to do to put off getting out. "You picked the wrong truck. It isn't worth much, and we're all but broke. You might as well let us go. We won't say anything

about it. What woman in the road? I don't remember any woman in the road. You, Jimmy?"

"Nope."

The armed men were now all around the truck. One tapped on my window with a rifle barrel and motioned for us to get out. I took a deep breath and held it. Didn't want to show how scared I was. "We sure as hell have fallen in the shit, Jimmy."

"With a cherry on top."

I turned off the engine. We got out. The woman took Jimmy's gun from him and held it up above her head. "Look what I found!"

One of the men said, "Nice. And not one but two players."

I eyed the man. "Players?"

Some of the men laughed. Couple of guys held guns on us while a couple more patted Jimmy and me down to make sure we didn't have any extra guns in our coat pockets or underneath. One of them took my pocket knife and put it in his pocket.

I heard snow crunching and looked behind us. Down the road on foot came a big man with a rifle. He wore a white parka with the hood pulled up. "He the one who was in the ditch?" I asked the woman.

"I like your cowboy hat." She took it and put it on her head.

"Give it back. Too big on you."

"I like them big." She laughed. "Know what I mean?"

She walked away carrying Jimmy's gun and wearing my hat as the man in the white parka reached us. He was taller than me by a head. He shook back the parka hood and came up close. Mean looker. Greasy blond hair, scar down his left cheek and across his lips.

"You boys like football?"

Jimmy didn't miss a beat. "National religion of Texas, ain't it? What you think?"

The leader eyed Jimmy's cap. He took it off Jimmy's bald head and put it on. "Go! Longhorns!"

Jimmy spit in the snow. "Don't reckon I like you takin' my cap."

"If you're still breathing after the game, maybe I'll give it back."

My heart started thumping faster. "What's football got to do with us breathing?"

Scarface gave me a wink. "It's a tough game."

Jimmy screwed up his face and pursed his lips like he

might be going to spit on Scarface, then he changed his mind and swallowed. "Used to play me some football when I was a kid."

Scarface laughed and slapped him on the shoulder. "Well, hot dog!" He fired his gun three times quick in succession, aiming up in the air.

I remembered what the woman had said. "You letting the ones up the road know to come in? Two players all you need?"

Scarface frowned at me. "Get in the van."

Of course the van wasn't really stuck. They took us to the farm, hidden in a hollow a few miles down that side road. Place had a farmhouse still standing, garage, chicken coop, silo, and a big old barn.

The smell of dead'uns hit us before they opened the barn door and herded us in. A gasoline generator was making noise, giving juice to the lights that hung overhead down the length of the barn and some heaters that were blowing hot air here and there on the end where we'd come in. But it was still cold enough in the barn to make our breath frosty.

The wooden floor had been cleared off and white football field lines had been painted on it, some of them not too straight. One side of the barn had a thick wire screen running from floor to rafters, and they'd built a long bench behind the screen for folks to sit on.

Down the other end of the barn in the center of what was passing for an endzone was a bunch of dead'uns in a cage. All kinds—men, women, young and old, some fresher than others, a few so thin and rotted they were little more than tattered flesh and bones.

Scarface pointed with his gun to the field of play. "Welcome to the Dust Bowl, boys! We call it that because the Gourmets—that's your opponents down there in the cage— can be damned dusty. Their dead skin flakes off a lot when they get hit. Sometimes other things fall off, too. In the Dust Bowl, heads can really roll!"

Jimmy spit on the floor, but not near Scarface's feet. "Never heard 'bout no Dust Bowl, and I know me somethin' 'bout sports."

"You've never had enough money, old man, for anybody that knew about the Dust Bowl to have any reason to tell you about it. The people who are coming here to watch, they can pay what it takes."

Jimmy shook his head. "Wastin' their dough. Ain't gonna be much of a game. Dead'uns can't play 'em no football worth a damn, 'cause good football takes smarts."

"Oh, they don't play pretty, but it's good enough to please a crowd that really only wants to see someone get killed and eaten for real, like most have only seen in tapes of old newscasts and infomentaries.

"How it works is like this: When the customers get here and the Gourmets are let out, you boys get to try and make it to the other end without getting killed. Of course, if you get bitten even once, you'll be poisoned by the Dead Bug and become a Gourmet as soon as you die and wake up."

I let that sink in a little before I said, "What's the prize? We make it, Jimmy gets his cap back? And I get what?" Figured they meant to kill us anyway and let us wake up Gourmets, but maybe I could work a deal. "Can I join your gang?" Decided I'd better make it sound like I was really interested, not just trying to save my skin. "Because your gang's got to pay one whole hell of a lot better than patrolling for the damned State of Texas."

Scarface got a look on his face like he was feeling low. "Don't get your hopes up. No one's made it—" he nudged me in the ribs and laughed in my face "—yet."

Heard Jimmy laugh, too. "Well, kid, get ready to be the first to make it, 'cause I'm damned straight gonna get me my cap back."

Scarface tipped the cap on his head to Jimmy. "That's the old team spirit. Go, Longhorns! Hook 'em Horns! But if you boys change your minds, decide you don't feel like playing football today, here's what I'll do: shoot you in the legs, then throw you out there to get eaten. That way, the crowd won't feel too cheated."

I looked at Jimmy. "Guess we'll play."

"Guess so."

They took our gloves off, handcuffed our hands behind us, and fixed us on a short chain that was attached to the wall. "Don't take our gloves," I said when Scarface started to leave. "Might need them. Keep our hands warm so we can handle the ball."

"There isn't going to be any ball."

"Gonna need 'em anyways," Jimmy said, "to keep from cuttin' our hands on the dead'uns' bones when we rip 'em open and snap their necks."

I joined in. "That's right. There's plenty of ways to kill a dead'un, maybe some your customers might like as much as watching us get gnawed on."

"I almost think you both think you can beat this game. You can't. But I'll leave you your gloves. Why not? Maybe you

can do some really entertaining damage to a Gourmet or two before you fall. Showbiz!"

He stuck our gloves in our coat pockets, told one guy to watch us, then left with everyone else.

Pretty soon I heard some music in the distance and some whooping and hollering. Figured they were having a party up at the farmhouse. I caught the guard's eye. "Why don't you go on up and have yourself some fun? We're not going anywhere chained like this."

He ignored me and stayed, and we didn't find a way to get loose.

It must have been a couple of hours before customers started coming in. Fancy coats and expensive hats. Jewelry glittering on the women and even some of the men. All of them were laughing and having a good time, waiting for the show to begin, which Jimmy and me were in no hurry for.

I saw the red haired woman, still wearing my Stetson. She came in with another woman who had blond hair hanging long outside a green parka. Red pointed at us, gave us a wave. Blondie waved, too, then both of them laughed.

"Sure would like to get even with the ones doing this to us, Jimmy."

"All I want's my cap back."

"Wouldn't mind getting my hat back either, but how the hell we going to make it? They took my pocket knife—not that it would have been much use, not with its short blade. Of course they left me that pencil I took out of that dead'un's nose. But a pencil isn't going to help."

"Bet you can kill 'em with that pencil just fine. Bet it's long enough. Hold the end and shove it deep through an eye. Cram it in far enough. Me, I'm gonna use my fingers and hands. Saw a feller once what killed him a dead'un by hittin' it so hard in the nose its nose bones got drove up in its brain."

"Might work for one or two if we were quick enough—and lucky enough—to keep from getting bit, but there's going to be a whole bunch coming at us. We need an ax or a club."

"Kid, you know there's only one way to kill dead'uns. One at a time. Just gonna have to do it fast as you can, anyhow you can."

"You've been thinking deeply about it, I see."

"What you been doin'? Wishin' you was home?"

"Wishing I had a gun."

I saw Scarface heading our way.

"Here we go, Jimmy."

"Looks like."

Scarface looked us up and down. "All rested, are you? Time to play."

Jimmy spit. "Let me at 'em."

"Me, too. You going to let me join your gang, afterward?"

Scarface said, "Might let you patrol for us, catch dead'uns to become Gourmets."

"Maybe that's where our bounty money in the country has been going, Jimmy. They've been taking our game."

"Yeah. Might could be they owe us some bounties."

I nodded. "Right. You owe us—at least a job, afterward."

Scarface motioned to some of his men to come over. "Don't worry about after. For you boys, there isn't an after."

Jimmy laughed. "Might as well give me back my cap. You're forgettin' we kill dead'uns for a livin'."

They uncuffed us and shoved us to the field of play. I hadn't been to the bathroom since I'd stopped on the road that morning. Had to go bad, being so scared and all. Hoped I didn't end up going in my pants with people watching. Then I thought that was a silly concern. I had worse problems and then some. To hell with it.

The customers on the bench behind the screen cheered as Jimmy and I were forced to step on the makeshift field. Other places, armed men stood ready outside the screen. Downfield, somebody opened the cage then hurried away as the Gourmets lumbered out.

The men near us backed away. The dead'uns started shuffling toward us. Some got distracted by the people near their end of the field behind the screen, but most were coming toward Jimmy and me.

Heard Scarface holler, "Play ball!"

"That's for baseball," Jimmy said. "Got your pencil, kid?"

I took it out of my coat pocket. "Yeah." I looked at the pencil, put it back in my pocket. "I'll save it for later, when I'm really desperate."

"Good plan."

We both slipped on our gloves.

I pointed. "See how the ones that are more fresh are stronger and in the lead?" They were at mid-field now, which wasn't too far from us since it wasn't a real football field.

Jimmy nodded. "And I reckon the dead'uns up front'll be the hardest to kill."

"If we get past maybe the first six, the more rotted ones behind them might get taken out with a good kick or two."

Jimmy gave out a loud ol' yell all a of sudden that made me jump. He grinned at me. "Didn't mean to scare you."

I got his drift and grinned back. Hollered a loud Texas yell of my own. Then Jimmy and I walked side by side toward the dead'uns.

The crowd cheered.

I took the nearest one on my left, Jimmy the nearest on his right. Mine had a big patch of oozing decay on its throat. Looked like something had eaten half through its neck. Maybe cancer or just a dead'un's cold teeth.

Seeing that ugly patch and remembering what Jimmy had said to Scarface gave me an idea. Before I could think too much about it I shoved my hand into that neck wound and got a grip on its backbone just below the base of its skull. I jerked-twisted-jerked and snap went that spine. Dead'un went down. Wasn't real dead—its eyes were still moving—but even with its brain still working it couldn't move any more.

I had a flash of Jimmy standing over the dead'un he'd fought. Didn't know what he'd done to it, but he was already dealing with another.

I had two closing in on me. I kicked the knee of the one that was nearest, and it went down with a busted kneecap. Used my gloved fist that was dripping gore from the first one's neck to punch hard up into the next dead'un's nose, just like Jimmy had said might work. The blow made the dead'un stagger back, but it didn't go down.

The one that'd had its kneecap busted was crawling at me, ready to reach up and grab my leg. I kicked a big dent in its head, and it stopped moving. Could have kicked myself right about then for not remembering sooner that my bullhide workboots had steel toes.

I needed to deal with the one I'd punched in the nose and a couple more coming up, so I jumped back a few steps to give myself room, reached down, and took off my left boot. Holding it by its leather upper like a club, I rushed toward the dead'un I'd punched, feinted to one side, slipped behind it, and caved in the back of its head with the steel toe.

Gave out another loud yell and cratered another dead'un's skull, then another and another and another. I was faster than they were, and right then I hated them more than I was scared of them. Had a thought that if I'd been older and I'd had a steel-toed workboot back when I watched the dead'uns kill my folks and sister, things might have been damned different and then some!

Guess I went into one of those frenzies I've heard about, because I don't remember much more of the fight after that, just swinging that boot and swinging that boot and listening

to the crunch and crack of dead'un skulls caving in while I hooped and hollered and yelled like I was having the best time of my life. Maybe I was.

I began to come back to myself when there were no more dead'uns coming at me.

By then it had gotten damned quiet in that barn. Heard my own breathing, hard and heavy, as it frosted the cold air, but I didn't hear anything else. I blinked a few times to clear my vision. The folks behind the screen were staring at me with big eyes, most of them with their mouths hanging open, wide. Then they all started cheering and yelling and clapping their hands, and I saw something else.

I was standing in the endzone, and the only dead'uns that were still moving were the two that were down on their knees near the middle of the field, gnawing on Jimmy.

I gave another holler and ran down that field and clubbed one of them dead'uns so hard ooze shot out of its cracked skull. I clubbed the other one, too, and then I knelt by Jimmy.

He was dead. One of them had been chewing on his face and neck, the other on one of his arms. His red blood was everywhere. I was kneeling in it, and it was still warm. "Damn it, Jimmy," I said. "God damn it to hell!"

I stood up and looked for Scarface. He was walking toward me. Two armed men with him were pointing their guns at me. The crowd quieted down. "I can't believe it!" He was smiling big. "You actually did it! I salute you!" And he did. He raised his hand and saluted me like I was some kind of general. The crowd cheered. "Bet you'd like to club me, too."

"Damned right!" I lifted the boot. His men raised their guns.

"Is it worth dying for?"

"You're going to kill me anyway."

"No, I'm not. Unless you make me, that is." He glanced at the crowd. "And that'd be bad for business. You're famous now. You think this bunch won't tell others? On the sly, of course. It'll give us even more business. The Gourmets can be beaten! Makes it a whole new ball game, so to speak, especially for betting big bucks. And besides, if I shoot you, who'd help us patrol for new Gourmets? And who'd wear your friend's cap?" He took the Longhorns cap off his head and held it out to me.

I took it and threw it down on Jimmy's body. "I'm still going to kill you."

"Before long you'll like the money I pay you more than you'll want to revenge your fallen friend. What's your price?"

"Maybe I don't have one. No, wait. What'll it cost me to have someone put a bullet through Jimmy's brain before he wakes up hungry?"

"Do it." He motioned to one of his men.

It hurt to watch the bullet make a mess of Jimmy's head, but it meant he damned well wasn't going to wake up a dead-'un.

"Now, do you want to earn lots of money patrolling for me instead of getting next to nothing from the State of Texas? Or I do I have to have you shot—but not through your brain?" The shooter pointed his gun at me. "What's it going to be?"

Almost seemed I heard Jimmy's voice about then, and he was saying, "Kid, you know damned well you can't go and kill him right now with a damned ol' stinkin' boot. But by hell if there ain't plenty of other ways. And later'll be just as good. Still got that pencil?"

I grinned wide. "With a cherry on top."

"What?" Scarface said.

"I'm thinking about it."

I squatted down, put the boot back on my foot, then got Jimmy's cap and stood up. On his cap was his blood, and that made it better. I looked Scarface in the eye. "How much money are you talking about?"

"That's the spirit!" He grabbed my left wrist and raised my hand over my head, turned me to face the clapping and cheering folks behind the screens. He asked me, "What's your name? So I can tell your fans."

The cap was in my other hand. I put it on my head, felt Jimmy's cooling blood wet against my skull, and thought again about punching the pencil in my pocket through one of Scarface's eyes some dark night.

I jerked my left wrist out of his grip and lowered my arm to my side. "My name?" I faced him, grinned. "Just call me Kid." And I spit on the floor.

SUSAN

ROBIN D. LAWS

It had taken him until his fifth trip to the loading dock of the old sugar refinery before it finally came to him what the smell reminded him of: alligators. Saint Augustine's Alligator Farm, in St. Augustine, Florida. His parents had taken him there when he was a little kid. And in turn he'd taken Maggie and the kids during their own trip down there, just three years before The Rising. How could he have forgotten that smell? Thick, damp, loamy. Thousands of alligators lolling around, packed together in mossy water, shitting and pissing and screwing and fighting over chicken carcasses. Grinning up at you as their reek rose into the humid air. Like they knew their stink was going to stay on your skin and hair, root its way into the fabric of your polo shirt and your cut-off jeans and stay there for as long as it could. They might be penned up and put on display, those alligators, but they could still fuck with you. A little, last gesture of impotent reptilian malice. Well, this place smelled like that. It hit you as soon as the guy opened the big corrugated metal door. Forster was glad to have finally pegged the thing that had been nagging at him all this time.

Forster reached for his wallet to pay the guy but Tim, who'd come in behind him, put a restraining hand on his shoulder. The guy waved the two of them through with no payment exchanged. This was a new arrangement. Tim had paid the hundred bucks for Forster last time, but now he seemed to have some kind of comp privileges. It did not surprise Forster that Tim might be providing some kind of *quid pro quo* service for them. Even if he'd been able to rouse himself to curiosity over this minor detail, he knew better than to ask. If it was interesting enough to come up in idle conversation, Tim might drop a mention of it. Forster had established himself as worthy of trust.

They headed toward the steps that led up to the top level of risers. Tim liked to survey things from on high. Observe the bettors as well as, maybe even more so than, the competitors. The first couple of times, Forster had preferred to get closer to the action. Now it was fine by him to sit beside Tim.

On the way up the stairs, Forster stopped his hand just

short of getting a big splinter from the railing. It, like the rest of the bleacher structure, was chunked together from raw, unfinished lumber. The first time he'd been there it was all fresh and new, like it had been put up the previous day. Now it was starting to get grimy.

"Watch out for splinters," he said to Tim.

"Thanks," said Tim.

They were hardly at the top of the stairs when one of Tim's regulars was on them, panting like an aged sheep dog. Large, wide, bald face, distinguished mostly by his big comb-over and silver-framed aviator glasses. He wore a cheap brown suit, the polyester fabric pilling up at the knees. Matching brown tie, lighter brown shirt. Forster had him down for a government employee of some sort.

"Hecuba's gonna freakin' kick freakin' righteous ass tonight," the regular said. He put extra emphasis on the word "ass." "I can feel it. It's gonna be her biggest night yet."

Tim leaned his long body casually up against the railing and reached for the cigarette he'd tucked behind his ear. He didn't light it or anything, just played with it, tapping it against his left palm.

"Think so?"

"Know so."

"That kind of certainty . . . I don't know. What kind of odds we want to talk?"

Forster sidled past them toward the usual spot on the third-last bench from the top. The odds-making process was of little interest to him. He wasn't here to bet. He'd burned out on gambling a long time ago.

He lowered himself onto the hard bench and looked down at the other people. Immediately below him, a white-haired man spoke in a high, flutey voice to a broad-shouldered guy in a plaid flannel shirt. At least a generation separated them and something about the ease with which they sat together said to Forster that they were father and son. Directly over, a very obese young woman with stringy hair and a big white sweatshirt with a picture of border collie puppies on it unrolled a paper bag and took out a rattling package of cheese doodles. Down front was a row of Tamil guys, all of them in ski vests. The Portuguese, Chinese, and gangbanger delegations were also present in force. They waved fistfuls of hundreds at each other. Forster saw Tim's leather cowboy hat down there among them; he was weaving between the groups, making notes with his stylus on his knock-off Palm Pilot.

The place was fuller than it had ever been before. Word

was really getting out. Forster was surprised that the organizers were willing to let so many in. Too many people knew
now for this to go on for much longer. The cops would get
tipped off and come in the middle of the night with the heavy-
duty Gauzner sprayers. They wouldn't bust in during an
event, with the bleachers full. Too big a chance of things getting out of hand. No matter how much they'd have liked to
track down each and every spectator and see them slapped
with ten-to-fifteen for criminal facilitation, illicit custody of
PMAs, first degree.

Forster closed his eyes. The insides of his eyelids burned.
He needed more sleep. He wished he could close his nostrils,
too. Identifying the smell had done nothing to make it more
tolerable; just the opposite.

He must have nodded off, because he started when Tim,
sitting down next to him, leaned on his shoulder.

"Good action?" Forster asked, by way of conversation. Tim
nodded. Forster thought maybe there might be a hint of a grin
on him somewhere, but with Tim you couldn't always tell.

The P. A. made itself known with a squeal of feedback. Tim
shuddered, but Forster did not. Every freaking time they had
the mike pointed into the speakers. He'd come to expect it.

The voice at the mike did not trouble itself to rouse any
extra anticipation or excitement in the crowd. It was an uncon-
fident teenager's voice, occasionally cracking and inevitably
rising toward the end of each sentence. "Everybody get ready
for tonight's bout," it said. "Tonight we have the new challenger, Orkon the Eviscerator." The crowd greeted this news
with a ritual booing. Orkon was here as meat, just like all his
predecessors.

Heavy blue drapes parted down on the left side of the pit,
and out came two men in bulky padded suits, the kind used
for attack dog training. Riot helmets made them look like they
had bug heads. They wheeled in Orkon on an industrial-sized
upright dolly. Six wide leather belts, each with a huge rusty
buckle, secured the zombo to it. They had a big fake Viking
helmet with tinfoil-covered horns plunked on his head. Orkon
looked like he had some fight in him; he hissed and snapped
his half-missing teeth at the ring men as they wheeled him to
his corner. He wriggled and strained at the belts, but they did-
n't give. It would be good to start the match when he was still
pissed, so they left him in place and hustled across the ring
and through the drapes on the other side.

Forster could see a wave of doubt ripple through the guys
nosed up to the plexi-shielding in the front row. Maybe this

one was ready for Hecuba. Some bills changed hands. But then the voice announced the arrival of the current all-time champion, and the small crowd surged to its feet, stamping and whistling. They began to chant "He-cu-*ba*, He-cu-*ba*, He-cu-*ba*." Forster half-heartedly chanted along at first, but then left off, not sure who he actually meant to root for.

The ring men came back with the second dolly, this one bearing the shorter, stouter corpse of a woman. Forster had spent a certain amount of time thinking about her, wondering who she'd been before she got bit. There was something about her pear-shaped figure, her wide thighs and the vestiges of sandy, permed hair on the top of her head that, to Forster, said supermarket checkout clerk. Possibly a Wal-Mart greeter. Definitely something from the lower echelons, like that. Well, she'd found a distinction now she'd never had when she was breathing. More money had changed hands on her in the course of a couple of matches than she'd probably earned in her whole living existence.

Unlike her opponent, Hecuba was not moving at all. Those little lizard-smart eyes of hers were darting back and forth, but that was it. "Conserving her energy for the fight," Forster heard the white-haired dad say to his son, giving him a rib-nudge. The son must have been the newbie, Dad the old hand. Forster had listened to many of the bettors go on about how Hecuba knew exactly what she was doing, that she recognized somehow she was competing. She had that something extra, the motivation that made for a champion. Forster had not stirred himself to disagree but had seen nothing in her, other than the usual insensate, predatory stimuli-and-response behavior. She was just faster and meaner than the others, that's all.

The audience was clapping rhythmically now, the sound building itself up into a big crescendo. The organizers weren't much in the way of showmen, because they didn't wait for it to peak or anything. The announcer did nothing to build or shape the crowd's anticipation. Forster had to admit, though, that this actually gave the thing an air of authenticity, that he would have soured on it even sooner if it had been all faked up. Maybe they knew what they were doing after all.

The handlers casually reached into a toolbox that had been sitting center-ring the whole time, and withdrew from it a pair of plastic Super Soaker squirt guns, one bright neon green plastic, the other pink. Both were stained red-brown. Each ring man stepped back, took aim at one of the zombos, and let loose, drenching his target.

The guns held human blood. Zombos could not, under normal circumstances, be induced to attack each other. They could sniff out live from dead. The only way to make them go apeshit on their own kind was to spray them with the fresh stuff from a live victim. After witnessing his first match, Forster asked Tim where they got it, but Tim refused to speculate. Which answered the question, more or less.

The ring men retreated and, from backstage, one of them hit the remote switch that blew the micro-charges on the belts. Little plumes of smoke rose up from the dollies as the zombos staggered forth. From the way Orkon struggled with the restraints just a few seconds earlier, a bettor might have put his money on him being first to free himself and to capitalize on that freedom. But the bigger corpse staggered around, batting at the rising puffs of burned powder, as Hecuba crouched down, hissed, then made a run at him. She tackled Orkon, knocking him off his feet, and began to claw at his eyes with her jagged, extruded fingernails.

Tim leaned forward, biting his lip. One of the Portuguese guys got up on his bench and executed a little dance of exultation. Orkon squirmed out from under his attacker and flailed wildly at her head. As he lunged for the side of her throat, she scrabbled backward on the particle board flooring. He dove at her. She thrust herself upward and back, to a crouching position. Orkon rose to his feet, too.

The Viking helmet had fallen off in the melee's first moments. As part of the whole warrior theme, the ring men had strapped a belt, scabbard, and sword to Orkon's otherwise naked waist, and for a moment it seemed like he was going to pull the sword and go hacking at Hecuba's head with it. But instead, he tore the belt off and tossed it aside. Then Orkon threw his head back and shrieked; his gray tongue flopped past his chapped and peeling lips. Hecuba held her ground, pawing the flooring with her splayed left foot. Forster noticed there were a couple more toes missing than last time.

Hecuba braced for Orkon's charge, and he came at her headlong. She back-swatted him with her hand, though the force of the blow hardly seemed to register with him. He howled again, then thrust a punching hand deep down into her chest. Even Forster couldn't help but wince at the sound of cracking bone. Orkon kept his hand inside her, his shoulder muscles working like he was groping around for something. Another distinct snap followed. Finally Orkon withdrew his bile-smeared arm. He held something long and sharp-ended in his quivering fist: one of Hecuba's ribs.

The room went quiet as the bigger zombo took a step back, raised up the rib like a dagger, and then stepped forward to drive it down through Hecuba's left eye socket. Leaping from the flooring to put all of his weight behind the blow, the challenger knocked his prey down. Hecuba's limbs flopped like trout on the floor of a boat, then stopped. Orkon pushed his face deep into her gaping chest cavity, to feed. Moments later he staggered back, shaking his head from side to side as he spit chunks of unsatisfyingly dead meat from his jaws.

Then he did the thing every victorious zombo did, the thing that the organizers relied on to control their fighters. He smelled the sweaty, agitated spectators, and leaped like a frog onto the reinforced plexiglass. Blue sparks ran up the metal stanchions separating the clear panes. Embedded filaments too small to see carried the current to the zombo at every point of his contact with the barrier.

Orkon convulsed three or four times, then fell motionless to the ring's floor, face up and spread-eagled. The ring men dashed out and rolled their victor into a canvas tarp, which they pulled tight with what had to be several dozen sets of belts and buckles. By the end of the procedure, Orkon had opened his eyes and was irregularly blinking. The ring men hastened their buckling, and soon he was completely unable to move. They finished off by gingerly wrapping a ball gag around his slowly jawing mouth. A tentative-looking assistant, also fully geared in padded armor, piloted a gurney onto the stage. The ring men casually hefted the bagged zombo and flipped him onto the gurney, which they quickly wheeled off through parted curtains.

Forster could hear the blood rushing past his ears. Not a sound in the entire freaking place. He looked at the men across from him, saw their dropped jaws and checked his own to see if it was also swinging back and forth like the head of a drinking bird. It was not.

The serene expression on Tim's face as he rose to make his rounds through the arena showed that his money had been on Orkon.

Down front, a short, buck-toothed man wearing a fur cap sat staring at Hecuba's opened corpse, tears rushing down both of his capillaried cheeks.

✦ ✦ ✦

Tim sat across from Forster in their habitual coffee shop, his arms splayed across the red fake leather covering the backs of the booths. He had laid his hat down beside him, revealing his receding hairline, a feature accentuated by his habit of gelling his hair tight to his pointy-crowned skull.

"I had opportunity to smell-test Hecuba a couple days back," he said. "Much as they tried to mask it, you couldn't miss the formaldehyde. I mean, just count back the months to her first match. She had to be getting pretty squishy."

"I think I'm bored with this shit, too," Forster said.

"Don't tell me."

"I hardly felt anything at all this time."

The waitress came with their coffees. Tim ordered an open-face turkey sandwich with mashed potatoes. Forster glanced at the menu for the first time, scratched his neck, and said he'd have what his friend was having.

"What has it been? Just six times? And it's already paled on you."

"The process of my beginning to feel nothing seems like it's accelerating. It's the same curve, just faster now. Like I could plot it on a graph." Forster fished a ballpoint out of his coat pocket and began to draw a curving line, like the dorsal surface of a whale, on the diner's all-white place mat. "First is the fear—I feel my heart pumping—and from then I can begin to feel other things: elation, fury, a sense of connectedness to the people around me. Then the fear dies down. Revulsion comes in to replace it, and that's fine, too. That's feeling something, after all. I'll settle for revulsion, I think. Then thorough self-loathing. Even more unpleasant, but still feeling. Then this begins to leach away, too, leaving just this sort of flat . . . grayness. Like the people around me are actually a million miles away."

"Present company excluded, naturally." Tim inspected the cigarette he'd been fidgeting with, broke it up into three pieces, and deposited it, unsmoked, in the amber-colored ashtray.

"The drugs were the first, and they lasted the longest of all. There were so many different ones to try. And part of the experience is the people you're around when you're on them, and the things that happen. But the end of that curve was when I couldn't get a buzz off anything. All just maintenance. Big deal. The good time period: that lasted, what, eighteen months? Nearly two years?"

"Sounds about right. Plenty of people party-heartying then."

Tim would know; he'd been Forster's dealer from the start. The two of them had been in grad school together, way back. Now here they were again. Each was the only person the other could fully talk to. Tim had to dumb himself down around the lowlifes he worked with. References to Foucault or Godard strictly off-limits. The post-Rising labor market tolerated many quirks, but certain things you didn't discuss in the break room.

"Then the hooker thing," Forster continued. "That overlapped, but all told lasted me maybe a year. Little less."

"Lots of people find that alienating."

"The various fetish scenes—I know you don't want me to get into the details—"

He could see Tim tense up. "Yeah, keep it to vague allusions. That one time I asked. . . ."

"Each of those was its own separate curve. Things I never thought I'd ever see myself doing, then quicker and quicker, I was not only doing them but had gone through them. They were dead for me, passé.

"Okay, the S/M scene, that's so all-encompassing. That did last longer than some of the things before it. But still, same pattern. Part of me was hoping that this deathmatch thing. . . . It wasn't sexual, it wasn't bodily, it would be different. The spiritual purity of the degradation, it would last longer. And the first time—"

"A classic match. Hecuba's first."

"Thought I'd shit myself, I was so scared going in. Scared of a raid. Of it being a scam, of getting robbed and beaten. Of how I'd react when I first saw one of them again. Of maybe one of them getting loose, biting somebody, starting a cascade."

"And jeez, when the head went flying into the crowd. . . ."

Forster remembered his coffee and took a big drink of it before it cooled too much. "Yeah, maybe that was part of it. That first one was so . . . so . . . intense that from then on in, it was all downhill. If that third match—that awful drawn-out one where they just wouldn't go for each other—if that had been my first one, if it had built up more, maybe I'd still be feeling a jolt. But the whole time tonight, I kept waiting for it to kick in, and nothing."

"Yeah, that night, that was a classic, all right."

"But tonight, it was all just the same old dull feeling—the same non-feeling. And the people around me, I didn't feel like I was part of them, a member of their race, or even in the same room with them. Like I'm watching via a grainy, black and white security monitor. The only thing that got my blood pumping at all was first contact with that smell, and even that was only for the first few moments. You can get used to fuckin' anything, that's what I've learned."

"Ever given any thought to Africa? Or New Orleans?" Tim

was referring to places where the syndrome still raged. Most of the Third World writhed with it; their governments couldn't afford the full array of Gauzner technologies. They had plenty of the bombs but not enough spray units. Various outside funding proposals were snarled in the U.N. for the third year running. New Orleans was still under military quarantine, with only the most determined death's-heads getting through. The whole coastal region of Louisiana kept breaking out, for reasons the experts never managed to pinpoint. Urban legend held forth on the subject of a Gauzner-resistant strain, but proof remained elusive.

"Those places don't interest me. I keep telling you, it's not a death wish. I want to feel the opposite of dead. If I wanted to top myself, I'd just head out to the viaduct and jump. To expose myself to the infection again—you know what that would betray."

"Yeah. Of course." Tim pursed his lips. "I didn't mean to—all I was saying is, the gladiator thing, I was really hoping it would last longer for you."

"Yeah. Me, too." The waitress brought the food. Forster stared down at it, unhungrily. Tim dug in. The matches always gave him an appetite.

"Look," said Tim, between oversized mouthfuls of mash potato and gravy. "I knew this time would come, though not so soon. And you know I sympathize with your malaise. And admire the headlong way you pursue it. There for the grace of god and all that.

"So."

"There's this thing. I been keeping it in reserve for you. I'm only in the preliminary stages of hooking it up. The people who handle this, they're not my usual circle. You'd say they're several circles away, okay? So what I'm saying is it's all chancy. Can't guarantee anything. And if it does go through, these are some crazy, nasty mofos and I can't extend any kind of my usual dispensation. If things go wrong, it's all on you, right?"

Forster sat forward. He felt like his heart had started up again.

"It's really freaking sick, okay? And if this doesn't do it for you, I tell you, my wad is shot. There's no further frontier I'm capable of pointing you toward. But, jeez, if you're into it, it should last you more than six lousy times. Now I know you know the kind of discretion I expect of you. So don't be insulted if I repeat that this has absolutely, in no circumstances, not a word breathed to anyone except for me. This is not like the thing tonight, where they're inviting in half the world and its uncle. Okay?"

"Come on. Tell me."

Tim looked around for eavesdroppers. "Like I say, it's preliminary. It might not come off."

"Come on."

He leaned forward and spoke *sotto voce.* "How would you like to fuck one of them?"

✝ ✝ ✝

He walked home from the subway, rock salt crunching under his boots, his breath illuminated by orange streetlights. The very idea of it had given him a hard-on, his first in months. The bitter chill of the air invigorated him. He strode up the concrete steps toward his building's foyer, reaching into his pocket past the freezer-bagged supply Tim had sold him, to his keys. As he unlocked the front door, he saw, through its glass, a slim figure wearing a hooded coat. Forster could not see her features, but knew her frame. Sephronia. Her presence utterly deflated him, threw him back into the gray again. He resigned himself and opened the door.

She stepped toward him. "John, I've been waiting for you, hoping you'd—I'm sorry, but this is the only way."

Forster stood before her, paralyzed, not knowing whether to stand there and take it or shove past her wordlessly.

She took another step his way, and lowered her hood, revealing the harsh pink and unwholesome smoothness of the scar tissue that covered her face and entire skull. She'd left off her wig. The gesture was one of remonstrance. Forster knew he should be feeling bad, but had forgotten how.

"I need you to see me," Sephronia said. "To look into my eyes."

He had done this to her, tenderly, over a period of weeks, with a portable acetylene cutwelder. She had consented to the act, sure, but in the expectation that he'd keep her around. That it was a sealing of the permanency between them.

"Please, at least say something."

"If I could think of something to say, I would."

She made a third step toward him. He thought he might flinch from her, get backed into the mailboxes, but found himself standing his ground.

"I've been thinking," she said. "That you didn't see the degree of commitment I had ready for you. That you needed to see how far I am willing to go for us."

She pulled back her coat's fake-furred left cuff to reveal,

at her wrist, a freshly cauterized, naked stump. "I did this to show you."

Forster finally found what it took to brush past her. "That's sweet, honey, and I wish I could care." He slid-clicked the lock on the interior door and slipped through. She tried to catch it and hold it open, but he closed it quickly. He headed to the stairs without looking back at her. As he walked up toward his apartment door, he tried unsuccessfully to make himself feel guilt for what he'd driven her to, or, if not that, at least empathy for her state. Most elective amps started with their off-hand, but Sephronia did everything with her left.

She'd find someone. The amp lifestyle was one of the fastest-growing out there. She'd get over him and settle down with some young, apprehensive stump-lover anxious to abase himself before her every crippled need. Maybe if he knew she'd end up worse off than that, he'd be able to conjure up the proper remorse.

✢   ✢   ✢

Forster looked again at the slip of paper with the address on it. He'd expected another disused industrial site, like the one where the fights were held. But this was an old restaurant with papered-over windows. "New Harmony Restaurant," said the sign that hung overhead. "Delicious Meals," with the word *delicious* in quotation marks.

His hard-on was back, after having deserted him again. The anticipation had made him feel real, for the first couple of weeks. By week three, with still no phone call from Tim, it trickled away. With anyone else, Forster would have concluded he'd been taken in by a line of bull, but he trusted Tim better than that. Tim had made clear that his arrangements might not come through. By the time the call came, Forster had given up on the whole prospect. Yet here he really was, he told himself, really standing in front of the place where he was going to get to fuck a zombo.

There were three doorbells, and he'd been told which one to buzz, and how many times to hit it. As he followed his instructions, it occurred to him that the sex of the subject had never been mentioned. He thought it would be better if it were female. Despite his expanded experiences of the aftermath years, he hadn't completely shaken his preference for women.

They kept him standing there for a while, stamping his feet against the sharp cold. Finally a small tear opened up in the butcher's paper that lined the glass door. Dark, heavy-browed eyes appeared.

"Yeah?" said a voice muffled by the glass.

"You got some videos for me to return?" replied Forster, providing the prearranged response.

The door opened. The man behind it was mountainously tall and fat, wearing a food-stained khaki T-shirt stretched too tight across his belly and man-tits. His long beard and shaggy dark hair were all of a piece. He didn't step aside to let Forster in until Forster took a step toward him. He glowered suspiciously down. Forster understood this as the intimidation necessary to the arrangement. Still, a little talk from the guy could at least indicate what was expected of him next. He looked around at the interior of the building. The restaurant fixtures had been completely torn out. Busted pieces of gyprock lay on the floor amid a dusting of plaster. Most of the golden wallpaper had been torn off the walls, but a few pieces remained, and they were stained the color of rust. Could well have been blood; the place might have been a massacre site. This had been one of the city's worst-hit neighborhoods.

Two men appeared from what was probably the former kitchen. One wore a Juventus soccer jersey over gray wool slacks and had a heavy gold chain-link bracelet around his hairy wrist. The other was skinny and looked like he should be working in tech support somewhere, with a white dress shirt, bushy carrot-colored hair, thick-framed glasses, and an overbite.

Juventus-jersey did the talking. "You're Forster?"

Forster nodded.

"Cash up front."

Forster reached casually into his coat, pulled out the roll, and tossed it to Juventus, who plucked it from the air and, without looking at him, passed it back to Tech Support. "Count this," he said. Tech Support rolled away the thick rubber band, dangling it off his thumb as he riffled through the bills nearly as fast as a machine would. Juventus pocketed the entire amount and left the room.

Man-Tits lumbered forward and pointed toward a wooden door, painted white. "She's down there." Forster had been in some pretty brusquely run brothels before, but this was the epitome. It was perfect.

Tech Support evidently felt the lack of amenities and beat Forster to the door, opening it wide for him. He gestured for Forster to precede him down the dark stairs. For a moment, Forster's shoulders tensed up, ready for a conk from behind. But he'd already given up all but pocket change. They had no good reason to cack him.

Forster heard a switch flicked behind him. A utility light hung from a wooden ceiling beam. The staircase led down into a dingy corridor. There were more rusty stains on the white-washed walls. Under the stairs stood a row of unplugged refrigerators.

"So," came Tech Support's voice, "do you, uh, live in the city, or have you come down maybe from somewhere else?"

Forster was uncomfortable with them even knowing his real last name. The guy had to be fishing for clues they could use in an after-the-fact blackmail operation. "No offense, but I'm not really in a frame of mind for chitchat."

"Right. Sure."

Forster reached the end of the staircase, expecting Tech Support to follow and point him toward the room where she'd be waiting. Instead the guy sat himself down on the second-last step. He brushed some lint off a pant leg. "Look, the others only care about money. For you to do your business and go." He had some kind of subtle speech impediment, but Forster couldn't narrow down exactly what. "But there's a right way and a wrong way to, uh, go about this." He stopped, clearly struggling for the exact right phrase. "Look, you've got to treat Susan in a certain way. You can't assume just because of her condition that she isn't feeling what's happening to her."

Tech support's eyes were watering up. He stuck a finger in past his glasses to rub at an eye. "Try and be—I know gentle sounds funny. It's not the right . . . I guess try and be receptive to her mood, to the kinds of movements she makes." He swallowed hard. "Don't just force yourself and pump, pump, pump. That makes Susan very unhappy, very unsettled for days afterward. For you, this is just a one-time thing. In and out. Just try to understand and don't be a jerk." He looked searchingly up into Forster's face, presumably looking for a nod of assent or something.

Forster gave him nothing. The guy was creeping him out. He'd felt fine until this. "Which door do I go through?"

Tech Support stood, pulled on his sleeve. "It's not just for her sake I'm asking. It's much better if you let Susan take the lead. You'll like it a lot better, I swear. Really."

"Which door?"

Tech Support pointed to a door at the end of the hallway. Forster walked down to it. He looked back and saw Tech Support looking at him forlornly. The guy was draining his jolt. Forster turned around.

"You aren't going to be standing outside the door, are you?"

"Well, uh, I'm supposed to . . . in case there's a problem."

"But there won't be a problem, will there? Everything is well secured, right?"

"Yes, yes." He started to approach. "I've readied her. You won't have any problems. Just be—"

"Because, no offense, but I don't want to be aware of your presence. Right?"

Tech Support nodded quickly, up and down. "Right, right." He pivoted and scampered up the stairs.

Forster waited until he heard the upstairs door close. He turned back toward the door at the hallway's end. He stopped to take a deep breath, to try to refocus himself, to get the awareness of what he was about to do surging through his body again. He took a big snort of air like it was coke. And another. He put his hand on the door handle and stepped into darkness. It smelled both like alligators and like formaldehyde. Immediately a noise started up, a low punctuated growl, like a cat struggling to choke up a hairball. He reached out and groped for a light switch. Fluorescent lights flickered and then grudgingly went fully on.

She lay face down on what looked like a hospital bed, pastel green paint chipping off its metal frame. They'd spread her out, strapping each leg to one of the bedposts. To accomplish this, they'd twisted both of her ankles severely. Her skin was paler than the specimens Forster had seen at the zombo matches, making obvious a complex of purple bruises around the restraints. As he stepped closer toward her, her growling upshifted into a sort of frenzied pant. He could see her trying to lift and turn her head to see him. A brittle mass of peroxide hair wildly haloed her head, hardly moving as she thrashed. As far as Forster could tell, she'd have been an average-looking woman in life, tall and thin-boned but no particular beauty. The bleached hair was out of character with the rest of the corpse: undoubtedly a post-mortem addition. She shook the bed frame but could not budge it from its moorings; it had been bolted into the concrete floor. There was some give in the bolts, though. He wondered if they knew. He would tell them afterward. The presence of a little risk made it better.

Forster took another step forward. He slowly moved his fingertips toward the back of her thigh. He left them in the air for a moment before bringing them brushing against her ashen flesh. It felt rubbery and not ice cold, but cool. Her flailing intensified and he pulled his fingers away. He leaned in to study the surface of her skin. White lines crisscrossed it, and

Forster was curious to know what they were. On close inspection, they seemed to be bloodless, open, scabless cuts, perhaps made with a thin blade like a box-cutter's. Maybe they were just artifacts of handling.

A pair of black fake-satin panties had been put on her; they were at least a size too small, and her dead flesh puckered at the waist and leg holes. Forster's hand went out toward them. Then he stopped, and remembered to look around the room for holes in the walls or ceiling. Starting with the places that would afford the best view of his face, he quickly spotted a drill-mark, and checking it out close, a pinhole lens. He withdrew a deck of Post-It notes from his jacket pocket and fixed the gummed edge to the wall, just above the hole. He glanced back at the door, saw that it had a cheap brass slider to bolt it shut. He slid it. Forster turned back toward Susan and her black panties. Without looking too closely, he shoved them to the side. He was rock-hard.

He unclipped his sleek gold-and-silver belt buckle and unzipped his fly. She had stopped her screaming and thrashing. He looked again at Susan. He stepped back. He bit his lip. He checked himself; he was still hard. He zipped up his fly and buckled his belt.

He sat down on the cold cement floor.

Well, Forster thought, *who'd have thought? I've found it. I've found the place. The place below which I will not go.*

Well. It had been well worth the money. He breathed in deep. He would remember the air he was breathing. He ran his hands together. They felt real and solid for the first time since the night when it all happened. He ran his fingers over his face. That felt real, too. He felt that he was inside himself. Not above or outside, but inside.

He walked over to Susan and moved her panties back into place. The contact started her to shrieking again. He backed off, startled. He had to look away from her. He sat down again. His chest felt like he was back on speed.

Wow. A place below which I cannot go. Wow.

He unbolted the door and opened it. Juventus and Man-Tits were standing right there, with Tech Support off to one side.

"You didn't take too long in there," Juventus said, expressionless.

"You know what? I've discovered I'm not up to it. I thought I would be but I'm not."

Juventus rolled his tongue thoughtfully under his closed upper lip, his eyes still empty. "Then we have a problem."

Forster felt dampness at the collar of his shirt. He knew that to get through this, he would have to fake the very detachment that had just fallen away from him. "I'm not asking for my money back. I've just decided I don't actually want to fuck the zombie, that's all."

Juventus shoved him back into the room. "You're going to fuck that zombie."

"What? What do you care? You have my money."

Juventus shoved him again. He pointed to the Post-It note on the wall.

"You'll excuse me," said Forster, wishing his voice wasn't rising so high, "if I decided I didn't want streaming video on your website of me porking a zombo."

"But you haven't porked jackshit," Juventus said. Another shove. "Raising the question of whether you're a cop. So to prove you're not a cop, you're going to fuck that zombie and I'm going to stand here and watch."

Forster momentarily took his eyes off Juventus and looked behind him, at Tech Support. He looked very unhappy, too. Afraid this would be tough on Susan, no doubt. She was hissing and dry-retching again. Forster glanced down and saw that the bolts holding down the bed were even looser than before.

"You can't just make a guy fuck something. I mean, if you don't got the wood, you don't got the wood."

Juventus smirked. "We got an injection to help you in that area. For twenty-four hours, you'll be a rebar." He made a vague waving gesture; Tech Support opened a plastic case and handed a syringe to Man-Tits.

Forster leaped up to try and grab Juventus by the ears. Juventus punched him hard in the gut and he doubled over. Forster duck-walked backward and sank to his knees at the head of the bed, gasping. Man-Tits advanced on him. Forster reached over to the belt holding Susan's left hand to the bedpost and wrenched open the buckle. She bolted upward, her freed arm arcing over to the other wrist.

"You crazy motherfuck!" Juventus said, wide-eyed and frozen. "Get the sprayer!" he yelled.

Susan ripped the other belt in two and wrenched herself upward, heaving the bed out of its moorings. It flipped up with her and its head-beam clipped Man-Tits on the temple as she lunged for him. She and the bed landed on Man-Tits and shook around. He howled as the bed bounced up and down and blood began to pool out onto the floor. Tech Support was gone from the hallway. Juventus reached for an ankle holster, pulling a small pistol and firing shots into the bed, probably hitting Man-Tits as well as Susan. Then her claws snaked out and grabbed his leg, pulling him off balance and onto his ass. She clawed into his thigh, opening an artery. Juventus groaned and clamped his hands over the wound. Susan slashed away the bindings on her ankles, wriggled from under the bed, and began to gnaw on his crotch. She sank her fingers into his skull and banged his face repeatedly into the concrete. When Juventus went motionless, she whipped around to face Forster, crouching as Hecuba had.

Tech Support appeared at the doorway, holding a gleaming, unused Gauzner sprayer out before him like an assault rifle. His face was beet red, his nose leaking snot. "Susan!" he yelled. "Susan!" Until she finally turned around.

"Susan, you got to listen to me," he said. She wove in the air before him, like a cobra before its charmer. "Susan, please. I don't want to have to use the sprayer. You do understand the sprayer, right? Just calm down. Everything can be all right. Just us now. No more others. You've taken care of these two. That's all you need to do."

She darted forward and ripped his belly open. She clamped one hand around his jaw-line and lifted him up over her head and against the wall. She banged him against it just like she'd smacked Juventus against the floor. Tech Support hadn't died yet and was pleading with her the whole time, though with her grip on his windpipe Forster couldn't make any of it out. She began to keen, almost like she was singing a note. Forster circumnavigated the crumpled bed and Man-Tits' already-shuddering corpse to grab the sprayer. Gauzner designed it to be operable even by a small child in emergency circumstances. Forster pointed it at Susan's back, pulled its big trigger, and watched the blue liquid hit her, slackening and melting the muscles of her back. She fell like a sack. He sprayed her some more, then pointed it under the bed to douse Man-Tits. Then he did Juventus and Tech Support, before they even started moving.

Forster dropped to the floor himself, when it became clear the lot of them were topped. He sat there gulping, and thought about what had happened during The Rising, when the intruder bit Maggie, who then passed it on to the kids. How when they came for him his instincts had taken over, the pick-axe in his hand. How he'd dug it into their skulls, instead of doing what he'd later wished he had done: let them take him, too.

He'd piece out the exact reasons later, but right now what he knew was he'd come alive again. Silently, he thanked Susan for the resurrection.

NUMBER OF THE BEAST

KENNETH LIGHTNER

POLICE FILE: MURDER CASE OF PROFESSOR AMELIUS CAINE

INVESTIGATIVE REPORT

OFFENSE: Probable Murder
VICTIM: Caine, Amelius, Professor
CASE NUMBER: 327-8053-666
DATE: 29-1-01
INVESTIGATING OFFICERS: Det. Tom Hasser, Det. Richard James

CRIME SCENE NOTES
January 29, 2001; 10:30 A.M.

Crime scene discovered by RPS deliveryman. Campus Patrol officer Adam Grange responded to the 911 call and immediately taped off the area. As the body was obviously deceased, Officer Grange then waited for NOPD Detectives to arrive and take charge. Crime scene appears intact and uncontaminated.

Found body lying on the exterior side of the loading dock. Head pointed north, legs were skewed off at odd angles. Refer to Polaroid photographs taken by Det. James.

Also found and photographed blood trail leading all the way back into a lab area within the building (Room S15). Found and photographed blood spatters inside lab area. Blood spatter patterns are consistent with blood flying off a swinging object, which suggests the murder took place within the lab. Blood samples taken.

One room discovered nearby was severely burned inside. Discovered a military flame thrower that may have caused the burn marks. No burn marks found on body.

Recovered numerous samples of hair and fiber.

Discovered the diary of one Jake Senzer on the body. The contents of the diary, if they were not so blatantly fictitious, would explain the state the body was in. However, given they deal with zombies and a mad scientist's lab, one can only assume this is merely a coincidence.

CORONER'S REPORT

OFFENSE: Murder
VICTIM: Caine, Amelius, Professor
CASE NUMBER: 327-8053-666
DATE: 29-1-01
INVESTIGATING PATHOLOGIST: Dr. Simon Frenlich

NOTES:

January 29, 2001; 2:00 P.M.

State of the body suggests that death occurred at least two days prior to discovery. The body shows severe trauma to the head and evidence of biting or gnawing around the head and the legs. The head was missing most of the brain tissue and both legs were missing about 80% of their muscle tissue. Found scoring on the leg bones consistent with animal teeth. The number of tooth marks discovered on the bones suggests a dog or group of dogs fed off the legs and gnawed the bones before the body was discovered.

There were multiple wounds severe enough to cause death. However, in my opinion, most were inflicted after the victim was already dead.

Based on bruising discovered around the neck, I believe the cause of death to be asphyxiation by strangulation. The blunt trauma to the skull may have occurred near the same time and may have contributed to the death.

All hair and blood samples recovered at the scene of the crime match the DNA of Dr. Caine.

ACTIVITY REPORT

OFFENSE: Murder
VICTIM: Caine, Amelius, Professor
CASE NUMBER: 327-8053-666
DATE: 3-2-01
INVESTIGATING OFFICERS: Det. Tom Hasser, Det. Richard James

Attempted to locate Jake Senzer for questioning. Found one Daisy "Dee" Hubert, who last saw Senzer on January 2nd.

Apparently, Ms. Hubert sent him to Dr. Caine to participate in a research project. Ms. Hubert also admitted that Mr. Senzer was a heavy user of heroin. Ms. Hubert stated, "Most likely, Jake killed the professor for money and drugs."

DIARY OF JAKE SENZER

JANUARY 1:

I am addicted to heroin.

I've been addicted now for ten years.

I try to quit each New Year. Once I stayed clean for the entire month of January.

This year has to be different. I'm starting this diary so I can finally admit the truth to myself. Last October, I found out Josh was HIV positive. If I don't quit soon, I'll end up just another dead junkie the world forgot.

Once I had dreams of what my life could be. Dreams never come true on heroin.

I'll start feeling withdrawal soon, and this shit is already depressing me. You might think a little depression is the least of my worries right now. You'd be wrong. I get through the withdrawal every time I try to quit, but every time I start right back up again as soon as the depression hits. Withdrawal is a physical effect you either manage or don't. Heroin has a tighter grip than that though. After withdrawal comes the depression. I know the pain of withdrawal will end. I can never see the light beyond the depression.

Fuck it. The truth is I'm a heroin addict, and I need a score right now.

JANUARY 2:

OK, I'm off the wagon in record time this year. I made it till noon yesterday. But maybe this diary thing takes longer than an hour. I've decided to keep it up. The heroin has so little effect on me these days, I can easily write while I'm high.

I guess I should describe my day yesterday. After giving up on the diary, I went out to stock up. Last month Dee met this professor she claimed could get medical morphine. Dee lives in the Garden District near the Tulane campus, in a ratty shack some asshole landlord decided wasn't fit for students anymore. I live a little farther downriver near Napoleon Ave., so I rode the St. Charles trolley out toward campus and walked about six blocks over to her place. Apparently this deal was working out great for her, because she was dealing to a whole pile of wastoid students. They were all strung out in her living room with the radio blaring some trashy teen music. Nothing makes me more nauseous than bad pop music. I knew Dee had taste as well, so I figured she'd hide in the back and wait for the customers to leave. I found her in her bedroom, bombed out of her skull. She had earphones on.

Dee and I go way back to a time when we were both just like those punks in her living room. I studied journalism for two years before the habit left me with no extra money for tuition. She hung on for another year of pre-med before succumbing to the needle as well. We'd done it a few times at the beginning, but heroin takes priority over your love life. Fortunately, we stayed friends.

When I asked about the morphine she told me this professor was hooking her up in exchange for sending him some candidates for a research gig he was doing. He needed long-time addicts and paid for their time in morphine.

"I'd sell you some of mine, but I'd have to overcharge you. Why don't you meet this geezer and get some for free? You'd be doing us both a favor if you mentioned I sent you."

I needed something fast and when I felt the need, friendship was irrelevant.

"Gimme something now, and I'll meet this dude for you after."

"I'll loan you some until you get back," she replied.

A doctor will tell you that morphine and heroin are the same basic drug. It just ain't so. Heroin is a street drug. It's made for the street, by the street, and in the street. The street taints its effect. Morphine is made in a nice corporate factory with the intention of helping people. It has a smoothness and placidness all its own. Life was good. I kissed Dee on the cheek, took her directions, and headed out. I didn't bother with the geezer . . .

JANUARY 3:

I'm in the grip right now. I thought I'd try writing a bit to take my mind off it. I can't go back to Dee until I meet that geezer anyway. God, my body aches everywhere. The small hole where I injected yesterday feels like a freakin' gunshot wound.

I can't do this right now.

Sign me up as a medical experiment.

JANUARY 5:

I'm in a small cell. There's more to this research than Dee led on. The professor gave me my diary though, and encouraged me to write everything down. That sort of gives me a bad feeling about this, because I don't think this experiment could be legal. If he's letting me write about the experience, he must not be planning on me ever getting out of here.

I met the professor in his office two days ago. I was coming down hard, and I needed a fix right there. He said no problem. He tied off my arm and shot me up like a real pro. Only it wasn't just morphine. I woke up here fifteen minutes ago when the professor gave me back the diary. He took everything else I had. I'm even wearing one of those stupid hospital gowns. Where am I?

JANUARY 19:

Two weeks ago I woke up stretched out on a steel operating table. Restraints held my arms and legs so that I could barely wiggle. Fear started to work on my head as the drugs wore off. (Now we all live in terror of the drugs wearing off; they're all that make me capable of writing.)

"I think you'll need some more morphine today," the professor said, when he saw that I was awake. "You'll need it today like you've never needed it before in your life."

I turned my head toward the voice and saw the doctor pushing up a small table with various medical implements on it. I spotted the needle first and a part of my brain calmed. As long as I was high, he could do whatever he wanted. Looking back, I can't believe I felt that way. I'm really hopeless.

The next things I saw looked like twelve-inch bolts, but they were all shiny and sterile looking. I wondered what he could possibly do with those. I tried to strain my head around and see what might be waiting for me.

"Ah, you want to know what's going on? Are you sure? Some things are better left unknown."

He spun the table around and tilted it so I could see. God, trying to remember makes my head spin. I never dreamed such a horrible fate could await anyone. I've seen friends waste away from AIDS and this made my stomach turn. What force inhabits the professor that allows him to do it?

He grabbed my arm to tie it off. I should have been anticipating the high, but I could only stare in horror. In front of me were six human beings hung up like sides of beef. They had pins or rods inserted on either side of their waist. The rods must have gone in all the way to the hipbone, because they seemed to support most of the body weight. A large frame, in turn, supported the rods and suspended the bodies in midair. It looked as if more rods were in their backs to support the upper body, but I couldn't be sure from my angle. Where the rods penetrated the skin, blood oozed out and stained the leg below. Worse still, every one of them still lived. The professor had hung them in this state without otherwise harming them.

I recognized them. They were those loser students from Dee's place, and they were all staring blankly ahead, stoned out of their minds.

"You're the last one," the professor said. "Once you're in place, we can begin the experiment. You see, once we begin, you won't have the strength to move around for a few weeks. I find these brackets are much easier than worrying over bedsores. They can be set to automatically rotate to avoid blood pooling. I invented them for coma patients. However, apparently they weren't *humane* enough for mainstream hospitals. As if a coma patient cared. . . ."

At last I felt the sweet ecstasy of the morphine. All the tension and horror disappeared and I groaned. The doctor picked up one of the bolts and smiled at me. I didn't care anymore. I smiled back. I knew when he started drilling the bolt into my waist. I could hear the flesh resisting; I could feel the rod as it passed through my muscles. I even felt a little pain through the drug haze as it screwed into my hipbone, but I couldn't make myself care. I just smiled as he held up the next bolt, and I stared at one of the hanging bodies as he put it in my back. I noticed stitches across the forehead of the body I was staring at.

"Now to give you a number. Identification after the experiment has sometimes been difficult. I can think of no way to avoid that problem except to brand directly on the skull."

He strapped down my head, cut through the skin on my forehead and pulled it back. I could feel the warm blood running down the sides of my head, and still I didn't care. When the burner hit my skull, I could smell the burned flesh. It didn't even make me hungry.

"OK, your number is 659. Ah, that's it. We're done. Now we can get on with the meat of the experiment."

He sewed up my forehead and moved an empty frame over the table. He carefully clamped me in and hung me next to the other six bodies, then began to explain the next step. At least, this is what I remember of his explanation. Maybe it's what he said. Maybe it's something from an old black-and-white horror flick I watched once on late-night TV.

"I have recently returned from Haiti where I studied under one of the local Voodoo priests," the professor began. "He taught me a lot of crap about how to fool a villager into thinking you had power over him. He also showed me an insect he claimed could make zombies out of men. He told me he had, of course, never tried it, but his master had used it once as punishment against a man who stole from him. The insect

was a rather large beetle. He told me it carried a powerful magic that creates zombies if it is mixed in the victim's blood.

"I took samples of the beetles back and studied them. It turns out they carry a very interesting virus. As you can see, I am still experimenting with it, but here's what I can tell you: It does not kill you outright; in fact, it seems to spend a great deal of its energy keeping your body alive. However, it only does this for certain areas of the body. It completely disables your immune response. It is more powerful than AIDS in this respect, as parts of your body may succumb to gangrene within a week. The virus protects the lower brain and, to a lesser extent, your muscle tissue. The rest it feeds off of and leaves open to bacterial attack. It also feeds off some of the invading bacteria, eventually reaching a balance point where it sustains the brain and muscle tissue indefinitely.

"I choose this group—you fine specimens—because the virus also suppresses natural hormone production. You see, gangrene is very painful and the previous patients had no ability to produce any natural painkiller. They stayed awake the entire time, screaming, until they lost hold of their sanity and began attacking and eating anything that moved within reach. I eventually had to destroy them. However, thanks to your, uh, 'hobbies,' your hormone production in this area is already suppressed. You have also learned to deal with the pain of withdrawal. My hope is that with a regular maintenance of drugs, you could live forever with this virus. Granted, society could never accept your appearance, but sacrifices must be made to gain immortality!"

"Regular maintenance of drugs?" one of the wastoids said. "Sounds perfect." We all agreed. Somehow, the rest of the doctor's speech went unnoticed.

Like I said, it's hard to tell if that really was what he said, or if I'm only remembering some movie dialogue I once heard when stoned. I am, however, pretty clear about what happened next. I wish to God I wasn't.

He walked over to a work area and slid a small glass cage out from behind some beakers. It contained two large, very ugly beetles and a huge amount of brownish slime. When he removed the lid, you could feel death hovering in the odor it released. He grabbed one of the beetles and stuck a needle directly in the center of its body. He pulled back the plunger and drew in a sickly yellow fluid. He returned the bug to its cage, then fed it a pound of hamburger meat from the cooler.

He walked to each of the smiling teen addicts in turn, and injected a small amount of the fluid into them. "Normally, I'd

be much more careful about sharing needles between people like you, but in this case, it hardly matters." I noticed they all seemed to go unconscious shortly after the injection. He injected me last.

I awoke two days later, but that's only a guess. Things from here on in get sort of fragmentary. Anyway, the morphine had long since worn off. Pain wracked my body. I couldn't move without a horrible grinding pain in my joints. I discovered the seven of us were still hanging in the doc's contraptions. I just cannot express the pain and discomfort I felt. Even to try would take the rest of this small diary's pages. I knew the pain of withdrawal. This was beyond even that, but, over the sad years, I had learned to endure.

Despite the doc's claims, my fellow inmates were not adequately familiar with pain or withdrawal. As each came awake, he or she started screaming. One threw up. Another shouted obscenities at the professor. Yet another thrashed about in a vain attempt to break out of the rack.

This last one soon lost any resemblance to humanity. He twisted and screamed. He frothed at the mouth like a rabid dog. Finally, he made one last lunge to free himself. The effort broke his pelvis. The snapping sound broke into my thoughts and finally I could no longer endure. I screamed with the rest as his body sank down on the steel peg that no longer supported his weight. I imagined a broken bone shard sliding up into his intestines as the body drooped lower. I screamed louder. Blood oozed from the elongated entry point of the peg, but it was not a healthy red. It had turned dull orange and was as thick as molasses. I knew that stuff was inside me as well—is still inside me—and I shouted curses at the crazy old man with what little energy I could muster.

Finally, a green light came on behind all the racks in my sight and a small mechanical arm swung out with an injection needle. It moved slowly and gave each of us our "regular maintenance of drugs." All but one, for in sliding down, the last subject's body had moved beyond the needle's reach. Six of us were silenced, but the last cried on until all he could do was sob. Something the doc had done to us kept the poor bastard alive and conscious, despite the horrifying pain. I guess I might have gone mad just listening to him, but the morphine afforded me detachment. The six of us no longer cared. Perhaps this made the broken kid's misery even worse.

The next several days went on like that—pain, morphine, pain, more morphine. The doctor removed the seventh member of our group, so at least the morning screaming subsided

slightly. I learned later that the doctor burned him alive. Apparently it's the quickest way.

The professor finally took me off the rack after over a week of observation. He told me that since I seemed in control of my wits between doses that he would try me in a cell. He left the others strung up to see if they would ever adapt. Meanwhile, he returned my diary and encouraged me to write. Ironic that I started writing this to get off dope, and now I can only think straight enough to write in it while I'm on the stuff.

January 20:

I woke this morning with intense pain around the wounds left by the rack pegs. However, my jailer came down promptly and rid me of my concerns with a quick hit of morphine. Afterward, he examined the wounds through the bars. He told me that gangrene had set in, but not to worry, that was a normal reaction to the virus. In fact, he said, I actually had a very light case relative to how long I'd had the virus.

Light case of gangrene? I'm no doctor but gangrene is deadly, right? Don't they usually chop off limbs to keep it away? I should have asked him these questions, but the morphine had me in its embrace.

January 22:

Today the doctor brought my five fellow victims down and put them in the cell opposite mine. They were unconscious when he brought them. He told me they had not adapted to their state at all, and he no longer planned to waste morphine on them. He had six new subjects to work on and needed the old ones out of the way. Numbers 660 through 665, I thought.

I got a close look at them before they woke up. The doctor was right. My leg looked great compared to theirs. Their bodies were covered in black splotches that looked like the gangrene on my waist. In the worst spots, the skin was peeling away and falling off to reveal the same yellowish goo we were injected with. No one would believe these people were—and are—still alive. They look and smell as if they died two weeks ago and have been rotting ever since.

However, they are alive—or at least they aren't dead yet. I know this because one of them screamed. His stomach was grossly distended and he was grabbing around it trying to relieve his pain. The screaming woke one of his buddies, who groaned and turned to him. I expected him to yell "Shut up," or something even less polite, but instead he simply growled and barred his teeth. When his friend just wouldn't stop his

screaming, the other one stood over him and kicked him hard in the gut.

I cannot describe the horror of what happened next. I felt something slip in my head when I saw it. The other five have become nothing more than animals, and I feel myself ready to fall to their level. No one could witness what I have seen and remain sane. That we are no longer fully human is obvious, but still I hope to retain my mind. The diary helps a little in this, which is why I keep it up.

What happened after the kick. Right. I'm working up to that.

Well, the guy's stomach must have been distended with gas created from the rotting process, because when his friend kicked him, it exploded. Black rotting flesh flew off in all directions leaving a gapping hole where his stomach and intestines should have been. The disgusting pus-yellow fluid oozed up to fill the cavity. I couldn't imagine any life remaining in what was left of that body, but it sat up.

And it smiled.

It looked happy, as though the explosion had released it from the pain it had been suffering.

The sound woke the remaining three and they all five walked over to the far wall and started scrapping bits of flesh off and *eating them.*

I will fight to hold onto what humanity I have left, but there is a part of me now that shares their hunger.

JANUARY 24:

Today I write to try and explain what is happening to my mind. I know now it is slipping, and I will soon become like the five across from me. I write in the moments of lucidity granted by the morphine. After a short hour or two, I will return to the pain and the hunger. Each day I feel it scramble back faster. It won't be long before the drug has no effect at all. The professor seems not to notice though. My moments of clarity convince him of the experiment's success. Ironic how he seems to trust me more and more as I begin to trust myself less and less. You might think I feel as if some other entity controls my actions. The truth is, I know exactly what is happening. The pain puts me in a different state of mind. It brings out all of my hate, all of my rage. And now, since the events of two days ago, I feel an extreme hunger. I haven't eaten since the beginning of the experiment. Amidst the anger and hate, I realize the only food available to me might be the professor himself. I plot his death and for the satisfaction of my

appetite. The five across the hall in the other cell make their desires known by their growling and lip smacking whenever the prof comes near. I know that only through subtlety will I eat. . . .

JANUARY 26:

This morning I couldn't remember why I was here. I re-read this journal and when I read, most of my memories camed back. However, I know things are slipping. I did not know all the words I used before. Maybe some words like "HIV" were just bad spellings, but I swear I use to know what they all meant. This morning the drug man come down and hozed the room across from me with a fire-shooting thing. Isn't there a name for those? Anyways, it smelled so good. He said he done the same with the last group as well. I am the last test man. Tomorrow he plans to try a game with me, I will play with my food and then eat.

The final entry was heavily blood smeared and written in a rough scrawl. What follows is our best guess at the content.

JANUARY 28:

I free.

No more drugs.

Old man dead. I kill him when he played game with me. I eat his leg. He tastes good.

Afterward, he changed to be like me, but I banged his skull. He no more moves. Since he like me, I mark his skull with 666. Don't know why.

I think maybe this book his. I leave book with him after.

Maybe I eat more leg. Something in his head smells very good.

Brains.

Good.

CORONER'S REPORT ADDENDUM

OFFENSE: Murder
VICTIM: Caine, Amelius, Professor
CASE NUMBER: 327-8053-666
DATE: 30-1-01
INVESTIGATING PATHOLOGIST: Dr. Simon Frenlich

NOTES:

January 30, 2001; 9:00 A.M.
Re-examined body on request of Det. Hasser, who asked

*me to check the skull of the deceased for markings. Request
sent via e-mail yesterday.*

*Deceased skull does indeed have a crudely etched "666"
on the forehead.*

ACTIVITY REPORT

OFFENSE: Murder
VICTIM: Caine, Amelius, Professor
CASE NUMBER: 327-8053-666
DATE: 3-4-01
INVESTIGATING OFFICERS: Det. Tom Hasser, Det. Richard
James

*Having still not located Jake Senzer, we went to 2013-C
Wirth Place, the residence of Daisy "Dee" Hubert, with a search
warrant. No one answered the door for five minutes, so Det.
Hasser kicked in the rear kitchen door to gain entry.*

*Discovered large puddles of blood in the kitchen area.
Amongst the blood were found bits of skin and muscle. Two
sets of bloody footprints led from the puddles out the door. One
set of footprints was identical to similar prints found near Dr.
Caine.*

Ms. Hubert was not in the house.

DAWN OF THE LIVING-IMPAIRED

CHRISTINE MORGAN

"Welcome back to *Daybreak Coast to Coast*, with Elaine Kristin," the pre-recorded announcer said.

Elaine turned her megawatt smile into Camera One, her impeccably coiffed caramel locks falling over the shoulders of her rich turquoise blouse.

"In just a while, we'll be joining home styles consultant Frances Meade, who'll be showing us how you can decorate your house for the holidays with the contents of your recycling bins! But first, in our continuing effort to keep you up-to-date on events here and around the world, we have two special guests with us to discuss perhaps the most controversial issue of our time."

Elaine shifted her gaze to Camera Two, knowing that an inset screen would now be showing scenes from some of the choicer news segments and home video clips they had on file. Nothing *too* icky, of course, nothing to put the millions of viewers off their breakfast. The sponsors wouldn't appreciate that.

So instead of the infamous and grisly footage of what had happened at last month's gala Entertainment Achievement Awards—a bloodbath that had made Elaine Kristen *almost* forgive them for snubbing her in the morning show host category for a third year running—the booth ran the ones of the disinterred milling aimlessly outside of a closed mall like impatient shoppers before a big sale.

"Since the first of them rose and walked away from their mortuary slabs and caskets six months ago," Elaine went on, ignoring the small sound of pained disapproval from her left, "their numbers have increased drastically, in an epidemic that has affected nearly every nation. Each government has taken its own steps to combat what is seen as both menace and health risk. Solutions have primarily taken the form of military action, violent eradication and disposal."

Camera One panned back to include Elaine, her comfy dove-colored chair, and the fake windows that looked out on a photo mural of a sunswept, smog-free cityscape. It was no place that could ever be seen in reality, consisting as it did of computer-melded snippets of New York, Los Angeles, Seattle, and Chicago.

"Here in America, the land of the free," Elaine chirped, "the efforts of the military have run into a roadblock. I'm speaking of the so-called 'zombie rights movement.' With me today to discuss the movement are General Jason Gillespie, recently retired member of the U.S. taskforce organized to deal with the situation. . . ."

Gillespie, sitting to her right, nodded brusquely into the camera. His steel-gray hair was cropped close, his dark eyes both hooded and piercing. A sort of stern charisma, all iron and resolve, radiated from him, despite the knotted white scar that scrawled from his eye to his chin, and the obvious prosthetic that replaced his left arm.

"Good morning, Elaine," he said with a voice both deep and harsh, the sort of voice that belonged shouting orders from the top of a trench while bullets stitched the air.

Elaine nodded pertly and continued: "And Doctor Karen Wyatt-Anderson, noted psychiatrist and president of NALI." Elaine shifted her position to face the other woman. "Doctor Wyatt-Anderson, we'll begin with you. Can you tell us a little about your organization?"

Karen Wyatt-Anderson was a cool winter-eyed blonde in a severe navy-blue suit and silk blouse. Her features were aristocratic and patrician. Her spine was even more rigid, her shoulders more stiffly held, than the general's.

"Yes, Elaine," she said. "To begin, I must object to your use of the term 'zombie rights.' NALI stands for the National Alliance for the Living-Impaired, and we are dedicated to correcting the damaging misconceptions revolving around our clients."

"They *are* zombies," rumbled Gillespie, rubbing fitfully, absently at the prosthetic as if he could feel sensation in the phantom limb.

"That's like calling those with a mental illness 'nuts,'" Wyatt-Anderson countered sharply. "It is a hurtful term. NALI would like to see it stricken from popular usage. Along with several others."

"What others?" Elaine asked.

"The frequent and derogatory or belittling phrases involving the word 'dead,'" the doctor replied. "Whenever someone refers to someone else as 'dead meat,' or claims to be 'dead on their feet,' it reflects poorly on our clients."

"Your clients dig themselves out of their graves and eat people," Gillespie pointed out. "It's a contagion, it's spreading, and it needs to be dealt with. Decisively, and soon."

"That's the very attitude NALI is seeking to change."

Wyatt-Anderson returned her attention to Elaine, seeking sympathy. "These people—yes, *people*—are our friends and neighbors, our families. They deserve to be treated with the dignity and respect they had in life. They should not be feared, reviled, or hunted down."

"But haven't they changed, doctor?" Elaine said.

"They're not the same as they were, no. But neither is someone who has suffered a debilitating brain injury, or fallen into a coma, or been stricken with a mental illness or decline in cognition. Yet in those cases, the afflicted are still cared for. Their basic needs are still met."

"Basic needs!" The general leaned forward. "Lady, the only basic need a zombie's got is to chow down on human flesh! I've *seen* these things in action. I was in New York during the big July breakout. I saw one bunch of them overturn a bus-load of kids and dig right in!"

"How did you handle the July breakout?" Wyatt-Anderson shot back. "By gunning down thousands of the living-impaired, in direct violation of their civil rights."

"Damn straight! They're not people anymore. They're corpses. Their civil rights went out the window the minute they pulled themselves out of the ground and started helping themselves to brain take-out!"

Elaine knew there was a time to intervene and a time to sit back and let the interviews take their course. This was the latter. She discreetly picked up her coffee cup—emblazoned with the sponsor's logo, naturally—and sipped as the studio audience enjoyed the argument.

"It has been consistently proven that the living-impaired retain rudimentary memories of their past lives and habits. They are able to recognize familiar faces—"

"And bite 'em off to get at the gooey bits," snarled Gillespie. "They need to be wiped out."

"Destroying them is not the answer!"

"What is? We could have had this country cleansed by now, if you people hadn't come along whining about tolerance. What would you rather do? Get 'em all in a circle, hold hands, sing 'Kumbaya'?"

"With proper treatment, the living-impaired can be brought to a reasonable level of functioning."

"What sort of treatment?" Elaine interjected smoothly.

"Primarily therapy and medication—"

"God bless America," the general muttered as a curse, rolling his eyes. "Therapy!"

Doctor Wyatt-Anderson ignored him and went on speaking

to Elaine, who was nodding encouragingly. "Their desire for flesh, which is simply another form of addiction, can be treated with a patch."

"A patch?" Elaine urged.

"The Necroderm C-Q," she explained. "It's a time-release appetite suppressant combined with a craving inhibitor."

"Does it come in a gum?" someone from the audience called snidely.

"No," Wyatt-Anderson said, "but there is a liquid form that can be injected in stronger doses. We use that to stabilize clients in crisis."

"Suppose that you can control their addiction," Elaine said. "What then?"

"Then we enroll them in a series of programs. Anger management. Coping skills. Job training. We help them and encourage them to manage their symptoms and compensate for their condition, with the goal of being able to exist in a non-restrictive environment."

"Non-restrictive . . . you mean on their own?"

The general muttered a comment, but it was lost as the doctor continued her explanation.

"Yes, Elaine, but to get them out on their own involves a slow, tedious process. At the moment, we have over six hundred of the living-impaired placed in residential facilities, and thousands more in more intensive hospital-style settings. But millions more are out there, desperately in need of our services. The hardest part of our job is outreach, getting help to these people. Thanks to the efforts of those like the general here, most of the living-impaired are afraid to come forward."

Elaine nodded sagely. "Recent statistics have shown that the living-impaired population now outnumbers the homeless and the mentally ill," she said. "When even those people couldn't receive adequate help, can NALI realistically offer their services to everyone?"

"Sadly, Elaine, we can't. NALI just doesn't have the staff or resources to extend all the help we'd like. Funding for our programs is practically nonexistent. We depend almost entirely on private donations from families who have been touched by this tragedy. But you mentioned the homeless and the mentally ill. The living-impaired population hasn't so much outnumbered them as it has absorbed them."

"Yeah, they feed on the ones they can catch," Gillespie said. "The bums, street people, winos, loonies. If they leave enough meat on the bones, then those sorry bastards get up and start walking, too."

The doctor swept him with a scathing look. "With the drastic decline in those populations, one would expect that there would be considerable funding left over. Money that had been going toward mental health and housing rehab programs could, and *should*, be funneled into ours. Yet that's not happening, Elaine, and it needs to be."

"What about the Center for Disease Control?" Elaine asked. "What's their stance? I had heard that this was being treated as a communicable disease . . . postmortem infectious necrivorism, I believe was the term. Lots of people are concerned about how to keep themselves safe."

Gillespie nodded, eyes glittering. "One bite, and they've got you. Don't I know it! All they have to do is break the skin and there's not a damn thing anyone can do. When they had me and were pulling me out of that evac chopper. . . ."

Elaine shuddered in genuine sympathy. She'd argued bitterly with her producers over whether or not they could show *that* clip, the one in which, to avoid being dragged down or bitten by the trio of gray-green corpses clinging to him, Gillespie had given the order that had cost him his arm. Little wonder he was having trouble holding to the military's usual polite, but firm stance on the subject. Then again, the general was retired and thus removed from the control of handlers, and a notorious hothead—both of which helped make him such a flashy guest.

The general was rumbling, with an almost cheerful grimness, through his war story, but Wyatt-Anderson was intent on spoiling it for him. "The key to containing the spread of the illness," she interrupted, "is to avoid exposure." Her icy tone made it clear that she believed that the general had cost himself his arm, and nearly his life, by provoking the attack. "The use of universal precautions, to prevent the introduction of the infected material—"

"Zombie spit," said the general. "The thing to do is eliminate the *source*. If there were no goddam zombies, no one would have to worry about catching it. We find them, shoot them, burn what's left, and there you go. End of story, end of danger."

"Is that how you'd handle other contagious illnesses, General?" Wyatt-Anderson asked. "AIDS, hepatitis, TB? This isn't the Dark Ages, and we will not treat patients like condemned criminals! They are victims of a terrible, terrible disease. We owe it to them to *help*, not draw plague circles around them!"

Elaine, responding to increasingly urgent signaling from

her producer, cut in with another of her brilliant smiles. "We have to take a short break for some important messages, but we'll be back with General Gillespie and Doctor Wyatt-Anderson in a few minutes to take questions from our studio audience. And we'll also meet Barb and Danny, two of NALI's success stories."

The sign switched from ON AIR to OFF, and canned elevator music issued from the speakers over the audience. A couple of crew members came onstage to check and fiddle with this and that, and Elaine motioned for a refill on coffee.

"You're bringing some of those things out here?" asked Gillespie. His face had reddened, making the pale scar stand out in vivid relief.

"Don't be afraid, General," Wyatt-Anderson said condescendingly. "The counselors have everything under control."

"How *do* you keep them under control?" Elaine asked. "It's fine and well to talk about universal precautions and not getting bit, but when you're dealing with a new . . . a new client, how do you even get close enough to slap the patches on them?"

"Some direct methods are necessary," the doctor admitted. "They can be stunned or subdued by an electrical charge. Before the effects wear off, we get them under restraints to begin treatment."

"Waste of time," growled Gillespie. "Waste of money. You think you're going to rehabilitate zombies, put them back in regular society? That's crazy, that's all it is. Crazy."

"Thirty seconds," warned one of the production assistants.

Elaine thanked him with a nod, and got up. She smoothed her skirt—white with a tropical floral pattern in shades of turquoise—and took the handheld microphone.

"And . . . we're live in three, two, one!"

"Welcome back," Elaine said brightly. "We've been listening to some rather opposing viewpoints on today's topic. Doctor Karen Wyatt-Anderson, president of NALI, supports compassionate caregiving and treatment for the living-impaired. Retired General Jason Gillespie feels that zombies are a threat and must be handled with extreme prejudice. Now let's see what our audience thinks."

She held out the microphone to a clean-cut young college boy in a cableknit sweater. "Hi, Elaine, hi. I'm Jeff. My question is for the doctor. Do you, personally, work with the zombies? Er . . . with the living-impaired?"

Wyatt-Anderson gave Jeff a cool, lofty look. "In my capacity with NALI, I work very closely with the staff of several hospitals and facilities. My main function is in training and education."

"So that's a no?" he pressed. "You don't work personally, hands-on, with the stiffs? You don't have to look at them, smell them, worry that they might take a chunk out of you?"

"I have seen several living-impaired clients," she said.

Jeff looked straight into the camera and hoisted one eyebrow knowingly. Elaine thanked him and moved on to a portly man possessing the jowls and the sorrowful eyes of a basset hound.

"Albert Lawry here," he said, gaze fixed on the microphone. "I just . . . my wife Helen. . . . She died a year ago. . . . I was wondering, Doctor, if you could help me find her? She was buried in Oregon, with her parents, and when everything started I went to the cemetery, but she wasn't there. Do you have a list or something?"

"I'm sorry, Mr. Lawry. Most of the time, our clients have no identification. We try to track down their records, but it's a slow process. If you call NALI, at 1-888-555-3323—"

"That's 555-DEAD," Jeff announced, drawing a laugh from the audience and a flush of chagrin from the doctor.

She regained her composure, but if telepathy were real and could kill, there'd be one attractive twenty-something laid out on the floor. "If you call NALI and leave your name and information, we can contact you should we locate your wife."

Elaine moved to the next waving hand, which belonged to a teenaged girl with intricately beaded and cornrowed hair. "General Gillespie, my dad is in the Marines, and he says that zombies can only be killed if you blow their heads off or burn them, is that true?"

"I hardly think that's an appropriate question!" Doctor Wyatt-Anderson snapped.

The general faced the girl. "As near as we've been able to tell, the only way to stop them is to take out the brain. Fire might do it eventually, but in the meantime, they'd still be running around. And I'll tell you one thing . . . may be hard to believe, but a fried zombie stinks worse than a regular one."

Karen Wyatt-Anderson's lips had drawn together in a line so thin and tight that they'd almost disappeared. "I must once again object to your choice of language. These are *people* we're talking about. Wives, husbands, sons, daughters, mothers, and fathers! You demean and degrade them by referring to them in those terms!"

A thin, almost frighteningly intense woman with long dark hair popped up beside Elaine, pushing aside an anxious grandmotherly type. "They're *dead*! Can't you get that through your politically correct skull?"

"They've come back. Not all the way, granted, but they've made the effort."

"Effort! Some alien germ or solar radiation makes the corpses walk, that's all it is! Not God, not their own free will! Who would want to come back as something like that? Who'd want to live like that? I say that putting them out of their misery is doing them a favor, not sending them to some twelve-step program!"

Savage applause, not the least of which was from the general, greeted the woman's remarks. Mixed in were cries of "You said it!" and "All right!" and one man chanting, "Bring out your dead! Bring out your dead!"

"Why don't we?" chirped Elaine in her most vivacious talk show hostess tone. "Let's bring out Barb and Danny, and hear what they have to say!"

Jeff and the man who'd been chanting the Monty Python dialogue both cupped their hands around their mouths to make megaphones and called, "Braaaaaaaiiiiiiiinns!" in slow, dragging imitation of the undead.

The good doctor stood up. "I will not have them subjected to this blatantly hostile abuse! NALI's purpose is to increase public awareness and help our clients."

"Maybe it would help for everyone to see the progress they've made under treatment," Elaine suggested. "Instead of the negative, sensationalized images of their kind most of us have seen."

"Progress!" Gillespie snorted. "Couple of zombies, hosed off and put in clean clothes. Maybe you can train 'em like animals, but they're still flesh-eating monsters. Suppose you bring them out here and they decide it's an all-you-can-eat buffet?"

"Barb has been flesh-free for eight weeks," Wyatt-Anderson said huffily. "Danny for almost as long. They're proof that the patch and the treatment are effective, two of our most compensated clients."

Elaine caught the eye of one of the backstage crew, and he responded with a nod.

Moments later, a small group emerged from the side door of the set. Three men and a woman, all in pristine white lab coats, ushered in two shuffling figures.

An appalled, fascinated "Ooooh!" came from the audience, accompanied by a shifting rustle as they all leaned forward to get a good look at the necrivores.

The larger of the two, introduced as Barb, must have been a huge woman in life and hadn't diminished much since. A drab mustard-colored sweatsuit neither concealed nor flattered the drooping swell of her belly or the pendulous melon-sized breasts that bobbled like loosely filled sacks of gelatin. Her behind was truly mythic in its proportions, and with her head bent down against the glare of the studio lighting, her chins descended to her chest in a series of mushy folds.

They'd obviously made an effort to get her presentable. Her skin was doughy and blue-gray, but she was clean and not visibly maggot-ridden. What was left of her brown hair had been drawn neatly back in a scrunchied ponytail. She had the sadly sweet face of so many hopelessly obese women, hinting at the beauty that might have been hers had her life taken a different turn.

It would have taken about eight Dannys to make up one Barb. The smaller of the pair couldn't have been more than ten years old when he died, and the evidence of his death was present in the form of a malformed dent in the side of his head. It was the sort of injury one might expect to see when a kid disregarded the helmet law and came to grief with one of those zippy little scooters.

The ghost of an impish smile lurked around his slack, dry lips. He wore jeans and an oversized football jersey and high-top sneakers like any other kid. Yards of spice-scented wrappings might have suited him better, for he appeared wizened and dry, more mummified than rotting. His dark skin had taken on a hue and texture reminiscent of ash-coated beef jerky.

General Gillespie made a sound somewhere between a moan and a snarl as the two zombies shambled closer. Their attendants stopped them at the center of the stage, Cameras One and Two zooming in for close-ups.

Both of their patches were in plain sight, pasted to the sides of their necks just below the ear. In a final bizarre touch, the patches were for some reason the gleaming plastic pink-tan that used to be called "flesh" by the crayon people, a color that didn't match the skin of any race of the living, let alone the dead. On Barb and Danny, it was as hectic as a clown's vivid red cheeks.

Doctor Wyatt-Anderson crossed her arms smugly and threw Gillespie a silent "Told you so!" as the nervous tittering and revolted gasps of the audience gave way to murmurings of pity.

Elaine was surprised to find that she understood their

feelings, for there was something unspeakably tragic and solemn about the pair. They stood slouched by both in the poor posture of death and the inescapable defeated hopelessness of their circumstances.

Danny goggled at the nearest camera. One of his eyes was milky but otherwise normal; the other was distended from the socket as if it had been popped out and replaced without true concern for the fit. That orb was roadmapped with broken veins, and a purpled corona engulfed the pupil.

The bleak incomprehension in their stares changed as they took in the sight of the studio audience, dozens and dozens of healthy humans. The glint put Elaine in mind of reluctant dieters confronted with a bakery window.

What must we look like to those glassy gazes? the host wondered. *A parade of meaty limbs and delectable torsos?* She thought about the old saying—you can't help someone who didn't want to be helped. What was the treatment doing to the living dead? As far as she knew, as far as anyone knew, they came back with only one driving impulse: to eat. And now that had been taken away from them. What did that leave?

"My God," Elaine heard herself say. "This is terrible!"

"The growth rate of the living-impaired population," Wyatt-Anderson said, "has leveled off thanks to the increase in cremation as a form of funerary services. But there are still millions of them out there, and they need your help."

Gillespie shook his head. "What they need is to be sent back where they came from. That one lady was right—this is no way to be!"

Barb swiveled slowly in the general's direction. Watching her move was like watching the gaseous atmosphere of Jupiter rotate, bands of flesh shifting and sliding at different rates. A whiff of her odor reached Elaine. Mostly soap and talcum powder, but underneath was a faintly rancid, wholly repugnant reek of spoilage.

The general realized with evident, utter horror that he was the focus of three hundred-plus pounds of zombie attention, and took an involuntary step back.

"Deaaad," Barb said, forcing the word sluggishly through liquefying vocal cords.

"Dead," Danny seconded, his voice more clear but raspy as a file on sandpaper.

"And they should stay that way," said someone from the audience. Elaine recognized the intense brunette without needing to look. "Dead things should stay that way. This is wrong. Can't you see that? Wrong!"

Doctor Wyatt-Anderson stepped forward to argue, but Barb's chins tripled and then receded as she nodded. "Rrrrrrronnng!"

Her pudgy, sausage-fingered hand floated up as if tied to a helium balloon. It wandered aimlessly around her head for a moment, pulled strands of hair from the scrunchie to hang lank in her face, and then found the edge of the patch. Two of her fingernails peeled loose as she dug at it.

"Barb, stop it," said one of the attendants.

Danny squinted up at his behemothic companion, some dim understanding welling in his muddy eyes.

Barb's patch came unstuck with a grisly squelching noise, tearing away a spongy mat of flesh with it. "Dead!" she shrieked. "Dead-dead-dead!"

The attendants rushed in, bringing heavy-duty tazers out of concealed holsters. Elaine, rooted to the spot, was buffeted as the audience yielded to instinct and thundered for the exits.

"Dead-dead-dead!" Danny parroted, and ripped the patch from his own neck so vigorously that he nearly beheaded himself. The ivory knobs of his vertebrae poked through like stepping stones.

"Stop her!" Wyatt-Anderson ordered above the din. Then, incredibly, "We'll never get funding like this!"

It was, Elaine would later think, a pretty crappy set of last words. Barb lumbered forward with the force of a charging rhino, and crushed the doctor's rib cage with one swing of her massive arm.

Still unable to move, hypnotized by the spectacle, Elaine observed with detached marvel the way the impact sent ripples through the zombie's flab.

Barb seized Wyatt-Anderson, pulled her close as if going for a kiss, and clamped her jaws on the doctor's shoulder. Elaine, in a space beyond terror now, batted at Barb's face with the microphone and squashed her nose into a soggy ruin. Barb let go of her victim.

An attendant grabbed for Danny as Doctor Wyatt-Anderson's body was hitting the ground. The dead child writhed snake-fast and got a mouthful of muscle, eliciting a scream that was more fear than pain. And it was a lot of pain.

Barb stepped mostly over but partly on the fallen psychiatrist, cracking bones like twigs underfoot, and reached for her next meal. Elaine thrust out the microphone in a defensive effort and Barb chomped into it, masticating furiously at the spongy black covering before spitting it aside.

Someone dropped an iron safe onto a solid hardwood

floor. Or at least that was what Elaine's first thought was as a colossal *boom* resonated through the studio. It wasn't until the side of Barb's skull blossomed out in a pulpy yellow and gray spray that she realized what had happened. The giant body went down so hard that it should have set off car alarms in the parking lot outside.

Elaine very nearly went down with it, as Barb's flailing hand snared the front of her blouse. She was yanked backward to safety by the college guy in the cableknit sweater—Jeff.

General Gillespie, his uniform jacket all askew and a holster tucked into the rear of his pants, was waving a gun roughly the size of a small cannon. He squeezed off a wild shot just as Frances Meade, *Daybreak Coast to Coast*'s answer to Martha Stewart, came rushing onstage to see what all the fuss was about. She went flying back in a crimson spray that clashed horribly with her pale green outfit.

Elaine saw that even though the cameramen had fled, the lights and the ON AIR sign were still working fine. Camera One had been knocked aslant and was getting nothing but stampeding feet. Camera Two, however, was getting everything.

Electricity leaped and sizzled as the attendants tried to tazer the ravenous smaller zombie into submission, but Danny was having none of it. The taste of hot blood and warm meat was in his mouth for the first time in weeks, and he was not going to be denied.

Elaine, knowing that this show would either make her career or destroy it, tore away from Jeff and rushed at the general. He was yelling incoherently, blasting away. It was a pure miracle that more of the panicked studio audience hadn't been hit. She snatched at the gun—wincing, but not pulling away from the touch of the hot barrel—and wrested the weapon away from him.

Danny was atop the bitten attendant. Grisly snacking and slurping noises could be heard even above the rest of the cacophony.

Elaine slammed her dainty turquoise-blue pump down on Danny's back, set the barrel of the gun to the back of his head, and with a grimace that she somehow knew resembled the way her mom looked when fishing around in a turkey for the giblet packet, pulled the trigger.

The recoil was instant and tremendous, slamming up her arm with such force she thought she had dislocated her shoulder. But the bullet plowed through Danny's small and already cracked skull, out the other side, and lodged in the thrashing attendant's face, saving him from the basic fate worse than death.

Only one NALI attendant remained, the other two having remembered pressing appointments elsewhere. In a total loss of sanity, he pointed his tazer at the morning show hostess. General Gillespie, wanting his toy back, had the bad luck to interpose himself in time to take the volts. He collapsed, twitching and jerking.

"It's all right!" Jeff yelled, pointing at the motionless bodies of Barb and Danny. "They're down! Both down!"

His words took the edge off of the furor, but it all went to hell again a split second later.

With a sudden convulsive lurch, Doctor Wyatt-Anderson pushed herself upright. She held herself awkwardly, with half of her ribs caved in and one arm dangling crazy-jointed and limp.

The remaining attendant, Jeff, and Elaine all shouted a word that would have been edited out or bleeped on tape, but they were still live, still rolling.

Wyatt-Anderson's gaze fell upon them. Formerly haughty and cold, it was now filled with a mindless hunger. Her lips drew back to expose a view that would have been right at home in a toothpaste commercial. She darted forward and swiped a handful of manicure at them.

On raw reflex, Elaine fired again. The shot hit Wyatt-Anderson between the eyes and took most of the top of her head off. The doctor cartwheeled in a tumble over the gore-splattered dove-gray chair that Elaine vowed never to sit in again, and came to rest in a heap at the bottom of the window with its fake cityscape.

"Wow," said Jeff shakily. "I guess she wasn't just president of the National Alliance for the Living-Impaired . . ."

It was the insanity of the moment, or the reek of blood and decomposition that made them take leave of their senses. But the rest of the surviving trio came in with him on the end.

"She's also a client!" they chorused, and finally someone in the control room had the good sense to go to commercial.

TRINKETS

TOBIAS S. BUCKELL

George Petros walked down the waterfront, the tails of his coat slapping the back of his knees. An occasional gust of wind would tug at his tri-cornered hat, threatening to snatch it away. But by leaning his head into the wind slightly, George was able to manage a sort of balancing act between the impetuous gusts of wind and civilization's preference for a covered head.

The cobblestones made for wobbly walking, and George had just bought new shoes. He hadn't broken them in yet. Still, the luxury of new shoes bought the fleeting edges of a self-satisfied smile. The soles of his new shoes made a metronomic *tick-tick-tick* sound as he hurried toward his destination, only slowing down when he walked around piles of unloaded cargo.

Men of all sorts, shapes, and sizes bustled around in the snappy, cold weather. Their breath steamed as they used long hooks to snatch the cargo up and unload it. George walked straight past them. He did not put on airs or anything of the sort, but he hardly made eye contact with the grunting dockworkers.

His destination was the *Toussaint*. George could tell he was getting closer as the quiet suffering of the New England dockworkers yielded to a more buoyant singing.

George detoured around one last stack of crates, the live chickens inside putting up a cacophony of squawks and complaint, and saw the *Toussaint*. The ship was hardly remarkable; it looked like any other docked merchantmen. What *did* give one a reason to pause were the people around the ship: they were Negroes. Of all shades of colors, George noticed.

Free Negroes were common enough around the North. But to see this many in one area, carrying guns, talking, chatting, flying their own flag—it made people nervous. Ever since the island of Haiti drove the French from its shores and won its independence, their ships had been ranging up and down the American coast. George knew it made American politicians wonder if the Negroes of the South would gain any inspiration from the Haitians' visible freedom.

The crew stood around the ship, unloaded the cargo, and

conducted business for supplies with some of the Yankee shopkeepers. George himself was a shopkeeper, though of jewels and not staples of any sort. He nodded, seeing some familiar faces from his street: Bruce, Thomas. No doubt they would think he was here for some deal with the Haitians.

The smell of salt and sweat wafted across the docks as George nodded to some of the dockworkers, then passed through them to the ship's gangplank. One of the Haitians stopped him. George looked down and noticed the pistol stuck in a white sash.

"What do you need?" He spoke with traces of what could have been a French accent, or something else. It took a second for George to work through the words.

"I'm here for a package," George said slowly. "Mother Jacqueline. . . ."

The man smiled.

"Ah, you're that George?"

"Yes."

George stood at the end of the plank as the Haitian walked back onto the ship. He returned in a few minutes and handed the shopkeeper a brown, carefully wrapped parcel. Nothing shifted when George shook it.

He stood there for a second, searching for something to say, but then he suddenly realized that the tables had been turned. Now *he* was the one who wasn't wanted here. He left, shoes clicking across the cobblestones.

✦ ✦ ✦

In the room over his shop George opened the parcel by the window. Below in the street, horses' feet kicked up a fine scattering of snow. When it settled by the gutters, it was stained brown and muddy with dung.

The desk in front of him was covered in occasional strands of his hair. He had a small shelf with papers stacked on it, but more importantly, he had his shiny coins and pieces of metal laid out in neat, tiny little rows. George smiled when the light caught their edges and winked at him. Some of the coins had engravings on them, gifts between lovers long passed away. Others had other arcane pieces of attachment to their former owners. Each one told George a little story. The jewelry he sold downstairs meant nothing. Each of the pieces here represented a step closer to a sense of completion.

He cut the string on the package and pulled the paper away from a warm mahogany box lid. The brass hinges squeaked when he opened it.

Inside was a letter. The wax seal on it caught George's full attention; he sat for a moment entranced by it. The faint smell of something vinegary kicked faint memories back from their resting places, and Mama Jaqi's distant whisper spoke to him from the seal.

"Hear me, obey me. . . ."

George sucked in his breath and opened the seal to read his directions. *There is a man,* the letter read, *right now sitting in a tavern fifteen or so miles south of you. You should go and listen to his story. . . .*

There was a name. And the address of the tavern.

Who was Louis Povaught? George wondered. But he didn't question the implicit order given. Layers of cold ran down his back, making him shiver. Automatically, without realizing it, he pulled something out of the box and put it in his pocket, then shut the lid. As he donned his coat and walked out of the shop to find a carriage, he told Ryan, the shop's assistant, that he would be back "later," and that he should close the shop himself.

✦ ✦ ✦

Hours later, the sky darkening, George's cab stopped in front of the Hawser. A quick wind batted the wooden sign over the door. George paid and walked inside. It was like any other tavern: dim, and it smelled of stale beer and piss. He looked around and fastened his eyes on a Frenchman at the edge of the counter.

Frenchman, Negro, Northerner, Southerner, English . . . to George, all humanity had seemed more or less the same after he'd met Mama Jaqi. Yet even now he could feel that he was being nudged toward the Frenchman. This is the man he was supposed to meet. As irrational as it may have seemed, George carefully stamped his new shoes clean, leaned over to brush them off with a handkerchief he kept for exactly that purpose, then crossed the tavern to sit by the stranger.

The Frenchman—who would be Louis Povaught, George assumed—slouched in his seat. He hardly stirred when George sat next to him. The barkeep caught George's eye, and the shopkeeper shook his head. When he turned back to look at Louis, the man was already looking back at him.

Louis, unfortunately, hadn't spent much time keeping up his appearances. A long russet-colored beard, patchy in some places, grew haphazardly from his cheeks. His bloodshot eyes contained just a hint of green, lost to the steady strain of enthusiastic drinking.

"I think, not many people walk in here who do not order drink," he declared. "No?"

George pulled out his purse and caught the eye of the barkeep. "He'll have another." George looked down and pulled out paper money, leaving the shiny coins inside.

"And you," Louis said. "Why no drink?"

"It no longer does anything for me," George explained. He reached his hand in the pocket of his undercoat. Something was there. Like something standing just at the edge of his vision, he could barely remember picking it up.

Now George pulled it out. It was a silver chain with a plain cross on the end. The shopkeep held it between the fingers of his hand and let the cross rest against the countertop.

"I have something for you, Louis," George heard himself saying. "Something very important."

Louis turned his tangled hair and scraggly beard toward George. The chain seductively winked; George locked his eyes with the entwined chains and followed them down to the rough countertop. Such beautiful things human hands made.

Louis' gasp took George's attention back to the world beyond the necklace.

"Is this what I think it is?" Louis asked, reaching tentatively for it. His wrinkled hands shook as they brushed the chain. George did not look down for fear of being entranced again. He did not feel the slightest brush of Louis' fingernail against his knuckle.

"What do you think it is?" George asked.

Louis turned back to the tavern.

"My brother Jean's necklace," Louis said. "On the back of this, it should have engrave . . ." Louis waved his hand about, "*J. P.* It is there, no?"

George still didn't look down.

"I imagine so."

Louis leaned back and laughed.

"*Merde*. So far away, so damn far away, and that bitch Jacqueline still has talons. Unlucky? Ha," he spat. "Do you know my story?"

"No," George said. "I do not."

The barkeep finally delivered a mug of beer, the dirty amber fluid spilling over the sides and onto the bar top where it would soak into the wood and add to the dank and musky air. Louis took the glass with a firm grasp and tipped it back. It took only seconds before the mug contained nothing but slick wetness at the bottom.

Louis smacked the mug down. "Buy me another, damn

you," he ordered. George tapped the counter, looked at the barkeep, and nodded.

Stories, George thought, could sometimes be as interesting as something shiny and new. He would indulge Louis, yes, and himself. He handed Louis the necklace.

"Jean was much the better brother," Louis said. "I think it broke my father's heart to hear he died in Haiti. My father locked himself in his study for three days. Did not eat, did not drink. And when he came back out, he put his hand on my shoulder, like this—" Louis draped a heavy arm over George and leaned closer; his breath reeked of beer "—and he tells me, he tells me, 'Louis, you must go and take over where you brother has left off.' That is all he tells me. I never see him again."

Louis pulled back and scowled. "And Katrina, my wife, she is very, *very* sad to see me go away to this island. But I tell her it is good that I take over the business Jean created. I will make for her better husband. My brother has left me a good legacy. Hmmm. I did good business. I made them all proud. Proud! And you know what," Louis said, looking down at the necklace, "it was all great until Jean walked into my office three month later. It was . . . I'd seen his grave! There were witnesses. . . ."

"Business was good?" George interrupted. "What did you do?"

Louis ran a thumb around the rim of his glass.

"It didn't cost much. A boat. Provisions. We bought our cargo for guns . . . and necklaces, or whatever: beads and scrap." He opened a weathered palm. There was nothing in it.

"What cargo?" George interrupted. This was the point. It was why Mama Jaqi had sent him.

"Slaves," Louis said. "Lots of slaves."

"Ah, yes," George said. Mama Jaqi had been a slave.

"I made money," Louis said. "For the first time I wasn't some peasant in Provencal. I had a house with gardens." He looked at the shopkeep. "I did good! I gave money to charity. I was a good citizen. I was a good *businessman.*"

"I am sure you were," George said. He felt nothing against Louis. In another life, he would maybe have gone with Louis' arguments. He remembered using some of them once, a long time ago. A brief flash of a memory seared George's thoughts: he desperately blabbered some of the same things Louis had said, trying to defend himself to the incensed Mama Jaqi.

Quickly George shook away the ghostlike feel of passion. He needed to prod Louis' story along. He was here for the story, but he wanted it over quickly. Time was getting on, and he had to open the shop tomorrow. He would have to finish Mama Jaqi's deed soon. "What a shock seeing your brother must have been," George said at last.

"I thought some horrible trick had been played on me," Louis said. "I had so many questions about what had happened. And all Jean would do was tell me I had to leave. Leave the business. Leave the island. I refused." Louis made a motion at the bartender for more beer. "I was still in Haiti when it all began. Toussaint . . . the independence. I lost it all when the blacks ran us all off. I slipped away on a small boat to America with nothing. Nothing."

The Frenchman looked at George, and George saw a world of misery swimming in the man's eyes. "In France," Louis whispered, "they hear I am dead. I can only think of Katrina remarrying." He stopped and looked down at George's arm.

"What is it?" George asked.

Louis reached a finger out and pulled back the cuff of George's sleeve. Underneath, a faint series of scars marked the shopkeep's wrist.

"Jean had those," Louis said. The barkeep set another mug in front of the Frenchman, and left after George paid for it. "Do me a favor," Louis said, letting go of the other's sleeve. "One last favor."

"If I can," George said.

"Let me do this properly, like a real man. Eh? Would you do that?"

"Yes," George said.

Louis took his last long gulp from the mug, then stood up. "I will be out in the alley."

George watched him stagger out the tavern.

✢ ✢ ✢

After several minutes George got up and walked out. The distant cold hit him square in the face when he opened the door, and several men around the tables yelled at him to hurry and get out and shut the door.

In the alley by the tavern, George paused. Louis stepped out of the darkness holding a knife in his left hand, swaying slightly in the wind.

Neither of them said anything. They circled each other for a few seconds, then Louis stumbled forward and tried to slash at George's stomach. George stepped away from the crude attempt and grabbed the Frenchman's wrist. It was his intent to take the knife away, but Louis slipped and fell onto the stones. He landed on his arm, knocking his own knife away, then cracked his head against the corner of a brick.

Louis didn't move anymore. He still breathed, though: a slight heaving and the air steaming out from his mouth.

George crouched and put a knee to Louis' throat. The steaming breath stopped, leaving the air still and quiet. A long minute passed, then Louis opened an eye. He struggled, kicking a small pool of half-melted snow with his tattered boots. George kept his knee in place.

When the Frenchman stopped moving, George relaxed, but kept the knee in place for another minute.

The door to the tavern opened, voices carrying into the alley. Someone hailed for a cab and the clip-clop of hooves quickened nearby. George kept still in the alley's shadows. When the voices trailed off into the distance the shopkeeper moved again. He checked Louis' pockets until he found what he wanted: the necklace. He put it back into his own pocket. Then he stood up and walked out of the alley to hail his own cab.

✜   ✜   ✜

The snow got worse toward the harbor and his shop. The horses pulling the cab snorted and slowed down, and the whole vehicle would shift and slide with wind gusts. George sat looking out at the barren, wintry landscape. It was cold and distant, like his own mechanical feelings. He could hear occasional snatches of the driver whistling "Amazing Grace" to himself and the horses.

Mama Jaqi had done well. George felt nothing but a compulsion for her bidding. *Obey.* . . . No horror about what he had just done. Just a dry, crusty satisfaction.

When he got out, George paid the driver. He took the creaky back steps up. He lit several candles and sat in his study for a while, still fully dressed. Eventually he put his fingers to the candle in front of him and watched the edges turn from white, to red, to brown, and then to a blistered black. The burned skin smelled more like incense than cooked flesh.

He pulled them away.

Tomorrow they would be whole again.

George lifted the silver necklace out with his good hand. He set it on the shelf, next to all the other flashy trinkets. Another story ended, another decoration on his shelf.

How many more would it take, George wondered, before Mama Jaqi freed him? How many lives did she deem a worthy trade for the long suffering she had known in her life? Or for the horrors of George's own terrible past? He didn't know. She'd taken that ability away from him. In this distant reincarnation of himself, George knew that any human, passionate response he could muster would be wrong.

Even his old feelings would have been wrong.

Long after the candles burned out, George sat, waiting.

MURDERMOUTH

SCOTT NICHOLSON

If only they had taken my tongue.

With no tongue, I would not taste this world. The air in the tent is buttered by the mist from popcorn. Cigarette smoke drifts from outside, sweet with candy apples and the liquor that the young men have been drinking. The drunken ones laugh the hardest, but their laughter always turns cruel.

If they only knew how much I love them. All of them, the small boys whose mothers pull them by the collar away from the cage, the plump women whose hair reflects the torchlight, the men all trying to act as if they are not surprised to see a dead man staring at them with hunger dripping from his mouth.

"Come and see the freak," says the man who cages me, his hands full of dollar bills.

Freak. He means me. I love him.

More people press forward, bulging like sausages against the confines of their skin. The salt from their sweat burns my eyes. I wish I could not see.

But I see more clearly now, dead, than I ever did while breathing. I know this is wrong, that my heart should beat like a trapped bird, that my veins should throb in my temples, that blood should sluice through my limbs. Or else, my eyes should go forever dark, the pounding stilled.

"He doesn't look all that weird," says a long-haired man in denim overalls. He spits brown juice into the straw covering the ground.

"Seen one like him up at Conner's Flat," says a second, whose breath falls like an ill wind. "I hear there's three in Asheville, in freak shows like this."

The long-haired man doesn't smell my love for him. "Them scientists and their labs, cooking up all kinds of crazy stuff, it's a wonder something like this ain't happened years ago."

The second man laughs and points at me and I want to kiss his finger. "This poor bastard should have been put out of his misery like the rest of them. Looks like he wouldn't mind sucking your brains out of your skull."

"Shit, that's nothing," says a third, this one as big around as one of the barrels that the clowns use for tricks. "I seen a woman in Parson's Ford, she'd take a hunk out of your leg faster than you can say 'Bob's your uncle.'"

"Sounds like your ex-wife," says the first man to the second. The three of them laugh together.

"A one hundred percent genuine flesh-eater," says my barker. His eyes shine like coins. He is proud of his freak.

"He looks like any one of us," calls a voice from the crowd. "You know. Normal."

"Say, pardner, you wouldn't be taking us for a ride, would you?" says the man as big as a barrel.

For a moment, I wonder if perhaps some mistake has been made, that I am in my bed, dreaming beside my wife. I put my hand to my chest. No heartbeat. I put a finger in my mouth.

"I'm as true as an encyclopedia," says my barker.

"Look at the bad man, Mommy," says a little girl. I smile at her, my mouth wet with desire. She shrieks and her mother leans forward and picks her up. I spit my finger out and stare at it, lying there pale against the straw, slick and shiny beneath the guttering torches.

Several of the women moan, the men grunt before they can stop themselves, and the children lean closer, jostle for position. One slips, a yellow-haired boy with tan skin and meat that smells like soap. For an instant, his hands grip the bars of the cage. He fights for balance.

I love him so much, I want to make him happy, to please him. I crawl forward, his human stink against my tongue as I try to kiss him. Too quickly, a man has yanked him away. A woman screams and curses first at him, then at me.

The barker beats at the bars with his walking stick. "Get back, freak."

I cover my face with my hands, as he has taught me. The crowd cheers. I hunch my back and shiver, though I have not been cold since I took my final breath. The barker pokes me with the stick, taunting me. Our eyes meet and I know what to do next. I pick my finger off the ground and return it to my mouth. The crowd sighs in satisfaction.

The finger has not much flavor. It is like the old chicken hearts the barker throws to me at night after the crowd has left. Pieces of flesh that taste of dirt and chemicals. No matter how much of it I eat, I still hunger.

The crowd slowly files out of the tent. Through the gap that is the door I see the brightly spinning wheels of light, hear the bigger laughter, the bells and shouts as someone wins at a game. With so much amusement, a freak like me cannot hope to hold their attention for long. And still I love them, even when they are gone and all that's left is the stench of their shock and repulsion.

The barker counts his money, stuffs it in the pocket of his striped trousers. "Good trick there, with the finger. You're pretty smart for a dead guy."

I smile at him. I love him. I wish he would come closer to the bars, so I could show him how much I want to please him. I pleased my last barker. He screamed and screamed, but my love was strong, stronger than those who tried to pull him away.

The barker goes outside the tent to try and find more people with money. His voice rings out, mixes with the organ waltzes and the hum of the big diesel engines. The tent is empty and I feel something in my chest. Not the beating, beating, beating like before I died. This is more like the thing I feel in my mouth and stomach. I need. I put my finger in my mouth, even though no one is watching.

The juggler comes around a partition. The juggler is called Juggles and he wears make-up and an old, dark green body stocking. He has no arms. His painted eyes make his face look small. "Hey, Murdermouth," he says.

I don't remember the name I had when I was alive, but Murdermouth has been the favorite name the others call me lately. I smile at him and show him my teeth and tongue. Juggles comes by every night when the crowds thin out.

"Eating your own damned finger," Juggles says. He takes three cigarettes from a pocket hidden somewhere in his body stocking. In a moment, the cigarettes are in the air, twirling, Juggles' bare toes a blur of motion. Then one is in his mouth, and he leans forward and lights it from a torch while continuing to toss the other two cigarettes.

He blows smoke at me. "What's it like to be dead?"

I wish I could speak. I want to tell him, I want to tell them all. Being dead has taught me how to love. Being dead has shown me what is really important on this earth. Being dead has saved my life.

"You poor schmuck. Ought to put a bullet in your head." Juggles lets the cigarette dangle from his lips. He lights one of the others and flips it into my cage with his foot. "Here you go. Suck on that for a while."

I pick up the cigarette and touch its orange end. My skin sizzles and I stare at the wound as the smoke curls into my nose. I put the other end of the cigarette in my mouth. I cannot breathe so it does no good.

"Why are you so mean to him?"

It is she. Her voice comes like hammers, like needles of ice, like small kisses along my skin. She stands at the edge of the shadows, a shadow herself. I know that if my heart could beat it would go crazy.

"I don't mean nothing," says Juggles. He exhales and squints against the smoke, then sits on a bale of straw. "Just having a little fun."

"Fun," she says. "All you care about is fun."

"What else is there? None of us are going anywhere."

She steps from the darkness at the corner of the tent. The torchlight is golden on her face, flickering playfully among her chins. Her breath wheezes like the softest of summer winds. She is beautiful. My Fat Lady.

The cigarette burns between my fingers. The fire reaches my flesh. I look down at the blisters, trying to remember what pain felt like. Juice leaks from the wounds and extinguishes the cigarette.

"He shouldn't be in a cage," says the Fat Lady. "He's no different from any of us."

"Except for that part about eating people."

"I wonder what his name is."

"You mean 'was,' right? Everything's in the past for him."

The Fat Lady squats near the cage. Her breasts swell with the effort, lush as moons. She stares at my face, into my eyes. I crush the cigarette in my hand and toss it to the ground.

"He knows," she says. "He can still feel. Just because he can't talk doesn't mean he's an idiot. Whatever that virus was that caused this, it's a hundred times worse than being dead."

"Hell, if I had arms, I'd give him a hug," mocks Juggles.

"You and your arms. You think you're the only one that has troubles?" The Fat Lady wears lipstick, her mouth is a red gash against her pale, broad face. Her teeth are straight and healthy. I wish she would come closer.

"Crying over Murdermouth is like pissing in a river. At least he brings in a few paying customers."

The Fat Lady stares deeply into my eyes. I try to blink, to let her know I'm in here. She sees me. She sees me.

"He's more human than you'll ever be," the Fat Lady says, without turning her head.

"Oh, yeah? Give us both a kiss and then tell me who loves you." He has pulled a yellow ball from somewhere and tosses it back and forth between his feet. "Except you better kiss me first because you probably won't have no lips left after him."

"He would never hurt me," she says. She smiles at me. "Would you?"

I try to think, try to make my mouth form the word. My throat. All my muscles are dumb, except for my tongue. I taste her perfume and sweat, the oil of her hair, the sex she had with someone.

Voices spill from the tent flap. The barker is back, this time with only four people. Juggles hops to his feet, balances on one leg while saluting the group, then dances away. He doesn't like the barker.

"Hello, Princess Tiffany," says the barker.

The Fat Lady grins, rises slowly, groans with the effort of lifting her own weight. I love all of her.

"For a limited time only, a special attraction," shouts the barker in his money-making voice. "The world's fattest woman and the bottomless Murdermouth, together again for the very first time."

The Fat Lady waves her hand at him, smiles once more at me, then waddles toward the opening in the tent. She waits for a moment, obliterating the bright lights beyond the tent walls, then enters the clamor and madness of the crowd.

"Too bad," says the barker. "A love for the ages."

"Goddamn, I'd pay double to see that," says one of the group.

"Quadruple," says the barker. "Once for each chin."

The group laughs, then falls silent as all eyes turn to me.

The barker beats on the cage with his stick. "Give them a show, freak."

I eat the finger again. It is shredded now and bits of dirt and straw stick to the knuckle. Two of the people, a man and a woman, hug each other. The woman makes a sound like her stomach is bad. Another man, the one who would pay double, says, "Do they really eat people?"

"Faster than an alligator," says my barker. "Why, this very one ingested my esteemed predecessor in three minutes flat. Nothing left but two pounds of bones and a shoe."

"Doesn't look like much to me," says the man. "I wouldn't be afraid to take him on."

He calls to the man with him, who wobbles and smells of liquor and excrement. "What do you think? Ten-to-one odds."

"Maynard, he'd munch your ass so fast you'd be screaming 'Mommy' before you knew what was going on," says the wobbling man.

Maynard's eyes narrow, and he turns to the barker. "I'll give you a hundred bucks. Him and me, five minutes."

My barker points the stick toward the tent ceiling. "Five minutes? In the cage with that thing?"

"I heard about these things," says the man. "Don't know if I believe it."

My mouth tastes his courage and his fear. He is salt and meat and brains and kidneys. He is one of them. I love him.

He takes the stick from the barker and pokes me in the shoulder.

"That's not sporting," says the barker. He looks at the man and woman, who have gone pale and taken several steps toward the door.

Maynard rattles the stick against the bars and pokes me in the face. I hear a tearing sound. The woman screams and the man beside her shouts, then they run into the night. Organ notes trip across the sky, glittering wheels tilt, people laugh. The crowd is thinning for the night.

Maynard fishes in his pocket and pulls out some bills. "What do you say?"

"I don't know if it's legal," says the barker.

"What do you care? Plenty more where he came from." Maynard breathes heavily. I smell poison spilling from inside him.

"It ain't like it's murder," says Maynard's drunken companion.

The barker looks around, takes the bills. "After the crowd's gone. Come back after midnight and meet me by the duck-hunting gallery."

Maynard reaches the stick into the bars, rakes my disembodied finger out of the cage. He bends down and picks it up, sniffs it, and slides it into his pocket. "A little return on my investment," he says.

The barker takes the stick from Maynard and wipes it clean on his trouser leg. "Show's over, folks," he yells, as if addressing a packed house.

"Midnight," Maynard says to me. "Then it's you and me, freak."

The wobbly man giggles as they leave the tent. My barker waits by the door for a moment, then disappears. I look into the torchlight, watching the flames do their slow dance. I wonder what the fire tastes like.

The Fat Lady comes. She must have been hiding in the shadows again. She has changed her billowy costume for a large robe. Her hair hangs loose around her shoulders, her face barren of make-up.

She sees me. She knows I can understand her. "I heard what they said."

I stick out my tongue. I can taste the torn place on my

cheek. I grip the bars with my hands. Maybe tomorrow I will eat my hands, then my arms. Then I can be like Juggles. Except you can't dance when you're dead.

Or maybe I will eat and eat when the barker brings me the bucket of chicken hearts. If I eat enough, I can be the World's Fattest Murdermouth. I can be one of them. I will take money for the rides and pull the levers and sell cotton candy.

If I could get out of this cage, I would show her what I could do. I would prove my love. If I could talk, I would tell her.

The Fat Lady watches the tent flap. Somewhere a roadie is working on a piece of machinery, cursing in a foreign language. The smell of popcorn is no longer in the air. Now there is only cigarette smoke, cheap wine, leftover hot dogs. The big show is putting itself to bed for the night.

"They're going to kill you," she whispers.

I am already dead. I have tasted my own finger. I should be eating dirt instead. Once, I could feel the pounding of my heart.

"You don't deserve this." Her eyes are dark. "You're not a freak."

My barker says a freak is anybody that people will pay money to see.

My tongue presses against my teeth. I can almost remember. They put me in a cage before I died. I had a name.

The Fat Lady wraps her fingers around the metal catch. From somewhere she has produced a key. The lock falls open and she whips the chain free from the bars.

"They're coming," she says. "Hurry."

I smell them before I see them. Maynard smells like Maynard, as if he is wearing his vital organs around his waist. The wobbling man reeks even worse of liquor. The barker has also been drinking. The three of them laugh like men swapping horses.

I taste the straw in the air, the diesel exhaust, the thin smoke from the torches, the cigarette that Juggles gave me, my dead finger, the cold gun in Maynard's pocket, the money my barker has spent.

I taste and taste and taste and I am hungry.

"Hey, get away from there," yells the barker. He holds a wine bottle in one hand.

The Fat Lady pulls on the bars. The front of the cage falls open. I can taste the dust.

"Run," says the Fat Lady.

Running is like dancing. Maybe people will pay money to see me run.

"What the hell?" says Maynard.

I move forward, out of the cage. This is my tent. My name is on a sign outside. If I see the sign, I will know who I am. If I pay money, maybe I can see myself.

"This ain't part of the deal," says Maynard. He draws the gun from his pocket. The silver barrel shines in the firelight.

The Fat Lady turns and faces the three men.

"I swear, I didn't know anything about this," says the barker.

"Leave him alone," says the Fat Lady.

Maynard waves the gun. "Get out of the way."

This is my tent. I am the one they came to see. The Fat Lady blocks the way. I stare at her broad back, at the dark red robe, her long hair tumbling down her neck. She's the only one who ever treated me like one of them.

I jump forward, push her. The gun roars, spits a flash of fire from its end. She cries out. The bullet cuts a cold hole in my chest.

I must die again, but at last she is in my arms.

If my mouth could do more than murder, it would say words.

I am sorry. I love you.

They take her bones when I am finished.

CALLIOPE

AARON T. SOLOMON

Amanda Stilman awoke to rivers of golden sunlight pouring gently through her window. The entire room was filled with sparkling warmth. She had kept the drapes pulled back and the window open to let the world itself coax her from sleep and draw her into the smile of another Texas morning. When the sweet summer air came through and brushed against her cheek, she arose, and on this morning, as she had done every morning for the last forty years, Amanda sat down before her vanity mirror, took in the flavor of a brand new day, and set about to groom her long, silken beard.

Age had robbed the hair of its luster, but Amanda didn't mind. She simply loved the beard's freakish appeal. Its inherent wrongness made her different, alluring, exotic. It had made her a carnival personality of some public note back in the day. In fact, it had made Amanda Stilman.

Ah, the carnival! With its smells of popcorn and cheap cologne, its sounds of children giggling and the barkers' rambling cries. At the carnival, Amanda actually meant something. She remembered how the marks would arrive in droves just to gawk at her and gesture. Although there were many so-called "bearded ladies" playing the circuit in her time, none were as beautiful or vivacious as she. When Amanda Stilman took the stage at the Show of Natural Wonders, every eye in the house followed her closely, intensely, as she danced in slow and voluptuous circles to the wild midway noise . . . and to the distant piping song of the calliope, of course.

Nothing spoke more profoundly of the carnival than the calliope, and to Amanda, there had never been a more beautiful sound. It was the calliope that gave her stage appearances their haunting sincerity, their true carnival appeal. But thinking about it now only broke her heart. Amanda missed her old life more than ever these days, for she belonged up on that stage, unfettered and free to live her own life her own way. The stage gave her necessity and purpose, and a lot of money as well. She owed her very soul to the carnival stage.

Amanda—The Bearded Beauty.

It was her everything.

When the thoughts faded away, she sighed deeply, then

frowned. The bronze vanity mirror before her had drawn in all her memories and offered in return only a murky reflection. Years of tarnish had built up on its surface to cloud Amanda's beauty, and now she was just an old woman in a burned photograph. A forgotten no one. A dead mother.

But then an earnest tapping came from the open window, almost subtle enough to be drowned out by the song of the sparrows that frequently played in the oak tree outside. At first, Amanda thought nothing of it, but presently the tapping grew louder, pulling her out of the doldrums and drawing her attention to the window. What she saw there gave her a start.

Two strange faces peered back at her through the opening. Who could these strangers be? Both men wore dark masks of military design, and their curious eyes sparkled wide behind clear plastic goggles. One of them had beep tapping his gloved finger on the windowsill.

Amanda wondered if there was an emergency. Was she in any danger? It wasn't very likely, but hardly anyone visited the Sideshow Retirement Ranch anymore. Not even the museum was enough to draw a crowd. But it didn't matter. Although the men seemed awfully serious, they were visitors all the same, and if Amanda Stilman cared for anything at all these days it was company—even if they did wear such fearsome faces.

"Pardon me, uh . . . ma'am," said one or the soldiers. "Would you kindly step over to the window, please?"

How cordial he was. How delightful! Amanda felt the inclination to blush, except all the blood in her flaccid veins had dried up years ago. Her body was sallow, resembling a mummy carved from rotten chocolate. Still, she smiled at the men, raised a pencil-thin finger to stay their advances, and then returned to the vanity mirror to fuss her beard into shape. This was hard to manage, given that Amanda Stilman had died more than thirty years ago.

The soldiers exchanged a number of odd looks.

"Do you understand any of this?" asked the younger of the two.

"Never seen anything like it," admitted the other.

"Strange. It seems almost maudlin."

"'Maudlin'?" snorted the elder man. "It looks just plain dead to me."

"Well, yeah, it looks dead," agreed the younger. "But I'm saying it looks maudlin, too, like it's got something heavy on its mind."

"So, you plan on asking it questions? Wanna psychoanalyze the thing and find out how it feels about its mother? Maybe it'll tell you how its mother tasted, Anderson, and then you can report back to your college friends and sit in a coffee shop somewhere and go, 'Hmmm . . . that's interesting.'"

"Shush, Fred! It's moving."

Amanda faced them again, only now she was fixed up special. Light blue powder framed the shriveled holes where her eyes used to be, and she had smeared on gobs of bright red lipstick. Some of it was caked on her teeth and resembled blood—but it was only cartoon blood, since nothing at all seemed real anymore, to her or to the soldiers.

The creature pushed its chair back and shuddered to its feet.

Clack-Clack!

Clack-Clack!

Now those were serious sounds.

Both men were holding shotguns on Amanda, who stood absolutely still beside her precious vanity. She wondered why these nice boys would do such a thing, unless, of course, it was all just a game. Yes, that had to be it—a game. With a smile grown so wide it nearly yawned off her face, she started forward.

"What the hell?" mumbled Fred Bartlett, the elder soldier, as Amanda came stumbling toward them.

The creature's hands extended with subtle gestures, inviting the men into the house. Each step brought a flurry of dust from her creaking bones. The archaic nightgown she wore was modest, but still revealed more than the soldiers wanted to see. The sight of her desiccated flesh and all the cartoon blood smeared on her teeth and streaked through her beard was just too much. Much too much.

Fred Bartlett fired his shotgun.

Boom!—clack-clack—Boom!

Amanda Stilman's head burst like a mud-filled balloon. Her precious beard twisted up in the mess, floating on the buckshot's slipstream like a feather.

The corpse stumbled back. It felt for its head. Then Bartlett casually blew off its left shoulder.

"Stop!" Anderson cried, but he could not be heard over the backwash from the blast.

Amanda trembled. She reached for her shoulder and found nothing there. Her nightgown had fallen away to reveal a withered husk of a body, sickly thin from age and degradation. The sight was humiliating for the living as well as the dead.

"Fred!" Anderson yelled. "You've got to stop!"

Bartlett answered with a blast from his gun.

Amanda's chest punched inward, nearly pulling the rest of her body in with it. She hit the floor, pouring dust and rotten meat like blood. Another blast took off her right foot. Another blew her pelvis into splintery fragments.

Then it was over. At last, it was over.

Bartlett gave his young partner a look of disgust before leaving the window. When he was gone, Anderson gazed into the house at the woman's remains—remains that continued to flop around on the bedroom floor in a mound of their own debris. He wondered sourly what he had become to leave such things in his wake.

Less than a month ago, Steven Anderson's Ivy League dreams seemed ready to make the leap to reality. He was Harvard-bound, a member of PETA, and enamored of pacifism. Alan Alda was his personal savior, *Mother Jones* his scripture. All that changed once the dead came back. Things in the sticks went to hell pretty fast. The local officials quickly proved incapable of dealing with the threat, and the bigger cities had reportedly sucked up all the professional military help. Before he knew it, Anderson had been recruited by local hard-ass Fred Bartlett, an ex-Marine with some rather dubious Vietnam credentials, to push back the undead threat and forestall a local victory by the creatures.

They had spent their first night together at Bartlett's ranch on the outskirts of Korval, Texas, in a small wooden shack where Bartlett taught his new student the Tao of small arms fire.

"But why me?" Anderson had asked as he held a double-barreled shotgun at arm's length, terrified of the thing.

"You're young," Bartlett had replied casually. "Plus, you have a certain appreciation for life and understand what it's all worth. I always kinda figured that pacifist crap you spouted around town didn't come from your heart. Guess I was right. Otherwise, you wouldn't have even considered coming out here to help me against these things." He eyed the youth convincingly. "Truth is, I mostly asked you because you ain't likely to go off all half-cocked when the heat's on, like the other fools around here probably would. I can tell you ain't no hick, and I can tell that if you have to fight, you're gonna. And that's all I can really ask for."

Indeed, it truly was.

The idea that first night was to have Anderson prepped for urban warfare in less than twelve hours. During that time,

Anderson had attempted to reason with Bartlett and offer some alternate solutions to their problem. But he found no logic that could counter Bartlett's response to a world in which the dead tore up and out of the ground, no system of ethics that could excuse him from the fight. Anderson finally admitted that he could not sit idly by and let the corpses devour everything around him. He was alive, dammit, and they were not, so what rights did they truly own? It wasn't as if they were any sort of endangered species.

So Anderson shut his mouth and did everything he could to cooperate with the ex-Marine. It wasn't until they were finished training that first night, and the Texas sky was crispy white with sunshine, that he asked the question that had been haunting his thoughts:

"Why do you think they came back?"

Fred Bartlett said nothing at first. He just continued sitting on the hillside, drinking his beer and watching the sunrise.

"Who the hell knows," he said at length. "They just did is all." Then he studied Anderson with soft gray eyes, and a solemnity suddenly gripped him, made him darkly thoughtful. "I'll tell you one thing, though. All this crazy shit is changing everything. It's changed you already. It's working on me, the world—everything! It's a civil war, if you really need to define it. It's the dead against the living. And it don't really matter why things are the way they are. It only matters that the living win."

Those words seemed necessary: simple qualifiers for the gruesome task ahead of them. Words that continued to haunt them both as they sat in silence, watched the sun come up, and finished their beers.

In the days that followed, Anderson and Bartlett saw a lot of the living dead.

They had started with Korval's two cemeteries, which were blissfully small, and during the missions came to appreciate the complexity of their enemy. Among other things, it became immediately apparent that these creatures could see in ways other human beings could not—in the dark, for instance—and this gave them a world of advantage. Whatever had brought them back to life had endowed them with incredible perceptions. Anderson mused on this frequently. Bartlett cared nothing for speculation and devoted his thoughts entirely to putting the ghoulish things back in the ground.

Together, the men did a pretty fair job of it. In no time at all they had scrubbed the cemeteries free of unrisen bodies, which they later chopped up and burned as deadwood. They dealt with the few active zombies they encountered with equal ease. It frightened Anderson how quickly the destruction became routine. No remorse, no regret—nothing personal.

A few days later, the men returned home from a patrol to discover that the National Guard had all but taken over Korval, Texas. Young troops with machine guns stood idly along Main Street. A giant M-1 tank hulked at the intersection of Third and Doggett. It seemed the reports about the military being deployed only in the bigger cities had been premature.

Bartlett and Anderson soon found themselves standing before Commander Jake S. Corban, a slender man with starch in his joints, who had already heard about their local cleanup operations.

"You men are performing an exceptional service for your country!" barked the commander. "Unfortunately, my men cannot assist you at this time with clearing the rest of this sector of the living impaired."

The news reports, it turned out, had been accurate after all; the Guard unit was merely on its way to Dallas. However, since Anderson and Bartlett had things in their own neck of the woods pretty square, it behooved the commander to give them at least the air of official sanction. By noontime, with everything said and almost nothing done, Commander Jake S. Corban marched his troops down Main Street and out of Korval, Texas. In their wake they left something they called a "survival packet," and its contents quickly turned the pair's bleary eyes bright.

Included were a couple of black, SWAT-style uniforms complete with masks and goggles; a pair of high-powered Mossberg shotguns; and a large, military-issue flame thrower, which was, perhaps, the most kick-ass thing Fred Bartlett had ever been presented in his life. To him, utility was the highest art form.

These new toys were used successfully at the McMillan Farm, where the men had to gun down and torch an entire family of redneck cadavers. They had proved useful again and again, until this very morning at the Sideshow Retirement Ranch, where Anderson had witnessed another demonstration of life's contempt for death. But watching Amanda Stilman's body get blasted to quivering pieces set him back a page, made him reflective and cautious of himself. He had, in short, begun to wonder if the muck of this private war had not completely polluted his soul.

It troubled him fiercely to remain so close to the dead

woman's body. He felt like a barbarous intruder. Leaving the window, he sulked over to where Bartlett was standing in the shade of a nearby oak tree. Though he knew the reception would be far from amicable, Anderson would taken anything right then just to get out of his own head.

"Why didn't you shoot it?" the old man snapped. "I was there, you was there, it was there—and you didn't shoot. I wanna know why."

"I don't know, really," Anderson said to his feet. "I guess I just wanted to see what it would do."

"You did, huh?" Bartlett leaned his shotgun against the oak tree. Then he shrugged out of the flame thrower tanks strapped to his back and set them aside. "Why?"

"Didn't you notice how it acted?" Anderson replied, his voice muffled by his black, ventilated mask. "It didn't act all crazy like the others."

"Doesn't matter."

"But it does, Fred. It does because it seemed almost—"

"Let me guess—human? They all seem almost human!" Bartlett shouted, his face purpling with frustration behind the headgear. "You think this is easy for me—like I got some kind of bloodlust, or something?" He stepped up to Anderson and tapped him firmly on the chest. "We had to eliminate an entire family over at the McMillan place, kids and all, and you held up fine. But you break down over one stiff—one you don't know, and who don't know you."

Anderson was flabbergasted. "I can't explain it. I don't really know what happened back there. I'm sorry."

"Well, you better figure it out in the next ten seconds, 'cause this is the very last place on our list. When we're through here, we're through it all. You understand me?"

"Yes, Fred," Anderson whispered raggedly. "I understand completely." And he meant every word of it.

They fell into a pensive moment in the shadow of the sprawling ranch house, which resembled an old Spanish manor with its red-tiled roof pitched high like a mountaintop. Over it all spread the vast Texas sky, unmoved by the events unfolding beneath its expanse. Again, Anderson felt himself lost in a cartoon, and understood how Tolstoy must have felt when he declared the world to be utterly absurd.

The moment ended. Bartlett shoved the flame thrower tanks into Anderson's arms, snatched up his shotgun, and marched toward the house. "Come on," he said. "We cleared an entry point. Let's get in and get this over with."

Despite his considerable size. Bartlett managed to climb

through the window with ease. At the McMillan Farm, all of the dead had been piled up at the front door waiting for them, and Bartlett assumed it would be the same here. They'd tried to check the other windows, but found them blackened or the rooms within too dark to see. They had been lucky with Amanda's room, and since it was easily cleared, here they would enter. Anderson passed the tanks inside and bumbled his way in after them.

What remained of Amanda Stilman continued writhing on the floor. With a firm kick, Bartlett sent it flailing into a shady corner. The room was murky, dark, and filled with the smell of make-up and spoiled meat. On an old oak dresser was scattered a collection or framed pictures, now spattered with dried blood. The stuff had been painted on the walls, too, in splashes of dark brown. Amanda's bed was a tangled mess of sheets, dust, and human sauce.

"What's that?" Bartlett gestured to a piece of folded yellow paper on the floor by Anderson's feet.

Anderson picked it up and looked it over while Bartlett shrugged the flame thrower back onto his shoulders. Unable to see clearly enough to read, Anderson pulled the mask and goggles from his face, letting a jangle of dark brown hair fall to his armored shoulders. "It's a brochure," he observed. His face was veiled in sweat. "Something about 'The Museum of Wonders Past.'"

"That's where we are, kid. What does it say?"

Anderson read selectively: "'Visitors will discover antique carnival memorabilia . . . an authentic working calliope . . . and for those who dare, a grim collection of the very oddest of oddities—Pickled Punks.'"

"What the hell is a Pickled Punk?"

Anderson shrugged and continued. "'Down below, in the Vault, visitors will discover some of the greatest names in sideshow entertainment. . . .'" His voice trailed away.

"What is it?" Bartlett asked, and met with Anderson's faraway gaze. "What's the matter?"

"People have been buried here, Fred. The Vault is a private cemetery."

"You mean, they keep stiffs down below?"

Anderson nodded regretfully, his young face ravaged by stress. He'd had enough—enough of cemeteries, of rotting corpses and clotted blood and things that were dead but didn't act like they were dead. The stench of roasted flesh was clogged in his nose. The sight of all the blood made him want to gag. Then a private darkness came closing in, crashing down like a wave of ink until even the streams of sunlight coming through the open window grew thinner and thinner and threatened to wink out, completely and forever. . . .

Bartlett's gentle hand came down on his shoulder and squeezed tight. The old Marine had removed his own mask and studied Anderson with fatherly concern. Despite a skin thick as leather and a demeanor to match, Fred Bartlett could sometimes be more tender than he cared to admit.

"You've got to stay with me on this," he said. "I've got your back, kid, and I know you got mine. Nothing in here can touch you as long as I got your back. Understand?"

"Yeah," Anderson stammered. He found himself blinking rapidly, as if he'd been suddenly pulled from a deep sleep. "Right. I've got your back, Fred. Everything's cool."

Bartlett smiled warmly. "That's good to hear."

"But . . . a lot or people have died here." Anderson's eyes took in the blood-smeared walls, and he recognized for the first time how little of it had come from the bearded corpse. "This is going to be bad. I can feel it."

"I know. And that's why we gotta handle it. So let's get in there, do our job, and get back home."

Anderson took a deep breath, let it out slowly. He hefted his shotgun and said, "Let's get this over with."

Bartlett winked at him approvingly. Then he turned to the bedroom door with both hands on his gun. "Just like McMillan," he said. "Only, no surprises this time. Get the door, would you?"

Anderson crossed to the door, grabbed the knob with a gloved hand, and glanced back at Bartlett.

"Open it!" Bartlett barked.

Anderson flung the door wide and stepped back, bringing his shotgun up defensively. But the threshold was empty. A dark hallway lined with closed doors stretched deep into the house. Nothing moved at all. Bartlett stepped warily into the hall with Anderson close behind.

Carnival pictures, carnival posters—the walls were covered with images of carousels and Ferris wheels, barkers and magicians. Quietly, and with braced backs, they checked the other doors, all of which opened into empty bedrooms in far worse shape than Amanda's. The windows and walls and floors had been blackened by dried blood and other waste. Anderson imagined all the gore must have come from the residents of the house who'd been living when the dead rose, poor souls who'd had no idea that their illustrious past would one day creep up the cellar steps to claim them.

The men regrouped in the hallway, which eventually opened up to a much larger room. They paused at the doorway. Through syrup-thick darkness, diminished only by a single red light, Anderson could make out display tables, fancy chairs, and hanging tapestries. Still no movement, though.

"Keep an eye out," Bartlett warned. "There's plenty of crap in here that compromises our maneuverability. And remember: Even if a dead toddler comes at you, just blast it. I don't want a repeat of what happened in the bedroom."

"Just blast it," Anderson confirmed.

His hands were fused to the shotgun as he and Bartlett stepped brazenly into the heart of the Museum of Wonders Past.

It was a true museum, one dedicated to preserving the Technicolor ghosts of the traveling carnival. In one corner stood an ancient wooden ticket booth, restored a decade past with fresh paint; a red light still glowed inside. A high-bell and its heavy mallet sat in another corner. Throughout the room, display tables containing ticket rolls, preserved costumes, photographs, and juggling props were set up in confusing, mazelike angles. It was a complex landscape, one, as Bartlett had already noted, not conducive to close-range combat.

Beside the ticket booth was a doorway that opened into the deepest shadows Anderson had ever seen. When he read the sign above it, a greasy lump of tension worked its way down his throat. . . .

The Vault.

"Don't worry about that room yet," Bartlett assured him. "We'll do that one last. I promise." He gestured toward the far wall and cocked a smile at his partner. "Besides, this over here is far more interesting."

And he was right. The entire wall was built of mirrors that had been carefully broken and glued back into shape, forming a dazzling reflection of a shattered room. Very disorienting. The two men appeared shattered as well. A fractured cartoon. There was a doorway somewhere in the middle of that clever wall, nearly hidden by the spectacle of glass surrounding it, and was itself formed of mirrors, which twisted away into a hallway of reflections on reflections on reflections.

The Hall of Mirrors.

"You've got to be kidding me!" Anderson spat. He had to blink away the dizzying image before it overwhelmed him completely.

Then came the smell, sighing from the walls like a hot metal vapor mixed with raw meat and cabbage. The dead were coming, and somewhere deep in his gut, Anderson knew there would be a lot of them.

"They're on their way!" Bartlett hollered.

"I know! But from where?"

As if in reply, a shuffling sound echoed from the Hall of Mirrors. Both men trained their weapons on the glimmering threshold, trembling slightly and breathing through their mouths to avoid the awful stench.

"Aim higher!" Bartlett gestured toward Anderson's gun with his own. "Take off its head first. We gotta get rid of those teeth right away."

"I know," Anderson growled defensively, though he raised his aim nonetheless.

Together they skirted the tables for clearer ground. The vapor grew thicker. Before Anderson could wonder what would happen next, an image appeared at the entrance to the hall: a dark flurry of movement, distorted by myriad reflections large and small. It was all rags and skin and yellow teeth.

When it emerged, both men fired at once. A dozen mirrors exploded, blowing shards of glass into sparkling arrays—but the monster kept coming, unscathed. Somehow, they had missed it entirely. When it finally got clear of the mirrors they saw why: The thing was tiny. It hobbled toward them unsteadily, arms out to its sides like a little boy pretending to fly. Was it a child? Some kind of chimp? In fact, it was neither of those things.

"It's a midget!" Bartlett screamed. "Aim low, low, low!"

Too late. The tiny monster leaped at Bartlett in a surprisingly graceful arc—arms outstretched, mouth open—and clamped around his left leg. As the midget worked its teeth on his kneecap, Bartlett howled madly and hopped about on one foot. "Get it off me!" he demanded. Bartlett wedged his shotgun between himself and the thing and tried to pry the it loose.

Anderson moved fast, but never made it to Bartlett. A stunning weight crashed down on his shoulders, crumpling him to the floor. Through a gush of delirium came Bartlett's voice screaming about something behind him. Behind who? Behind Bartlett? Behind Alan Alda? What the hell? Then a tremendous grip took hold of Anderson's uniform and heisted him straight off the floor, into the presence of death itself.

The stench was unbearable. It poured off a tattooed giant stuffed with rotting muscles. A very dead carnival strong man. And with a colossal hand it hauled Steven Anderson all the way up to its skeletal face, which was nothing but raw gray bone framed with tattered flesh.

Anderson wailed, kicked, and squirmed, but for nothing. "Fred!" he shouted, but his partner was too busy with his own attacker to do more than grunt. There was no one to help him at all. He stared, paralyzed with fear, as the strong man's jaws opened wide.

Finally Anderson remembered his shotgun. With a roar, he rammed its barrel up through the giant's lower jaw, snapping it shut. Then he jerked the trigger and blew the monster's skull to pieces.

The strong man fumbled backward, dropping Anderson roughly. It struck a display table, crashed over it, and spilled across the floor amidst a scattering of broken glass and carnival momentos.

As the echo of the blast subsided, Bartlett shouted, "Get ready!" He had finally gotten the purchase he needed to use his makeshift lever. "The little bastard's coming loose!"

Anderson scrambled toward them just as the midget lost its hold. It popped free of Bartlett's leg and slid across the floor with a shred of SWAT-style uniform locked in its jaws. Anderson snatched the thing up by the scruff of its neck and held on tight.

Bartlett raised his gun and cried, "Up! Throw it up!"

Anderson did so with all his might, and for a second time that day the midget made a graceful arc through the air. But this trip ended when Bartlett pulled the trigger of his gun and reduced the thing to clots of bone and skin.

Behind them, the strong man staggered to its feet. Anderson spun and fired, opening a hole in the monster's breast, but it was not enough. The giant kicked its way past the fallen display case and kept right on coming. Anderson fired twice more, but wide of the sizeable target.

"Come on, Fred!" he yelled over his shoulder.

"Hold him off a minute. I'm busy."

"What the hell are you doing?" Anderson cried.

"Just a second, Steve." Bartlett fumbled a new batch of shells into the Mossberg. "Just one more second. . . ."

But Anderson didn't have a second. The strong man grabbed him again with its heavy hands, squeezed hellishly tight, and swept him off the hardwood floor. The monster pressed him up over its missing head, then threw him across the room—over display cases, over Fred Bartlett—and into the far wall beside the Vault. Anderson struck high and hard, barely missing the ticket booth in the corner. He smashed down into the floor awkwardly. When he hit, something in his right leg snapped.

Anderson tried to move, but his knee didn't work anymore. Then the pain came surging up through him, crippling his lungs, making it difficult to breathe.

"Fred," he gasped. "Fred, where are you?"

Bartlett was busy at that moment with the strong man, which had caught sight of him with its weird eyeless vision and lurched forward with clutching hands. Bartlett backed off clear of the tables, luring the creature away from his partner. Behind him in the corner, by the mirrored wall, loomed the high-bell and its heavy mallet.

When Anderson pulled himself together and saw this, he reached for his gun, but he had lost it in his trip across the room; he could see it lying well out of reach on the other side of the ticket booth, teetering on the edge of the Vault. Whimpering, he pulled himself up using the booth as a crutch and started for the gun, but each step wanted to drag him in and down to a darkness away from this nightmare, into the safety of oblivion. Yet he shook off the pain and made those steps and soon he was at the doorway. Bending painfully, Anderson reached out with a trembling hand

A low, horrible moaning rolled from the Hall of Mirrors. Anderson froze and turned away from the Vault. Bartlett froze and turned away from the strong man. Even the strong man froze and turned away from its intended victim. And the terrible wailing rose in pitch and clarity as the mirrored threshold grew dark with reflections of twisted, clawing flesh. Anderson was right about their numbers—the dead here were many— and they emerged from the Hall of Mirrors in a storm of tangled limbs and gnashing teeth. Their empty eyes searched for meat and found Bartlett close by. In seconds, the mob would be upon him.

The ex-Marine stumbled back into the corner and onto the high-bell's platform. Its heavy mallet plopped to the floor. He was trapped. Mindless of the dead horde squelching toward him, he threw a determined snarl at the strong man. With a Southern shine in his cold gray eyes, Bartlett leveled his shotgun at the hip and fired.

A huge lead slug punched straight through the strong man's gut and smacked into the far wall. The rotting Goliath slid back across the floor, fell to one knee, and then clambered up to its feet. Meanwhile, the dead were piling up around Bartlett, reaching out with hungry fingers, forcing him farther into the corner. Nevertheless, he kept his gaze fixed on the strong man; he knew he was going to die, but he was going to fell the headless beast.

Anderson could stand it no longer. He swooped up his shotgun, slid a round in the chamber, and opened fire. Two scrambling monsters collapsed in a spew of dust, but two more simply took their place. The mob was a hydra. Despite the futility of it all, Anderson fired and fired again, though he could see no clear target through the tears in his eyes.

The zombies surged, crushing Bartlett into the corner. The high-bell went sideways and clanged sharply to the floor. He tried to break free but the corpses held him, and they grabbed his SWAT-style uniform, the straps of his flame thrower tanks, his arms, his skin—and then tore into him, searching for arteries, for blood, for the thing he possessed that had been robbed from them long ago: life.

Anderson shrieked like a madman and limped toward the mob. He fired his weapon but heard only sharp, hollow clicks. The Mossberg was empty. No time to reload.

"Go!" Bartlett yelled from the writhing pile of bodies. "Get out . . . now!"

The old Marine's shotgun barrel pushed out from the quivering heap and leveled on the strong man a final time.

"You bastard!" he spat through a gush of blood. Then he pulled the trigger.

Ka-boom!

The monster's awesome chest ruptured with impact. Its headless body wheeled backward out of control, right for Steven Anderson, who stood paralyzed with a useless gun in his hands, knowing he had to move but forgetting how. The creature struck him with all the subtlety of a freight train, and once again Anderson left the floor. This time he did not strike the wall, but instead felt as if he had passed right through it. And in those lucid seconds when the world turned into manifold shadows, he understood that he had been knocked back through the open doorway . . . and into the Vault.

There followed a moment of blissful flight, as if the cartoon reality had become friendly and he could maybe hang in the air forever. Then the moment ended and down he went, crashing head-to-belly-to-shoulders-to-back over sharp wooden stairs that ended, finally, at an earthen floor.

He struck bottom and slid across the dirt, twisted up into a lumpy knot, until he crashed into an object at the other end of the room. The thing clunked hollowly in protest, but Anderson lay without care in a tangled heap, aware of little more than darkness and pain. Not even the Mossberg, which had landed by his side, mattered to him anymore.

Silence.

But that was only a momentary illusion. As Anderson regained his senses, he heard the voice of his partner, in all his suffering; Bartlett's cries wavered over the moans of the dead that were tearing his body to pieces. And that wasn't all. As if awakened by Anderson's presence, something wet and horrible sloshed about in the dark basement, just out of reach. Whatever it was came no closer, even when the cries from upstairs grew to monstrous shrieks of agony, and then diminished to gurgling gasps of defeat—and then stopped altogether.

Anderson shook all over. He pushed himself up on rubbery arms and leaned back against the large object behind him. When his head bumped against it, a slight metallic ring echoed through the room.

Up above, the dead were stumbling around each other, crunching on the fallen glass, bumping into display cases, moaning like disappointed children. Through the gloom, Anderson watched the staircase: At its head was the rectangular threshold where torn and bloody shadows had begun to congregate. The sloshing sound down in the basement grew more demanding, as if calling out to the mob with reports of the intruder. Before long, the first of the creatures found the doorway, paused, and then peered into the darkness with its special vision.

Anderson's hand fell from his lap and struck the Mossberg. He scooped it up absently, fished a couple rounds from his utility pocket, and began loading the weapon. Then he tried to stand, but his broken leg gave out and he pitched sideways. His outstretched palm came down flat, on some kind of pedal switch mounted on the floor. A sharp clank echoed off the concrete walls. The entire room seemed to growl.

In truth, it was a generator that was growling, and its sound frightened Anderson, alerted the monster in the doorway, and made the sloshing thing slosh like it had never sloshed before.

Slowly, gently, the Vault came to life. A long string of bare lightbulbs blossomed to life across the ceiling. Their jaundiced glow was dim, but enough to reveal the churned up graves to Anderson's right. The emptied holes stretched into the still-dark recesses of the Vault, patiently awaiting the wandering tenants that now gathered at the upstairs doorway.

The sloshing came from a long wooden shelf that owned the wall to Anderson's left. Large glass jars sat upon it in a neat row. The containers were filled to their brims with pale, yellowish liquid, in which floated an assortment of deformed human fetuses. They were malformed, twisted creatures—some with two screaming heads, others with none at all. These were the Pickled Punks of which the brochure had boasted so indulgently. And they clawed at the walls of their glass wombs, dead eyes bulging like sour eggs, searching for life in the darkness.

The absurd, cartoon reality pushing in on Anderson was filled once more with horrible sounds, the most haunting emanating from directly behind the young man.

He glanced back, but could not recognize the wall of pipes and colored switches for what it was. Yet the singsong music wheezing from it was unmistakable. It started out slowly, too slowly. Then, like an old vinyl record slowly being brought up to speed on a turntable, the despondent music of the carnival calliope grew into a whirlwind tempo and filled the Vault.

The mob of corpses had finally begun squeezing through the doorway. Myriad arms and faces and knotted hair pushed like a singular thing down the stairs. The remains of the strong man was among them, pawing over a pair of conjoined twins that crouched, crablike, by the railing. A wolf-faced monster snapped at something with alligator skin, and a fat man was stomped underfoot by others who were impatient with its bulk. At last, something gave way, and the whole menagerie came tumbling down to the landing.

The first one to stand lost its head to Anderson's gunfire. When it collapsed, the wolf-thing took its place. Undaunted, Anderson aimed and blew off one of its scrawny legs. The next shot smeared its face into fuzzy gelatin. Anderson, finally accepting his part in the cartoon, smiled at the sight.

The wild calliope music gusting through the room made Anderson laugh, too. In fact, everything was to him funny now. He could barely keep his amusement from overwhelming him with fits of screaming laughter. The irony of the situation bludgeoned him like an oversized mallet. His entire life he had talked about equality and unity, and here it was at last—the ultimate equality—shambling toward him with ex-Marine on its breath, wanting to take in everyone it found, regardless of race or creed or color, and make them part of it.

Anderson decided that he was a hypocrite for resisting. A bark of crazed laughter burst from his lips and he lowered his gun. The calliope's song became a shrill shriek in his ears.

But the dead did not claim him. A frenzied movement erupted within the struggling mass and something ripped its way up through the pile of tumbled bodies with enviable strength. At last, a ravaged dead man broke through the crowd and stood glowering before at their fore, its gray eyes red-rimmed and hot with death fever.

Fred Bartlett.

Yards of sloppy organs hung from his ravaged stomach and trailed off into the crowd. The tumbled zombies were rising up behind him, gathering at the landing for a final assault. Bartlett's glowing eyes held on his former partner fiercely, and in his gaze Anderson recognized just a glimmer of that old Southern shine. Somehow, Bartlett had managed to deny that part of himself to the mob, to clutch that shred of individuality and hold it somewhere within his hollow, bloody frame.

With a surge of strength, Fred Bartlett pushed back against the mob. At the same time he twisted around to face them, exposing the two black flame thrower tanks strapped to his shoulders.

The gesture silenced Anderson's laughter. The young man understood exactly what the old Marine wanted him to do. He brought his gun up and drew a bead on his partner. "Got your back, Fred," he whispered.

Just before he pulled the trigger, in that final instant, Anderson swore he saw Bartlett glance back at him and wink approvingly.

The buckshot spat across the room. and struck the gas tanks, breached their thick metal skins, and flipped them inside-out with a violent concussion that fractured the air itself. Then came the shrapnel, the raging wall of fire—and the cartoon world was swept away into a devouring wave of brightness and blackness.

The explosion was the very last thing Steven Anderson ever heard . . . except for the calliope, of course.

The calliope.

The calliope played on.

PROMETHEUS UNWOUND

MATT FORBECK

This story was written several months before the events of September 11, 2001. Rather than delete or modify it, and allow terrorism to dictate our actions even in this relatively inconsequential manner, we present it as written in its entirety. The author, editor, and publishers would like to take a moment to recognize the true heroes of the day, the fine people who risked—and, in far too many cases, lost—their own lives to save those of people they never knew. May we all be so brave.

TOP SECRET: EYES ONLY

NOTE: This script has been submitted for approval by the director of the NSA. It was written by our agent—codename: Spud—who was on the scene of the recent disaster in New York City. Raw footage of many of the incidents depicted has been recovered from Spud's hidden camera. The stock footage referenced in the script has been secured by our field agents. Reenactment footage can be created as necessary.

The director is debating whether or not to have this film made. Would this help allay the panic in the streets, or would it amplify it? Time is of the essence. Have your response on the director's desk first thing tomorrow morning. If it's positive, we can be in production overnight.

SCENE ONE

New York City. Dusk falls over the skyscrapers, which cast long shadows into Brooklyn and beyond, almost as if reaching toward the encroaching darkness rolling in from the east. The golden rays from the west cast everything into sharp, noirish contrast. The hues of the dying light bring a sepia-toned nostalgia to the place, but we know that it's only a matter of time before the light fades and night swallows the land. The strangest thing—something that any native New Yorker would recognize at once—is the lack of lights in the cityscape. Something is clearly rotten in the Big Apple.

SPUD [VOICE-OVER]
Death falls upon New York City.

The camera sails in closer, as if a cape was carrying it in for us.

> SPUD [VOICE-OVER]
> And when I say "Death," I don't mean the
> Grim Reaper.

Flash to a picture of that serial killer, the GRIM REAPER, who ran around LA a few years back, right up until the FBI nailed him. He's there in his full skull-mask, reaching out with that bony finger of death he had.

He appears out of the darkness, as if reaching for the audience. Then he's gone.

> SPUD [VOICE-OVER]
> I mean DEATH. The real damn thing.

We swing in closer. Past the twin towers of the World Trade Center. We're heading uptown.

> SPUD [VOICE-OVER]
> New York City. The Big Apple. The City that
> Never Sleeps.

The camera finally spots its destination: the Empire State Building. The golden rays of the sunset are fading now.

> SPUD [VOICE-OVER]
> Well, you can be sure that no one around
> here is sleeping now.

Zoom in closer, to the top of the building. We can see that someone is strapped to the base of the antenna atop the skyscraper, spread-eagled like some modern-day Christ on an X-shaped cross of steel girders.

> SPUD [VOICE-OVER]
> Not even the dead.

The camera swings in hard toward the figure on the tower. We recognize the man there now, PROMETHEUS, by the remnants of his trademarked blazing-white-and-yellow costume. It's in shreds, as is most of his body. We can see that his belly has been opened up, and his guts and organs are hanging loosely out of his chest. We can almost see the front of his spine.

A group of zombies crowd around Prometheus. There are all sorts of dead people, of all races, genders, and physical types. The dead are feeding on him.

The most amazing part of the scene is Prometheus. He heals faster than most people can breathe. And he's healing now. You can actually see the intestines growing back, the liver filling out the places that have been chewed off. This is one man who's going to be a long time dying.

PROMETHEUS
[Screams]

Zoom in tight on Prometheus' mouth. It's opened wide enough to swallow someone's head, and we can see where his cheeks have been shredded and are healing again. The genesis of a regenerating eyeball swims dangerously in a lidless socket in his head, and we can see clawlike, dead fingers scrabbling at his skull, trying to get at his brains.

Fade to black. Roll opening credits. End with the following:

To suffer woes which Hope thinks infinite;
To forgive wrongs darker than Death or Night;
To defy Power which seems Omnipotent;
To love, and bear; to hope, till Hope creates
From its own wreck the thing it contemplates. . . .
—Percy Bysshe Shelley, *Prometheus Unbound*

SCENE TWO

Fade back up. Intersplice footage of the battle between the FBI's capes and the criminal known as PANDORA with the interview SPUD did with Prometheus. Start with a shot of a plane flying into JFK.

SUBTITLE
Three days ago.

SPUD [VOICE-OVER]
I flew in from LA to do a documentary about the men and women of the FBI's special forces unit: the Commission. Call them capes, powers, goons, dupes—whatever you like. These men and women are the real power behind the throne these days. All I can say is I'm glad they're on our side.

It's a sunny day. Spud gets off the plane, and two FBI agents are there to greet him. They reek "Fed": dark glasses, earpieces, well-concealed shoulder holsters, and all that. They hustle Spud into a limo, where Prometheus awaits. He's in a black suit and a blacker mood. With a brusque motion from Prometheus, the limo takes off for the city.

                    SPUD
          Mr. Stein. I'm pleased to—

                    PROMETHEUS
          Drop the formalities. Call me "Vic."

                    SPUD
          Vic, then. I'm surprised to—

                    PROMETHEUS
          See me out of my costume? That get-up is
          for photo-ops, or when I'm on the job.

Cut: Prometheus in full costume, arrayed along with the rest of the Commission. Cut back.

                    SPUD
          Aren't you afraid that your—

                    PROMETHEUS
          Enemies will find me? Hardly. I was
          unmasked on national television back in
          1996. Since then, I've lived with it.

Cut: An unmasked Prometheus as he strides out of P.S. 33, dragging an unconscious RUMPELSTILTSKIN behind him. His costume is ripped and torn, but his body is already healed. A blinding number of flashbulbs go off. Prometheus seems unaware of, or unconcerned by the cameras. Cut back.

                    SPUD
          The fame. Has it been difficult adjusting to
          it?

                    PROMETHEUS
          A bit. I'm an officer of the law, not a politi-
          cian.

Cut: Prometheus in full costume again, this time with his mask pulled back. The PRESIDENT is pinning a medal on his chest in a White House ceremony. Cut back.

                    SPUD
          Not yet, at least.

PROMETHEUS

Not ever.

SPUD

What can you tell me about what happened
with Pandora?

Cut: Series of shots from a TV news helicopter. Prometheus
and Pandora—who is fully aflame here—battle it out atop the
Empire State Building. DEMOGORGON, a monstrous demon,
takes on the rest of the Commission in the background.
Demogorgon is winning. Cut back.

PROMETHEUS

Not much more than what's already been
in the news. Before the incident last week,
Ms. Esperanza—a.k.a. Pandora—had been
at the top of our Most Wanted list for over
three years.

Cut: Interior of a school gymnasium. The skins of children
flap from the basketball hoops, their corpses arranged in a
bloody circle around a pentagram drawn into the court's center jump circle. Cut back.

PROMETHEUS

We were informed by sources that Pandora
had concocted a grand plan to open a gate
to Hell in the heart of New York City.

SPUD

Seriously? Hell?

Cut: A quick montage of pictures of demons and devils in art
and architecture throughout history. Finish with a close-up of
Pandora grinning out at the viewer. Cut back.

PROMETHEUS

Affirmative. Her plan apparently called for
the gathering of a large number of corpses
to be used in a blood sacrifice to a demon
named Demogorgon. After she brought the
demon into our world, it would be under
her control, and she could then unleash
mayhem upon the world.

SPUD

And that's exactly what she did.

PROMETHEUS
Until we stopped her, yes.

Cut: Another shot of the scene above the Empire State Building during the battle with Pandora. Prometheus—large sections of his skin burned black by Pandora's hellish magic—stands over the dead, extinguished Pandora, who is covered with blood. In the background, Demogorgon disappears into a rift in the sky. Cut back.

SPUD
But your victory had its price, didn't it?

PROMETHEUS
Agent Asia, she . . .

Cut: Still above the Empire State Building. AMERICAN EAGLE soars down from the heavens, holding AGENT ASIA in his arms. Her neck is twisted at an unnatural angle. Cut back.

SPUD
I'm sorry. It was an inappropriate question coming so soon after . . . If you'd rather not—

PROMETHEUS
I'd rather honor my wife by talking about her, not remaining silent.

Cut: Agent Asia's funeral at St. Patrick's Cathedral. The crowd is a virtual who's who of capes and other prominent members in both local and national law enforcement. Both the President and the ATTORNEY GENERAL are in the front rows. Prometheus kneels in the very front, his hands covering his tear-stained face. Cut back.

PROMETHEUS
Agent Asia sacrificed herself to save both the lives of her fellow agents and the life of every resident of New York City.

SPUD
Very true. But I understand there has been some tension between you and the other members of the Commission since then. Word is that you blame them—especially American Eagle—for not protecting her as they should have.

Cut: Outside St. Patrick's, Prometheus tears into American Eagle. Madness gleams in his eyes. The fight rages on for a full minute before the other members of the Commission separate the two. Cut back.

> PROMETHEUS
> After my wife's death, I was understandably distraught. It's only been two days, so I'm still coming to terms with it.

> SPUD
> I want to thank you again for agreeing to talk with me on camera, despite your obvious grief.

Prometheus waves off Spud's concern coldly, barely concealing a wave of disgust.

> PROMETHEUS
> My superiors didn't offer me a choice. Besides, that's not an issue.

> SPUD
> Then what is? How about your relationship with your team members? How are you ever going to patch things up with them now? I understand death threats were made.

> PROMETHEUS
> The situation has been blown out of proportion by the media. I didn't mean—

Prometheus' mobile phone rings. He fishes it out of the breast pocket of his suit coat.

> PROMETHEUS
> Excuse me. What? Repeat that. You're certain? Damn. Driver!

The limo screeches to a halt.

> PROMETHEUS
> The World Trade Center. Now!

The limo pulls a quick U-turn in heavy traffic, throwing Spud against a door. Prometheus remains perfectly in place. Horns blare as the car squeals away. The DRIVER runs all sorts of lights to get to his destination at top speed. As the limousine nears the World Trade Center, the driver slows to a halt.

PROMETHEUS
Driver! What's going on?

DRIVER
There's a disturbance in the street, sir.

Prometheus motions for Spud to move aside so he can peer past the driver and into the street. A large number of ragged, battered-looking people are storming the entrance of the building. Guards are shooting at them. Bullets pummel into the people, but they keep coming on. Only those shot through the head actually fall to the ground and stop moving. They're zombies.

A number of zombies suddenly notice the limo and charge toward it.

PROMETHEUS
Run them down.

DRIVER
But, sir!

PROMETHEUS
Do it! Head straight for the underground
parking ramp. Now!

The limo leaps to life, burning rubber. It runs down the creatures in the way. A FEMALE ZOMBIE is plastered across the windshield, which has cracked at the impact of her head, spiderwebbing beneath her. We can see that the flesh has been torn away from her skull, leaving only patches of hair on the scalp. The female zombie's teeth are exposed in a skeletal grin.

PROMETHEUS
Out of the way!

Prometheus shoves Spud aside roughly. He draws his gun and fires one round right past the driver and into the female zombie's head. A huge hole appears in the windshield, right in the center of that spiderweb break. The female zombie falls backward and spins off the limo as it careens toward the parking structure. She leaves three fingers clinging to the near edge of the hood.

The limo races around the side of the building, mowing down more zombies. The gate to the parking ramp is closed, but the driver rams it.

SCENE THREE

The observation deck of South Tower of the World Trade Center. Looking out past the North Tower, we can see the Empire State Building in the distance. The entire rest of the Commission is here, waiting for Prometheus. As Prometheus and Spud exit the elevator, they are met by American Eagle, still sporting a shiner from his fight with Prometheus. The two do not shake hands. Most of the people on the deck—many of who have served with Prometheus for years—refuse to meet his steely stare.

AMERICAN EAGLE
[points at Spud]
What's he doing here?

Prometheus gives American Eagle a savage grin, happy to be the bearer of bad news to a man he clearly still has issues with. These two have been at each other for years, but it's obviously gotten worse in the past couple days.

PROMETHEUS
He has friends in high places. I confirmed
with the head office on the way up. We're
stuck with him for the whole ride.

American Eagle stares at Spud for a moment, unbelieving, then turns and walks away, shaking his head. At the window, he stops and beckons Prometheus over, offering him a pair of high-powered binoculars.

AMERICAN EAGLE
It's Pandora.

Prometheus barely restrains himself from sneering at the man as he refuses the binoculars. He knows that American Eagle doesn't need them, and he's not willing to admit inferiority to him in any way. The tension is thicker than the East River.

PROMETHEUS
Brilliant detective work.

Cut: A telephoto lens shows the top of the Empire State Building in sharp focus. The observation deck is swarming with zombies. Among them, we can see Pandora guiding things. She looks like the living dead as well.

PROMETHEUS
Air strike?

AMERICAN EAGLE

There's a concern about collateral damage. There are thousands of people in there.

PROMETHEUS

Alive or dead?

AMERICAN EAGLE

Mostly alive. We've confirmed at least several hundred. Pandora's zombies seem to be holding them as hostages. They're not directly attacking the people in the building, but they won't let them leave.

PROMETHEUS

Options?

AMERICAN EAGLE

We've been asked to take out Pandora in a surgical strike. It's hoped that this would somehow damage the zombies.

PROMETHEUS

You've been watching too many movies.

AMERICAN EAGLE

The one thing we can't figure out is how this happened.

Prometheus snatches the binoculars from American Eagle. He stares out at the Empire State Building for a moment, then returns the binoculars. He's even more disgusted than before.

PROMETHEUS

Look at the people closest to Pandora.

AMERICAN EAGLE

People? You mean the zombies?

PROMETHEUS

I said look at them.

American Eagle peers intently at the Empire State, then gasps.

AMERICAN EAGLE

They're . . . the same people Pandora sacrificed to Demogorgon. . . . Dear God.

PROMETHEUS
God had nothing to do with it.

SCENE FOUR

A shot of the New York City skyline. The shadows are getting longer, darker. Smoke and screams trail up from the street. Spud, Prometheus, and other members of the Commission sit in a military helicopter as it sails above the rooftops. The members of the Commission who can fly trail along outside. From the grid of buildings we focus on one rooftop where a lone WOMAN has been cornered by a crowd of zombies. She jumps, but American Eagle peels off from the formation and saves her.

PILOT
We're almost in position.

Prometheus sidles up to the helicopter's open hatch and spits into the wind. He wears double holsters for twin automatic pistols, one of which he currently has in his hands, ready to deal death to the undead. Dozens of extra clips of ammo swing from the holsters' harness. Most of the Commission lines up behind him. They each regard him nervously, almost shamefully. The flyers sail along outside, waiting for the signal. The chopper swings down over the observation deck of the Empire State Building.

PROMETHEUS
Let's do it!

Prometheus goes face-first out of the chopper on a rappelling line, catching himself scant inches from the observation deck. The others follow hot on his heels. He hits the ground firing with one hand while he releases his rappelling line with the other. He draws his other gun and continues firing without missing a beat. Each and every shot hits its target in the head.

The next few moments are filled with gunfire and zombie brains being splattered everywhere. Some Commission agents can fire plasma blasts from their eyes and hands, and they are having a field day with the zombies. Still, the zombies' numbers seem endless, and Pandora is nowhere to be seen. A rookie Commission agent, DARK JUSTICE, goes down, the zombies clawing open his skull before he hits the ground.

Prometheus works his way through the chaos, toward the doors into the building proper. As he does, American Eagle swoops in, firing away with his assault rifle at the zombies and then forcing his way into the building. Before he can follow, Prometheus is pushed back by a new wave of zombies.

After another few moments of desperate fighting, it's looking bad for the Commission. The tide of undead seems unending. Suddenly, a voice rings out over the crowd. Everyone freezes, including the zombies.

                    AMERICAN EAGLE
    Hold it!

American Eagle backs up out of the building's entry, and the zombies part before him as if he's a leper. He looks shaken to his core. Grinning madly, Pandora comes immediately behind him. She has Agent Asia in a chokehold in front of her, a gun to Asia's head. American Eagle stands between Prometheus and Pandora, keeping Prometheus from making a clean shot.

                    PANDORA
    Welcome to my parlor.

                    AMERICAN EAGLE
    Wh-What do you want?

                    PANDORA
    Nothing much, love. Just a place for me and
    my pets to call our own. Of course, my
    needs aren't exactly simple. A sophisticated
    woman like myself could hardly make do
    with something even as small as a city
    block. No, I think I need something more
    expansive, a place to hold all my pets. All I
    want is NEW YORK CITY!

                    AMERICAN EAGLE
    You're out of your mind.

                    PANDORA
    Am I? Already my pretties have taken over
    most of midtown. It's only a matter of time
    before I have the rest of Manhattan, maybe
    even by the end of the night. After all, every-
    one we kill joins our ranks.

                    AMERICAN EAGLE
    There's no way we can just hand over New
    York.

Pandora pouts beautifully and removes her gun from Asia's temple and points it at American Eagle. Asia doesn't seem to notice anything going on around her.

> PANDORA
> Really? Well, I suppose I'll just have to set-
> tle for killing you all.

Prometheus steps around from behind American Eagle and plants a bullet squarely into Agent Asia's skull. Her brains splatter all over Pandora and even American Eagle.

> AMERICAN EAGLE
> Dear God!

American Eagle staggers back, clearly in shock at what just happened. He turns to Prometheus, horrified.

> AMERICAN EAGLE
> Are you crazy? You just shot your wife!

Prometheus pistol whips American Eagle, who drops to the ground. Prometheus sneers down at his former friend.

> PROMETHEUS
> You moron. My wife is dead.

Prometheus turns to Pandora.

> PROMETHEUS
> Give me one good reason why I shouldn't
> do the same to you.

Still holding Asia's brainless corpse as a shield, Pandora throws back her head and laughs down the barrel of Prometheus' gun. Then she turns slyly serious.

> PANDORA
> Why, my dear Prometheus. You're welcome
> to try. Of course, if you do that, all of New
> York is doomed.

American Eagle staggers to his feet.

> AMERICAN EAGLE
> What are you talking about?

Pandora sweeps the barrel of her gun, indicating the scene spread out before them all.

> PANDORA
> I'm the only one who has any kind of con-
> trol over my pets here. Without me around
> to focus them, just what do you think
> would happen?

Prometheus shoulders past American Eagle and points his pistol right at Pandora's head.

> PROMETHEUS
> I say we find out.

> AMERICAN EAGLE
> Prometheus, put down that gun! Agent,
> that is a direct order!

> PROMETHEUS
> You lost your authority over me two days
> ago, George.

American Eagle steps back and raises his assault rifle to Prometheus' head.

> AMERICAN EAGLE
> Put down that gun, or so help me . . .

> PROMETHEUS
> You don't have the guts.

American Eagle cracks Prometheus on the back of the head with the rifle's butt. Prometheus falls to his knees, dropping his own gun. American Eagle kicks it away. He then grabs Prometheus by the arm and hauls him to his feet.

> AMERICAN EAGLE
> Get yourself together, agent. We're leaving.

American Eagle signals to the chopper. The PILOT dives down from the safe vantage point at which he had the helicopter hovering. The flyers start ferrying the others back into the chopper. American Eagle grabs Prometheus beneath the arms and begins to rise into the air.

> AMERICAN EAGLE
> You won't get away with this, Pandora.

> PANDORA
> Why, love, it seems to me I already have.

As American Eagle hauls Prometheus into the air, Prometheus pulls his second pistol from his shoulder holster and points it up at American Eagle.

PROMETHEUS
Put me down, you bastard!

AMERICAN EAGLE
Have you lost your mind?

Prometheus fires off a shot that zings past American Eagle's shoulder.

PROMETHEUS
I said, PUT ME DOWN, TRAITOR!

American Eagle looks down at Prometheus for a long moment. Then he lets go. Prometheus plummets directly into the waiting arms of dozens of hungry zombies.

AMERICAN EAGLE
[Shakes his head]
Whatever you say, Vic.

American Eagle flies back up to the chopper and gives the retreat signal. The flyers and the chopper spin around and head back toward the World Trade Center, leaving Prometheus to his fate. No one goes back to rescue him. No one even looks back.

AMERICAN EAGLE
Let's get out of here.

SCENE FIVE

Back at the World Trade Center observation deck. American Eagle is staring out toward the Empire State Building as Spud approaches him. Night has fallen over the city.

SPUD
So, just how bad is it?

AMERICAN EAGLE
Hm? Oh.

For a moment, American Eagle seems ready to lash out at Spud. Then he seems to realize the pointlessness of it, and his face softens.

AMERICAN EAGLE
It's about as bad as it gets.

SPUD
Come on. It's not hopeless, is it? I mean,
you guys have faced down worse than this
before and lived to tell the tale.

At that moment, the power goes out. Suddenly, the only near-by light comes from FIREFLY, a member of the Commission who is standing off to one side of the observation deck.

A non-costumed Commission SUPPORT AGENT steps out onto the observation deck from near the elevators. He moves directly to American Eagle to report.

SUPPORT AGENT
Not to worry, sir. We have all floors above
the 60th secured, and we have five chop-
pers on the roof.

AMERICAN EAGLE
Backup generators?

SUPPORT AGENT
Should be on line soon, sir.

American Eagle turns away, dismissing the support agent without a word, like some kind of king. He resumes looking out the window to the north. He seems transfixed by some-thing in the distance, but Spud can't figure out what. One of the Commission, a young woman by the name of PHASE, is looking through a set of binoculars in the darker side of the north wall. Suddenly she steps away and screams.

PHASE
OH MY GOD!

Spud dashes over to where Phase is standing. Her fellows in the Commission have rallied around her. Firefly holds her closely, comforting her. She is quaking like southern California on a bad day.

SPUD
What? What is it?

Phase points to the pay binoculars and stutters out her answer between sobs.

PHASE
It's him! It's Prometheus!

SPUD
What? You can see him through that thing?
He's still alive?

PHASE
Yes, he's still alive. But they're eating him!
They're eating him ALIVE!

FIREFLY
But with his healing powers . . .

SPUD
He's regenerating as soon as they tear the
flesh from him.

Cut: Through a telephoto lens, we see the details of the gruesome scene atop the Empire State Building. It is just as Phase
has described it, just as this script describes back in Scene
One. Only now we also can see that Pandora has cracked
open Prometheus' skull and is using her fingers to feast on his
brain. Cut back.

PHASE
We have to save him! What can we do?

American Eagle, still staring out the window in the direction
of the Empire State Building, just as he's been doing all along,
finally speaks up. The room falls deathly silent as all eyes turn
to him. The thick glass windows and the lack of air condi-
tioning, thanks to the power failure, make the place as quiet
as a tomb.

AMERICAN EAGLE
Nothing. There's nothing we can do.

SCENE SIX

Liberty Island. Spud and all the surviving members of the
Commission stand on the shore of the island, looking out at
the darkened skyline of Manhattan to the north and east. The
power is still working on Liberty Island, so behind them the
floodlights pick the Statue of Liberty out of the night. Distant
gunfire, the wail of sirens, and the occasional explosion punc-
tuate the unnatural stillness of the night.

American Eagle is talking with the same non-costumed support agent that reported in to him on the observation deck of the World Trade Center in Scene Five.

> AMERICAN EAGLE
>
> They've cordoned off the entire island?

> SUPPORT AGENT
>
> Yes, sir. Every bridge and every tunnel has been closed off to all traffic. Manhattan has been secured.

> AMERICAN EAGLE
>
> That's what you said about the World Trade Center.

> SUPPORT AGENT
>
> Sir—

> AMERICAN EAGLE
>
> Never mind.

American Eagle turns his back on the support agent, who scurries away. Spud approaches. American Eagle returns to staring off at the island.

> SPUD
>
> Excuse me?

American Eagle, clearly quite tired and distracted, turns back to face Spud.

> AMERICAN EAGLE
>
> Hm? Yes?

> SPUD
>
> So, um, what's the plan?

> AMERICAN EAGLE
>
> We strike at dawn.

> SPUD
>
> And by "we," you mean. . . ?

> AMERICAN EAGLE
>
> The Commission and the Marines.

> SPUD
>
> And me?

AMERICAN EAGLE

My orders are to bring you along. Vic was right. You have highly placed friends.

SPUD

At this point, I don't know if I'd call them friends. What are you going to do? I mean, how do you fight against an enemy like this? You can't just nuke it.

American Eagle raises an eyebrow, though it's unclear if he is amused or considering the comment as a serious suggestion.

SPUD

Right?

AMERICAN EAGLE

No. No, we can't nuke it. There's too much to lose there. And there could still be hundreds of thousands of people alive.

American Eagle turns back to peer into the darkened city once again.

AMERICAN EAGLE

There is no easy solution . . . but that doesn't mean we're dead yet.

SCENE SEVEN

Liberty Island. Dawn breaks over Manhattan, and even from this distant vantage you can smell the dead. It takes a lot to mask a stench like that. Spud spots American Eagle and goes over to get an update from him. Before Spud can speak, American Eagle spins to talk to him.

AMERICAN EAGLE

Do you hear that?

SPUD

[Cocks his head]

Actually, no. I don't hear much of anything.

AMERICAN EAGLE

Exactly. The fighting has stopped.

SPUD

Is that something good or something bad?

American Eagle glances at a handheld computer, upon which he has been receiving and reviewing classified updates.

> AMERICAN EAGLE
> Apparently it's something very good. From what anyone can tell, the zombies have all turned to corpses. They're just lying there.

> SPUD
> Maybe Pandora's mojo ran out?

> AMERICAN EAGLE
> Or maybe it's a trap.

> SPUD
> So how can you tell? I mean, you can't just go over there and ask the zombies whether they're alive or not, right? Right?

Close up on American Eagle. He looks at Spud as serious as death.

> AMERICAN EAGLE
> That's exactly what we're going to do.

SCENE EIGHT

The sky over Manhattan again. American Eagle is leading a group of flyers on a reconnaissance mission into the heart of the city. The Empire State Building looms large in the distance as the helicopter carrying Spud and a few other members of the Commission gets closer to the place where this all began.

As the chopper moves in toward the Empire State Building, we can see that Prometheus is still strapped to the base of the antenna. His clothes are in shreds, but he's actually looking much better than the last time we saw him. He may be covered with blood, but at least his skull is intact.

American Eagle lands right next to Prometheus. The rest of the flyers alight on the observation deck and begin inspecting the thick layers of corpses spread about the place.

> AMERICAN EAGLE
> Prometheus? Are you okay?

Prometheus looks up at American Eagle. For a moment, there is no recognition in his eyes. Then a wry smile cracks his face.

PROMETHEUS
Better'n ever, George.

American Eagle sets about cutting Prometheus down. As he does, Prometheus collapses into his arms.

AMERICAN EAGLE
What in God's name happened here?

Prometheus shakes off American Eagle's helping hand, insisting on standing on his own two feet.

PROMETHEUS
I keep telling you, God had nothing to do
with this.

Prometheus, still unsteady on his feet, looks down from his high vantage to the observation deck. He scans the casualties until he finds his wife's truly dead corpse. We zoom in close on what remains of her face, as if it is looking back at him.

PROMETHEUS
Get me down there.

American Eagle picks Prometheus up under his arms. The two sail smoothly down to the observation deck. American Eagle sets Prometheus down next to Asia's corpse.

Prometheus kneels and takes his wife's lifeless body in his arms. He bends his head and slowly begins to weep in silent rage. When he speaks, it's in a voice hoarse and thick.

AMERICAN EAGLE
What happened to the zombies? Where's
Pandora?

PROMETHEUS
Do you know that these "pets" of hers like
to eat brains?

Prometheus looks up at American Eagle. His tears have cut tracks through the caked blood on his face. A dark need for vengeance dances in his eyes. American Eagle steps back.

AMERICAN EAGLE
Yes.

PROMETHEUS
Did you know they ate parts of my brain?

AMERICAN EAGLE
Yes.

PROMETHEUS
You can see damned near everything with those eyes of yours.

Prometheus sets Agent Asia down gingerly, then stands to glare directly into American Eagle's eyes.

PROMETHEUS
Here's the funny part. See if you can follow this, George. Those zombies are used to eating the flesh of people they've just killed. They tore at me like starving wolves. But this body of mine is stubborn as Hell. It wouldn't give up the ghost. Finally they went for the brains anyhow. Pandora cracked open my skull herself. Then she scooped out my gray matter and tossed the bits to the zombies like some kind of doggy treats.

AMERICAN EAGLE
I know.

PROMETHEUS
I may be able to heal any wound, but that doesn't mean it doesn't hurt. If you prick me, I still bleed.

AMERICAN EAGLE
I know.

PROMETHEUS
I screamed so loud I ripped my vocal cords apart. But they healed right back up, so I got to scream again and again and again.

AMERICAN EAGLE
I KNOW, VIC! God damn it, I saw the whole damn thing.

American Eagle turns away. Prometheus stares at his back silently for a moment before continuing. As Prometheus begins to speak again, he uses one hand to roughly force American Eagle to face him.

PROMETHEUS
I haven't gotten to the good part yet. It
turns out that brains like mine don't really
die, not when they're in a zombie's stomach
anyhow. It has something to do with why
the ghouls want brains in the first place.
Their bodies use the gray matter—the
myelin, maybe—to keep their own nerves
in shape so they can keep moving, no matter how badly the rest of them may rot.

AMERICAN EAGLE
What are you saying?

PROMETHEUS
I'm saying that the zombies that ate my
brain were . . . infected by the stuff. Can't
think of another word for it. After a few
minutes, I realized I could actually control
them just by thinking about it. That's why
they're all lying down now.

A look of sheer awe falls over American Eagle's face. The rest
of the Commission members in the place have been collecting
around the two, listening to their conversation. The duo is
given a respectful distance, but every ear in the house is listening to what they have to say.

AMERICAN EAGLE
Do you mean to tell me that you fed your
brains to every zombie in Manhattan?

PROMETHEUS
Hardly. But Pandora did feast on my head
herself. She can control the undead on the
island. And now I can control her.

Wide grins of relief break out on the faces of American Eagle
and the rest of the Commission. American Eagle reaches out
and grabs Prometheus in a bear hug.

AMERICAN EAGLE
That's amazing, buddy! Christ, you did it!
You saved us all!

It takes a moment, but eventually American Eagle realizes
that Prometheus isn't responding. American Eagle releases

his embrace, and Prometheus pushes him away. As this happens, the zombies suddenly spring to their feet and start grabbing the members of the Commission. The air is filled with surprised screams.

> PROMETHEUS
> No, "buddy," I saved myself. As for you, you
> traitor—well, you're dead meat.

The zombies grab American Eagle, three of them holding fast on every limb, others tearing off his wings. As he struggles, Pandora steps forth from the roiling crowd and grabs American Eagle's head. He screams as she cracks open his skull and begins gorging herself on the soft stuff inside.

Spud, still safe up in the hovering helicopter, watches in horror for a moment before it becomes clear that few if any of the Commission agents are going to be leaving alive. And he doesn't want to face them dead. Spud dashes forward and screams at the pilot.

> SPUD
> Get us the Hell out of here!

The helicopter zooms away at top speed, heading for the Hudson River and safety to the west. Two wounded flyers who managed to escape zip past the chopper, torn and bleeding. We focus on them, showing that at least some hope remains. But as the camera pans back to the New York City skyline, the now-mad cackling of Prometheus rings out like a tolling bell.

FADE TO BLACK

Salvation

L. H. MAYNARD & M. P. N. SIMS

Maguire arranged the shotgun cartridges on the dining table and counted them again. Ten, plus the one he kept in a leather pouch hung around his neck. The one in the pouch he was saving—it was not to be used against them. It was his last resort, his final solution. From observing what had happened when he had shot the others he had worked out that the only way to finally finish them off was a headshot. Anywhere else on the body and the bastards just kept getting up and coming after him.

If the worst happened, and he was sure that eventually it would, then he would simply load his final cartridge into the shotgun, place the barrel at his neck, and pull the trigger. It should take his head clean off and stop him becoming like them.

But that was a few days off yet. There was still a chance he could get away. There was still a faint hope.

Leaving the cartridges on the table he went across to the window and looked out. The sun was starting to sink in the sky, the sunset a vibrant wash of orange and cerise, making the clouds look as though they were on fire. The quality of the light was lambent, painting the tops of the surrounding trees with gold, making them shimmer in the early evening breeze.

It all looked so peaceful, so serene, that Maguire had to force himself back to the ugly reality of his life. His eyes followed the line of the electrified fence surrounding his farm. There were small groups of them dotted every hundred yards or so along the perimeter. Some of them he recognized, some he didn't. Some were familiar faces to him: Eric Stapleton, the owner of the village shop; Jean Luff who ran the post office; Eddie Graves, the local bad boy, a tearaway whose petty crimes had seen him in trouble on many occasions with Tony Fisher, the village policeman. Fisher was there too, standing just beyond the fence with the O'Sullivan brothers, who owned the neighboring farm.

They stood there day after day, keeping up the vigil, held at bay by the static hum of the fence, but dedicated and relentless, waiting for him. Sometimes Maguire would become exasperated with them and loose off a shot from the gun, but those incidents were becoming less frequent as the supply of ammunition dwindled.

Did they really expect him to just go out there and surrender himself to them? No, not even he believed that. The sickness had robbed them of the ability for cogent thought. They were dead, empty husks in which the life force had been snuffed out, but reanimated as walking corpses. They could not reason, could not establish a rational thought pattern. They were just reacting to stimulus, much like plants or vegetables.

He was just the stimulus they were reacting to at the moment.

At least that was what Maguire told himself. It certainly made it easier for him when he was forced to deal with them. Blowing off the head of someone you once considered your friend is a traumatic experience, but one he had suffered on countless occasions. The thought that they were just mindless automatons assuaged the guilt and made it possible to continue. For a moment, when he blasted his wife, Jenny, he had been sure there was something in her eyes, some spark of acknowledgement of what he was about to do, but then she had closed her eyes, and his scream of anguish had drowned out the sound of the gun. And when it was all over he had hugged her headless body close to him for several hours, telling her, and himself, over and over again that he really had no choice. His existence after that had seemed very long, the days relentless, and the nights endless.

Maguire pushed himself away from the window and went into the anteroom to check the generator. The room was dusty and cold. It had once been used as a storeroom for his wife's jams and chutneys. She'd had quite a reputation for her preserves and pickles, so much so that it had become quite a lucrative sideline, helping the farm's economy, and balancing out some of the losses caused by the EU farming policy.

There were still all manner of jars on the shelves, but it was the generator and the hundred liter containers of fuel to run it that occupied most of the space in the room. He topped up the generator's fuel tank and checked the motor. Once he was satisfied everything was in order he went back to the kitchen to prepare himself some dinner.

He'd had to get used to eating alone after Jenny's death. For the first few weeks it had been terribly hard. Several times he cooked a meal and discovered he had laid two places at the table and cooked twice the amount he needed. Those evenings had ended with him drinking himself into a drunken unconsciousness.

Later, when the global ramifications of the sickness became fully known—before the cessation of all media—and the attacks on the healthy by, what the newspapers and television had christened "the undead," were becoming commonplace, Maguire had forced himself to eat in order to keep up his strength. Now, after three months without Jenny, and with the world's population all but destroyed, he was beginning to wonder if it was all worth it.

As he chewed the beef he had salted and preserved a month ago, Maguire fingered the pouch around his neck. It would be so easy now to kill himself. There was very little in the world worth living for. The things he had once thought important, the tiny hopes and fears he had considered part of his character, were all meaningless. The relentless terror of each day, of each night, had squeezed out any semblance of normality he had once known. What was now normal was just to breathe each breath and be pleased to have the chance to breathe another.

He remembered the first time he realized that Jenny was going down with the sickness. She had been sunbathing in the garden and had come in to pour herself a glass of lemonade. They were both aware of the seriousness of the sickness that was sweeping across the globe—the media had been filled with little else for the previous fortnight—but despite the heavily reported incidents of whole towns and cities being wiped out by the sickness, there prevailed an almost mocking skepticism about it that, to a certain extent, he and Jenny had bought into. And so when she reached down in front of him to get some ice out of the freezer and he saw the small gray patch of skin—no more than the size of a penny—on her shoulder, he nearly laughed. It was only when he saw the terror in Jenny's eyes when he mentioned it to her that the enormity of the discovery sunk in.

That evening they had both got very drunk, made love with a passion that had been lacking in their marriage for years, held each other and cried.

The progress of the sickness was alarmingly fast. Within twenty-four hours Jenny had developed a fever. Within forty-eight the gray patch had spread across her entire back, spread round to touch her breasts and was creeping up her neck under her hairline.

Twenty-four hours after that she died at his hands, as he blasted her in the neck with the shotgun.

Maguire finished his meal and dropped his plate in the sink to join the others that were there growing mold. There

were no mains to provide water to clean dishes. His entire water supply was kept in plastic containers in the spare bedroom. He could not waste that on washing either the dishes or himself. If he stank, it was too bad. He doubted the undead would bother too much about the smell as they disemboweled him and feasted on his entrails.

The reports of the cannibalistic attacks had been muted at first—the media instructed by their governments to hold back from reporting the widespread nature of the incidents—but gradually the attacks became too frequent and too violent to contain. And very shortly after that there was nobody left to report them—no newspapers being printed, no television and radio being broadcast. The world had died, with a speed that had taken everyone by surprise. Those who were left, those immune to the sickness, were so few it was only a matter of time before the undead would become the only inhabitants of a tired and ailing planet.

Maguire went upstairs to the bedroom and picked up his binoculars. He put them to his eyes and studied the faces of the zombies standing around the perimeter of his farm. He caught himself and swore. He had promised himself not to use that word to describe them. Yet the poor wretches who stood just outside the electrified fence and watched the house with their slack-jawed, imbecilic but hungry expressions were creatures dragged from his worst nightmares.

He started as he saw a flash of green in the distance. He refocused the binoculars and looked again. There was a vehicle moving along the road, heading down toward the farm. It was a Land Rover, olive green, its windscreen protected by a makeshift steel grille. Peering out from behind the grille was a girl with dark hair tied back from her face. She was watching the road with a ferocious intensity, her eyes darting from side to side, scanning the undergrowth either side of the lane.

She did not have Maguire's advantage of seeing the lane from higher up, so as she approached she had no idea that the zombies were secreting themselves behind bushes and trees, slow idiot hunters lying in wait for their prey.

The girl in the Land Rover reached the fence and stopped. Maguire watched her for a long minute, watching *her* as *she* watched the farmhouse. She made a movement as though she was about to open the door. At the same time the undead creatures lurking in the trees moved forward slightly with anticipation. They could smell the hot, sweet blood of a healthy human.

"No!" The word broke from Maguire's lips as he realized

that the girl was about to get out of the vehicle to an almost certain death.

He wheeled away from the window and ran from the room. He took the stairs two at a time, nearly missing his footing and falling the rest of the way. He hammered into the ante-room and shut down the generator, then ran on into the kitchen and grabbed his shotgun, scooping up a handful of cartridges and dropping them into his pocket.

By the time he had opened the bolts of the front door and pulled the door open, the girl was out of the Land Rover and looking through the fence to the house. Already the zombies were creeping out from the undergrowth. The one who had once been Tony Fisher, the policeman, had positioned himself between her and the Land Rover, effectively cutting off her escape.

The girl realized she was in serious trouble at the same time that Maguire broke from the house, yelling at the top of his lungs. He ran toward the fence, shouldering the shotgun, and loosed off a shot wide of the girl. The blast took Eric Stapleton off his feet, removing his arm at the shoulder in the process.

The girl looked at Maguire's approaching form with alarm, then screamed as one of the zombies grabbed her wrist and jerked her arm upward toward its salivating mouth.

She yanked her arm away, lashing out with her other hand, catching the zombie on the side of the head, making it release its grip. But she was badly outnumbered and knew it.

"Help me!" she cried out to Maguire as he fired another shot. This one blasted Tony Fisher's head from his body, the head itself exploding like a disused wasps' nest, disintegrating into a gray, powdery cloud, dry and dusty, without blood.

As he approached, Maguire slipped another two cartridges into the shotgun and fired both of them, not aiming, just using the noise to scare them and make them release their grip on the girl. Where she had pulled up in the Land Rover there was a makeshift gate in the fence. It was barely indistinguishable from the rest of the fence, and the power flowed through it so it was just as hard to breach.

He untwisted the wires holding the gate in place, yanked it open, and spun the shotgun around in his hands so he was holding the barrel. Then, using the stock as a club, he forced his way through the zombies until he could grab the girl. She was swinging her fists, but was hopelessly surrounded. Eric Stapleton had got to his feet once more and, untroubled by his missing arm, grabbed the girl by the hair. Maguire smashed

him in the head with the rifle's headstock, hearing a satisfying crack as the heavy wood split the skull.

Stapleton toppled backward. Maguire pulled the girl through the gap in the fence and slammed the makeshift gate shut, twisting the two wires back in place. Then, panting loudly, trying to get his breath back, used another two cartridges to drive the zombies backward to give himself enough time to get inside and start the generator again.

The girl was crying as she followed Maguire to the house. She clutched the ignition keys in her hand so tightly they had broken the skin.

"How could I have been so stupid?" she said as she closed the farmhouse door behind her.

Maguire said nothing but disappeared into the anteroom to restart the generator. The girl moved to the window and looked out. The creatures that weren't swarming over the Land Rover were paying special attention to the body of Tony Francis, ripping pieces from it and stuffing the matter into their mouths. One of the more enterprising zombies was fumbling with the gate, trying to unwind the wire Maguire had secured it with.

The thing's face registered nothing as he freed one piece and dropped it to the ground.

"They're breaking through!" the girl called to Maguire. In the anteroom, Maguire sweated as he tried to bring the generator back to life. Each time he tried, the motor refused to catch. The girl appeared in the doorway. "One of them's untying the gate," she said.

Maguire looked up at her and glared as if to say, *What the hell do you expect me to do about it?* But he remained tight-lipped.

The girl approached the generator. "Shouldn't that be switched to 'On'?" she said, pointing to the tap on the fuel pipe.

Maguire cursed. He must have caught the safety cutout in his rush to turn the generator off. He flipped the switch over and tried the motor again. It started first time. From outside came a guttural scream as the creature attempting to undo the gate was hit by the full force of electricity as it surged back through the fence.

"Thanks," Maguire said gruffly. His voice sounded strange to his own ears and he wondered how long it was since he had spoken. *Probably not since Jenny died,* he thought.

He went into the kitchen and looked out at the fence. The creatures had backed away from the electricity and were busy pulling the Land Rover apart. The seats were out, lying by the

side of the vehicle, and one of the creatures was staring at himself in the rearview mirror he held in his rotting, gray hand.

Maguire ran up the stairs and checked the perimeter
fence with the binoculars. It seemed intact—no breaches in
his defenses, and he could see no creatures in the gap
between the fence and the house. When he came down again
the girl was staring moodily out at her Land Rover. She tossed
the keys in her hand. Suddenly she spun around and hurled
them at the wall, missing Maguire's head by inches. "Careful,"
he said.

"Stupid, stupid, stupid! I should be dead. If it hadn't been
for you, I would be."

He shrugged. "I'm Maguire, James Maguire. You are?"

"Claire Thomas."

He was aware he stank—it did not take the wrinkling of
her nose to tell him. He wiped his palm on the side of his
grubby jeans and stuck it out.

She shook it.

"Where are you from, Claire?" he asked.

"Oxford. I was working as a caregiver at a nursing home
there. That was until the sickness hit. Out of sixty residents
and half as many staff, I was the only one who didn't go down
with it."

"You were lucky."

"I thought so, too, at first. Now I'm not so sure."

He rounded on her. "Don't ever say that! Would you rather
end up like them?" he said, gesturing to the window. He sat
down heavily at the kitchen table and rubbed his face with his
hands. With a sigh he pulled them away and looked up at her
bleakly. "So what's it like out there? I take it you didn't come
straight here from Oxford."

"No, I tried a number of places first, but it's the same
everywhere. There are pockets of survivors, but most of them
would not let me get near. Most of them are armed—all of
them are hostile to anyone not part of their particular group."
She looked about the kitchen. "I don't suppose I could have a
cup of tea, could I?"

Maguire laughed out loud. The sound seemed strange to
him, but then it had been months since he'd had anything to
laugh about. "The great British cure-all," he said as he filled
the kettle from a water container and set it to boil on the
range. "Wars have been won by the British belief in tea as the
great restorative."

"Tea also lost us America . . . symbolically at least."

He stopped laughing. "Point taken," he said.

Later, when Claire had fallen asleep on the couch in the lounge, Maguire took himself up to the bathroom, and with some of his precious water he washed himself from head to toe, including his hair. Then with a pair of nail scissors he got to work on the beard, hacking off the bristles close to the skin, then finishing off with a reasonably sharp razor. It wasn't until the last of the beard was leaving his face that he realized what he was doing. He might try to convince himself that he was simply fulfilling a basic human function in cleaning his body, but the truth, as he well knew, was that he was doing it for someone else, and for a woman. Not to impress, surely, but not to repulse either.

As he patted cold water onto his face he looked at himself in the mirror. His skin was sallow, and there were dark half-moons shadowing beneath his eyes. The eyes themselves were tired and there was a hunted look in them. It wasn't the face to instill, or inspire, confidence, and he hoped the girl wasn't going to look to him for any heroics. It was as much as he could do to keep body and soul together. Losing Jenny had liberated him in a way. It made him self-reliant, possibly even selfish. Their marriage had been happy, if not exhilarating. In the dark, lonely nights, when he sat listening to the grunts and animal noises from the other side of the fence, he missed Jenny and her companionship. In truth, though, his loss was not as difficult to bear as he might have imagined. All those times over the years that he had considered what life would be like without her had prepared him for a solitary existence. Even so, he was surprised at the anticipation Claire's arrival had stirred within him.

Claire awoke to the smell of sizzling bacon. She wandered sleepy-eyed out into the kitchen.

"I was just coming to wake you," Maguire said.

She looked at him carefully. "You look ten years younger without the beard," she said.

"It's funny, I always hated beards. Never thought I'd have one. The eggs are powdered, by the way, so I've scrambled them."

"And the bacon?"

"Emergency rations. It won't be a regular occurrence."

She smiled. "You say that as though you expect me to stay."

He turned his back on her, concentrating on flipping the bacon in the pan. "Stay or go, it's just the same to me. It's obvious you can look after yourself out there, or else you wouldn't have got this far."

She put a hand on his shoulder and turned him to face her. "That's not what I meant," she said softly. "I don't want to go. Yours is the first friendly face I've seen in weeks. . . . God knows it's the first human face I've seen in weeks. I'm not going to walk away from it . . . that is, so long as you can put up with me here. You owe me nothing."

He turned back to the bacon and flipped it out onto a plate. He gave the scrambled eggs a stir and divided the pan between them. "Not *haute cuisine*, I'm afraid, but the best I can do in the present circumstances."

"It's a banquet," she said. "A veritable feast."

He put the plates down on the table and they sat and ate in virtual silence. He had boiled some coffee and it wasn't until they had drunk half a pot that they spoke again.

Claire asked him about his life before the sickness, and he told her about Jenny, about the farm, about his time at agricultural college before that.

"They told us there that we were the backbone of England, and I must admit it was a romantic ideal—growing food to feed a nation. They made it seem like a noble occupation . . . a vocation, almost."

"I can tell from the irony in your voice that it wasn't."

"Had the sickness not struck when it did, I suppose we could have hung on for another six months. At the end, Jenny was working behind the bar at The Feathers four nights a week just to put food on the table. Feeding a nation . . . there's a laugh. We could barely feed ourselves."

The conversation was halted by a crash from below.

Maguire gripped the side of the table and pushed himself to his feet. "They're in the house," he said.

He approached the door to the cellar, the shotgun cradled over his arm, his finger stroking the trigger. Glancing back, he said to Claire, "Keep a watch up here. I think the doors are strong enough to keep them out, and I shuttered the windows while you were asleep. You should be safe."

Her face was white and there was fear in her eyes. It was the fact that you could not reason with the creatures that scared her so much. They were brainless, driven only by their hunger for flesh and their thirst for blood. She had seen her younger brother turn and attack her father, biting a large piece out of the older man's neck until her mother had caved her son's skull with a poker. Claire shivered at the memory.

Maguire rested his hand on the doorknob and turned it gently. He pushed open the door, stretched his hand inside, and switched on the light.

He recoiled as he found himself staring into the dead eyes of one of the O'Sullivan brothers who was halfway up the cellar stairs. His sibling was at the bottom of the stairs, the wriggling body of a large rat gripped in his hand. He put the rat's head in his mouth and bit down, severing it from the still-writhing body. Maguire gagged as blood spurted out of the brother's mouth. Then he raised the shotgun to his shoulder and fired into the face of the brother on the stairs. The blast blew the man's head apart and he tumbled backward, colliding with his sibling. The two dead men went sprawling backward, and the rat's lifeless, headless body flew through the air.

Maguire rushed down the stairs with a cry, put the barrel of the shotgun against the other brother's head, and pulled the trigger. The sound of the gunshot in such a confined space was deafening, and it was a few seconds before he heard Claire screaming up above.

As he ran back up the stairs, Maguire fumbled in the pocket of his shirt, his fingers closing around two more cartridges. He broke the gun and loaded it, wishing now he had sawn the barrels down to make the weapon more maneuverable.

When he reached the ground floor he found the front door open. There was a figure silhouetted in the doorway—a man, his face gaunt, the eyes opaque, white-filmed. The mouth gaped open, giving the face a vacuous expression and revealing blackened teeth.

Maguire did not recognize him. He wasn't local. Not that it mattered. Maguire blasted him with both barrels and reloaded.

In the lounge Claire was grappling with Jean Luff. Jean, the placid grandmother, local post-mistress, and pillar of the church had her teeth buried in Claire's shoulder and was making a keening sound that set Maguire's nerves on edge. Even as he took in that awful sight, he was still trying to work out how they had got past the fence. Claire's gaze met his. There was terror and despair in her pale gray eyes.

Maguire reversed the shotgun and drove the stock into Jean Luff's face, shattering her cheekbone and making her release her grip on Claire's shoulder. Then he spun the shotgun in his hands and squeezed the trigger.

Jean Luff's head exploded, spattering them with dust and bone. The headless carcass dropped to the floor where it twitched a couple of times before falling still.

Without giving the corpse a second glance Maguire ran to the front door. He checked to see if there were any others, but the rest of the creatures milled on the other side of the fence.

He was suddenly angry with Claire. If she hadn't turned up in her bloody Land Rover, he would never have shut off the electricity, and the zombies would never have got inside the fence. He was angry also that she must have opened the front door and let in Jean Luff and the other creature. Now he had used all his ammunition and was defenseless. All he had left was the single cartridge in the pouch hanging around his neck. And he wasn't going to use that . . . yet.

When Maguire went back inside, all his anger evaporated.

Claire knelt on the floor, hugging herself, singing softly. She crooned a lullaby to the dead body of Jean Luff, as tears poured steadily down her cheeks. Her shirt was torn at the shoulder and Maguire could see blood beneath the hole where Jean's teeth had ripped the skin. He crouched down and wrapped an arm around her, coaxing her to her feet. "Come on," he said. "Let's go out to the kitchen. I'll put the kettle on."

She looked up at him, sniffed back the tears, and nodded.

"I need to look at that shoulder," he said a little while later, as she sipped the hot, sweet coffee he had made for her.

So far she had said nothing, not even when he had put the cup down in front of her. She was in deep shock.

Maguire went to the cupboard under the sink and pulled out a green plastic first aid box. He unclipped the catches and opened it. The contents were sparse, but at least there was a bottle of iodine and some gauze.

Claire unbuttoned her shirt and dropped it down to reveal the wound. Maguire hissed. It was worse than he had first thought. There was actually a piece of flesh missing. He would have to act quickly to cleanse the wound before infection set in. If he left it too long and blood poisoning developed, Claire was as good as dead.

In the first aid box he found a small cellophane envelope of sterile thread and a needle. He palmed them in his hand and went back to the lounge. He rummaged through a cupboard, his fingers closing around the neck of a bottle of vodka. He returned to the kitchen and poured several fingers of the alcohol into Claire's coffee. "Drink that. Then I'll make you some more."

She looked up at him with questioning eyes.

"I'm going to have to stitch you up." He looked away from her gaze. "It's going to hurt."

Claire nodded slowly, picked up her mug, and drank.

She cried out when he swabbed the wound with iodine, but after that, though the sweat poured from her brow and tears poured from her eyes, she made no sound.

He finished stitching, then smothered gauze with iodine and covered the wound, using several strips of tape to keep the dressing in place.

"How did they get in?" she asked.

"They must have come through a gap in the fence when the power was out. Did you open the front door?"

"I panicked. I didn't know how many there were down in the cellar. I had visions of an army of them creeping up the stairs. I just had to get out of the house. It was too claustrophobic."

He nodded. He could understand how she felt. He'd been shut up in the house for months, not daring to venture out any farther than the fence. He admired her courage, driving across country on her own. It made him feel inadequate. There was a perfectly serviceable truck in one of the barns. If he could only get enough fuel to run it, perhaps they should get away from here—try to find others in their position and band together. An individual stood no chance against the creatures. Maybe a group of healthy, rational humans would be able to systematically destroy the zombies and wrest control of the world back from them.

Claire was buttoning her shirt. It was remarkable to Maguire that within hours of her arrival, he had started thinking in the plural again. It was no longer what *he* could achieve, but what *they* could accomplish. What was also remarkable to him was the arousal he felt at seeing a woman partly unclothed. There had been times during the past few weeks when he had thought all normal human emotions were beyond him, merely consigned to memory.

She became aware that he was watching her and turned to face him, a wan smile on her face. "Thanks for the repair job," she said.

"How does it feel?"

"Sore. Where did you learn to do that?"

"I worked on a sheep farm as part of my training. Sheep were always snagging themselves on the fences. The farmer was a tightwad and thought the local vet charged too much, so he used to sew them up himself. Later he taught me how to do it."

She yawned. The sun had died in the sky and the night had closed in. The lights in the room flickered uncertainly as the power from the generator fluctuated. She shivered. "I don't want to sleep alone tonight," she said.

In truth, neither did he. He had been alone too long. He missed feeling Jenny's soft, warm body beside him. He missed the smell of her hair, missed her femininity. Having Claire beside him in the bed would not, could not feel the same, but he hoped it would stir his memories and make the memory of Jenny more real.

Claire undressed in the dark, though whether to save her blushes or his, neither really knew. The sheets still felt cold as she slid between them. She shivered and Maguire wrapped an arm around her, pulling her toward the warmth of his body. He buried his face in her hair, remembering the time when Jenny had cut hers short and how he had hated it.

She rolled over in his arms until their faces were inches apart and he could feel her breath fanning his cheek.

When they kissed it seemed the most natural thing in the world, and the lovemaking that followed was easy and gentle. There was no heat of passion, just two people fulfilling a common need, finding solace in each other's bodies. It was necessary—a brief life-affirming interlude in a bleak and unremittingly hostile environment. The only acknowledgement of the outside world Maguire allowed himself was to keep the shotgun down by the side of the bed, and the one remaining cartridge in the pouch around his neck.

Afterward they slept, and, for Maguire, it was the first night since Jenny's death that he'd done so without suffering nightmares.

Something tugging gently at his neck woke him. Claire was fumbling with the leather pouch. Maguire brought his arm across and grabbed her hand; at the same time, he caught her gaze and glared at her. "No."

She flushed and took her hand away. "I'm sorry," she said. "I was just curious to see what was in there."

He sat up, his face relaxing, the frown smoothing out. He took the pouch from around his neck and opened it, tipping the cartridge out into his hand. "Salvation," he said.

She looked puzzled. "I don't understand."

"It's all I have to stop me becoming like them."

"I still don't—"

He formed a gun with his hand—his index finger the barrel. He put it to his head and mimed pulling the trigger.

Claire closed her eyes and shuddered. "Oh, I see." She pushed herself from the bed. "I need a cup of tea."

As Maguire watched her walk from the room, watched her smooth nakedness, he saw something that made a chill run through his body. He almost groaned, but managed to contain it until she was through the door. Then he lay back against the pillow and screwed up his eyes to fight back the tears. One thing he had learned since all this had started was that life was unfair, so bloody unfair that it was almost a sick joke. Only he did not feel like laughing.

He reached down to the side of the bed and his fingers closed around the barrel of the shotgun. Maguire broke it and slid in his one remaining cartridge. There could be no mistake with this shot; it had to be clean and accurate.

Claire stood at the sink, staring at the shuttered window, imagining the figures standing, waiting just outside the electrified fence. She wondered how Maguire could have stayed here so long by himself, how he could survive in these siege conditions without going totally mad. It was a question she could have asked him if she had turned, for he had just walked into the room. But his movements were silent. She heard nothing as entered, or as he aimed the shotgun at a point an inch below the hairline at the base of her neck. Only at the faint sound of the breath Maguire exhaled as he pulled the trigger did she suspect his presence, and by then it was too late.

He stood for a long moment feeling the breeze from the shattered window on his face, and then crouched down beside the decapitated body. His fingers traced the patch of drying gray skin, about the size of a tennis ball, on the back of Claire's thigh.

Salvation, he thought bitterly.

Maguire got to his feet and opened the back door wide, then went into the anteroom and shut down the generator. The silence crashed in on him like a wave. He walked to the front door and opened that, too. After one last look at the zombies at the fence, he smiled grimly to himself and went through to the lounge to wait.

TAKE, EAT

JOHN C. HAY

Old Mrs. Wilkerson was the first. Father Helias had just climbed into the pulpit, was shuffling his notes and getting ready to give his sermon when he noticed her. He was surprised to see her in the back row, since the front pew had been her domain for so long. Some of the other members of the congregation had noticed her as well, and there was much whispering and furtive glances as they feigned paying attention to Helias in the pulpit. Mrs. Wilkerson didn't seem to notice the commotion though. She just sat in the back row, head lolled to one side, wearing the blue dress she had been wearing three weeks ago, when Helias had buried her.

Helias had heard stories about the zombie problem. Occasionally word would leak out that the dead were coming back to life in some part of the state and killing people. Nothing on the news, of course, but that wasn't the sort of thing you put on the six o'clock news anyway, at least not if you didn't want to start a panic. Thankfully, Mrs. Wilkerson didn't do any of the things he had heard about; no running around, no attacking other members of the congregation. She just sat there, like she had every week before her death.

Bemused, Helias looked down at the papers in his hand. He was supposed to give a sermon on Vanity, and it struck him as suddenly useless. He had always tried to make his sermons applicable to both the week's lessons and to the congregation as a whole, but here was a parishioner who came before God with no sense of vanity at all. She had no concern for how she might look, or what others would think of her. On the spur of the moment, he changed the topic of his sermon to Pride instead, and used the parable of the Widow's Coins to drive home his point: Just because she was dead didn't mean Mrs. Wilkerson wasn't welcome. The congregation muttered and whispered as he spoke, but Helias felt that they understood.

He finished the sermon, moving on to the celebration of the Eucharist. When the time for Communion came, the members of the congregation stood more or less calmly, forming a line, waiting to kneel at the rail and receive the bread and wine. Mrs. Wilkerson stood at the end of the line, shuffling up the aisle with difficulty and an obvious lack of coordination. Still, she made the effort, even though the taut skin of her knee split as she lowered herself to the kneeler in front of the rail, showing bone the color of old ivory underneath.

Helias' head swam a little, and for a moment his heart pounded in his chest with fear and revulsion. Every fiber in his body screamed at him to run, but then his conscience took hold. How could he preach the acceptance and love of God, and not accept this woman in front of him. His inner voice cried out to him: *"Inasmuch as ye have done it unto one of the least of these my brethren, ye have done it unto me."* What was this wretch before him, if not the very least of God's people? Not even the biblical lepers and prostitutes would have associated with her. Weighed down by the pity and sorrow that filled him, Helias' heart slowed and he suddenly understood the true nature of ministry.

Mrs. Wilkerson's sightless eyes followed Father Helias as he worked his way along the rail. He couldn't actually give the sacrament of Communion to the dead; it didn't seem right somehow. As a last minute decision, he laid his hands upon her and blessed her, as he would anyone else unable to take the sacrament. It seemed to work for her, though. She stood afterward, and Helias could swear that the dead woman almost smiled before she shambled back down the aisle and out the door.

✛ ✛ ✛

The next Sunday, there were three. Mrs. Wilkerson, of course, who had reclaimed the front right pew, where she had sat for the twenty-five years that filled the space between her husband's tragic death and her own. Father Helias assumed that there must not be enough left of Mr. Wilkerson to reanimate, or else he would have been there beside her. The other two zombies were sitting in the back row, as Mrs. Wilkerson had the week before. There was a woman that Helias didn't recognize, and another man that looked, at a distance, like Stan Walsh, though there was some substance staining a lot of the zombie's face, so Helias couldn't be sure.

It would be something of a shock if it were Stan; he always brought that unruly mob of a family with him. This zombie was alone, and the Walsh clan was nowhere to be seen. It seemed to Helias that there were considerably fewer parishioners this week as well. He assumed that the majority of folks had decided to pack up and leave town. To be honest, Father Helias had thought about leaving, too, in the early part of the week. But he had decided in the end that his duty was to the congregation, in case they needed him. He didn't want even a single person to come to the church on a Sunday morning, and find that God had shut His doors and made for the high ground, now that it looked like Judgment Day was at hand.

When the time came for Communion, Mrs. Wilkerson did as before, waiting for Father Helias to lay his hands upon her and bless her before she returned to her pew. He noticed that she looked a little worse than she had last week, her skin more pockmarked, the dirty blue fabric of her dress stained with more dark patches, the nature of which Helias decided not to contemplate. The other two followed her lead, kneeling at the rail when their turn came and waiting for his blessing.

Helias realized, now that he could see him up close, that it was Stan Walsh after all. It looked as though he had been caught in a fire of some kind; the lower half of his face and neck were blackened and charred, his lips burned away to reveal cracked and stained teeth. The priest blessed both of them as he had Mrs. Wilkerson, and they rose silently and shambled back to their seats and waited, then left with the rest of the congregation.

The week after that, there were twenty-five. Stan had brought Mrs. Walsh this time, and two of their oldest children, though the rest of the family was still absent. Mrs. Walsh's right arm looked to be burned fairly badly, and Helias wondered if it was from the same accident that had done such damage to Stan's face. Many of the other zombies were congregation members who had been alive at the start of the week. Helias was happy to see that being dead didn't interfere with their sense of duty to the Almighty, even though the number of living eyes staring back at him from the nave was steadily shrinking.

Those eyes remained focused on Helias as he celebrated the Mass, and he felt their gaze like a physical touch. From time to time he would hear someone sobbing in the congregation and would be touched that someone else was as moved by the power of Christ's sacrifice as he was.

By now, the people who remained in town were trapped. The National Guard had finally placed a quarantine on the place: No one was allowed to leave, and no one was allowed to come in. Apparently, what was happening here was happening all over the country, and the government had decided it needed to be brought under control. Helias wondered if any of the other Episcopal parishes in the afflicted areas were receiving the sort of new conversions that he was, but he couldn't call them to discuss the matter; the phones had been out since Tuesday.

The second week after the quarantine was the first Sunday that the dead outnumbered the living. They sat there, many in the same pews that had been their habit while alive. It was as though Sunday was a ritual from which even being dead provided no escape. As long as they could move, they would come to church. In fact, the word seemed to be spreading that Helias didn't turn anyone away. The Robinson family was sitting near the back of the church, and they were devout Baptists. At least they had been—before. Apparently the lack of a Rapture had caused them to reconsider their denomination. Mrs. Wilkerson was still there, of course, sitting in the front row. Helias noticed that her left eye was mostly missing, and assumed she had run afoul of one of the many crows and vultures that had begun frequenting the town since the quarantine. He stifled a nervous little chuckle as he moved to the pulpit. *A crow is a foul fowl*, he thought to himself.

It was a special Sunday for Father Helias as well. In light of the change in composition that his flock had undergone, he had decided to step outside the liturgical calendar for his Gospel. Every eye and every empty socket was turned to face him as he read from Chapter 11 of the Gospel of John: "Then said Martha unto Jesus, Lord, if thou hadst been here, my brother had not died. But I know, that even now, whatsoever thou wilt ask of God, God will give it thee. Jesus said unto her, Thy brother shall rise again."

Staring down at the congregation from his pulpit, Father Helias made up his mind in an instant. These were his flock, and if nothing else, it was his responsibility to minister to them, so that when they finally earned their rest they would go to the bosom of the Almighty. Helias performed the Eucharistic prayer with conviction and at the appropriate time each member of the congregation lurched up the aisle and knelt at the rail. He smiled down at Mrs. Wilkerson, who waited patiently as she did each week, her single eye milky as it watched him back. He lifted up the Host between them and mumbled the words before offering it to her, whispering the words *The Body of Christ*.

She leaned away, one corner of her mouth pulling down as she turned away from the Host. Slowly, she turned her head from side to side, her mouth working silently. Nonplussed, Helias simply blessed her and went on. He did not try to offer the Host to any of the others.

✝ ✝ ✝

It was Wednesday, and Helias sat in his living room look-ing out at the streets. Except for the absence of movement, it could pass at first glance for any other small midwestern town. Then one would begin to notice the silence, broken only by the occasional raucous squawk of a crow. There were no children laughing, no dogs barking, not even insect sounds, other than the now inescapable buzz of flies.

Helias knew he needed to go out there. The refrigerator was nearly empty, and he wasn't about to allow himself to starve to death. He refastened the taut starched white Roman collar and went out the door. The grocery store was only a short walk from the rectory, but every street presented the same image: sudden emptiness, as though everyone had just packed up and left in the middle of what they had been doing.

He was almost to the store when the first zombie lurched out of an alleyway for him. He hadn't seen them outside of the church before, and was quite astonished at how fast they could move when they wanted to. The thing actually had hold of Father Helias before the priest even recognized him. The revenant stared dumbly, perhaps confused when his potential victim didn't scream, or struggle, or even fight back. The priest simply returned the creature's gaze, his eyes staring back into those lifeless, clouded orbs, before saying sternly, "Curtis Johnson. I haven't seen you in church lately."

What was left of Curtis looked more confused than it had before. Then he actually appeared ashamed, bowing his head as he released the priest. Other zombies had begun to gather, and Helias noticed that some of them were carrying arms, or legs, or sometimes just unrecognizable chunks of meat. He avoided thinking about the implications of that, and turned and traveled the rest of the way to the grocery.

All along his path more dead waited, and sometimes they would reach out and try to touch him as he passed. They weren't trying to grab him, just to brush his shoulder or his arm. He began to bless them as he went. And their numbers grew. After Curtis' initial charge, no zombie tried to hurt Father Helias. They just stood there, watching him, waiting.

While he was in the grocery store, an idea came to him. After making a quick mental list, Helias gathered the supplies he would need to put his plan into motion. He thought for a moment about leaving money in the market, by the cash reg-ister, but then decided that it was unnecessary. He was very likely the only living person left in town anyway.

The zombies were still crowded along Helias' path for the

walk back, and as before, he blessed those that he could reach. They watched him with a kind of silent reverence as he walked back to his home, carrying his bag of groceries.

That Sunday marked the first time that Helias was the only person in the church who still needed to breathe. On the way to the pulpit, his eyes fell on the ice chest he had stashed beneath the tabernacle, and once more the thought of blasphemy gnawed at his mind. But before him sat his new flock, and their patient, unblinking eyes rekindled his resolve. He stepped into the pulpit and began the Gospel, reading from Matthew 25:

"And he shall set the sheep on his right hand, but the goats on the left. Then shall the King say unto them on his right hand, Come, ye blessed of my Father, inherit the kingdom prepared for you from the foundation of the world: For I was hungered, and ye gave me meat. . . . And the King shall answer and say unto them, Verily I say unto you, Inasmuch as ye have done it unto one of the least of these my brethren, ye have done it unto me."

He celebrated the Eucharistic mass as normal, but when the time came to bless the gifts, he instead took a plate of small, quarter-sized chunks of meat from the cooler. He laid his hands upon the flesh as he continued the blessing, his eyes closed. He could hear, though, the stirring of the congregation. At the appropriate time, the zombies lurched and shuffled to the rail, and knelt patiently as Helias walked along the row. He held up a morsel of meat in front of each dead face, and then gingerly placed the flesh upon the waiting tongues. Each zombie waited until his fingers were clear before rising and chewing the meat and silently returned to a seat. At the end of the Mass, once Helias dismissed them, they filed slowly out of the church again.

The priest decided to count the experiment as a success. He could continue to minister to his parish and, with God's blessing, he was able to give full sacrament to the poor souls who had become his charges. He made plans to go out on Monday to get more meat from the grocery, so that he could continue his mission.

On Monday, as he came out of the house, they were waiting for him, lining both sides of the street as he walked along, reaching out to touch him, awaiting his patient hand, his forgiving smile. Helias took time to smile at each one, blessing them simply, and they would seem to smile in return. They were his flock, and their obvious love of him lifted his spirit. He walked among them, filled a shopping cart with meat from the grocery store and headed back to the rectory. As he was almost to his home, there was a commotion. A zombie lurched out into Helias' path. It was Stan Walsh, and in one hand he carried an arm, still twitching with unnatural life.

The crowd parted and watched, and another zombie, Stan's wife Jenny, stepped up beside him. The shoulder of her dress was stained with blood where her unburned arm had recently come off. Helias felt a moment of nausea, then an overwhelming feeling of sadness, even pity for the scene before him.

"Wait right here." he said, and dashed into the house.

All he had was some heavy black thread and a large needle, but he tried to make it work. Jenny didn't seem to feel any pain as Helias pushed the end of the bone back into her shoulder socket and began the slow process of securing it there. In all, it took him close to an hour, one large stitch after another. In the end, it wasn't pretty, but she no longer had an empty sleeve just hanging at her side. She was able to flex her hand some, and even move her arm a little, but Father Helias doubted she would ever have normal use of the limb again. Still, he consoled himself that it was better than no limb at all.

And Jenny seemed truly touched by his efforts. An expression of joy spread across her slowly rotting features as she knelt down and pressed her lips to his shoe, then rose again and stepped out of his way to stand beside her husband.

✢ ✢ ✢

Two months after the quarantine was imposed, the meat ran out. Father Helias had realized that this day was bound to come, since the quarantine prevented any transport in or out of town, but he had always hoped his supply would hold out a bit longer. There was nothing that could be done though. He had begun a Great Work, and the word was spreading. Nearly the entire population of the town came to Mass on Sundays, and he began to suspect some were journeying from neighboring towns as well. There were certainly plenty of folks that he had never seen while they were alive. Every Sunday brought more of them, and soon they filled the pews of his little church and stood in the back as well. Always quiet, always respectful, they waited their turn, and at Communion he would bless each one of them, then offer them a snippet of meat, which they would take gratefully.

From time to time there would be one waiting for him on his doorstep, an unfortunate who had suffered some terrible injury that Helias was to heal. The priest had taken good wax string and large bore needles from the craft store, and would sit patiently and do the best he could to put the poor soul back together again. He found a copy of *Gray's Anatomy* in the library and tried, for a time, to use the images in the book as a guideline, but the real thing never looked like Dr. Gray's delicate line drawings. In most cases, the best he could hope for was to push things more or less back where they belonged, and close the holes before they fell out again.

Helias didn't know how he was to carry on with his mission now, though. He had given out the last of the meat as Communion last Sunday, was surprised he'd had enough for everyone, actually. In the end there had been just a single piece left, and this he'd eaten himself.

Despondent, the priest left his home. He was unsure how to proceed. He needed guidance—and decided to look for it in the only place he had ever found it.

There was a crowd of zombies waiting for Helias as he made the short walk to the bright red doors of the church, and he blessed them almost absently as he wandered past. If they noticed the haste of his benediction, or the weight he carried in his heart, they gave no sign. They just stood, following him with their clouded eyes, and waited.

Inside the church, there was no solace to be found. The cross hung above the altar, its shadow falling on the priest as he knelt at the rail. Over and over, one phrase beat down into his skull: *Inasmuch as ye have done it unto one of the least of these my brethren, ye have done it unto me.* The image of Christ among his faithful came to him; of Christ and his disciples sharing together, the Last Supper; of Christ, taking the bread up and blessing it. *Take, Eat, this is my body. . . .*

The inspiration came to Father Helias slowly, but in the end, he knew what he had to do in order to carry on.

✦ ✦ ✦

The church was more full than ever before on that Sunday, and the sight gave renewed life to Father Helias. He rose into the pulpit for the Gospel, and from there he looked out upon the congregation. Dead eyes watched him as he recounted the story of the Last Supper. He finished the Eucharistic celebration proper, then stepped in front of the altar as he proclaimed, "Take, Eat, this is my body, which is given up for you."

As a single entity they seemed to understand, moving forward, approaching for Communion. Helias stood at the gate to the rail as they came, then opened it and retreated a few steps, clearing the way for them to enter.

Old Mrs. Wilkerson was the first, as always. She approached Father Helias nervously, her single milky eye wary. She stopped a moment, as though unsure of what to do next, her jaw hanging slack behind receding lips. Father Helias looked at her, not even seeing anymore the ruptured pustules or the slowly liquefying tissue in her ravaged eye socket. He touched her cheek and whispered, "It's okay," before he placed his forearm into her mouth.

She bit down after a moment, and the pain nearly blinded Father Helias. He wanted to pull away now, to abandon with what he started, but he looked up again at the cross that towered majestically over the altar and grew resolute once more. Mrs. Wilkerson pulled her head back slowly, reverently, her face smeared with his tissue, tearing the mouthful of Helias' arm away with her. It was almost worse than if she'd been savage about it; the pain dragged out rather than being sudden and done.

Stan Walsh stepped up next, leaning over to sink his jagged, burned teeth into the priest's shoulder. Helias couldn't take it; he screamed at last, crying out, "Not my will, but thine, be done!" and as Jenny Walsh tore into his calf his legs finally buckled.

Fortunately, Stan was there to catch him, and as he was held upright, the pain seemed to fade away. The zombies continued in two single-file lines, all the way down the aisle and out the door into the street beyond. In pairs they approached him and took their modest bites from the Communion he offered. Father Helias saw them all, and opened his arms wider, smiling.

SIFTING OUT THE HEARTS OF MEN

WARREN BROWN & LANA BROWN

Our dear mothers and our wives would not like to know the truth of life in this alien country, so when my brother soldiers and I have written home, we have been careful to tell them only how different and how longingly the same the country looks, the extent of the few kindnesses the local people have been willing to offer, and that, tired, we have slept well at night.

I wonder, though, if our mothers and our wives and our fathers and our sisters and, God forbid our children, have learned yet, have somehow got an inkling, of the horror.

When the rebels started up, there was no question that our Union would whip them right soon. Our families now know the folly of that hope. More than four years later we have whipped them not enough, and they us more than we ever expected, and the situation has grown bleaker than I think my family, in their gray house in the city, could picture from their dreams alone.

I pray they still need their dreams to picture it; I pray they have not seen it close. Probably, I think, they have not. The dues of war surely are paid first and most horribly in the field. I'm headed home. I pray to leave this behind.

I thought, when I killed my first man at Bull Run, and was not killed myself but saw so many killed before me, when I first smelled the rotting bodies, bloating in the sun when we could not get them in the ground fast enough, or at all, that war was something different from what any woman could imagine. I thought, when I heard legless men screaming to be killed, when I saw the doctors do no better to the boys than the rebels at their worst, I believed no mother could, as my mother did, admonish her son to war.

But killing is the least of war. You stop wondering at the killing, at having killed, that you will kill again, when you worry more that your belly is empty and your shoes worn through or stolen from you. You want a biscuit more than you do salvation. A drink of rye more than to go to heaven. You forget what heaven is supposed to be like, because you are in hell and the two do not marry.

I am going back now. Gus and I talked it over and we think

the two of us together might make a go of it. The rebellion has died out, and Billy Yank and Johnny Reb no longer hate each other, but watch their brother soldier's back. Like so many men, Gus and I have stopped caring about the Union, or the honor of our names. We have stopped worrying that women will not greet us on the street if we have not fought like men.

To be a man is not what it was.

I thought, when I first killed a man, and when I first went hungry, that war was the deepest hell you could go to. But there's worse things than death and pain, worse things than killing another's kin. There's coming back after.

At first we couldn't even tell one from the other. The boys are so dreadful pale and sickly, their skin a rash of sores, their clothes in such rags, so many of them wounded here or there but still staggering, that the first ones got too close.

Our company had been marching all day and half into the night, tired, wet, and so boiling was the heat the sergeant had allowed we could march without our shirts. I had lagged behind some, considering if I should chuck my kit right there and fall down asleep, as I was sure I could. *Who would miss me?* I asked myself. But they shot deserters in those days and I took one more step, then another, then another.

I heard something behind me. It was dark, the moon covered in the clouds that had worked to drench us all day. I saw one of the boys, one I didn't recognize in the dark, and he walked even more bone-tired than I. I stopped and reached a hand out to him, as you did a fellow soldier then, but something about his face made me look twice, and I pulled my hand away. His uniform bulged at the belly as if too small for him, an unlikely sight among foraging troops; and then I saw the devilish mass below his neck. His chest was torn away as I had seen so many times, his lifeless heart burst forth unnaturally. I did not know what to make of it in my mind, but I screamed, Gus tells me, and I ran, thank God, for he was reaching for me and surely I would be one too now if I hadn't. He lurched forward as the boys turned to see what new horror could possibly make an 1860 man cry out, and he got hold of Samuel Miller's arm and bit it clean through, and Samuel's screams were added to the night.

The night was horror like none since, for none knew then to shoot them clean through the head, and he trampled on and tore two others despite our shots, until one of us hit him between the eyes on pure luck. But that night was the last that the men breathed sound; for once he fell, we thought the misery was done. Samuel and the others cried a merciless long time until they died, and by morning we knew the plague was hell indeed, for they rose up again, and we murdered our soldier brothers without a thought, except to save ourselves.

The officers, bound by that epithet to carry on and carry us too, ordered us to bury the men and strike out again. But they could not look at us straight. Hours to days and days to a week, we gleaned there were hundreds of the risen, all through the countryside. We had but one message from a passing rider, that there was no help in the direction we were going; we received no orders at all. By week's end, we determined to save the precious ammunition we had for the dead, and let the rebels alone.

We went on this way six more days, marching to no particular place, for there was no particular place that would receive us safely. We killed perhaps two hundred of them, and ran from a thousand more. We found they could not climb a tree after a man, but that a man would be trapped forever if he tried the trick. On the sixth day, Gus found himself so much accustomed to the target that he killed the major, who had been missing since dawn, with a single shot at fifty feet. There were but twelve of us left then, all the officers gone, and Thomas Greanley said we had a better chance each man for himself. No man had very much to say in dispute, and it was decided. As near as we could calculate, we were not far from the ocean, and many of the men saw in that direction some hope of help, or final reckoning. Gus and I determined to pair up, as we both wished to head dead north.

I hoped that the plague had not reached the cities, or if it had they had found some way of curing it. My families— mother and father and sister, and my dear wife Ruth and little son Jack—were in the Union capital, and I placed my bets on that city, where our able president had dealt so nobly with the danger of disunion. If any man could save his people from this calamity, Abe Lincoln could.

✜ ✜ ✜

For a time Gus and I made good progress, in one day traveling better than twenty miles where the land was flat and dry and the woods thick enough to hide us but well passable. Perhaps our spirits once lifted at the thought of home lifted our strength also, but for how long can raised spirits endure in the fear of Second Coming, or the coming of Lucifer himself? Our pace soon flagged with our strength. The land had grown more inhospitable, offering rocky ground and ravines in our path, which in the drizzle and overcast skies seemed sometimes like the mouths of hell from which the walking dead had sprung. We had hoped to locate mounts to carry us north, but horses have vanished from the land, or are found only as carcasses, alive with bluebottles and maggots. I think that our fatigue is so great sometimes that we would gladly leap astride the rotting beasts if they too should rise as the human dead have risen and urge them like riders of the Apocalypse toward our homes and loved ones. But the plague seems visited upon man and man alone. For a fact we hoped this was the literal truth before we came upon the mother in the road.

We were five days into our homeward trek, and had stayed the night in a derailed boxcar, its doors barricaded against the terrors of the night. Our meager rations of hardtack and jerky had been consumed, and we had set snares for rabbits or partridge, or whatever small game might spring the trap. Our plan as always had been to alternate the night watch, but hunger and fatigue took their toll and both of us slept, slept that is until the wailing of the babe broke the quiet of the early dawn. I awoke after Gus, in time to see him, Navy Colt in hand, sliding the door aside with his great arm. Quick to follow him and making sure a cartridge filled the breech of my carbine, I descended to the ground and beheld yet another thing that no man should behold.

It had not been a baby's wail that had awakened us. A babe there was indeed, pressed to its mother's breast where they stood in the road, the light of the rising sun making them a master's portrait of life and love, a glowing hope that all our dreams had not fallen into blackness. But the picture burned away as we saw that the scream was delivered from the young mother's lips, that her girl child even gray in death suckled with cold delight at the blood that flowed from the rent flesh of her mother's breast. Of all we had endured thus far, this scene exceeded the worst. So much so that Gus, a hard strong man, fell to his knees and sobbed as the young woman wailed again, clutching her dead but living child even closer in a hopeless embrace. I could not bear it and raised my Spencer to end the mother's pain only to find Gus before me, the cold eye of his revolver staring at my own face.

"You will not shoot a living woman, Tommy Barnes, before my having shot you first."

His manner was straightforward and without bluster, and I knew that for a brief moment he was mad, and I knew also that he would kill me dead.

"She will not be a living woman long, Gus. You have seen enough to know it."

"I have seen men take bullets meant for other men too. And I have seen men carry others across battlefields on their shoulders when they had no chance."

We stood looking at each other, and as my piece was cocked I am ashamed to say I considered feigning my consent, then shooting my friend in his madness when he presented the chance. But he was my friend and I lowered my Spencer and we went to her and used all the strength we both had in us to separate her from the baby. We watched her for an hour, and in her delirium she spoke enough to tell us that her name was Amy Chester, that she had folks in Baltimore and would we please let them know she and the baby were all right. We promised her we would. It was only when she slept that we did for it, and only when she awoke with empty eyes, approaching us in unclean hunger, that Gus himself killed her.

✛　✛　✛

It is now three days since we buried poor Amy Chester and her child. Our progress north continues slowly, but we have had good luck with game. I cannot help but think as we eat the rabbits and birds that maintain our strength that we ourselves are the game of the carnivorous dead who were once our brave comrades and our equally brave enemies. If in sacrament we take the bread as the body of Christ, have we his children somehow now become the sacrament of the damned, our own flesh taken to celebrate the reign of the legions of hell? Such thoughts can not be borne by sane men. And Gus and I do ponder in our despair whether our wits have departed us.

He carries the locket of Amy Chester wrapped in a Confederate dollar upon which is written the particulars of her people. He has shown me a likeness of his own wife, Rebecca, taken by cholera a year before the outbreak of the war. The resemblance between the two women is strong, and explains in part I think his adamant defense of Amy. He had not spoken much of Rebecca before, and never shown her picture.

✛　✛　✛

On Tuesday we came upon a large group of Negroes close by the side of the road. Men, women, and children there were, set in a neat camp with several wagons, and mules to pull them. The men were well-armed, some with Henry rifles, and drew down on us as we approached. In our ragged state it took us some convincing to show them we were not Confederates, but their leader, who went by the name Benford Blue, was a reasonable man who accepted us for what we were, and pulled from his kit a corporal's insignia, holding it next to mine.

"So you two boys sick of the fighting too?"

I could see that Gus did not well approve Blue's manner of speaking, and before I could stop him he was bound to reply.

"And I think I have seen things that would make the whites of your eyes go whiter, and stared them down too, you darkey son of a bitch."

Several of the men approached closer at this and I thought we would fare no better than rebels at their hands at that moment. But Benford Blue waved them back. He stood before Gus and raised up his buckskin shirt to reveal a livid rough-healed scar.

"A Confederate bayonet did that, Union man." He turned to show a net of slash marks on his back. "And a sergeant on the Union side did this when I was a green recruit and a white man said I was a thief. The rebel is dead and the liar is dead too. They both saw it was Benford Blue who killed them, saw him face to face, as you see me now." He lowered his shirt, and raised one leg of his pants. "And the man who did this was already dead, soldier." Benford Blue smiled down at the scabbed red sore. "Now he's dead for good."

I was overcome by terror, though my mind told me the Negro was not one of the dead himself. But how could it be? How could he survive what no other had? Gus had begun to back away; I could see he was ready to run. I started after him, but something told me these Negroes were our hope. If Benford Blue had survived, he must know how to answer the horrible punishment God had inflicted.

I leaped upon my friend, tumbling us both to the ground. "They're alive, Gus," I whispered as he struggled with me. "This place is safe."

The Negroes shared their mess with us and even Gus was grateful. The women held the children back from touching us or playing near. I could see from their dress that some were freedmen and others must be recent slaves. They had banded together, as had we with our rebel brothers, to arm against the unexpected enemy. As to Blue's miraculous survival, it resulted, as he explained with what I believe was no small satisfaction, that his people had discovered no secret, only a mystery. No black man or woman or child that they knew of had been afflicted. They hid in fear just as did we whites, but only as they would from wild animals. They were safe from the living death.

We beseeched them to shield us, and I reckon we weren't the first. Benford Blue would have none of it. It strengthened our case not at all that we could not have been afflicted, that we showed no sores or wounds that would bind us to rise after death. Blue said he could not be sure of it, because we were white men.

After a night they sent us on our way, standing guard so we would not be tempted to turn back, though we were in spite of it. But we walked on just the same.

✝ ✝ ✝

We were some two days walk north from Benford Blue and his band when we found ourselves on the bank of a mist-covered river we judged to be the Rappahannock.

Having taken such pains to avoid towns and their mass of people in our journey north, we were at something of a loss to determine exactly where we were. But we agreed that it would be best to follow the river northwest, skirting Richmond, which lay somewhere north of the river. Neither Gus nor I had any desire to meet up with a body of Union soldiers, who this far to the north might not look kindly on our desertion of our duties regarding the now almost forgotten war.

We had seen few of the walking dead for some days, and I dared hope that the plague had indeed confined itself to the battlefields we had left behind. With these thoughts of affirmation and accompanying visions of my dear loved ones, whom I prayed waited in a neat clapboard house in the capital, I put my hand on Gus' shoulder.

"I think we will see the Potomac before too many days more journey, my friend."

He replied with something of a smile, "I believe you are right, Tommy."

It was then the monster came at us out of the mist. Its dark bulk loomed into view eerily silent, like some Leviathan come from out of the depths to join the risen dead. We had been too subject to queer and monstrous sights of late and had become quick to fight or run. Before I knew what had happened Gus had raised his revolver and let fly a shot at the thing, the report of his Colt so close by it nearly deafened me.

The huge shape defined itself now and we beheld an immense ironclad very like the Confederate *Virginia*, against which the Union's *Monitor* had prevailed off Hampton Roads. That this ship wore the Union colors suggested she had been captured from the rebels and turned to the use of our Navy.

We could hear the huff of her engines now, and could see the smoke from her stack as she churned the water toward us. I expected at any moment she must turn to follow the curve of the river, but instead she continued toward us and we sprung away as her prow drove into the bank and she came to rest with a horrible rending sound as a full third of her length reared up on shore with a force that ripped her funnel from its fastenings and brought it crashing forward onto her deck. A great hiss of steam escaped from amidships and the sound of her engines lapsed into silence.

Gus and I stared at each other.

"Where is her crew?" I asked when I could speak.

He shook his head. As if in answer a steel hatch begin to rise on her deck, slowly, as if the man below had not the strength to push it to.

"They must be in a bad way," Gus said, hastening toward the great hulk, then finding a handhold on a stanchion and hoisting himself up onto the deck.

"Hang on, Gus. You don't know what you'll find there," I called to him.

He grinned at me. "Dead men can't run a ship, Tommy."

He pulled the hatch cover open and shouted a hello into the depths. A pale arm reached forth and gripped his ankle.

"To hell with you," he said, and leveled the Navy Colt and fired.

"Guess I was wrong, Tommy," he shouted, slamming down the hatch cover. It was the last thing I ever heard him say, for at that moment the ironclad seemed actually to take a great breath. Then I was lifted into the air and the world filled with thunder.

When I awoke I could find only pieces of the ironclad, and pieces of men. The boilers had taken Gus from life and the grisly crew from death. Driven barrel-first into a tree trunk like Excalibur into the stone was Gus' Navy Colt. Try as I might, I could not get it free.

✝ ✝ ✝

I was almost compelled to cry at being all alone in this god-forsaken world. I realized now that Gus was my tether to a willingness to go on. I fell to my knees, not to pray, for surely no prayer had been answered since the beginning of the plague, but to give myself up to the destiny of living death.

But as I sobbed on the riverbank, I thought again of my kindly young wife and our little child. I could not know, might never know, if they were safe or dead, or in that horrible purgatory in between, but I could not fail to try to reach them. I staggered to my feet again, and wandered northward.

I could not sleep and feared to lie down and try, so I

walked all night, and just as dawn broke I saw a town ahead. I no longer cared what I might meet there; I had no choice but to march as straight as my body would bear, and that I did.

Like the countryside in which it abided, the town was in that stage of panic that at first glance might be mistaken for the laziness of a Sunday afternoon. No one was in sight. The stores were boarded up and no sound escaped from within. I was afraid, more than of the dead, that there would be no one at all. I walked the boards next to the shops and saloon, and crossed the square to check the stables. As I stepped in front of the church doors, I heard a stifled cry: "Mister!"

I stopped and stared, and could make out no movement. But then the door came slowly open and a man whispered loud, "Hurry!" and waved me to him. I ran as well as I could in my condition, and was escorted inside, where perhaps twenty townspeople still held out hope. They looked me over closely and, accepting that I had not been infected, asked me if I had ammunition, and told me I could stay. They did not ask my story. I did not have to ask theirs. God had made our stories all the same. We had forged new gods: the carbine, the Gatling gun, and the cannon. The dead we made, and now we could not look away from them.

As I took my futile post at a window of the church, I looked my nameless companions over, for they might be the last of the living I would ever know. I saw in them more than the muted and dazed fear I had grown used to in my own face, reflected in Gus'. One woman held a newspaper and sobbed, and several others gathered round her. The men looked each other in the face with despair. I walked to the woman and took the broadside from her, and read that our beloved Abe Lincoln had been murdered.

Shot through the head. The great man. Could it be? The report said the event took place in a theater; did that mean our capital had not been afflicted, that the face of society was yet aswirl with pretty girls and honored gentlemen? Did they not know what horror the war had turned to?

Or was our captain himself a victim of God's retribution?

✣ ✣ ✣

It seems only hours ago I was drinking rye with Gus in camp, winning seven dollars from Ben Stuart with a queen-high straight, and he was cussing me and we were complaining about the cold and heat and other discomforts a man finds on the periphery of war. Now I hold my rifle on the windowsill in anticipation of the most brutal kind of killing that I have been called upon to do. To kill not the man himself, but his living soul, that would not give up because he fell.

And I wait for the final moment, to place a hole in my own brain. I know now I cannot spare my wife and child the torments of earth or hell. I can only spare the world the specter of my sin.

THE OTHER SIDE OF THEORY

DANIEL KSENYCH

"Retrieval Team confirming mark. Initiating descent."

The large twin-rotor copter, black-skinned and curved as if muscled, begins a vertical drop, spiraling slightly. Beneath it the tan plain, all wind-scoured rock and smooth sands, stretches to every horizon.

"Sir. . . ." The pilot's voice is rough, staticked, over the comm.

"What is it RT?" the voice comes back over his headset.

"Sir. It appears that the target is standing. And waving."

There is a pause over the channel. The voice returns.

"Confirm bio-readings, RT."

The pilot taps a pad mounted to his left, accessing a colorful graphic from one of the many terminals housed in the copter's bay.

"Bio-readings confirmed, sir. Within previously established parameters."

Another pause.

"So you're telling me that he's standing and waving and that there is zero internal biological activity?"

The copter nears the ground, whipping up dust into the bright, sunbaked air.

"Yes, sir. He's reading dead. But he's . . . Well, I can see now sir that he's smiling."

The copter touches down, easing its bulk onto wheel struts that have unfolded from its underside. A single figure, a man in a black jumpsuit, stands a dozen yards away. He has no equipment, no vehicle. There are no tracks in the sand to reveal where he came from, how he came to be in this isolated place.

"RT." The voice on the headset has changed. It's a woman now. "Get the grab-crew into containment suits. Zero communication with the target."

✣ ✣ ✣

The conference room is dimly lit, clean-lined. Twelve people, each in standard mid-21C formal wear, sit around the oval table. Polyuse keypads and display panels are mounted by their hands. A large, rectangular phosphorweave screen emits a steady glow from the wall they are facing in their swivel chairs. Dr. Kedea stands before the screen, silhouetted by its cold light.

As she begins speaking, elaborate graphs and diagrams, algorithms and complex equations begin to cascade across the screen.

"The results of our experiments have conclusively proved the existence of a fifth dimension. We have, on four occasions, successfully immersed a subject in this dimension and recalled him into—"

She gestures at the room and its occupants.

"—the four-dimensional world, three spatial and one temporal, that we routinely exist within.

"Teleportation is a reality."

One of the figures seated at the table speaks up, face shadowed and glasses reflecting the light from the screen.

"As I understand it, the accuracy of determining the re-entry point is far from one hundred percent."

Kedea nods. "That is only a matter of fine tuning the process. What is important is that we have successfully moved a human being from one point in three-dimensional space to another with a near-zero temporal lapse."

Another faceless figure speaks.

"What about the biological fallout?"

"Upon re-entry," Kedea responds, her voice even and confident, "the subject is clinically dead. All internal functioning has ceased."

A number of the seated people shift in their chairs.

"However," she continues, "in each case we have been able to resuscitate the subject with no lingering damage to his physiology or impairment to his neurological functions."

Images of a human body, sections highlighting and darkening, charts and numeric strings blooming and receding, scroll across the large screen.

"Ladies and gentlemen, your very generous funding has assisted us in ushering in a new age of scientific wonder. We hope your generosity will continue to help us explore this marvelous opportunity."

After each of the twelve people congratulate Dr. Kedea and confirm their commitments, they file out of the room and Mr. Octavius enters.

"You should have told them," he says in his soft voice.

Kedea taps the wall beside the screen. It goes dark and the room's ambient light brightens automatically.

"Not until we know more."

+   +   +

The chamber is rectangular, a cot against one wall, a sink and toilet on the opposite side. He stands in the exact center of the room, in his black jumpsuit, facing away from the one-way viewing window.

The attending technician speaks quietly to Kedea. "Notice his scalp. It's still clean shaven. No hair growth."

Kedea murmurs, "Twenty-eight hours."

Mr. Octavius glances at the row of monitors jutting from the wall beneath the observation window. Each of them shows a single flat line, each a different color.

"Has he . . . moved?" Octavius asks.

The technician continues to stare at the man in the chamber as he answers.

"Yes. He has walked about the room. Sometimes his gait has been casual, other times formal. His facial expression has also changed occasionally, from thoughtful to confused to relaxed. I had Psych Division analyze the footage but they haven't been able to come up with anything conclusive.

"He hasn't sat, slept, ingested, or excreted."

"Or spoken," Kedea adds, also staring at the man.

"Jesus," Octavius breathes, half-turning from the window.

"Environmental analysis?" Kedea asks.

"The room's clean," the technician answers.

Kedea smoothes her jacket.

"It's time we made contact."

+   +   +

Albert Parsons has been teleported five times.

Selected from an in-house recruitment program, Parsons has been an excellent test subject. Compliant enough to follow orders and undergo testing without complaint, aggressive enough to face the mystery before him with confidence. The first time his body was flooded with the choreographed radiation storm and lowered into the tank he made a Star Trek joke.

After re-entry and resuscitation he underwent extensive monitoring and re-testing. No biological, neurological, or psychological deviations from his previous patterns were detected. Parsons remembered nothing of the journey between activation of the tank and awakening in the bay of the retrieval copter. He described the experience as "exhilarating."

He received cursory briefings on the theoretical topography of the dimension he traveled through: an Escherian structure both surrounding and penetrating all points in three-dimensional space, existing outside the entropic forces of the observable universe from which the perception of linear time is derived.

"Sure," he said, "but theology has never been my strong point."

It is this statement that Kedea is remembering as the door to the chamber slides shut behind her and Parsons turns to face her.

There is nothing out of the ordinary about his appearance. He is the same man she selected six months ago, the same man she has launched out of this world into another and called back again five times now. His eyes are the same calm, friendly eyes that looked out at her from the tank just over twenty-eight hours ago. Except, she notes, he isn't breathing.

The room is quiet. The hum of the technology that habituation makes silent, ever-present in the corridors and labs of the complex, is absent here. So it is a loud quiet.

Parsons is looking at her. She notes the recognition in his eyes, perhaps a hint of welcome in his smile. Outside the complex, the corridors and labs and tests, outside the science of it all, she has felt happy for Albert Parsons. She likes him and feels proud of him and for him. She has felt pleased that he has gotten to do this amazing thing. Her assigned observer in Psych cautioned her against projecting her own feelings of accomplishment onto her subject, a warning to remain sensitive to his own experience. Parsons, possessing his own crude but effective sensitivity, once made a point of thanking her for this opportunity. Always quick to put others at ease.

His manner hasn't changed. She still feels comfortable with him, standing a few paces away from him in the chamber. Except for the hard and uncompromising fact, stated clearly and definitively by the monitoring sensors imbedded in the walls of the room, that he is dead.

Parsons gestures to the cot, offering her a seat. She shakes her head, begins to smile instinctively but can't make it happen against the weight of the fact. He notices and his eyes soften in sympathy.

"Albert," she says, inviting him to talk.

He shakes his head, but it doesn't seem to be a refusal.

"You can't?" she asks.

A single nod.

Feelings well up inside her. This never happens here, in the complex. Everything here is codified and delineated. The only unknowns are those that are predicted and designated. Late at night she has woken up alone in bed, feeling. It is an overwhelming thing for her and she always answers it by driving out to the complex and running simulations or studying results.

She is feeling now, a deep sadness, some fear. A lack of something. The absence of something inside her that will be able to help this man she has made. That she doesn't understand where the feelings are coming from is as much the problem as the feelings themselves.

"Albert. Help me understand."

He begins to walk toward her.

✦ ✦ ✦

The alarm sounds at 3:11 P.M. Internal Security arrives at 3:12 P.M. They wear white, chunky plyalloy body armor laced with MEM bioresponse fibers. Full musculature and respiratory enhancement, self-contained medical support suite. Variable-dose chem batons in hand.

They quickly observe and assess, and at 3:13 P.M. the six-man team breaches the chamber.

Octavius had to trigger the alarm—the first time he has ever heard the peak-to-valley-to-peak siren inside the complex. The technician was and is in shock, arms slack at his sides, repeating "Holyfuckholyfuckholyfuck."

Parsons casts Kedea's body aside as the door slides open. Her ruined skull smacks wetly against the smooth floor. An arcing filament of her blood trails through the air between her head and Parsons' mouth, red mouth, as if in slow motion.

The first two guards close on Parsons, thrusting with their batons. He swats one weapon aside with a speed and fluid grace never demonstrated in his physical tests. Grabs the other just under its tip, a molecule-wide crystalline delivery system. Yanks it forward, pulling the guard toward him, wrenching the baton free and reversing it. Puncturing, impossibly, the tinted visor and burying the baton deep into the guard's skull. Swinging the corpse at the end of the shaft sideways into the other guard, both crashing to the floor.

The next two guards are in right behind them, one with orders to get to Kedea, except Parsons is between him and his target. Parsons punches his fist through one guard's chestplate and chest, backhands the other across the head, tearing the head free of the neck.

"Holyfuckholyfuckholyfuck."

"It's not going to work," Octavius says flatly as one of the remaining guards manages to plant his baton into Parsons' shoulder. The chemicals discharge into his bloodstream but travel nowhere. In moments the guard's white armor is splattered red.

Octavius finally manages to move, stepping forward toward the door panel, hand reaching out to press it. His finger meets the smooth plastic and the door hisses out from the wall.

Until Parsons' hand grabs its edge and it stops.

At 3:14 P.M. the situation goes critical.

✛ ✛ ✛

"My best guess as to what's happening is—"

"Yeah, yeah," Commander Harrison cuts Octavius off. "I've been to the movies; I know how this is going to play out. Let's just cut to the final scene."

Harrison shoulders his rifle and moves toward the exterior communications terminal. Keys in the priority-one military channel. The ops center is dark except for the low red emergency lights and the flickering monitors. Omashay, the only other staff member they managed to rescue on their frenzied dash through the complex, is sitting in a chair with her face pressed into her hands.

Octavius puzzles out Harrison's logic and gasps.

"You're calling in an erasure strike?"

Such a strike was prearranged as a last-ditch protocol given the potential consequences of their work. Only to be initiated after evac and never for the reason facing them now.

"I am," Harrison replies. "Unless this is the scene where we learn they've cut communications."

✛ ✛ ✛

3:11 P.M. Parsons' teeth sink into her brain and the information begins to download. Everything that follows is residual 4-D processing of the data before the final directive sets. Just like Parsons' behavior—she understands immediately—his waving, his facial expressions and attempts at communication. Residue.

"Your model is wrong," she hears Parsons' voice say. Then a burst of silence. Then noise followed by more silence. And again. Oscillating, rising and falling into each other, an audio yin-yang symbol. Until the duality of it collapses and/or breaks open into something new and/or old beginning and/or ending.

She has sudden and total awareness of her body. The final rush of blood through her veins. The endless geography of her skin. The perfect synchronized community of her organs fragmenting into stillness and solitude. The technology of her skeleton.

"That which is everywhere and nowhere is death."

It is Parsons' voice and/or her voice.

There is something elegant to the receding activity in her body. And her memories. Entire sections of her childhood, her years at school, shutting down like a power outage and/or coming on-line into a unified, undifferentiated field. During the 2040s resurgence of the pre-century psychedelic subculture she read the Tibetan *Book of the Dead* tripping on Scape. This is nothing and/or everything like what it described.

"We have been invading death for millennia."

She sees time as a strand of DNA and/or electric current spiral-arcing out of three spatial dimensions, penetrating into and/or consuming a fourth.

"This is wild!" she hears the voice of a junior technician whose brain Parsons has just cannibalized shout as it joins with hers from somewhere a few minutes farther down the time current. Hundreds more voices are joining hers and his from the future as Parsons stalks the corridors and labs killing and feeding on technicians, engineers, and guards. Killing and feeding on the science. She is alongside him, there in the future, her body moving, strong and swift and unbound. She does not speak, understanding that language is a creature of time and space.

"And now death is fighting back," they say outside time and space.

Here, now, sprawled on the floor of the chamber, she, her corpse, begins to move.

✛ ✛ ✛

"Don't," Omashay says, pointing the sidearm Harrison gave her.

"Jesus," Harrison says with much more resignation than surprise.

Octavius reflexively steps away from her, stammering. "What—?"

"I'm sorry," she says, "but I'm the secondary character whose scientific curiosity overrides her good sense."

"Omashay!" Octavius shouts, trying and failing to sound authoritative. "We have to—" Then he realizes he's arguing in favor of suicide and stops.

Harrison drops his rifle from his shoulder and squeezes the trigger. Omashay jerks backward, her back tearing open with the exit wound, but not before she gets a shot off.

It goes wide and totals the comm terminal.

Octavius stammers some more.

Harrison slams a fresh clip into his gun, moving toward the door.

"Alright. It looks like this is going to have to be an action movie."

✢ ✢ ✢

Asante and Morgan are holed up in an antechamber off one of the laboratories. It's been red low-light and silence for hours now. A reinforced plastiglass window looks out from the small sitting room into the lab. Through it, earlier, they watched the quiet and fast-moving crowd of coworkers, each with his or her skull crunched and bloody, storm the lab and murder Vanderbelt, Mootabi, and Craigen.

Morgan cried for some time, from fear and from guilt for locking the antechamber door before her friends could get inside. Asante stood by the window, observing the slaughter, fists clenched. He felt, strangely, rage.

They both watched as Vanderbelt, Mootabi, and Craigen stood back up and fell in with the others.

Then main power cut. The hum of the complex faded slightly and the red lights came on as the backup generator activated. Some of the men and women in the lab moved out into the corridor. The remaining seven, including Morgan and Asante's work team, lined up at the window and stared inside. Their faces, those that weren't too torn and disfigured, were serene. Their gazes unwavering.

Hours passed.

Asante had a nervous breakdown after the first hour. He screamed and screamed at Morgan, at the small room and the furniture, at the faces watching them through the window. Eventually he collapsed in a corner, sobbing.

Morgan said at one point, "God damn Kedea, that bitch."

During the second hour Morgan calmly and reasonably pleaded with the people outside the glass to let her and Asante go. Asante, meanwhile, began hallucinating. He saw dozens then hundreds of tiny reptilian creatures crawling and flying about the room. They secreted colorful paint-like fluids into the air that swirled together and formed shapes: landscapes, his mother's face, scenes like news footage.

During the third hour Asante and Morgan sit on the floor opposite one another. They share stories from their past, discuss their work and families. They form a mutual, implicit understanding that they are dying. Then that understanding metamorphoses into an unspoken revelation that they have, in fact, been dead all along and that they are on the verge on being born. Their conversation becomes oddly religious and they talk about what is happening as if it is some sort of divine intervention. They undress each other and have intense, passionate sex as the people watch from beyond the glass.

Then, holding hands, they walk to the door and open it.

✚ ✚ ✚

When Harrison charges out of the ops center, firing into the group of silent people waiting outside, Octavius closes the door behind him. The violent stuttering of Harrison's automatic rifle gives way to his violent screaming and then silence.

Octavius sighs and takes a seat, sliding a laptop in front of him. He begins typing.

> *Some property of the fifth dimension, or perhaps the fifth dimension itself—if you'll forgive my anthropomorphizing—has co-opted test subject Albert Parsons' biological structure and re-engineered it to function as a probe. A remote vehicle capable of acting as a discrete unit of 5-D—*

He pauses, searching for the right word. Force? Energy? Those are 4-D concepts.

> *—as a discrete unit of 5-D xxxxx within 4-D spacetime. The behavior of this unit and the xxxxx it embodies (literally) appear to act not unlike a virus, spreading from host to host. The mechanism of transmission appears to be the ingestion of one host's brain matter by another.*

It feels good to be writing it down like this. For this first time since Parsons' retrieval Octavius feels he has a measure of control over the situation. Then he feels a dull pain in the back of his skull. *Psychosomatic*, he assures himself. Until he hears a voice inside his head.

"The act is symbolic."

It is Kedea's voice. *God damn Kedea, that bitch*, he thinks, surprising himself.

"The act of devouring the engine that generates the invasive four-dimensional construct of reality, which is itself entirely symbolic in nature."

The pain is increasing. That time the voice sounded like Parsons' and/or Harrison's.

> *I am currently experiencing some psychological and possibly physiological disturbances. This could be a result of the stresses of the situation. Or possibly a side effect of the spreading 5-D xxxxx.*

"Nothing is happening," he hears the voice and/or voices say. There is an accompanying stab of pain and rush of . . . something through his mind. He has the sense that it is moving at a velocity approaching beyond velocity, an event horizon bordering utter stillness and/or complete motion.

"Slow it down, slow it down," Octavius murmurs to himself. Lowers his fingers over the keyboard.

This is symbolic.

"You are processing residue from three minutes into your future—" now it sounds like his voice "—when you transcend the illusion of opposition and exit the ops center and join us."

The pain is flaring in his skull. He breathes deeply and stares at the words on the other side of the screen. A minute passes. He watches how the words have invaded the perfect silence of the blank screen, pretending order, their meaning only rough and noisy. Another minute passes. His vision blurs, from tears perhaps, and the distinction between words and screen blurs. He types.

What is on the other side of theory?

Octavius stands and walks toward the door.

INSPECTING THE WORKERS

JIM C. HINES

Kris Dobson approached the man by the wall, staring unabashedly at his body. The streetlight tinged his skin a pale yellow, and accumulated grime had stiffened his clothes like cardboard. Brown hair painted greasy swirls across his scalp. One curled lock fell into his eyes as he scraped graffiti from the old steel mill wall. Without stopping, he reached up and tore out the offending lock. Kris thought he was a marvelous specimen. He couldn't have died more than a few days ago.

The strobe light in her hand flashed twice, and the corpse's arms dropped to his side. Now effectively "dead," save for a few hardwired brain functions, he raised one hand and formed the ASL letters *S* and *N*: Situation Normal.

"The zombies understand that light?"

Kris wasn't surprised that Mrs. Gillespie had ignored her instructions to stay back. This was the same woman who had barged through the front doors of Reanimation and Revitalization, Inc., and refused to budge until she talked to the president. Faced with the prospect of physically dragging a screaming, struggling seventy-year-old woman out of the lobby, security had backed down. The president did the same thing, once the problem worked its way up to his level. R&R had enough public relations trouble without Mrs. Gillespie.

As a result of managerial cowardice, Kris now had to babysit a tourist as she did her rounds of the Detroit reclamation project.

"They don't really 'understand,'" Kris explained impatiently. "They have light sensors in the earlobes that are programmed to override the brain functions with a few basic commands. We use the strobes to activate the override, and our tests indicated that sign language works better than spoken language." *Especially given how quickly tongues tend to decompose*, she added silently.

The top of the zombie's ear had worked loose. Kris brushed the hair aside for a closer look. A partial tear, but salvageable. She grabbed a small tube from her vest pocket and used her teeth to pop the cap free. With her other hand, she scrubbed bits of scab and dead skin off with an old toothbrush.

She dabbed a few drops of clear blue fluid on the ear and pressed it into place against the zombie's head.

"What's that?"

"Superglue," Kris said. "We try to keep them from losing skin cohesion, and glue creates a better seal than stitches. They live longer that way."

She caught Mrs. Gillespie's wince and realized she had slipped again. Bad choice of words. But she couldn't help it. Regardless of their legal status, her zombies were still alive, at least to her. Their brains functioned, though with only five to ten percent of the normal electrochemical activity. More importantly, they could still do work—which put them one step above at least half of Kris' coworkers.

She finished her inspection and glanced at the ID tattoo on the zombie's neck. *3.2, KD*—one of last week's batch, and one she had released herself.

"Doesn't that hurt them?"

Kris shook her head. "We cauterize the pain receptors when we install the microbatteries." Then, knowing what the woman *really* wanted to know, she said, "Your husband never felt any pain."

Before she got stuck answering any more questions, Kris flashed a green double-strobe, and the zombie resumed his duties. Kris watched him go, admiring the movements. This latest batch incorporated slow-release capsules of formaldehyde, which seemed to be working perfectly. Any stiffness in the zombie's movement was no worse than Mrs. Gillespie's.

"They should be allowed to rest in peace."

Kris sighed. In the few hours since they had met, she had listened to this routine six times. She glanced longingly at her strobe light and wished she could design one that worked on the living.

She didn't bother to ask why, if Mrs. Gillespie was so opposed to R&R's work, she had permitted her husband to sign the papers giving them full rights to his corpse. One glance told Kris everything she needed to know. While Mrs. Gillespie had probably dressed in her best clothes for her trip to the R&R office, her best left much to be desired. Tightly stitched repairs scarred her flowered blouse and olive slacks, and those shoes were ready to fall apart. If she couldn't even afford a new outfit, how could she have hoped to cover the medical and funeral expenses for her husband? For that reason, Jack Gillespie had made the same choice as hundreds of Detroit residents, and signed his body over to R&R in exchange for full coverage of his debts.

"You people promised he would be buried after two weeks," Mrs. Gillespie said, her blue eyes hard as rock. "I've been to St. Mary's every day, and he's not there."

Here it was, another PR nightmare. "As I explained back at the office, sometimes we lose one."

Mrs. Gillespie took that without flinching. "Yes, I've heard your story. 'Scavengers,' right? But we've been here for hours, and I haven't seen a single wild dog. Not even a lost cat. Nothing but your poor slaves."

Kris sighed. She had hoped that Mrs. Gillespie wouldn't notice that flaw in the theory. The truth was, they didn't know why the workers occasionally vanished.

"How do you know Jack isn't still working? If he's not dead, how long until you give him peace?"

"The longest a worker has lasted is twenty-two days, and that was in a lab. Their bodies cannibalize themselves for fuel. First they burn up fat, then the muscle, and after two weeks, there's nothing left." Kris stopped to examine another zombie. This one had a fiberglass sliver through his right hand. She gently slid the sliver free, then sealed the wound with a drop of glue.

Without looking up from the zombie's dry palm, she said, "Jack is dead, Mrs. Gillespie."

They resumed walking. Thankfully, Mrs. Gillespie had run out of things to say for the moment, and her cold silence was a welcome change.

The impatience Kris felt for people was one more reason she so often found herself the butt of jokes back at the office. She didn't *really* prefer the company of the dead over that of the living. She simply wasn't very good with people. Given time, she could probably master the social skills most of her coworkers took for granted, but she had other things—more important things—to do, like proving that the Detroit restoration project could succeed.

As they moved closer to the center of the five-mile test area, Kris looked around, impressed at the job her zombies were doing. The old buildings had been scrubbed and cleaned until a bit of dignity shone through once more. Up ahead, a row of fifteen green dumpsters held a block's worth of trash, leaving the area clean and unspoiled. Even the fire hydrants gleamed yellow from a fresh coat of paint.

As an unexpected bonus, the bums and the gangbangers had quietly abandoned the area. To the superstitious, a single walking dead man made a better deterrent than the entire Detroit police department.

Kris smiled to herself. Her zombies *worked*. With every new version, they grew more efficient. Soon they would be able to move beyond testing. Another month at most.

"That's him!"

The loud cry made Kris jump.

"That one in the green jacket." Mrs. Gillespie pointed to a clump of zombies working at an old post office.

"Let me check." Kris held her strobe overhead and flashed a stop command. The dead workers promptly stopped.

For the first time, Mrs. Gillespie looked uncertain. She glanced at the group of zombies, then back at Kris.

"What's the matter?" Kris asked, puzzled.

Mrs. Gillespie looked away. "He was my husband."

Kris was not entirely devoid of compassion. "Wait here."

She walked over and checked each of the workers, paying special attention to the one in the green jacket. "I don't think this is your husband," she called out.

"But that's his jacket. I'm sure of it."

Kris rolled her eyes and signed, *Take three steps forward*, bringing the zombie into better light. "Mrs. Gillespie, this zombie is female."

"Oh. I see. Well, that would be just like Jack, to give his coat to a woman. He's very old-fashioned, you know."

Kris ignored her, distracted by a shadowy figure that ducked around a corner up ahead. She had checked the schedule before coming out tonight, and nobody else was supposed to be here. There shouldn't have been another living person for miles.

"What's the matter?"

If someone had broken into the project, her job was to report it to the police. The last thing she should do was drag a civilian along to investigate.

But filing a report that would mean abandoning her zombies to a potential vandal or saboteur. One person do could do a lot of damage in the time it took the police to respond.

"Nothing's wrong." Unfortunately, lying was another of those skills that Kris had no talent for.

"Bull," Mrs. Gillespie began hotly. "I raised five kids in my time, and I know a lie when I hear it. What are you hiding?"

Kris blinked, surprised at the edge in the woman's voice. "I'm not hiding anything." Feeling uncomfortably like a child again in the face of the older woman's wrath, she opted to retreat from the confrontation. "We should go back," she added quickly. "You must be worn out from all this walking."

It worked, and Mrs. Gillespie stiffened indignantly.

"Girl, if you think that after all the work I did to get here, I'm just going to give up and go home, you can forget it." She pointed her chin at the other zombies. "Now don't you think you should do something about these poor souls?"

Kris glanced at the frozen zombies. They would wait forever in that state, or at least until their bodies broke down. She strobed them to "life" and signed *Back to work*. As one, they continued whatever duty had been programmed into them.

Kris hurried up Pine Street and past a row of brick apartments, searching for the intruder. She felt quite smug about the situation now. If anyone questioned her decision to stay, she could say it was Mrs. Gillespie's idea to investigate, and Kris had been ordered to cooperate with her guest.

She managed another glimpse of her prey. She thought it was a male. He wore a dark coat and a red baseball cap. But she lost him again as she waited for Mrs. Gillespie to catch up.

"Why the hurry?" Mrs. Gillespie was breathing hard, and Kris forced herself to slow down. She didn't have time to stop for an ambulance if the old woman had a heart attack.

"I get off work at dawn, and I want to finish so I can get a little sleep tonight."

"No work ethic at all." A disdainful sniff indicated Mrs. Gillespie's opinion of those priorities. "Besides, you expect me to believe us moving at this pace has nothing to do with the man in the red hat?"

Kris stared.

"I'm old. I'm not blind. We'll make better time if we cut through King Park."

"Are you sure?"

"I lived in this city for seventy years."

Kris shrugged and let the older woman to take the lead.

The park inspired another wave of pride as Kris surveyed the work of her zombies. Tall, muted streetlights created the illusion of twilight, even at five in the morning. The pond was especially beautiful. The sidewalk around the edge had been bleached clean, and the zombies had dredged all algae and muck from the water. But the ducks hadn't yet discovered the newly inhabitable pond. Either that, or they were a bit wary of the zombies. There were no fish, either, which made the place feel incomplete. Kris decided she would have to take care of that the next time she was out. Maybe she could pick up some goldfish on the way to work tomorrow.

"The sun's coming up," Mrs. Gillespie commented.

"Good. Zombies are sensitive to UV," Kris explained. "They'll hole up inside, and that will make it easier to find our friend."

"Is that him?"

Kris stared. She was right. Up ahead, a bent figure hurried toward the old Ford plant on Sixth Street, a small bundle tucked under one arm.

She frowned.

"What is it?"

Kris had programmed all of her zombies to return to one of three safehouses to wait out the day. The auto plant was one of those three. The fact that he knew about the plant made her more suspicious that he was a saboteur, or else a competitor from one of the other biotech firms. She wished again that she could ditch Mrs. Gillespie and go in alone.

"Are you sure you're up for this?" Kris asked, knowing what the answer would be. "There are a lot of zombies in there. You could wait here, if you wanted."

Mrs. Gillespie's snort was answer enough.

They slipped through a chain link fence at the edge of the park and emerged into a throng of slow-moving zombies, all patiently funneling through the door of the plant. Fortunately, the dead were programmed to yield right-of-way to the living, and Kris dragged Mrs. Gillespie through the crowd and into the plant.

Small groups of zombies stood around the main floor of the plant, with more arriving all the time. But the building was enormous, the space broken only by the occasional I-beam, so it wasn't crowded. Most of the zombies continued their duties, scrubbing already-clean walls and floors or polishing the steel beams. Each beam glistened like new to a height of about ten feet—the highest the zombies could reach. Kris hoped that the next batch would be coordinated enough to use ladders.

"Oh my God." Mrs. Gillespie had gone white.

Kris stopped scanning the crowd for the man in the red hat. "It's okay," she reassured the older woman. "They won't hurt you."

"You don't understand. I just saw Jack."

Not now! If she had to babysit Mrs. Gillespie, she at least wanted those keen old eyes to help her search. "I thought I explained it to you—your husband is dead." A bit harsh, but she didn't have time to be gentle.

Kris followed Mrs. Gillespie's outstretched arm. She saw zombies in all stages of life, from a woman whose skin still showed a faint pink flush to one zombie who had rotted to the point where even Kris couldn't guess its gender. With so many walking corpses, Kris wasn't surprised that one reminded Mrs. Gillespie of Jack, but this wasn't the time for such nonsense.

The older woman grabbed Kris' arm. "Miss Dobson, I lived with that man for thirty-eight years of my life. I may have been confused before, when that woman had his jacket, but I'm telling you now that my husband just walked in there." She gestured again. "Into that room."

Kris looked. The door in the far wall bore a name plaque, which the ever-efficient zombies had polished into a golden mirror. "Probably the foreman's office," she muttered.

"I don't care if it's Satan's office. I'm going to find my husband."

Kris doubted the man with the red hat would be on the main floor, so she needed to check the office anyway. Besides, maybe this would convince Mrs. Gillespie that her husband was truly gone.

They followed another zombie through the door and into the office. The windows had been painted over, probably by an earlier batch of zombies who didn't know any better. The only light came from a single fluorescent bulb in the ceiling. But it gave off enough of a glow for Kris to see the eight zombies huddled in the center of the room. Unlike the workers outside, these looked up as Kris and Mrs. Gillespie entered.

"Jack," Mrs. Gillespie whispered.

Kris' eyes narrowed as she examined the zombies. None were fresh, but none appeared worn enough to be Jack Gillespie. Shining her flashlight on "Jack," she checked the teeth and skin for signs of wear.

"This one's only about a week old," she said softly, trying to cushion the blow. "He can't be your husband."

Mrs. Gillespie ignored her and knelt down beside the dead man. He looked at her, and Kris swore she saw a flicker of recognition cross those cloudy eyes. Very slowly, the zombie raised a hand and touched Mrs. Gillespie's cheek.

Kris' heart began to beat faster. This wasn't right. No zombie should react like that. And the others were displaying too many signs of alertness as well.

She shoved Jack's head to one side to read the identifying tattoo. *1.2-KD*. She jerked her hand back like she had touched flame. This zombie was over a month old. Scientific excitement warred with fear, and fear won.

"We, uh, have to leave," Kris said, trying to keep her voice calm.

Mrs. Gillespie waved a hand and laughed. "My husband isn't going to hurt me. None of them will. Isn't that what you've been telling me all this time?"

Another zombie came into the office. Kris' tension grew as

he positioned himself between the living women and the door. Kris didn't consider that he might be blocking her in on purpose. The zombies' brains weren't capable of such planning.

Then she saw the man in the red hat step into the office. The *zombie* in the red hat. But that was impossible. If he was a zombie, he should have stopped before, when Kris had used her strobe light.

Enough of this. She raised the strobe and flashed a red *Stop* command.

Nothing happened. The red-hatted zombie turned to face Kris, and she saw his features for the first time. They were unremarkable, save that one of his ears had been ripped off.

The light-sensors were implanted in the earlobes.

A glance around the room confirmed that every zombie had lost his or her left ear. The electrical system that should have paralyzed their brains was disabled.

Stop, she signed, hoping they could still understand ASL.

The zombie in the red hat cocked his head and held out the creature he had been carrying.

"Oh God," Kris whispered. Mrs. Gillespie, struck dumb with horror, merely trembled.

Everything started to make sense. The bums vanishing. The animals missing from the park, the scavengers from the streets.

For an instant, Kris knew the pride of motherhood. Only hours before she had explained why zombies couldn't survive beyond two weeks: Their bodies consumed themselves until they essentially starved.

But life adapted. Even electrically and chemically preserved life adapted.

The zombies tore apart the gray tomcat. Jack Gillespie studied his wife as he began to eat from the cat's thigh. Horror and fear overcame Kris' pride.

"We have to go," she repeated. "*Now.*"

The zombie still blocked the way. *Move away*, Kris signed furiously.

He ignored her. In desperation she tried the strobe again; perhaps some of the zombies might remember what it meant.

The dead man at the door narrowed his eyes. One hand touched the torn gash of his ear.

"Run, Mrs. Gillespie!"

There was no answer. Kris glanced back and realized why. The old woman now shared the tomcat's fate.

Rational thought failed. Kris lunged for the door, trying to knock the zombie aside. But fingers grabbed her ankle, and she crashed to the ground. Her chin cracked against the concrete, and her vision went white. She could feel blood dripping down her chin.

When her vision cleared, she looked up into the face of Jack Gillespie.

As she watched, the dry, torn face split into a smile.

LAST RESORT

MICHAEL LAIMO

The desert never seemed so alive. Nothing had ever been so hard as leaving it all behind.

Jack peered over at Bryan, the boy's face anemic under the bite of the late afternoon sun, harsh rays blaring through the windshield. The nine-year-old stared back at his father for the briefest moment, then set his empty sights back across the shimmering asphalt of I-75. His blistered lips gently parted as though to say something, but nothing came forth. Silence. Jack knew better than to get his hopes up by now.

The sign for Las Vegas Boulevard came into view and Jack took the mini-van across the unmarked drift of sand hiding the road. The wheels kicked up clouds of dust as if cloaking their entrance; the stuff blanketed the cracked windshield. He turned on the wipers, chasing away only minimal amounts of sand, just as the wheels skidded harshly into a deeper drift. The mini-van fishtailed toward the side of the road, and for a moment Jack thought it might get stuck, but it snagged something solid and cleared the obstruction. At the end of the off-ramp, he looked up and saw the once-famous Las Vegas Strip, its two-mile stretch of hotels never looking more dead. No lights. No sounds. No movement. A harsh contrast to the shimmering desert plains behind.

"What do you think?" he asked Bryan. Getting an answer from his son was as much a long shot as finding a working slot machine, one no less willing to pay out. He put a hand on Bryan's shoulder; the boy flinched, eyes straight ahead, the sweat long dried up from his emaciated frame. "You think we'll find anything here?"

Bryan stared straight ahead, unanswering.

Jack turned the steering wheel, started down Las Vegas Boulevard. "Let's find out, shall we?"

A minute later they passed the familiar diamond-shaped *Welcome To Las Vegas* sign that for years had ushered in hundreds of millions of thrill-seekers to their preferred places of contribution. It stood barely recognizable, like a rotting scarecrow, half its letters circling the base of the steel post in crumbled pieces. To the left Mandalay Bay towered silently into the gray sky, a giant now set in dead stone by the darkest of all

Medusas. Lifeless taxis and cars crowded the entrance, spilling mummified bodies from unshut doors and broken windows. Having never visited Vegas at its zenith, Jack could only fantasize at the gaiety and excitement that had once thrived here. The photos he'd seen, the movies, the paintings—it'd all looked as though a grand celebration were taking place. Fourth of July, but even bigger and better and more stimulating than one could ever fathom. Now it looked mournfully unremembered, as dazed and as desperate as the two of them might've appeared, if anyone had been around to see them: wounded, straying into town, stomachs crying for food, eyes in search of shelter, minds in search of solace.

Ahead, the Strip was clogged with hundreds of abandoned vehicles, some inverted, some piled three high. Slowly Jack turned left onto Paris Avenue. "Might as well find some food first," he told Bryan, staring at the road ahead and knowing quite well it didn't matter which path he took, what choices he made for them.

Winding around a number of wind-stripped cars, Jack chanced another look at his son. The boy's body trembled, near seizure, fingers clawing his chest, eyes looking through the side window at the atrophied bodies in the road and weird brown weeds growing out of those corpses not covered in sand. *Lucky me*, Jack thought, keeping his attention ahead. This stretch of road lead, virtually unobstructed, all the way to Paradise Avenue. He turned left past the shattered ruins of the Hard Rock Cafe.

Ahead a number of smaller motels flanked the sidewalk, the remnants of cars and taxis stripped, useless, at the curbs. Farther down, a few small stores lay deteriorating like defeated soldiers hurled aside in the heat of battle, their corpses picked at by vultures who themselves had no time to savor their winnings before also being devoured. Other local businesses—a drug store, a deli—were boarded over, the wood splintered in places to reveal a terrifying blackness within their husks.

To the left Jack saw a diner, its wrap-around front window fully destroyed. A sign hanging from a rusted post out front whipped about in the wind, the bitter shrill of its rusty hinges shooting across the lifeless street like the wail of a starving cat. He pulled off Paradise into the lot of the small eatery, sheets of sand thrashing Bryan's closed window. A white Buick LeSabre sat alongside the convenience store next door, its owner long gone and forgotten, perhaps rotting beside the video poker game he'd come to play.

The wind picked up again, sand billowing on all sides of the mini-van in more driven whirls. Instantaneously the sun dipped behind the soaring hotels, the cold of night racing in to spread its darkness over Jack's thin grip on faith, like massive, tenebrous wings.

Jack set the van in park and got out, walked around the front of the vehicle to Bryan's window. The boy pressed quick-bitten fingers against the glass, eyes dried of tears cast somewhere beyond Jack's presence. Absent of desire.

"I'll be back, kiddo. I'm just gonna check and see if there's any food, okay?"

Bryan panicked, hoarse voice wailing over a dry, swollen tongue, through yellow teeth. His eyes bulged, hands pounding the window then searching for the door handle that wasn't there. Jack slid open the side panel of the mini-van, removed a shotgun and pistol from the back seat. He checked to make sure they'd both been loaded, then reached over to the front seat, ribs jutting against the tattered cloth interior, and handed Bryan the pistol. The boy quieted.

"You won't need this . . . but take it just in case."

Jack shouldered the rifle, closed the side door, then stepped toward the diner. The winds surged, stronger somehow in the sun's absence. Sand battered his face, a hot sheet bringing pain, nearly blinding him. He squeezed his eyes shut and wiped away granules drawn to the moisture of his tears. Wrapping his arms around his head, he tackled the three sand-buried steps to the entrance of the diner and went inside.

The counter, stools, booths were wrecked, the glass displays smashed, dishes and utensils strewn everywhere. Stepping over a fallen stool, he peered behind the splintered counter-top. The empty eye sockets of a uniformed waitress stared back at him from the floor. The flesh had been eaten clean from her bones, only patches of mold-buried muscle and tendon remaining on her arms and legs. For a moment Jack imagined he saw something wriggling down there, something beneath the tatters of her uniform near the hollow of her stomach—something bigger than any insect he could name.

He pulled back, at once assuring himself that it was just a shadow . . . just a shadow . . . just a shadow cast by the setting sun through a shard of glass still in the storefront window frame. Jack turned away, a writhing feeling in his stomach reminding him of the thing's latent presence, promising him that it knew he was nearby . . . that it *smelled* him, wanted him. That he had much more to offer than its present host.

Swallowing a dry lump, he stepped back to the front of the diner and peered outside toward the mini-van. Bryan, still in the front seat, stared back at him, white fingertips pressed against the window. Jack's thoughts were torturesome, tears moistening his dry eyes, his once-beautiful Little-Leaguer now a poor nine-year-old pushing forty. The remnants of his mother's features had long vanished, resigned to two years of torment, of suffering, of pain. Jack held up an index finger, mouthed *I'll be right there.*

The boy stared, unanswering.

Jack turned and entered the kitchen.

The place was destroyed, glass and garbage everywhere. He pulled a cigarette lighter from his pocket, kept it in hand; he would need it soon, as only one small window in the rear provided light. Pans, empty cans, dishes littered the floor, doors ripped free from ovens, an open freezer revealing a barren interior. A microwave lay shattered on the tiles near the sink. Shelves, emptied of all canned goods. Everything coated in sand.

Again Jack wondered if Las Vegas could be *the* town harboring individuals who'd outlasted the scourge. After thirteen days out from their former sanctuary, Jack had seen no signs of life. Nothing in Dallas, nothing in Phoenix and all the small towns in between. Dead or alive.

After Phoenix, he had decided that here, in this city of sin, people of great importance—those who'd held high seats in the social stature court—might gather. Las Vegas would draw those who retained the influence to put them in touch with the select crowd, the ones collaborating to create shelter, the *smart* people who had known where to hide when it all ended.

Jack peeked out the kitchen door, across the counter and beyond the empty window frame. Bryan's fingers moved from the window to his mouth, jagged nails driven to the spaces between his rotting teeth. Jack wondered, *What could be easier than taking the gun, putting Bryan out of his misery, then doing the same for myself? A single, clean shot to the temporal lobe, ensuring paralysis of after-death brain activity. But would it definitely work?*

He'd seen corpses rise up with their heads nearly lopped off, half-moon craters leaving just a single eye for sight, a gaping void where the lower jaw once existed—signs of unsuccessful suicide attempts. Such creatures had walked the land for nearly two years, spreading disease, famine, their numbers increasing too fast for those humans still alive to make heads or tails of the plague. The risen dead fed on living flesh, an instinctual response triggered deep in the still-active subconscious mind, eating eating eating until there were no more *living* human beings left to eat. All the animals, too—the dogs, cats, birds, perhaps even the fish, though Jack hadn't yet an opportunity to test the waters.

The corpses returned to death through the ravages of starvation, cannibalism, ultimately becoming subject to myriad insect-borne diseases. With everyone and everything dead—people, animals—the swarming carcasses could no longer nurture their sparked intuitions and suddenly ceased to walk, as if some higher authority had pulled the plug.

What if Bryan and I die, Jack pondered, *only to return to the same unyielding quest for nourishment?*

Jack sifted through a foot-high drift of sand. Found an unopened can of beets. He used his hunting knife to strip the lid, speared three juicy purple disks, and sucked them down. They were hot, sour. He searched on, found nothing of value but considered taking a handful of green fuzzy things that might have once been potatoes. He ate half the can of beets, then exited the diner, leaving the green things behind.

He smiled halfheartedly at his son as he approached the van. Bryan pressed a palm against the window, face looking weird, doll-like: drawn without emotion. Jack slid the side door open, placed the shotgun on the seat, then reached over and handed Bryan the beets. He watched as the boy plucked them with his soiled fingers, opening his mouth just enough to put them in. Jack closed the door from the inside and climbed over into the front seat. Bryan's cracked lips had beet juice all over them. Jack couldn't help but think how much it looked like blood, how the boy looked more dead than alive.

How easy would it be to simply end the suffering with a pull of a trigger?

He started the car, noting the need for fuel. Before driving away he looked over at Bryan and the gun nestled between the boy's delicate thighs. Bryan sipped beet juice, then offered the can back to his father. Jack downed the rest in one gulp as he took the car across Sands Avenue, back toward Las Vegas Boulevard.

✛ ✛ ✛

The night was dark, thirsting for Jack, Sharon, and Bryan, as the family of three went about their evening, unaware of the unconventional circumstances taking place around them. Not an hour prior, every dead and not yet buried thing—man and animal alike—had animated and at once taken pursuit of warm flesh for consumption. Dead people ate living dogs; dead dogs ate living people. No prejudices existed. If it was dead, it wanted to eat you: man, woman, child, animal.

Jack owned three twenty-four hour convenience stores. Sharon picked up Bryan from Little League, met Jack at six as he made the rounds collecting the day's receipts. The first stop proved to show no great day of business, the take nearly half the usual amount. The second stop, his largest store, was unattended, the on-duty clerk having seemingly made himself off-duty. Jack checked the schedule. David was written in for the five-to-ten shift. Damn, the new guy. "David?" he called.

And then he saw: a young woman rising up from behind the counter, blood and gristle covering her face. Sharon screamed; Bryan's jaw clenched in shock; Jack tried to yell, but couldn't understand the unconscionable events taking place in his store. The girl held up what must have been David's arm, jammed it to her mouth, savaging the bicep with her teeth. The fear-hesitation succumbed to mortal terror and Jack, Bryan, and Sharon began screaming, unable to tear their sights away from the flesh-chewing woman in front of them, the woman who reached down and ripped something else free from the unseen body, something wet and gut-wrenching, then rose back up with steaming organs slipping through her fingers, slapping the floor, the meager pieces in her grasp finding their way toward the enthusiastic gnaw of her teeth.

Jack picked up his son, Sharon frantically grasping the sweat-soaked polyester of the boy's baseball jersey, stumbling over her husband's feet as they careened outside, away from the horror inside. The door of the mini-mart slammed shut behind them, leaving them abask in the moonglow of the night. The living dead awaited them in the parking lot, more than twenty bodies staggering aimlessly about, moaning incoherently in response to the threesome's hysterical cries. Then the dead were suddenly running after them, arms outstretched, mouths gaping, tongues lolling, the whites of their eyes moving in instinctual jerks like moths fluttering about a bright light.

The family screamed uncontrollably. They returned inside the store, Jack locking the door, one then two then suddenly ten or more ashen people slapping the glass-front, staring in, banging aimlessly into each other like eager piranha eyeing a meal on the non-water side of the fishtank. Heavy breathing and crying filled the store, pounding hearts pressuring their ears. They stood there, Jack, Sharon, Bryan, all of them staring in awe at the clawing cluster of insane people pressing their wounded, colorless faces against the glass.

A scream filled the air. Sharon's terrified voice wrenched Jack's soul just as surely as the sight of the flesh-eating woman tearing a hunk from his wife's trapezoid with a swift lock of the jaws. The most influential woman of their lives fell to the floor in unfathomable pain, her shoulder gushing blood in mad spurts as the flesh-eating woman chewed her prize, gazing at Jack and Bryan. She then dropped the half-eaten lump and came for them, mouth gaping, arms outstretched, suddenly eager to collect more warm flesh.

Jack grabbed Bryan and carried him down the aisle to the coolers that stocked beer and milk and soft drinks. He released his son, then grabbed a can of insect repellent and sprayed it at the oncoming ghoul, all the while retrieving a cigarette lighter from his pocket. He flicked it, the flame emerged, and he raised it to meet the spray of the repellent. Flames shot out, four, five feet, and then more as the woman caught fire, howling as if rats were stuck in her throat. Arms flailing wildly, her blazing body knocked into the counter and sent blistering candies to the floor in a shower of color.

Jack screamed for Sharon, she limping beside Bryan as he helped her into the back room. They locked the door behind them, went down into the basement, locked that door behind them, at last falling together into a familial heap at the center of the room, crying, trembling, wondering what would happen next.

✛ ✛ ✛

Unlike the fronts for Treasure Island or The Stardust, the canopied approach to The Mirage allowed for the mini-van to pass right through.

"Come with me," said Jack, stopping behind a stripped taxicab.

Bryan's eyes still had clouds in them, Jack noted, but it felt good to see him moving. Jack reached into the back seat, grabbed the rifle; Bryan brought the pistol he held in his lap. They stepped over bones and mummified bodies, the green felt mat with the white Mirage script out front rotting and stained with blood. The glass doors at the entrance were shattered, the shards still scattered across the marble flooring inside. Shriveled bodies lay everywhere, many missing limbs. The trees inside lived on, the branches growing above and beyond the smashed greenhouse dome. The huge fishtank behind the check-in desk remained intact, the water long evaporated, the fish turned to bone. The slot machines and gaming tables were utterly destroyed, casualties of war.

"We go to the top floor," Jack said. "That's where the important people would've gone."

They found the steps and climbed and climbed and climbed, taking breaks every three or four floors to catch their breath. On the twenty-first floor they rested longer, and Jack used this time to think of Sharon and their time in the basement of the mini-mart, his mind's-eye watching her get sicker and sicker as the wound in her shoulder festered, spread its unstoppable infection; how she stopped eating and how he and Bryan had to tie her to the pipes so she wouldn't hurt them. For she'd lost all recollection of who she was, had become an animal with no thoughts, only instincts, instincts that offered no help to her as she grew weaker and weaker, until she could no longer breath. Her body had withered to a fraction of what it once was.

Jack tried to shake away the bubbling memories, didn't want to but could not help but recollect what happened a few minutes later, when Sharon came back to life with the desire to eat suddenly upon her again. How they sat there watching her moan and wail and reach for them, how she gnawed through her own limbs like a captured shrew, intent on devouring her husband and son.

He also didn't want to remember how he had used a baseball bat to beat her head into a bloody pulp, smashed it until only her body remained, twitching for hours as the unlife seeped from it and finally released its uncanny grasp. How they stared at her body for days, then bagged it and put it on the highest shelf in the stockroom, away from the cans of food that lasted them nearly two years.

On the thirtieth floor, it appeared the entrance had been barricaded at one time, shafts of splintered wood just beyond the ajar door. Nails jutted from the jamb like thorns, hundreds seemingly inefficient in their commitment to restrain the enemy. Just beyond the entrance, Jack saw withered bodies, those full of limb and riddled with ancient gunfire. The gruesome stench here intensified, even after the whole world had gone to rot and it seemed impossible for anything more offensive to assault his nose. Father and son managed to squeeze through the available space—just as the flesh-eaters had done years ago. Dozens of motionless bodies lay twisted throughout the lengthy corridor, skin like leather taut against crumbling bones and shattered skulls.

"This way," Jack said, pointing to the left. He eyed a massive doorway at the end of the hall, a suite once fit for presidents and kings. "What do you think?"

Bryan nodded.

"Hello!" Jack called, knowing that if people were still alive here, they might assume them to be the enemy and shoot them just as they had the flesh-eaters.

They climbed over and around the head-wrecked corpses, some piled three high, unmoved since meeting their second fates. At the door. Jack tried the knob. Locked. He knocked. "Hello! Is there anybody here?"

Silence. At first. Then, a faint, painful cry.

"Stand back." Jack placed a hand on Bryan's chest. The boy staggered back, staring at the door. Jack raised the rifle and blew away the lock, making a head-sized hole. The door inched open. In a cautious way, Jack pressed his fingers on the warm door and pushed forward, slowly revealing the suite's interior.

At first he saw nothing, a room stripped of furniture, a shattered floor-to-ceiling window with tattered curtains billowing in a strong, whistling breeze, gray dusk-light seeping through and illuminating the room in wavering strips. Metal shelves lining the walls held a handful of empty cans and jars, remnants of a food supply long exhausted.

The soft cry he heard moments earlier had gained strength and volume with no door to block its reach. Once a whimper, it had become a moan rife with anguish. With hunger.

Its source appeared.

On all fours, an unclothed ghoul, skin green and craggy, crawled in from a doorway leading into another room. Its left eye was a dark, gaping socket from which fresh blood ran down and doused its lower jaw. It tried to stand but failed, both feet worthlessly reduced to shredded stumps and exposed ankle bones.

Thoughts flew through Jack's burned-out mind as if charged with an outside power. *When there's no more food, then everything dies. Even the dead. If this one's still alive, then there must be—must've been—someone alive here to feed it.*

He raised the rifle in a jerk, blew the demon's head away. Bryan didn't so much as flinch. "Let's see if there's anyone here," Jack said as he stepped over the dead thing and peered into the room.

What must have been a master bedroom suite for the rich and famous had become a playground for the devil's work. Perhaps twenty people had hid here two years past, when the dead took over the earth. And here they had remained in their shelter, a place that had once provided adequate sanctuary from the hell thriving thirty floors below, co-existing until their food supply ran out and they starved to death and started coming back to life, first one and then another. The strong killed the reanimated things off and tossed them into the hallway, attracting even more ghouls that blocked their only route to further sustenance, until they could no longer escape, until the dead outnumbered the living and made food out of them. Until only one remained, this last thing that had eaten the warm, dying remnants of the last human beings in this hotel, abandoning the mangled stew of body parts only to investigate the warm *living* human beings who had entered its domain.

"Bryan," Jack said staring at the festering mass before them. "We should try another hotel. What do you say? The MGM?"

Jack turned to face his son.

This time, the nine-year-old answered his father.

He shoved the barrel of the pistol into his mouth and pulled the trigger.

✦ ✦ ✦

The desert never seemed so alive. Nothing had ever been so hard than leaving it all behind. Jack drove in silence, his blistered lips gently parting as though to say something. Nothing came forth. Jack knew better than to get his hopes up by now.

The sign for Denver, Colorado came into view and Jack took the pick-up across the unmarked drift of soil hiding the road. The wheels kicked up clouds of dust, as though in effort to cloak his entrance.

Once, long ago, he had read about a bomb shelter hidden deep in the mountains of Colorado, a place that would shield those inside from an atomic bomb or nuclear missile.

Surely there would be people there.

He saw the Rocky Mountains in the distance. He prayed to no one in particular with the hope of finding sanctuary there, all the while eyeing the rifle on the seat next to him, promising himself that Denver would be his last resort.

SAME NIGHT, DIFFERENT FARMHOUSE

GREGORY G. KURCZYNSKI

Henry Kemper sat quietly at the bar, sucking the last drops of Coca-Cola from the ice in his glass.

It's getting so I can't even tell if I've been here before, he thought as he looked the place over. *Every one is the same. The same stench of rancid beer mixing with the stale smoke hanging like a toxic fog over the worn-out pool table. The same dark scars of cigarette burns on the wood-grain Formica bar. Over it all, the jukebox endlessly playing the same overplayed classic rock or pop crap that everyone listens to more out of boredom than enjoyment. One more nameless place where the frustrated and broken come after their workday to erase the memories of their failed lives with cheap liquor.*

Henry shuffled the small pile of bills and coins sitting in front of him. *Please let me find her here tonight. Just let her be here, so I never have to set foot in another one of these stinking places as long as I live.*

"Another Coke there, bud?" The bartender, a sagging, older man who had introduced himself as Al, gave him a tired smile. "We do have something stronger here, if you like."

Henry pushed his empty glass back toward Al, took off his glasses and wiped at them with the bar napkin. "Another Coke, thanks. Got to drive, you know."

"Another Coke it is. Wish everyone had your common sense." The barkeep refilled the glass, took a dollar from the pile, and went off to take care of the few remaining blue collar regulars having one for the road so they wouldn't have to face their wives and kids sober. Henry nursed the Coke, his attention drawn to the television over the bar. The local newscast was just beginning.

"Leading the news tonight, the outbreak of mass hysteria first reported late this afternoon in Pittsburgh and surrounding locations appears to be spreading throughout the country."

Bored, Henry shifted on his barstool. *Why do they always make these things so damned uncomfortable?*

The news anchor continued. "Reports are coming in from New York, Boston, Cleveland, and here in the Detroit area of people, seemingly in a drugged or incoherent state, committing random attacks on citizens. Law enforcement authorities state that, as yet, there is no motive or pattern to the attacks."

"There are some sick bastards in this world, don'tcha think?"

Henry turned to his left, toward the girl sitting two stools down from him. She was smiling in his direction. "Don'tcha think?" she repeated.

Henry had noticed her the moment he walked into the place, and ever since, his self-control had been tested to the breaking point. Who wouldn't want to stare? Mid-twenties, petite, pale skin, short-cropped dark hair. She had a cuteness about her, the look of a mischievous pixie. Now that he could take a longer look, though, Henry saw that her eyes betrayed a certain desperation. They offered up a silent invitation to anyone willing to help her escape the dead-end life in which she found herself trapped.

I can rescue you, Henry thought, heart thudding. *With your help, and a little understanding, I can rescue both of us.*

But he said, "Yeah, there're some sick ones out there," and moved his eyes back to the television to hide his eagerness. "People can't be too careful."

"I'm Jennifer." She reached out her hand—soft and warm, bubblegum-pink polish on her not too long nails. "My friends call me Jenn."

"Nice to meet you, Jenn." He summoned up a smile—the shy one he'd been working on. Not goofy, but non-threatening. Best to seem a little awkward in her presence, as if actual conversation with an attractive female was a bit overwhelming. "I'm Henry."

"Mind if I join you, Henry?" Jenn didn't wait for a reply, picking up her beer and cigarettes to move next to him.

Henry tried not to stare as she removed her leather jacket; her small breasts heaved beneath her pink T-shirt, a pink that perfectly matched her nail polish. Jenn sat back, taking a long pull of her beer. Henry guessed it was the third or fourth she'd had since he'd come in.

The last of the happy hour drunks across the bar were settling with Al, getting ready to call it a night. Henry smiled to himself. *I can't believe how smoothly this is going.*

"Whatcha grinning about?"

"I was just thinking you're awfully friendly for someone who was just making an observation about all the psychos out there. You don't know me. Aren't you afraid I could turn out to be one of these crazies they're talking about on the news?"

Henry gave a small cough as Jenn lit a cigarette, blowing the smoke into a lazy cloud over their heads. On the television, Peter Jennings was interviewing a psychiatrist about what could possibly cause so many people across the country to become bloodthirsty killers. *As if anyone ever really cares about reasons,* Henry thought.

"Oh, you look pretty safe to me," Jenn giggled, reaching over to loosen Henry's tie. "A lot safer than most of the assholes who hang out here. But you don't look like the type that usually drinks in a rat hole like this. What brings you in here?"

"Just in from out of town on business. Felt like stopping off before I head home."

"Back to the wife and kids, huh?" Jenn glanced quickly at Henry's left hand, swallowed down the backwash in her beer bottle, set it on the bar and motioned for Al to bring her another.

"No, no wife and kids. Never got married."

"Guy like you never married? I don't believe it! Why not?"

"I guess I haven't found the right girl yet. What about you? Here to meet your boyfriend? Husband?"

"Trying to get away from one is more like. Joey and I broke up a couple days ago. Had a fight, bastard hit me, I moved out. Now he's trying to make up, all sorry and stuff. Can't get rid of the sonuvabitch. Seems like I attract all the jerks."

"His loss. Maybe he'll come around."

"The only thing I hopes he comes around is a sharp corner at ninety miles an hour with bad brakes. I really thought he was going to be the one, you know? But he's not worth putting up with that kind of grief."

"It's amazing the things a person will endure for true love," Henry said, regretting the statement immediately. "What I mean is, maybe Joey being gone is for the best. You don't want him around when the real love of your life shows up, now do you?"

Jenn was silent for a moment, appraising Henry with a sidelong glance. "I do believe you're right about that, sir. And there's no telling when Mr. Wonderful is going to show, is there?" Henry tried not to notice as her hand slipped to his knee and she leaned closer, his senses overcome by the intoxicating scent of jasmine and baby powder.

"To true love, then," Jenn said and clinked the bottom of her bottle against Henry's glass. She slipped off her stool, caught herself and straightened. "Oops," she giggled, then righted herself, trying to look sober and not quite succeeding. "Hey, Al, can I get that beer?"

Al brought another beer. "Sure you need this one, hon?" he asked. "Don't want you getting in trouble driving home."

"I'll be fine, Al. My car's not here anyway. I'll get a cab or walk or something." Jenn rummaged in her purse to pay for the drink. Henry beat her to it.

"My treat," he said.

"Thanks. You didn't have to do that."

"I know, but I wanted to. Hey, are you hungry? I'm out of here in a bit anyway and I need to get a bite. Maybe you'd like to join me. I can always take you home."

Jenn smiled, lowered her head, and even seemed to blush. "Are you sure that's a good idea? I mean, how do you know I won't whack you over the head and start slicing *you* up?" She grimaced slightly as she took a sip from the fresh bottle.

"It's a risk, but I think I can take care of myself. Besides, the odds are in my favor. Statistically, female serial killers are virtually unheard of." Henry sucked in an ice cube from his nearly empty glass and crushed it in his teeth. With a gesture to the TV he added, "Seriously, you should let me take you home. It doesn't sound like a very safe night for a walk."

Don't push it, he groaned silently. *You might still blow this if you aren't careful.* What he said was, "At least let me call you a cab. Of course, I'd feel a lot better seeing that you got home safe and sound myself."

"Well, since you put it that way," Jenn said, her speech slurred slightly. "How could I deny such a charming and concerned gentleman? Tell you what. I have to go to the little girl's room, but when I get back, we'll finish our drinks and go."

Henry admired the cut of Jenn's tight jeans as she walked off to the ladies' room. Once she was out of sight, he ordered another Coke. He watched Al turn away to refill the glass, then pulled a small vial from his jacket pocket and poured its contents into the beer bottle.

The TV news continued its coverage of the mass murders, the anchorman reporting on the increasing carnage in the same bland manner in which he might offer up the weekend forecast. "Eyewitness accounts now describe victims of the attacks as not only being mutilated, but partially eaten. . . ."

"Jesus," Al said as he returned with the Coke. "I know it's a dog eat dog world, but this is freakin' nuts! Sorry, but once you finish those, I'll have to ask you to call it a night. No way I'm staying open with all this crap going on."

Jenn returned from the ladies' room, sat down, and took a long, slow drink from her beer, smiling in anticipation. Henry smiled back, and a warm feeling, a giddiness he hadn't felt for years, swelled inside him. *Yes, this one's definitely going to make up for all the failures in the past.*

Once he'd gotten to a deserted stretch of state road, away from streetlights and passing motorists, Henry pulled the car to the shoulder. Quickly scanning the road for any oncoming traffic, he pulled Jenn from the passenger seat. *Man, is she out*, he thought as he wrestled with her limp form, nearly losing his balance and tumbling to the gravel shoulder with her in his arms. *Never seen it work this fast, even with the beer.*

A cold shiver crawled up his back as the unthinkable occurred to him, only to be replaced a moment later by a rush of relief as he felt her weak pulse beating beneath the two fingers he laid on the side of her throat. "I really should be more careful with that stuff," he murmured. "It's not like I'm a goddamned pharmacist."

The duct tape made a loud ripping sound as he tore it from the roll in long strips to bind her wrists and ankles. He'd learned long ago that he couldn't be too careful. She was under now, but there was still at least fifty miles between here and home, and the last thing he needed was to try and handle an early wake up and drive at the same time.

Always remember Marie, Henry reminded himself. *You almost wrapped the car around a tree trying to calm her down. And you never were able to get the mess out of the upholstery.*

Checking the strength of the tape one last time, he lifted Jenn from the ground and dumped her into the back seat. As he moved to cover her with a blanket, Henry was frozen by a sudden wave of emotion that nearly suffocated him. He gazed at her sleeping face, pale as ivory in the moonlight. *So beautiful*, he thought as he reached out and tenderly stroked her cheek, wiping away a string of spittle that hung from her halfopened mouth.

"No, you won't be like all the others." He kissed her softly on the cheek before covering her. "You can't be. You'll be the one who can make the pain stop for both of us. I know it."

Henry closed the door on Jenn and walked around to get into the driver's seat. *Love and pain,* he thought, *permanently linked like life and death, light and darkness. It's impossible to conceive of one without knowledge of the other.*

"None of the others could understand that," he whispered as he slipped behind the wheel. Glancing in the rearview mirror at the blanket-shrouded woman, he added, "But you will. You have to."

Henry started the car, pulled back onto the road, and turned on the radio. A talk show host was taking calls.

"Next we have Joe, who says he's encountered one of these cannibal killers up close and personal. So, you're telling me that you know one of these murderers that's out terrorizing the countryside?"

"Yes, sir."

"And that person is your Uncle Bill, who you say died of lung cancer two days ago?"

"That's what I'm saying, yes, sir."

"And there's absolutely no way you could have been mistaken about who you saw."

"Well, being dead and all, he was starting to look a little gamy, if you know what I mean. But the guy I saw was, without a doubt, Uncle Bill. Right down to the suit and tie my aunt picked out for him to be buried in."

"Bullshit," Henry growled. The dead never came back. He knew that better than anyone.

He switched to an oldies station and turned his attention back to the road.

✛　✛　✛

It had taken over an hour to arrive at the old farmhouse that Henry's grandmother had left him in the will. Lost on twenty acres in the maze of corn and cow manure that was rural Michigan, it was the one place that Henry could truly be himself, fulfill his purpose. The house needed a lot of work, but it had a cellar, a deep well out behind the barn that was perfect for disposing of failures, and plenty of privacy. Henry didn't need anything else. Except for Jennifer.

Now, in the dimly lit cellar that was Henry Kemper's most personal corner of the world, she lay on her back, tied spread eagle to a wooden frame that rested atop the large metal trough Henry had found in the barn. *So much easier than having to mop up the floor*, he thought. *Or clean the bathtub. . . .*

Once, early in his search, Henry had tried using the bathtub, but it took three gallons of bleach and the better part of an afternoon to get the stains out of the grout.

Henry walked slowly around the sleeping form, admiring her slim waist, the curve of her hips. He knelt, leaned in close, and brushed away a few unruly strands of hair from her face. The scent of jasmine and baby powder had faded, but was still strong enough to send his senses reeling. *So beautiful. . . .*

"Jenn," he crooned softly. "Rise and shine, love. We've got so much to talk about. Such a big night ahead for us."

Jenn stirred fitfully, a small child being roused from a deep slumber. She snapped to life as she realized she was immobile, confusion turning to horror as her eyes focused on Henry and then the dark red stains on the cinderblock walls behind him. A little moan escaped her throat as her gaze took in the objects hanging from the ceiling, some of them glistening wet in the flickering light of the candles scattered about the room.

Henry put his hands to his ears, anticipating the scream he knew would come. It always did.

"Let me out of here, you sick fuck!" Jenn thrashed about, squirming and pulling against the bonds that held her.

"And I will let you go." Henry whispered, voice like oil on a calm pool of water. "I want to let you go more than anything. But you have to understand something first."

Jenn screamed again, until the sound was choked off by the rubber ball Henry thrust into her open mouth. After he had secured the gag with duct tape, he said, "Can we talk now?"

She turned her head from him, tears squeezing from her tightly shut eyelids.

"Come on, there's no need to shut your eyes. It's not that bright in here. Don't you like candles? I think they set a nice romantic mood."

Henry took her face in his hands, turned her head, forced her to look into his eyes.

"We were getting on so well back there in the bar, don't you think? That doesn't have to change now. We've both been looking for it—true love, I mean."

Jenn whimpered, her eyes locked onto Henry's. He relaxed his grip and walked to the corner of the room. Jenn lifted her head as best she could, her gaze following him to a table set with candles and some shiny objects she couldn't quite make out.

"I told you it was just a matter of finding the right girl. I found her once, you know." His voice broke, making him sound lost and frightened. Henry turned from her. *Can't let you see me like this. I don't like it—can't stand it any more than you can, love. There's just no other way.*

He fingered one of the shiny slivers on the table, but then put it down. Instead he picked up a faded photograph in a weathered gold frame.

Henry walked back to Jenn, held the picture close so she could see it in the dim light. The photo showed a dark-haired girl, no more than fourteen years old, her smile beaming like the summer sun as she frolicked on the beach.

"This is Annie," Henry said, voice monotone, almost a whisper. "My sister. I loved her more than anything in the world." He looked at the picture, stroked the glass with his fingertips. "I tried to make her understand my feelings, but she just cried, said it was wrong . . . that I was bad. . . ."

Turning from Jenn for a moment, Henry wiped at his eyes, and then whirled back to face her. "I didn't want anything to happen to her, I just wanted her to be quiet, to help her see how much I loved her." He stalked back to the table, which was draped with a dingy white cloth like an unclean altar, and set the picture back in its place. "People have no idea how much that hurts—knowing that she won't return my feelings, that she's not ever coming back. . . ."

Henry took up the silver sliver again.

"I guess it's just not possible to feel true love without unbearable pain. Look at you and Joey."

Jenn's eyes widened in fear as Henry moved closer. She tried to scream, but only choked on the gag.

"But you're different from the others. I know that you could love me. You've shown it."

Jenn nodded, and after a moment Henry leaned in to remove the gag. She gave a squeal as the tape pulled free, then coughed the ball from her mouth.

"Henry, it's okay." Jenn's breath came in panicked gasps. She shifted, tried to reach out to him, but the ropes cut into her wrists. "I do love you. I'll do anything you want, just—"

"No!" Henry cried. "It's easy to say, easy to lie." He spat out the last word as if it were poison. "The others said the same thing, but they were all liars. They couldn't handle the pain that comes with true love! First you have to feel the pain, and then you can know how love feels . . . how I feel!" He inhaled sharply, a rasping breath. "Christ, do you think I enjoy this?"

Jenn quieted, shrinking back like a small creature trapped in a corner. Her voice was nearly inaudible as she said, "Please don't kill me."

"Killing you is the last thing that I want," Henry replied, once again in control. "Don't you see? It's not about death, it's about love. And pain. Just let me help you get past the pain, and you'll understand."

The scalpel in Henry's hand glimmered in the candlelight. Jenn fought as Henry kissed her forehead and replaced the gag, silencing her cries. When he raised the scalpel, he gazed at it as if it were a holy relic. His eyes followed its path as he brought it down and sliced her T-shirt open. In the soft light, her skin was as pale and smooth as white marble.

"Shhhh. It won't be long," Henry said, caressing Jenn's tear-stained face. "Besides, from what I've learned from the others, it's only the first few cuts that really hurt."

✛ ✛ ✛

When it was over, Henry sat on the worn sofa, motionless amongst the living room furnishings that had been fixtures of the house since he was a small child. After his grandmother had left him the house, Henry didn't have the heart to change anything; even the crystal bowl filled with now-petrified hard candies that no one ever ate, even when his grandmother was alive, kept its place on the dark wooden coffee table.

He wiped his tears away with a blood-stained shirt sleeve, cradling the jar containing his sister's heart in his other arm. He remembered how difficult it had been to get it, how clever he'd been to break into the funeral home in the middle of the night. He'd worked quickly, removed the heart with only a jackknife and a pen flashlight. Even now, all these years later, there were times when he couldn't bear to be without it, to be without at least a part of Annie near him.

His memories of Annie were soon overwhelmed by bitter thoughts of Jenn. As he pondered what had gone wrong, Henry stared straight ahead. The television droned on just a few feet in front of him, but he didn't hear it.

"This just in: National Guard units have been mobilized across the country to assist in dealing with the epidemic of violence—"

Not fair, he thought. *You were just like all the others. Why couldn't you just see your way through to the end? I was there, waiting, holding you, crying for you. . . .*

"For those of you just joining us, it appears that the unburied dead are returning to life, attacking and feeding on the living. Authorities recommend that people stay in their homes and stay tuned to television or radio for further information. . . ."

But, no. You couldn't make the effort. You took the easy way and faded out like all the other lying bitches. Well, they're rotting at the bottom of the well, and you'll be joining them soon. But it didn't have to be like that. He moaned and clutched at the jar in his hands. *Not fair!*

The television screen shattered in a shower of sparks as Henry's treasured jar struck it. He screamed, overturned the sofa, battered the walls with his fists, anything to release his rage. Tripping over the coffee table, he fell forward, cutting his hands on the broken glass from the television. Eventually

Henry lifted himself from the floor. Exhausted and sobbing, he righted the table and began to place the spilled candies back into the cracked bowl.

Movement at the edge of Henry's vision caught his attention, and he turned to face the entrance to the cellar. She stood silently in the doorway, lines of dark, drying blood a sharp contrast on her pale skin. Henry wiped the tears from his eyes, looked again. She was still there, moving slowly toward him, jerking like a marionette with a few broken strings.

"Jenn!" He ran to her, caught her as she tripped and fell. "You know now, don't you?" Cradling her in his arms, he searched her eyes confirmation. He found none in that glassy stare, but still hoped beyond hope. "You really do love me."

Henry's heart leaped as Jenn clutched him tightly, leaned her head back, parted her lips. He closed his eyes, waiting, anticipating . . . and screamed as she buried her teeth in his throat. The pain exploded through his entire body.

They fell to the floor, the Jenn-thing chewing at his neck, jaws locked and unyielding. He heard a wet ripping, nearly fainted from the agony as bubblegum-pink fingernails tore at his abdomen. Henry feebly pushed her away, his mind focused only on the unspeakable sensation, like a white-hot knife being plunged into his soul. Then the truth of it seized him. Henry stopped fighting and began to laugh.

I knew it. I was right all along. . . .

The laughter became an agonized howl as Jenn's hands opened something deep inside Henry. She pulled her head back and a crimson geyser erupted from his throat wound, spattering the wall. The blood ran down in narrow rivulets that Henry watched in detached fascination. The gory stain reminded him of the ink-spill pictures the doctors had shown him one afternoon after his sister went away. Even though they told him he was supposed to see things in the ink stains, he never could, and the one on the wall now was no different.

Turning back to Jenn, Henry gazed into her vacant eyes and smiled. With his last bit of strength, he reached up and brushed a lock of blood-clotted hair from her forehead. The agony he felt gave way to a cold numbness—and the utter serenity that came with the realization that his search was finally finished.

My love, Henry thought as the world began to go dark. *I knew you would understand. I was right, you see: There is no true love without unbearable pain.*

MIDDLES

ROBERT E. VARDEMAN

Harold Clements didn't know whether to take the initiative and sit without being asked or to continue shifting nervously from foot to foot. He found it impossible to concentrate on what the vice-president of his division was saying, and he needed to know.

"Harold!" she snapped. Susan Greene leaned forward, her banker-style leather chair creaking ominously. "Pay attention. What's been happening with you?"

"What? Me? Nothing," Harold answered. "I'm sorry."

"Sit down and quit fidgeting," she said, obviously irritated at him. Susan Greene wore her dark hair short, almost mannishly, although that was the only part of her physically that Harold could ever consider masculine. She had clawed her way up the corporate ladder better than most men and held on to her position tightly. He looked at her more closely and found he could not take his eyes off her slender white throat, pulsing with vitality. Her breasts were full and strained the fabric of her crisp white blouse, but that vein in her throat held him captive with its promise.

Harold swallowed hard and tried not to think of the blood surging up and down her veins and arteries, feeding her quick, brilliant brain. The tasty brain. Would eating her brain increase his intelligence?

"Harold!" she snapped. "Stop gawking like that." She leaned back in the high-backed banker's chair. Again he heard the creaking of fine leather as her trim, athletic body moved against it. A vein in her forehead throbbed as her anger mounted.

Pulsing blood. To her brain. Her fine, tasty, succulent wonderful brain. He had to eat soon. It had been too long, almost a month, and he felt his grip on normalcy slipping.

"Normal," he said, hardly knowing he spoke. His voice came out like a rusty gate hinge.

"You *aren't* acting normal, Harold. We have the big project coming up. The one in Thailand? You remember Mr. Underhill briefing us?"

"The Erhial Corporation needs cheap labor. We can g-get it in Thailand."

"All those willing young workers toiling away for us at fifty cents a day. We *need* the reduction in labor costs. The Mexicans are killing us in the *maquiladoras*. Fifty percent wage increases in the last two years. Not acceptable."

Harold felt sweat beading his forehead. He wanted to wipe it off, but that would show weakness. He was strong. He was strong enough to hold back the . . . urge.

Tasty brains. Gooey, squishy brains. Susan Greene's brains fed by the powerful artery pumping in her throat. Tear out the throat, rip off the top of her head—the blood would never show against her jet-black dark hair—eat the brains. Scoop them out, gobble them—

"Harold!"

Susan's sharp voice brought him back.

"Susan, I am so sorry. I was down in Mexico at the, uh, ma-maqui—"

"*Maquiladoras*," she said caustically. "They were supposed to furnish us cheap workers along the border. All they seem to have done is provide a way of screwing the company and giving you some weird disease."

"Virus," Harold said weakly. He gripped the arms of his chair, trying not to think how much he needed to feed. Without a steady source of brains he slipped into mindless killing rage. With the fresh brains, with enough of the *right* brains, he could maintain.

"Maintain," he said, not even knowing he'd spoken.

"Are you sure you didn't go to some cathouse and get the clap or whatever STD the Mexican whores are filthy with now?"

The words shocked Harold into clarity. He sucked in a breath, held it, and then released it slowly to settle himself.

"No, of course not, Susan. I don't do such things." He hoped she did not hear the lie in his voice. He went to brothels, especially when sent to out-of-country manufacturing sites, but to feed. Harold had to be more careful because he did not want to get some weird virus. He had heard of kuru and other brain-borne diseases. Dipping his dick in the filthy holes between a whore's legs would never happen. But what disease could he get from their infected, feeble brains?

He needed higher class, clean brains. His belly rumbled and his vision blurred as he thought of tearing the top of Susan's head off to expose her brains to his voracious hunger.

"Harold, this meeting is not working. If you can't do your job, let me know right now. I can get Fowles or Munson."

Harold snorted in contempt. He wondered if Susan Greene

was a lesbian. She carried the sisterhood thing too far. Kathryn Fowles was another ball buster, like Susan, and Misty Munson was a joke. He had to feed. Now.

"What's wrong with you?" Susan asked, startled. "It's as if you were a cell phone off link and you just came into a new transmission area."

He stood, towering over her. He started to jump onto the desk and take her where she sat, before she could get out of the chair. That would be best because she wouldn't be able to put up much of a fight. But Harold held back at the last instant. This wasn't the plan he had followed for eighteen months. He dared not be caught, and there would be such a mess when he scooped out handfuls of Susan's tasty brains. Stick to the plan. Don't deviate. It worked. As it had six times before.

He turned abruptly and started for the door.

"Harold? Can I do anything? Call a doctor?"

"I need to meditate," he said. "I'm off my game today. I'll get back with you about the factory in Thailand."

"Make an appointment with my secretary," Susan said coldly.

Harold hardly noticed how he had been dismissed summarily. It wasn't likely he would be put in charge of the project now, no matter that it was a career-maker in the company and that he had earned it. Feeding was more important.

In keeping with the plan, he left the executive offices, took the elevator down, and began the selection process.

Harold walked up and down the hallways on the third floor of the corporate office building, glancing into each tiny breadbox room. He had a list in his office on the tenth floor, but did not want to take time to study it for a likely candidate. All the middle-level managers toiled away at jobs no one understood, least of all them. They shuffled papers, looked important, and got paid for showing up. And if they stopped showing up, it was often weeks before anyone noticed because their jobs were meaningless.

"Seth," Harold said, stopping in front of an office he had chosen virtually at random. He thought Seth Anderson—that was the name on the plate beside the open door—was on his list. He couldn't remember.

"Mr. Clements?" the young man said, looking up from an open ledger. He seemed to be adding figures, writing down his result, and then tossing the paper into his wastebasket. Harold wondered if he should warn him to shred everything. Never leave a trail, paper or blood.

"I need to see you, Seth."

"I—I'm not Mr. Anderson. He took a job with another company. I'm his replacement. José Rodriguez, sir."

Harold fought down a tide of panic. He knew Seth Anderson was gone. He had torn open the man's head and devoured his brains a month ago.

"Another job?"

"Well, no one knows. He didn't show up for work one day and then rumors started. You know how it is—corporate headhunters always looking for recruits with brains and determination."

"I, uh, yes," Harold said, struggling to cover his confusion. He was losing it. He needed brains. He was becoming one of them. A zombie. Mindless, crazed, centered on nothing but senseless killing to get at savory brains.

"You took over his job, didn't you?"

"Yes, sir."

"I've got an assignment for you. It might take the rest of the day, so bring your briefcase and anything else. You can go home directly from the warehouse."

"Warehouse? I didn't know we had a warehouse in town, sir."

"The Erhial Corporation has real estate everywhere, José," he said in a confidential tone, putting his arm around the young man's shoulders and guiding him toward the back stairs. It wouldn't do if anyone saw them leaving together. That meant questions he didn't want to answer. As it was, the damned surveillance cameras were everywhere. He had to be so careful, so very careful.

"Go on down to the lobby. Take the stairs. I'll be down in a couple minutes. I have to grab some notes from my office."

"Yes, sir," José said as eager as a puppy dog to please. He thought he was being dealt into a top level project.

So much for high IQ brains, but Harold needed food. Now.

✛ ✛ ✛

"The warehouse must cover an entire block," José said, looking around the dirty, abandoned structure.

"It does," Harold said. His hands shook now. But he had to follow his plan. Step by step. He had to. He felt his intelligence draining and the plan helped keep him on target. "Where did you park?"

"Out back, where you said," José said.

"Good, the police wouldn't find the car there for a week or two. By that time I can get rid of it."

"What?" José turned, startled. "You're joking, aren't you, Mr. Clements?"

"I know a chop shop that loves the racy little sports cars you middle management types drive. A BMW?"

"A black Z3," José said proudly. "But what did you mean about a chop shop?"

"A place that cuts up expensive cars so they can sell the parts," Harold said, going down his checklist to be sure everything was in place.

"You are kidding, right?"

"Where are you from? Our office in Mexico City?"

"No," José said, anger mounting. "I'm from Miami."

"Cuban?"

"Yes."

"Good. I haven't had any ethnic food since I was in Mexico," Harold said, turning. He felt his control fading and the *hunger* coming on him. There was no need to restrain himself now. And he didn't. Before José Rodriguez could scream, Harold had his bony fingers wrapped around the man's throat, throttling life from him. Even before José died, before his heart stopped pulsing blood to his brain, Harold had clawed his way past the cranium and exposed the gray matter hidden underneath. It oozed out as he scooped and gobbled, feeding noisily.

Only when the last sinuous fold of the slick, savory brain tissue vanished into his mouth did Harold feel almost human again. Normal. For a while.

He started his clean up. José was middle management and would never be missed because no one knew what his job was—and no one cared. Before Harold had the last speck of blood licked off the concrete floor, he was already choosing the source of his next meal.

✛ ✛ ✛

José had not given up enough to let Harold pass for human long. His hands still shook a little, and he felt the flesh of his face sagging and turning putrescent. Worst of all was the way his mind refused to come up with the details needed to perform his job adequately. Susan Greene was on his case and seemed intent on destroying his career. He needed more brains to climb back to normal for the afternoon meeting with the CEO concerning the Thailand factory.

It was a risk, but one he had planned for when he was still in full control of his faculties. He had always been an expert planner. Always. And now it would stand him in good stead.

Harold walked along the corridor outside the middle management offices, looking for his next meal. He hurried past José Rodriguez's empty office. No one had noticed the man's disappearance yet, but then they had never really noted his successor's abrupt departure, either.

The plan worked. Harold had to stick to it, especially now that his faculties were becoming more brutish.

He stopped and looked left and right. To his left was a cute little ash-blonde he had noticed a couple months ago. He swallowed and closed his eyes, thinking how her blood would stain her blonde hair as he ripped off the top of her skull to expose her brains. She wasn't going anywhere in the company, either. She didn't have the aptitude.

She would make a good meal.

But Harold turned his back on her and went into the other office. "Gort-heads," he had called kids like this when he was in grade school, kids with heads that looked like mushrooms. A large skull did not always yield a big harvest of brains; he had discovered that soon after he had become a zombie—and had learned how to hold off the intellectually numbing aspects of being a zombie by appropriate, selective feeding.

More brains. Many, many, many more brains. But quality. Quality brains held down the urge to feed as often.

"Can you help me out a minute?" he asked.

The gort-head looked up. Mushroom-shaped skull. Thoughts of chanterelle made Harold's mouth water. Brains and mushrooms. Succulent. Tasty. Just what he needed to fend off the worst effects, to get back to normal.

"Sure, what can I do?" The way the gort-head answered told Harold he had no idea who was demanding a bit of his time. He knew Harold was upper management but probably didn't even know his name.

"I've looked over your record and have something that's right down your alley," Harold lied. "Come to the copier room in ten minutes. Bring your résumé with you."

This galvanized the man into action. Copy room? Résumé? That meant an upward career move.

What it really meant was that Harold knew the surveillance camera in the corridor outside the copier room was broken and that he could get in and out without being seen. He arrived fully five minutes before the manager.

As the man entered, Harold pounced. He drove him facedown to the floor, onto the drop cloth left last week by the copier repairman. Before his victim could shout, Harold broke his neck. Then he feasted. Fully, messily.

Cleanup took longer than usual because Harold didn't want any trace left in the room. He bundled the body in the drop cloth, then shucked off the disposable plastic raincoat he had worn for the feeding and tossed it on the mangled corpse. Harold licked his lips, checked to be sure he didn't have even a drop of blood on his clothing, then wrapped up the bundle and glanced into the corridor. Two secretaries came up, clutching sheaves of papers to be copied and chattering like magpies.

If he had spotted them before he had dined, Harold would have panicked. Now he was in control again. He smoothed nonexistent wrinkles on his suit coat and stepped out, exuding an air of confidence appropriate to a top manager.

"Ladies, you're out of luck today. The copier is broken."

"Oh, you men," said one, flirting with him. "It's probably out of paper."

"Does it smoke when it's out of paper?" Harold asked easily. "I had to pull the 220 volt plug after it gave me a shock. I think it fed back into the computerized control circuit." Dazzle them with bullshit. It always worked, just as his plan to get more brains always worked.

"I suppose we can use the copier on the fourth floor," one said to the other.

The one who had been flirting with him glanced over her shoulder as she followed her friend, giving him a quick smile. Harold knew better than to have anything to do with a secretary. They were always missed right away. Better to stick with mid-level managers.

He ducked into the copier room and dragged the wrapped corpse out. Harold felt stronger now and easily hefted the body over his shoulder. Freight elevator doors at the end of the corridor took a few seconds to pry open because the elevator was on another floor. Harold dumped the corpse down three stories to land with a dull thud on the elevator roof. He would retrieve it later for disposal, before it started to smell. Until then, it was safely hidden. Nobody ever looked at the topside of a dirty, messy freight elevator.

Whistling, Harold headed back for his office in the Olympus of the Erhial Corporation Building, ready for anything Mr. Underhill—and Susan Greene—threw his way.

✦ ✦ ✦

The meeting started well. Harold was well fed and in control again. He had held the zombie-deadness at bay with two meals in one day. But Underhill droned on and Harold felt his grip slipping. He glanced across the big cherrywood table in the conference room and saw Susan staring at him as if he were a bug under a microscope.

She wanted him removed so one of her lesbo lovers could take his place. That had to be it. He wouldn't give her the satisfaction. Working for Erhial Corporation was perfect for him. The company was wildly profitable and hired workers daily, employees no one would ever miss.

"What do you think, Harold?"

It took him a couple seconds to realize Underhill was speaking to him. He had been drifting, fighting off the zombie-numbed mentality that crept up on him and anesthetized the fringes of his mind. Although he had eaten well twice today, he needed more brains to keep sharp. More brains. He licked his lips, then remembered he had been asked a question.

"I agree, sir," Harold said. This was always a safe answer.

"You think we should expand the Thailand plant by half or only a quarter?"

"What you said, sir, is right on the money. I couldn't agree more with your appraisal of the situation." He looked across the table and saw Susan Greene mouthing, *Good save.*

And it seemed to satisfy Underhill. The CEO closed the folders in front of him and tucked them into his briefcase, even as Harold reminded himself to check the copier room one last time for any speck of blood. And to get rid of the body on top of the elevator. It wasn't any harder getting rid of two than it was one—he hadn't yet dealt with José's corpse either—but he had to figure a way to wheel the gort-head out of the building without being captured on a surveillance tape. No one would miss certain employees—living, breathing human beings—but the security guards would pounce on him if they thought he was stealing even one precious bent paper clip.

"Harold, we need to talk." Susan Greene stood over him. "About the Thailand project."

"Your office or mine?" he asked. She hesitated, then smiled just a little. He wasn't sure he liked it when she smiled.

"My apartment. Eight o'clock? We'll discuss it over dinner."

"Are you cooking?" he asked, amazed at her invitation. She had never hinted she wanted any social contact with him until now.

"No, I'll call out. I'm a terrible cook." She licked her lips, gave him a seductive look and then left the conference room. Harold couldn't help noticing the way she waggled her booty just for him.

He leaned back in the chair and decided he must have

scored big time with Underhill for Susan to be sucking up to him like this. Then Harold shot to his feet and hurried to his office, where he had the list of potential gray matter sustenance providers. He wanted to be in perfect shape when he met Susan, fully fed, at the top of his game.

And Harold had to admit he was feeling a bit dull around the edges right now, the zombie-mentality creeping up on him like a thief in the night.

✝   ✝   ✝

He rang the doorbell and looked around the hallway of the posh apartment building as he waited for Susan Greene to answer. The surveillance camera at the end of the hall had a detached wire dangling under it. In a ritzy apartment house like this, he was sure vandals had not done it. Probably one of those privacy freaks who complained endlessly about others spying on them and then demanded that the government keep surveillance cameras on speeders, drivers running stoplights, and even suspicious characters on public streets.

The door opened and Harold caught his breath. Susan looked radiant. The hard edge she always showed at the office was gone, replaced by a more . . . human look.

"I didn't expect you to dress up for me," he said, eyeing her. He saw the way the vein throbbed rhythmically in her white neck; the new hairdo, short hair swept back as if she stood in a strong sea wind; the clear, dark eyes fixed on him.

"Come in, Harold. We have a bit to discuss."

He looked around the apartment and saw Susan was not a woman who went overboard on frilly doilies or ceramic knickknacks that needed constant dusting. The room was appointed with functional furniture, almost what a man might select. It figured.

"Sit down. Let me get you a drink. What do you like? No, wait—let me guess. A Bloody Mary." She laughed delightedly and went to a small wet bar to fix the drink.

Harold took the glass she handed him and stared at it. "How'd you guess?"

"Oh, I wasn't guessing. I know a great deal about you, Harold." She sat on the far end of the black Naugahyde sofa, one leg curled under her as she faced him. Susan sipped at her Bloody Mary, peering over the rim at him.

"We've worked together for almost a year. I suppose we both know a lot about the other." He took a long pull at his drink. It had a sharper tang to it than he had anticipated.

"But I know more about you that you think," she insisted,

sitting her glass down on an end table. "I know how quickly you go through middle managers, for instance."

"Hard to keep good help," Harold said. His heart hammered, and he fought to keep a neutral expression. She couldn't know, not for sure. He mustn't react guiltily or Susan would catch on.

"Hiding . . . *things* around the office is risky behavior."

Harold felt as if he would explode. A thousand observations flashed through his mind in that instant: She was vulnerable. The Naugahyde sofa would clean up well if he tore the top of her skull off to eat her precious, huge load of brains. The rug might be a problem holding a bloodstain, but as he moved his foot back and forth, he saw it was a durable acrylic fiber. Soap and water would remove any obvious spots. It was the only way. . . .

Then again, she couldn't know for sure everything that had happened. Maybe she was trying to psych him out, make him confess to get more power over him. Or maybe she was talking about something else, some petty crime she suspected him of. Harold swallowed hard. He had to play along. Get closer to her.

"I don't know what you're talking about," he said, taking another quick drink.

"No, perhaps you don't," she said. "It's getting harder, isn't it?"

"What? Putting up with your snide comments and obscure accusations?"

"The body on top of the elevator—is that specific enough for you? And I know why, too." She shifted on the sofa and picked up her drink again. "You've lost your edge. You find your mental acuity creeping away, as it did in the meeting this afternoon."

"I did well. Underhill approved." He put down his drink with trembling hands and slid closer to her.

"Yes, he approved. He is a fool and never sees anything going on around him."

"Like me being a killer?" Harold felt the shakes starting and realized the nerves in his hands and feet were dulling. While he could still control himself, he got his feet under him for the pounce.

"Like you being a zombie."

Susan Greene's words shot through Harold's head like a flaming arrow.

She *did* know. He had been so careful. The plan. The list. No one could possibly miss a manager low on the corporate pecking order. Susan was fishing, nothing more. Guessing.

"You need a fix now, don't you, Harold? Brains. Hot, steaming brains. Scooped from a still-living head. Yes, I see how you are. You're like a junkie who has developed a tolerance for his drug of choice. You need them now to keep from shaking. You're losing your humanity and becoming a zombie. Completely."

He clumsily knocked over the drink as he lunged at her. Susan slipped away easily and laughed at him.

"You're farther gone than I thought, Harold. I should have guessed when you didn't figure out how important the factory in Thailand could be for you. You could have eaten nameless, faceless factory workers for years before anyone noticed."

He tried to shake off the fog of desperate hunger clouding his thoughts. "What are you s-saying?"

"I tried to give you a chance, but you are too far gone."

Harold growled and grabbed awkwardly for her. Susan pushed him back to the sofa with surprising strength.

"You could have gone to Thailand and fed to your heart's content. Instead, I'll go, because I understand how zombie-ism progresses. It must be pure hell losing your senses and existing only to feed."

He lunged for her again, and again she shoved him back onto the sofa. Harold Clements tried to scream as Susan's fingers wrapped around his throat, squeezing what life remained from him. His vision turned black, but he was still alive as he heard her cackle, "I always enjoy ordering out for dinner."

Her fingers ripped at the top of his skull and began scooping out his brains.

ONE LAST, LITTLE REVENGE

ED GREENWOOD

There are times in every life when dreams come crashing down. This was one of those times for me, and I just hoped I could make the crash as spectacular as it deserved to be.

The darkly gleaming, glossy boardroom table stretched away for a seeming mile from my fingertips. I'd never bothered with such fripperies when Prendergast Fireworks and Novelties had still been mine alone. My creation, all those years ago. My overgrown workshop, a place of dust and clutter and fun . . . until Dr. Martyn Stannergar had come.

I needed "the Doctor," of course, and all of the sly, gray-faced suits he brought with him. My clowning still delighted small children, but the dollars weren't coming in the way they once had. Computers and "adult" toys were the rage nowadays, and "Jolly" Roger Prendergast didn't do either.

I still don't. An ugly new building blocks the view from my office window, blotting out even the tiniest glimpse of the little valley and the stream that winds through it—and that building is full of young, unkempt people I wouldn't want to come within two blocks of, let alone have on my payroll. They stare into flickering computer screens all day long, playing endless games that all seem to involve gunfire and explosions and screaming death while they purport to be doing something that'll enrich us all at Prendergast. Their break-even point is only a year or so away, Stannergar tells me.

Still, it's his money . . . their money. I had none left. All they needed was my name and distribution network. Oh, and my reputation: the kindly old salesman in the clownish, wide-stripe mock business suit who drove from store to store, playing with toys, giving some away, and fixing broken ones. Prendergast's Warbling Spintops, Prendergast's Marching Martians, Wiley's Walking Spiders, and hundreds more. Heard of them? Of course not. They're *old* toys, from the "good old days."

Yes, the good old days, when men cared about their work and their good names—and the phrase "an honest day's work" didn't evoke a snigger from bankers and young suits alike.

Like Stannergar and the toadies ranged down both sides of the table, smirking at me in open contempt. They'd got what they wanted, and now it was time to snatch Prendergast's company away from the old fool and show him the door. Still penniless, and with nothing to show for sixty years of one honest working day after another. They'd called their security goons already, anticipating a scene; I could see tall, menacing men in uniforms peering coldly in at the doors.

"This is a day none of us wanted to come," Dr. Stannergar was saying soothingly, unable to keep a gleeful smile entirely off his face, "but—"

I held up a hand in a *stop* gesture, and—wonders!—the Doctor fell silent. I gave him my best kindly old geezer smile, and said in as humble a voice as I could manage, "I knew all along this day would have to come too, Martyn—"

He winced, hating my wise father act as much as ever.

"—and I can see that I've not kept up with the times, and that what little I still do here is holding Prendergast Fireworks and Novelties back. I'd hoped you'd level with me as I used to, when I had men who just weren't working out, but that's all changing, too. So it's for the best. I'll go now, happily and quietly, so long as you produce one last toy for this Christmas season. I think it's my masterpiece."

There was a stir up and down the table, and a lot of side-glances. I kept the smile on my face and in my voice. "If I've misfired again—well, it's only one season, isn't it? You own this last little surprise already, lock and stock, you do. . . . I just want a chance to see it sweep the world. All right?"

The glances were exchanged openly this time, as I calmly adjusted my bow tie and then folded my hands on the table. Not a trace of a quaver or the trembling that sometimes came. Good.

In the end, Stannergar nodded reluctantly. "You plan to show it to us now?"

I nodded. "I'll just fetch it from my office. One of the men you've so thoughtfully invited—" I nodded at one of the doorways; Stannergar gave me a hard look, but I kept all trace of sarcasm or anger out of my voice "—can accompany me, and I'll bring it right back here. If you agree to produce it, it'll be handshakes all around, I'll give you my keys, and at long last I'll be able to go home and watch Desi and Lucy on my new television. It's got color, you know. I must have missed a lot of episodes by now."

They all smiled tolerantly; none of them bothered to stoop to the minor cruelty of telling me how long Arnaz or Ball had been dead.

"You go do that, Jolly," the fattest of Stannergar's suited

sharks said, almost eagerly. "If you think you've got a masterpiece, I've got to see it!"

There was an awkward pause, and then a sudden chorus of enthusiastic and entirely false agreement, all around the table—except from Stannergar, who didn't bother joining in. He just sat there looking irritated that his self-scripted moment of glory had been disrupted. The great scene of power, wherein he smoothly and dramatically crushed the soul of an eighty-year-old man in a bow tie and a rumpled suit, and had him bodily thrown off the premises faster than a Prendergast Rushing Moon Rocket.

Dear, dear. He'd never be able to tell his grandchildren about it, now.

No less than four security guards accompanied me on my short, cane-assisted hobble to my office. They had the grace to look sheepish about it, however, and made no protest when I went around behind my desk into my back office, past the Singing Robots and the hanging cluster of Fly by Night glowplanes, and closed the door in their faces. The bolt was as large as my wrist, and well-oiled; they'd need a cutting torch to get through it in anything less than an hour. After I'd secured the lock, I went to the closet in the corner, opened the door, and embraced the shiny firepole within—hey now, what good is it being president of your own novelties company if you don't give yourself a carload or two of, well, novelties?

Two Screaming Eyes went off as they were supposed to, whirling past me in the shaft like tiny firebolts. Appropriate; I was going forth into battle at last. Years after I should have done so, but better late than never.

The gigantic flatulence cushion at the bottom made my landing as gentle as . . . well, I'll spare you the lame joke. It took me just two steps to reach the closet that opened only to the little key on the end of my keyring. We were right behind the furnace—excuse me, "HVAC unit"—and so it was amid the deafening thunder of burners and blowers and suchlike that the door yielded and I found myself staring at: me.

It smelled a little, yes, but who knows—maybe I did, too. There was a reason I'd worn the same bow tie and rumpled suit all this past year, as Stannergar's confident smiles grew ever wider. Project Nightstalk, in all its glory.

Six strong, now. All of them once men who'd worked for me, toymakers who'd have toiled for "Father" Prendergast right into their graves. The inventors of the Walking Spider and the Bubbling Aquarium on Your Finger Ring and the Smacktail Dog; Dabble, the Dancing Duck; and dozens more. Great men, geniuses. Principled men, too. They'd refused to make the Doctor's cruel and rude adult "toys," and found no joy in the shoot 'em up video games the younger designers played. They were all past their eightieth or ninetieth year, so the computers themselves had been quite beyond them.

Stannergar had almost fallen over himself in his gloating rush to fire them. They'd barely shuffled back to their sagging old homes when he slapped them with unfounded lawsuits, accusing them of stealing "his" secrets—innovations they'd come up with down the years, and shared freely with me, as I had my inventions with them. Their only crime had been to live in the houses I'd built, around the factory. Right in the way of Stannergar's planned glass box of a building. They'd stayed on working because they loved it—but to Stannergar, they were just men to knock down and administer a good kicking to.

Red had come up with the gloop that kept cowhide supple and seemingly alive. Danged if it didn't work on humans, too, skin and flesh and all. Prendergast's Crawling Masks—later Prendergast's Haunted Masks—had come from that. Wiley had been the one to link the little car motors to batteries, and later to nerves, making a cat with paralyzed hind legs walk again. Later, he'd been the first *real* genius amongst us: He made Bob Jimry's shattered arm work again, the whirring little motor driving fingers and wrists and elbows to move as well as before the accident.

One by one, heartsick at all the police and the sneering lawyers and the gloating lawsuits, they'd died. I suspected some of these same security goons had helped Bob Jimry to his last breath—I don't see how he could have broken his neck falling *up* a flight of porch steps, the key to his locked front door still in his hand. Or hit himself three times on the back of the head doing so.

I paid for all of the funerals—and buried none of them. Wiley had made dozens of his little motors, and I worked for days in my cellar, next to the freezers that usually held moose from Red's hunting trips. Wiley was the first I managed to get standing. Then Red, and Bob Jimry, and Hallahan. Giving them a chance to get their revenge on the monster who'd hounded them to death. It was the least I could do.

My contribution had been the preservatives that kept them from collapsing entirely back to the earth that spawns us all. That and a little fiddling with the motors, which led to the creation of the small box that controlled their movements from afar. Years, that "little fiddling" had taken.

God knows I've never been a brilliant man, and even less a miracle worker—they were still dead men, their brains gone, their eyes empty and staring. But from time to time I fancied they were *looking* at me. I hoped, somehow, that wherever they might now be, they were aware of what I was doing to their bodies, and why. I hoped they were more enraged at Stannergar than at me.

I had six walking corpses in all, and latex masks for each, to make their skull-like, rotting faces into my own kindly collection of wrinkles, big nose and all. But only this one, staring back at me out of the closet, wore duplicates of my suit and tie.

I stared critically at its hair, ruffled it with my hand to more closely resemble what the mirror on the closet door was showing me, and steadied the cardboard box in its hands. *Prendergast's Special Surprise*, the box read, just to give them all something to think about, and beneath that label I'd written the comment: *Number 13. Not one of my best, but it does the job.*

I gave those words the crooked smile they deserved and took down the control box I'd spent so many years perfecting from atop Prendergast's Special Surprise. Switching it on, I watched the zombie unstiffen, turn its head to regard me, and open its eyes. Those eyes had been Red's once, but I tried not to think of that. Dust on eyeballs always looks a little strange, I think. I made it smile.

When it—Red—no, *it*—did, I smiled back and told it, "Break a leg, kid."

As it lurched past me to the service elevator, my zombie did not reply.

Hmmph. Kids, these days.

With a remote, I opened a door from the closet leading back to the hallways, a secret route that didn't pass through my office. Then I sat down in the big, comfy chair, sneezing at the dust, and switched on the bank of monitors. Spying is what screens are for, Stannergar, not playing games. Not nice ones, anyway.

The boardroom flickered into grainy, purplish life, and I pulled a rod and made that monitor slide out to hang in front of me. I was in time to see my own grand entrance.

Unspeaking, I went to my seat, set the box on the table, and started pulling out beakers and stoppered test tubes and little containers with oversized old radio switches and coiling wires trailing out of them. The men around the table smiled at the dust on things, and at the little show I made myself do, patting the heads of little lightbulbs that I'd painted faces on.

The Doctor surveyed the mismatched and moldering odds and ends, and managed an indulgent little laugh. "Really, Mister Prendergast—"

My double straightened, gave him a smile of triumph that the mask didn't quite convey, and brought its fist down hard on the test tubes.

I'd forgotten just how strong my zombies were. Stannergar's precious boardroom table split for quite a way down its length, and the sleep gas I'd meant to distribute around the room by tossing the test tubes boiled out like smoke. It was a mess. Just like my first three Prendergast's Pecking Penguins, who'd enthusiastically battered their little heads to shards breaking my workbench. Their stuffing went everywhere, too. We were finding it for months afterward.

Back in the boardroom there were shouts of alarm, and men shoved their chairs back and got to their feet in a hurry. Damn. I wasn't even sure the sleep-stuff still worked after all the time it'd been in storage. From the control room I made my double bow and thrust its hand down the front of its pants.

That made the security men—those that were left, that is; the others would still be sitting uneasily in my office—halt in their various charges forward, and peer at my double in amazement. Zombie fingers pulled the switch beneath the rumpled trousers.

I stopped watching, closing my eyes and turning my head away from the monitor just before the terrific crash came.

The room shook, a long, rolling boom that spilled more than one monitor to the floor, amid sparks and shards of glass and spitting, swaying wires. Around me, the lights all went out, and then came back on again, along with an insistent ringing of alarm bells. And no wonder. Most of the top floor of Prendergast Fireworks and Novelties was gone, along with all the glass windows of that nice new building full of computers. There would be fires.

Thankfully, my way out was all a matter of unlocked doors and level passages, right out to the old overgrown shed at the back of the warehouse Stannergar hadn't gotten around to bulldozing yet, along with all of its Prendergast's Patriotic Saluting Generals and Jimry's Singing Parachutes and suchlike. Hmmph. He never would, now.

Well done, Red. Useful things, zombies. A pity I'd had to blow my best one up. But up in the warehouse, there were still five of me left. All I had to do now was get all of us off the premises before—

No such luck. Sirens were wailing and tires screeching

before my old legs brought me up the stairs into the ware-house's dusty gloom. Thankfully there was still one small, heavily barred window looking out across the parking lot.

Flashing lights, lots of them—and more arriving every moment. Police cars, not just ambulances and fire trucks. Not that there was much left of the old factory to salvage, anyway. As I watched, the blazing wreckage fell into the lower two floors, and there was a terrific explosion. Boilers and oil tanks and that new HVAC unit, no doubt.

As if in sympathy, Stannergar's new glass-box building collapsed, too. I chuckled. All I'd wanted was one last, little revenge, but these things have always had a habit of, well, getting away from me. . . .

There were men running toward me now. Of course they'd head here; this was the last building left standing, except for the gatehouse for the parking lot. I'd have to hide, or feign complete befuddlement, and somehow I didn't think I'd man-age to fool any angry young policemen just now.

What to do, what to do?

There were thuddings on the doors, and shouts. "Is any-one in there? Hello!"

What to—ah, yes. Of *course*.

"Hello? Is anyone *in there?* Say something!"

I hurried to the locked cubicle at the end of the ware-house, fumbling in the dark for the right key. The same little one, at the end. Yes. *Yes.*

The door opened and I stepped inside and slid the bolt home—just as light flooded into the warehouse and brought more shouts with it.

The flashlight hanging inside the door should have died long ago. It gave me only a few feeble moments of amber flick-ering, but they were enough. I threw the switch that turned off the rat-frying field, shouldered past a Jimry's Hugging Doll that was almost my height, and clambered up onto the sim-ple wooden shelf that held the rest of Project Nightstalk.

They were lying in a peaceful row, arranged like customers in the backroom of a morgue I'd once seen. Five moldering zombies, silent and intact, all of them wearing face masks to look like me. I crawled slowly over them all to the empty space at the end, and laid down, putting my hands at my sides. It wasn't so dark, after all; light was coming down from one dirty skylight, high above.

I was shaking. I was old, damn it, and this hurrying was-n't good for what was left of me. I lay still and stared up into the near-darkness, wondering how long I'd have to stay there.

They'd probably put guards on the grounds, and bring in a forensic team. . . . God, I might starve waiting!

I couldn't just wander out of the warehouse, because they were sure to search it if I did, from end to end and cellar to rafters. And when they found my zombies . . .

I shuddered, there in the dark, and tried not to notice the sickly sweet smell of rotting flesh from beside me. *Close* beside me.

I ground my teeth. They were false, and it hurt, but I had to—had to—

The smell was growing stronger. Yes, it was.

I closed my eyes, shuddered again—and then felt something touch my arm.

Something thin and crumpling, that rasped like paper. I opened my eyes and looked down my chest. It was a piece of paper.

And it was being held out to me by—by the zombie lying next to me! I turned my head, heaven knows I didn't want to, and it was *looking* at me. There, in the dark, its dead eyes darker holes in the gloom.

I tried to scream, but only managed a whistling wheeze. The thing that had once been Bryce Wiley drew back the paper and then thrust it at me again, tapping my arm and chest. I tried not to remember the boardroom table splitting under the force of a zombie fist . . . and failed. I felt in my pocket for my little box, dragged it out—and saw that it was shut off. Dark, its switches all down. I rattled it. Nothing.

The zombie slowly shook its head.

How could this be? It was moving, without any goading from my control box! Had I made a better toy than I could ever have dreamed of? Or—or—

The paper scraped insistently across my chest again.

God save me! Quailing, I reached out for it. There was writing on it, but damned if I could read it in the gloom.

I spread my hands, helplessly, as flashlight beams played across the ceiling high above and police snapped sharp challenges at each other. They sounded disappointed at the lack of immediately apparent criminals or stored drugs or lurking gangsters, and their voices faded. But I knew they'd be back. Back to search, and find.

There was a bad taste in my mouth now. Fear. I didn't want to die in a cell after months of being dragged from courtroom to police van to interrogation room and back to jail.

"It would have been better if I'd been in the boardroom," I whispered to myself. "Carried my own explosives."

The paper was snatched away from me, and there were scratchings. I turned my head, fascinated. Yes, the nearest zombie was writing something—and I could see the heads of others now, raised to peer over their fellow.

At me. I swallowed, fighting down fresh fear, as something metallic was passed down the row of zombies and held patiently out to the last one. It finished its writing, held the paper out to me again, and accepted the metal object: a watchman's flashlight.

The flashlight clicked on, held low above the page so as not to spill excess light where anyone wandering the warehouse might see it. I read the words caught in its beam: *No, Mr. Prendergast, your death wouldn't have made anything better. We need you. Children who love good toys need you. Stannergar must die, and every last one of his young idiots. All the sick games they've created. All computer games. We must do the smashing and slaying, to make sure. Clear across the country. Every man, and every game. All. Revenge!*

The undead hand turned the paper over to show me the older writing on the other side: *It's long past time we discussed working conditions and wages. We can wait forever, but we won't.*

I stared at the paper for a long time, and then turned to look into those dead eyes again and mimed writing something. The flashlight clicked off and a pencil was thrust at me. I was pleased to see that my hand trembled only slightly when rotting fingers brushed my own. Then I took the pencil and the flashlight snapped back on. In its small, bright circle I wrote carefully: *Yes. Revenge. Agreed. After, I'll be delighted to make you all full partners in the company, if I have one left. My equals. I might have some difficulty in doing anything for a time: Police.*

That hand reached out, took the pencil from me, wrote something, and then held the flashlight again for me to read: *Understood. Agreed. Give me the box.*

The box? Oh. I reached back into my breast pocket, took out the little control box, and handed it over. The zombie cradled my masterpiece gingerly, held it up where all of its fellows could see—and then curled its fingers together, ignoring the brief flurry of spitting sparks and falling knobs and springs. What it gently handed back to me was a crushed, wrenched sculpture.

I was wet with fear now. Trapped. Helplessly I watched the hands that had just crushed metal set pencil and paper aside, and then rise to its chin.

The zombie turned its face toward me as it peeled the mask. Most of its flesh came away with it, baring yellowed bone beneath, but it rolled the latex back only to its nose, and I realized suddenly that it—that Wiley—was trying to show me a smile.

Then it reached out for me.

I tried to scream again, but only managed a gasp. It extended its hand again, insistently . . . like a salesman who's tried to shake your hand and been ignored, and is trying again.

Oh. Wiley had once refused to shake my hand because I was his employer, and "'twouldn't have been right" to do so. A sign of disrespect.

I cleared my throat. It took me three tries before I could manage the words. "Is it 'right' now, Mister Wiley?"

That dark, rotting head nodded, slowly, and tried to smile again.

Wonderingly, I extended my hand.

With infinite gentleness the cold, cold flesh touched mine, matched its grip to mine, and we shook hands, there in the darkness.

There are times in every life when new dreams come leaping up, and this was one of those times for me.

The Cold, Gray Fingers
of My Love

PETE D. MANISON

Marcus Cobb detonated the charge. Silent in the lunar vacuum, the explosion sent a cloud of dust out of the tunnel, obscuring the slow-motion tumble of rock, rushing forward to engulf him where he stood, unprotected, in the open.

Sweet, lovely gray powder. He could almost imagine he felt the sting of the high-velocity particles as they embedded themselves in the skin. He closed the eyes at the last instant, though it took a supreme effort of will. No sense losing the oculars again. That would call for a replacement, and he'd grown somewhat attached to this tool.

The dust began to settle. He opened the eyes again to find the entire crater floor covered in a new layer of sediment. Virgin powder. Exquisite. With a sigh, he walked the body forward, pausing only once to look back at the footprints his bare feet had left in the dust.

✣ ✣ ✣

There was a new tool at the site, and as Marcus collected chunks of ore-bearing rock he watched it out of the corner of his eye. A female. Naked like the rest, her gray, lifeless skin shone in the halogen work-lights, every ridge and curve sharply defined, so like the beautiful, beautiful surface of the moon. Hairless, her head was held with a regal poise, suggesting mastery in the operator. Behind her ears, the silvery strands of the control antennae emerged like tiny metal antlers, flashing in the artificial light.

"Hey, watch what you're doing!"

Marcus pulled his senses back to his work just in time to watch his fingers make their fatal error. He'd been on auto-pilot, hooking a fresh battery up to one of the big cutters. Normally you pinched off the base energy grid before tapping a cell, but just this once, distracted by the female tool, Marcus had forgotten.

"Get down!" someone shouted over the radio receiver implanted in the auditory center of his tool's brain.

Marcus ducked behind the cutter, using its bulk as a shield. The countersurge from the energy grid made all the lights up and down the tunnel burn as bright as day. It only lasted a second, but that was time enough for the hydrogen extractor fifty yards away to overpressurize.

For a weakened seal to rupture.

For the tool standing beside it to be torn in half.

Marcus waited behind the cutter. In vacuum, explosions were beautiful but brief. A tool could watch them safely since there was no air to carry a compression wave. But the low gravity made shrapnel travel farther and faster than it would on Earth.

It came only two seconds later: the brief sizzle of rain—lethal, hot metal rain.

When it had passed, Marcus stepped out to look at the two halves of the tool, zombie flesh still twitching as it tried to follow control commands. It was impressive, exciting even. But not so much, Marcus thought, as the new female tool.

+ + +

Send and Return. Return and Send. Marcus liked one more than the other, and it wasn't Return.

Pain and confusion, an overload of sensory data: oxygen burning in the nostrils, moisture itching in the eyes. Hormonal urges cut across all lines of reason, making control an illusion.

Damn it all, Marcus thought as he Returned. *Damn this wetflesh.*

At least it wouldn't be too long before the next time.

Around him in the Dream Center, operators lay wrapped in their control cocoons. Those coming off shift had begun to move, brushing away leads and sitting up, shaking their heads as they tried to reorient. Was it the same for them? He wondered that a lot. This bulky guy next to him, rubbing his eyes, lighting a cigarette—was this just another job for him? Or did he relish every second in the deadflesh, as Marcus did?

"Nice job, jerkoff," the big man said.

Marcus shrugged.

Then he went home to Rosalyn.

"How was your day?" she asked over dinner, the same way she asked every night.

He grunted.

"We got a new strain in today," she said, scooping up a spoonful of peas. "Some kind of high-yield grain. Right out of testing. They say it'll double our . . ."

She went on and on. Marcus tuned her out. Their three-year marriage seemed to have lasted a century. Not that she was hard on the eyes. Slim and blonde, with green eyes and a cute little butt, she still turned heads whenever they went out. These days he barely noticed.

He glanced at the clock. Nine hours left before his next shift. Nine long hours.

"Care for a glass of wine?" Rosalyn asked after dinner.

"Sure," Marcus grunted.

He had two glasses, but that wasn't the cause of the malfunction, later in bed. Her skin was soft, responsive, warm.

Alive.

"What's wrong, Honey?"

He closed his eyes, remembering the beautiful gray flesh of the new female tool. It was easier after that. Much easier.

✛ ✛ ✛

The morning shift was delayed forty-five minutes for an impromptu safety meeting.

"Some of you guys are getting sloppy." Wendell Jackson, the shift coordinator, glanced briefly at Marcus. "We lost another tool yesterday. That's three this month. There's no shortage of corpses, after the Tycho blowout, but do you lugheads have any idea how much it costs to wire one up?"

Heads shook around the room. A few faces turned Marcus' way, but he ignored them.

"Ninety thousand dollars," Wendell said. "*That's* how much."

Someone whistled.

"Yeah, more than most of you runts make in a year, bonuses included. So tighten up, shitheads. Any more fuckups and I'll be wearing a tool myself, watching over you guys like a hawk. I don't want that, and I know you don't. So watch what you're doing out there."

People started getting up, heading toward the Dream Center.

"Cobb," Wendell said. "I want to see you in my office at the end of your shift."

Marcus shrugged. "Sure thing, bossman."

And then, mercifully, it was over. Habit guided him through the hookup, and Marcus stood once more on the dead lunar surface.

Ah, he thought, *sweet purity.*

Life in the habitat was so . . . organic. Moisture. The smell of unwashed bodies. Even the feeling of air on his skin had become an irritant. Out here, there was none of that. This flesh didn't feel, and there was no air to carry odors. It was just him, the gray lunar peaks, and . . .

There! He spotted the female tool at one of the collection bins, sorting ore by hand. Crouching behind a boulder, he watched her. The work could wait. Hell, *everything* could wait. Wendell was bluffing about wearing a tool, and even if he did, even if he caught him, what could he really do? Corpse-riders were a rare breed, and Marcus Cobb was one of the best. They'd have a devil of a time replacing him, and they knew it.

She bent over for a rock fragment that had rolled out of reach. Every muscle in her legs, up through her buttocks, seemed chiseled from stone, perfect. Light and shadow were the paints of this artform, her body the canvas. Marcus raised a hand unconsciously, thinking how it would feel to touch that naked deadflesh.

He thought of Rosalyn and felt a twinge of guilt. Marcus had never been unfaithful, never even considered it. He found the idea of trampling their wedding vows repulsive. Yet now he felt a quickening of desire, a vague pressure that reminded him of his trueflesh, back in the Dream Center.

The female tool turned, looking about as if sensing his gaze on her. Earthlight washed one side of her face in blue. Exquisite! Everything about her seemed perfect, the lean, simple form, so utilitarian—nothing wasted, nothing just for show. Deadflesh going where living tissue could never go. Every muscle stood out, as clear as an anatomical diagram. She was superior, Marcus thought. They all were.

If only he could forget. Forget that he wasn't really here, that this body wasn't his own. If only he could forget his weak, true flesh.

✞ ✞ ✞

"Honey, what is it?"

He'd gone limp again, right in the middle of things. With a sigh of resignation, he pulled out of her. The smell of her excitement caught in his throat.

"Marcus, we need to talk."

He turned away, taking deep breaths, trying not to vomit.

"Is it me? Am I not beautiful enough for you?"

He laughed.

"Dammit, will you at least *look* at me?"

He turned back over, reluctantly. Rosalyn's face was taut, her eyes hard. Anger. It wouldn't last, he knew. There would be tears. Fat, wet, salty tears.

He got up and dashed to the bathroom. When he returned, she'd put her nightgown back on and was sitting up in bed, her legs curled under her, a thoughtful expression in her eyes.

"What's happening to us, Marcus? I'm your wife. Don't I deserved an explanation?"

He stood looking down on her. A distant stirring reminded him of how much he had once cared for this woman. The idea that he might be losing her was offensive, too much to contemplate.

"Is there someone else?" she asked.

He laughed, thinking of the female tool. How could he ever explain?

"Our marriage is falling apart," Rosalyn said evenly, "and you're *laughing*?"

"I'm sorry," he said, at last sitting beside her. "I'm having, uh . . . problems at work."

She took his hand, looked deeply into his eyes. "Do you want to talk about it?"

He shrugged. "What's the point? You wouldn't understand."

"Go to hell!"

"Rosy."

"Don't you Rosy me! This isn't how it was supposed to be. My friend Carrie at the agridome suggested therapy. I thought we could—"

"Marriage counseling? Like that would do any good."

"Marcus! Listen to yourself! You're shutting me out. You're not giving me a chance. I wish I could understand what's happening."

Maybe. . . .

"There! You're doing it again!"

"No," he said quietly. "I'm listening. Look, maybe that's it. You can't understand me because you don't understand my work. But there's always room for another operator—we're shorthanded at the new mine. You could . . ."

Rosalyn operating a tool. A female tool. The two of them, together in vacuum, their gray bodies intertwined. . . .

"Forget it," she said. "We've had this discussion before. It's bad enough I *married* a ghoul; I'm not becoming one."

"Rosy, please—"

"Get out!"

"But—"

She pushed him off the bed. "Don't touch me! You're sick, do you hear? You need help."

He slept on the sofa that night, dreaming of cold, gray fingers that caressed him in his sleep, that touched him in unimagined places, in ways he had never known.

✢ ✢ ✢

At the worksite the next morning, Marcus couldn't keep his mind focused. Earth hung in the sky, so small he could blot it out with one hand. What would happen, he wondered, if his real body died while he was running a tool? Would his soul live on, inside this wasted flesh?

Nonsense.

He watched for the female tool all morning. Had he known her when she was alive? Was that what drew him to her? No. Not that. In life she would have been just like the others, smelly and imperfect, changing and changing again to expose first one flaw and then another. It was death that had transformed her, made her beautiful.

Just before the mid-shift break, Marcus finished wiring up a new charge. He gave the *clear* signal, or thought he did. But he must have forgotten, because when the explosives were detonated, a stout gray tool was caught in the blast. Marcus watched, fascinated, as a mountain of rock buried it undead. Arms and legs moved, even as more rock came down, crushing it.

Damn. Another black mark on his record. Another replacement tool required. Another fresh corpse, wired for sight and sound. Marcus stood for a long time, thinking about that, watching as the workers started digging their way down to the buried gray flesh.

✢ ✢ ✢

"Honey?" Rosalyn called when she came home from work. "Do I have the wrong apartment, or what?"

He called back a greeting from the kitchen. "Make yourself comfortable. Dinner in five."

He heard her gasp of surprise. She would be looking at the table, at the wine glasses and the candles. How well he knew his wife. At first she would shake her head, not believing, then she would slowly smile, knowing that she had won another round.

He served their plates, making sure that everything was just right. When she came to the table, wearing her favorite T-shirt and nothing underneath, she looked radiant, happy. It had been a long time since she'd looked that way.

"I don't know what I did to deserve all this," she gushed. "Mmm. It looks delicious."

Marcus sat across from her, looking into her green eyes as he raised his wine glass in a toast. "To us," he said. "Together, now and forever."

Their glasses tinkled together. She giggled. "Oh, Marcus. I had no idea you could be so . . . romantic."

They ate slowly, pausing frequently to look into each other's eyes.

"I'm sorry," he said when they'd finished the main course and started on dessert.

"Sorry?" she asked. "For what?"

He watched her take a bite of cake, tried to focus on every detail, so he would always remember this moment. "For not being a good husband," he said.

"Oh, Marcus. Don't say that. Maybe it was me. Maybe I should have been more understanding."

He finished his cake, refilled their wine glasses. "No. You've been perfect. Any man would be proud to call you his wife. But I'm different. My work, you know. My life. Sometimes I think you would have been better off with someone else. A plumber maybe, or a computer programmer."

"Nonsense. You've just been . . . confused."

He nodded. "Then you *do* understand. I'm so glad. Things will be different from now on, Rosy. You'll see."

She smiled warmly, her eyes sparkling in the candlelight. "Promise?"

He took her hand. "Promise."

"Oh, Marcus. I love you so much. I—" She blinked, shook her head.

"Rosy?"

"I . . . feel . . . funny. . . ."

He took her hand, helped her over to the sofa. "Just lie back for a moment. It'll be over soon."

"Mar . . . cus. . . ?"

"Don't try to speak. Just let go. Oh, Rosy, I love you so much."

Drool was oozing from the corners of her mouth. "Love . . . you . . . too. . . ."

Tears stung in his eyes. But he held her hand, all the way through, and when her flesh turned cold at last, he climbed onto the sofa and held her to him and slept the most peaceful sleep of his life.

+ + +

There was another accident at the mine the following day. Marcus walked his tool too near the intake of an ore smelter, which promptly sucked up the tool and disintegrated it.

Reprimands came.

So did a replacement.

And again an accident, this time a fall from a crater rim, all the way down to the bottom, breaking every bone in the new tool's body.

More reprimands.

Another replacement.

Rosy.

"My love," Marcus murmured as he worked, wearing her body. "Now we'll be together, always."

There were no more accidents at the mine. And Marcus paid no more attention to the female tool. People talked, for a time, guessing that he was depressed because of his wife's death, or that he volunteered for so much overtime as a way of working through his grief. He pretended not to hear them when they talked, though sometimes they made him smile.

And sometimes, when no one was watching, he would touch himself with the cold, gray fingers of his love.

On-line Zombies
and Dry-Land Skates

SCOT NOEL
(From an idea by Tim Yeager)

Brains. Jacob's own juicy encephalon seemed a tall price to pay, but not unthinkable for the right reward. Of course he could no more imagine his gray matter dangling from a spoon than he could imagine his own death, but Jacob was tired of having nothing, of waking chilled beneath dirty blankets while the trees laughed at him, their leaves trembling with the humor of his desires. At least he had a plan. Suddenly, without a thought to tickle it out of him, Jacob began to giggle, then to guffaw. He could not have said why, though the state of the world seemed reason enough for laughter.

"'Tyger! Tyger! burning bright, In the forests of the night,'" Jacob said, recovering. Unable to remember the rest, he reached for the crib sheet on the seat beside him. The line about "fearful symmetry" seemed appropriate to his circumstance. The car had no radio, and these days he used driving time to memorize what he could. If his brain was to be worth anything, he had to fill it with information more desirable than trivia, which proved its usual predilection.

The exit came just in time. Beneath the grime on the dashboard, a light now burned in sympathy with the engine. Cracked block. Hellfires at war beneath the hood. Jacob eased his clunker off the highway, up into the mall lot where its consumptive rasp soon drew attention. Dead eyes peeked over sunglasses set fashionably low on powdered noses. Ladies in silk brocade scowled at him from the walkways, flocks of them caught in the smoke of his dying Plymouth. Jacob could feel their contempt. They hurried on as if driven by the scent of funeral pyres.

Mall security turned down the row Jacob had picked, blue lights flashing. He found a spot. Pulled in. The late models on either side brought sweat to his lips. He had no fear of the steel- and mist-colored sedans, their windows alive with autumn light. In fact, an impulse to swing the door wide made him tap nervously at the handle before getting out. The cars about him were beautiful, and he coveted them and wanted to smash them all at once. Getting out of his own crate in their presence made him feel dirty.

"I got money," Jacob said defiantly to the blue lights pulling up behind him. He drew three soiled twenties from his pocket and held them out for display. The rheumy-eyed guard scratched, then sighed as if considering a boon for the unworthy. He looked to his partner, who scowled but cupped an ear as a voice came to life there. Jacob heard the tiny receiver crackle, while the unseen speaker said something unintelligible, but favorable

The guards were human. Neither wore dark glasses, and the stains on the rheumy one's shirt would have driven a dead man to distraction.

"You have one hour," the driver warned, opening his door to lean out. He hooked a thumb at the ruined metal Jacob had just exited and asked, "That thing make it out of here?"

Jacob nodded, though he doubted it. He'd started a rebuild once but had grown bored and, in the end, only bolted together enough to make it run. Envisioning a stream of transmission fluid already lapping at the bald minis on the front, he only smiled; this might be a one-way trip.

The guards let him go with a shake of their heads and a whispered comment he would never hear.

With a comic about-face, Jacob turned toward the glitter of commercial splendor. The mall lay atop the hill like a chromium castle, and the dead man who owned it was rumored to have a taste for brains. This was no small fact, but the heart of Jacob's scheme.

He looked at his hands, wiping them up and down along his jeans. Neither his hands nor his stained clothing were about to change, but what opportunities the world had stolen away, he was about to steal back.

"'By the livin' Gawd that made you, You're a better man than I am, Gunga Din!'" A little confidence went a long way to make him giddy. He knew all eighty-four lines.

Jacob entered the mall.

The smell hit him first. You might think a thousand people rotting head to bowels would double you into a retching fool, but the air hung heavy with musk and every perfume known to man. Cologne stung Jacob's eyes. He licked it off his lips. And the noise! Voices jostled in busy repartee, breathless voices passing in the rush. They addressed neither him nor their neighbors. Earring transceivers dangled above lace blouses and velvet collars alike. Lip studs served as cell phones. They consulted with palm devices. Inane chatter rose from the assemblage in the same way the voice of a stream bubbles up from its incessant motion.

As often happened, Jacob's thoughts took a minor turn. As he stepped through the scene, changed only by the decomposition of the milling crowds, he wondered what the builders of the first mall would think of their inspiration now? Less than a hundred years separated the original near Minneapolis from the mega-structure around him, not to mention the wide-eyed innocence of the 1950s from the jaded, or—if he could permit himself a zombie pun—the *jaundiced* lifestyles of the dead.

Another smell assaulted Jacob. Food. The fry court lay ahead. The scents made his gut ache, tempting him to part with some of his meager wealth. The smell of seared flesh and pickle relish all but made him drool. Why did the dead have to eat anyway? He turned and kept to his goal.

Clothing stores loomed everywhere, but not the one he wanted: Novae Nautical. The rotating, interactive 3-D map proved a jigsaw of floating colors. At last he found it. 313T green: lower gallery, south.

A dead woman draped in yards of billowing napery whisked in beside him like a ghost. She tapped at a small keyboard concealed along her hip. The monitor loop on her glasses must have hidden him, but on impulse he smiled and asked, "Can you see where—?" The bones of her neck cracked as she looked over her shoulder. A sudden turn and, smooth as ice, she was away.

"Hey, goddammit!" Jacob said. He huffed after her. "I just asked. . . . Do I have to have swarf in my head before you—"

The sound of tiny bearings and polyurethane wheels rushed in behind, then passed. He was wearing a waisted frock coat and drainpipe trousers, knees bent gracefully above a pair of in-line skates. The man turned as if defending the retreating damsel, his face hung in a permanent scowl. Jacob hesitated. Others merged in quickly, cutting Jacob off. The traffic became heavier and ruder as he moved to the mall's center, so he backed against a column, overwhelmed by the weight of numbers. More and more the bodies charged by on wheels, each as caught up in cellular chatter as his or her pedestrian fellows, as wired to the wireless network as the best of the yuppies before the Breakdown.

The dead moved with a purpose. Restless and quick.

A bookstore opened to Jacob's left, a bright disco of crystal and brass. One stream of shoppers curled toward its wide entrance, a river moving through an ocean. Recovering, Jacob joined its narrow strictures, but they gave him space as they could, the space any crowd might give a beggar in their midst, or someone who smelled really bad. A book signing lay ahead. The line moved like cattle to the slaughter, beef for the author's table. Jacob followed, sidetracked from his primary strategy, but drawn on by a morbid curiosity. He found himself jealous at the sight of someone receiving the attention he had always craved.

It went so fast. The clerks were alive but in no good humor, thrusting a copy of the book into Jacob's hands and expecting payment in a scan as he passed. Their smiles vanished at the alarm; still, the tide moved on, unstoppable.

Jacob opened the gilded volume. Dense black words filled the pages. They bore no capitals and seemed content to run in a train without commas. Periods and question marks appeared as chapter titles.

"He has all the words, but not in the right order," Jacob said aloud, trying to be funny. No one laughed. At least he understood. This was e.e. cummings and James Joyce gone mad. Advertising banners large as sails loomed over him, proclaiming something unintelligible about the tome in Jacob's hands. He found himself before the author, book open, a moving walkway cruising beneath his feet. With a single deadweight stroke, the sallow hand passed across the page. One line, half an X, and Jacob was on his way down, where an angry blonde with a nametag tore the unpaid for book from his hands.

He said nothing, but a line of recently mastered poetry came to him, something from Rilke: "'You who never arrived in my arms, Beloved, who were lost from the start'!" With that commentary he pushed aside childhood dreams of renown and concentrated on the plan at hand. If he could not have fame, he could at least have a taste of life beyond the bounds of shacks and open fields.

The line pushed him out and down, toward the store anchoring the south wing: Novae Nautical. He was there!

No voiceless urge hastened him to join the lemming flow. Unseen energies might whisper of toiletry needs to others, or of the revival of Oxford bags, but Jacob's was the most primitive of motivations. Even his pretext for visiting the mall had been crafted to be simple and convincing. Betty wanted something. The conniving woman back home.

Edged as his evaluation of Betty seemed, Jacob hoped it was not unfair. He was counting on the ineffable self-interest some women could possess, especially when the golden rule these days was that the dead made the rules and owned all the gold.

As he approached a neon tunnel spiraling upward into a neon heaven, Jacob peered about for those who might be watching. Nothing yet. Oh, there was contempt enough and the rough avoidance he had come to expect from the walking stiffs, but no gaze fixed him as a target. Perhaps the cameras nestled in their domes were on the alert. There was no way to tell.

"'Your eyes are moonlight on a gentle stream.'" Jacob said to no one, or to the cameras, though he didn't press the matter by looking their way. "'The stream has voice, and by that voice I know the way the stream has come.'" It was good stuff. Jacob Soule's stuff. "'Somewhere there are waterfalls and children laughing.'"

"Can I help you?" Crimson fingernails gestured before him. Sunglasses met his gaze like a blank stare. This one was a corpse, a floor manager no doubt. "Sir? Restrooms are for customers. Sir?" She spoke through pressed lips.

"'Birds take flight. A thousand winters turn to spring, and the stream gentles them, as you gentle me.'"

"How nice, sir. What is it you want?" The question revealed blackened teeth and a whiff of rotting meat.

"Something in clinging crepe, with a bias cut. Size ten. A dress, I mean. Blue?"

A slow adjustment of the shades lasted the time it took her to rake him head to foot with an unbelieving stare. It seemed as though she wanted to say a thousand words, but in exasperation said only these: "You won't even scan."

"I've noticed. I have these." He displayed his paper bills.

The manager gurgled in frustration.

"Isn't anyone listening?" Jacob asked absently, still holding out the bills but growing bored with the manager's intransigence. He started in on another verse. "'As if it makes no sense, or pales when next to reason—'"

"There are places," the woman interrupted, "where you might find something . . . blue."

"If she wanted something from the Mausoleum shops, I would be there!"

"Well . . . then." She bent at her perfect waist, head tilting toward the bills. "For this . . . a scarf perhaps. A blue bias, you said?"

"A dress! By the gods, how much could they be?"

The woman paused, her fingers making little pawing motions in the air. "I'm afraid we've nothing for you."

Jacob's belly shook. A dry, humorless laugh. Then he heard the soft approach of well-oiled skate blades from behind. He watched the manager straighten. A tight-lipped smile was hers.

"Mr. Jacob Soule?"

Turning, Jacob feigned being startled by the suits, three of them gliding in toward him on skates. He did a good job. His true reactions were more calculating. He plotted escape routes in case things went south and smiled inwardly at the fact that things were, instead, finally going in the right direction. The one who spoke, the long-boned one who towered over Jacob, eased in close and his wingmen with him.

"Mr. Eider would like to see you, Mr. Soule." Turning to the clerk, the tall one smiled, his breath fresh; it was his left hand that seemed . . . wrong. "The dress, please. On Mr. Eider's account. Deliver it to the woman at this address." The floor manager nodded and backed away, holding the card provided as if it were oven fresh.

Outside a De Lorean awaited. Its gull wing doors and stainless steel body were unmistakable. Two more dark suits, once young men in life, circled the car on in-line skates as if the parking area cleared around the De Lorean were their own private roller-disco. They talked to their lip studs and played virtual games on the inner surface of their sunglasses. Their fists twitched and turned to the beat of wireless real time combat, yet if Jacob took one step away from the path to the waiting car, they were there, gliding close. When the wind tricked open one boy's lapels, the glint of a holstered weapon caught Jacob's eye.

Rather than eliciting fear, the guards turned Jacob's mind down an arcane path, for the skates amused him. He recalled a tale from the eighteenth century about a London inventor names Joseph Merlin who attended a masquerade wearing one of his latest inventions, metal-wheeled boots. In a flair of showmanship, Merlin rolled across the ballroom while playing the violin, only to find the only brake provided was the wall-length mirror ahead of him. It seemed a fit metaphor for the innovations that had brought the zombies into being, with man running ahead on wheels of bio-compatible chips while playing a data stream violin and never considering that a way to slow down might be a good idea. Merlin recovered and dry-land skates became an elegant toy. The idea called the Global Cortical Network never had a second chance.

Easing himself into a seat covered in fresh plastic, Jacob nodded to the rigid suit behind the wheel. Only the zombie's cufflinks smiled back. Gold. The doors came down. The car pulled out and accelerated quickly. They drove for hours beyond the town, beyond the power grid, up a long highway that, at last, seemed totally unused except for the hum of the De Lorean along its winding curves.

"Mr. Eider appreciates antiques," Jacob said, referring to the car. It was the only conversation he was to have between the mall and the mansion nestled deep in a woodland hollow.

Ah Betty, he thought. *Praise be the mercenary spirit behind those dirty cheeks. May you be comforted in your hovel, dressed in blue.* She must already have the garment, or her money, or whatever price she had fixed for the sale of his brains. But that was what Jacob wanted. He had set her up. A lie told in the half moonlight, in the half-successful wooing of a maid had become the truth. He had taken on a new identity. The very tangled thought of the idea made him giddy. It was working!

At last they pulled into a great, brilliantly lit driveway before huge white doors. One barrier retreated upward into hiding, and the De Lorean pulled in to a spotless garage, coming to rest beside its twin.

Standing beside the second De Lorean was a heavyset man scrupulously decked out in a morning suit and topper. With a paisley scarf in one hand, he rubbed gently at the passenger side mirror. But more astounding than the sight of this anachronism was the second De Lorean itself. It was gold. To look at it beneath the bright lights of the garage proved a challenge, its edgy yellow spilling everywhere, a mercurial brilliance so great it was difficult to tell exactly where the car began and ended.

As the gull wing doors of the guest car lifted in that holy place, Mr. Eider stopped fussing at the mirror with his rag and stepped forward to help Jacob out.

"Welcome to my home, Mr. Soule. Your reputation precedes you. I am Constantine Eider."

Jacob thought to laugh, but the laugh had gone out of him. Looking away from the gold, head bowed, he found himself equally disturbed by the impossible polish of Mr. Eider's shoes. With nowhere else to focus, he looked up into eyes this creature was unashamed to bare. Liquid blue, vulnerable eyes. Intelligent eyes.

Looking into that gaze, Jacob reached for a verse but could find none in the entire length and breadth of his memory. For an eternity he was not sure he had ever known how to talk. He seemed trapped by those eyes.

"I know my blessings, Mr. Soule. The eyes are usually the first to go, are they not? I hope you'll join me for dinner. I promise an unforgettable repast."

It was then Jacob found his voice, but not for poetry. The oil in him set his hands to sliding uneasily along his jeans. One hand jerked out to pat the hood of the De Lorean he had arrived in.

"The sound when you turn, the first time to each side . . . it's the drive shaft. Not serious, just needs some Teflon." When Eider's gaze fell to Jacob's roughened fingers, Jacob found the good sense to finish with, "I would be honored to join you, sir." In flashes, he noted a gun rack, a workbench, and the lines to the house generator. All useful things.

Escorted to a suite within the great house, Jacob was encouraged to shower and dress for dinner. He needed no encouragement, peeling off his oily hand-me-downs as if they had been sewn together from refuse; the wastebasket in the room seemed too good for them. A liquor cabinet adorned by good whiskey stopped him short of cleanliness, and he downed a tumbler of the amber juice. Something in him blurted out with glee. He wanted someone to talk to. Yet the only inhabitant of the decorous apartment was a new suit of clothes, all plastic wrapped and waiting.

"I tell you, only two of those gold De Loreans were built," he confidently told the waiting duds. "1979 American Express Christmas Catalog, for gold cardholders. Hee, hee! Buffing out a dent in those gull wings could rack up twenty-five grand!" He looked around, found a bathroom bigger than the out-house he called home, and got to work with soap and water. "Time to raise the stakes maybe, eh?" For a place in the middle of nowhere, the water pressure was good and the house was ablaze with light. The steam and soap of the shower filled him with a scent as intoxicating in its own right as the whiskey that warmed him to his toes.

No more than an hour later dinner was upon him. The room to which two servants led him proved vast. Gilt chandeliers hung from a ceiling high enough to make cathedrals blush with envy. A marble table shone bare its white shoulders and exquisite skin, and upon it a formidable meal had been set.

It surprised him that nothing spoke of foreign or unpronounceable delicacies. In serving Jacob and Mr. Eider, the servants brought each man a deep dish of French onion soup, two double porterhouse steaks, a tureen of scalloped potatoes, a bowl of peas, a literal mountain of coleslaw, and three loaves of bread—one rye, one wheat, and one sourdough. A decanter of burgundy sat to each man's right. A vast dinner.

Jacob giggled and went to work. The burgundy eased his throat. A cut of meat warned his insides of the treat to come. When he looked up he noticed a screen had been placed before Eider, a low Japanese print of just the right height to hide the man's mouth as he consumed his meal.

At some level the poor beast knew what had happened to him, just as, at some level, all of the zombies were aware. Jacob chewed and stared, and stared too long.

"It's quite all right, Mr. Soule, for a man such as yourself to wonder. A poet." Mr. Eider dabbed at his mouth with a silken napkin and straightened in his chair. "What can I say? This meal, the clothes, the cars . . . all impulses, I suppose. Bits of movies and old stories floating on the net, coming to me like a dream. As I recall, it's much like wanting a woman. How much thought do you put into that, Mr. Soule?"

"More than you might imagine," Jacob warned, "but I understand the point. Unbidden impulses. The swarf in your head." He tapped his temple as if in understanding or sympathy, then took another drink, ate another bite. All of his fears dissolved in the sweet warmth of the porterhouse. He tapped his shoes happily together. "Do you think the net is still trying to direct the economy?" He was proud to be so conversational.

"My malls depend on it, Mr. Soule. Of course, I have my own curiosities. How does it feel to have nothing, to be a slave of the dead?"

"I . . . didn't know I was a slave," Jacob answered honestly, reaching for the bread. "Just dispossessed. It's been like this before, two economic classes and no middle. This time it took the Breakdown to make it happen; everyone with swarf in his or her head went to the floor with the network. We had imagined you were all down for the count, too."

"Perhaps it was a fitting end for the wired elite," said Eider. "Those nano-machines in our heads—the 'swarf,' as you say— they were too stubborn to lose."

"And not good enough to win. It only brought you back to life . . . sort of."

"Your woman sold you for less than I pay one servant for one month. Is that how good being alive is?"

"'She walks in beauty, like the night,'" Jacob said after a moment's thoughtful repose, "that's what did it. Tried to be a gentleman, show a little culture. Guess I gave myself away. As for poor Betty, how does it work? Do you have wanted posters up for me?"

"Not for you personally. Not posters. There are contacts, fees mentioned. Not long after someone enters my territory I hear of it—persons of note, that is. The way you live, Mr. Soule, is it what you desire, to wander from place to place, to hide who you are, to live with refugees in graveyards—?"

"It's the last place you zombies will come!" Jacob took a long, hard pull of the burgundy. "I was always a recluse, you know that. Media couldn't even get a picture. But that's beside the point. Why are we sparring?"

"A mean streak of mine!" Mr Eider said, smiling. "Ah, would you mind not placing your fork on the table, please."

Eider snapped his fingers. One of the servants reached the table at speed, annihilating the bit of grease and startling Jacob. *Ah*, he thought, *skates again*. His sigh became a laugh through the nose. At times it seemed the Global Cortical Network, or what was left of it, had a sense of humor.

"I apologize if James startled you. Did you think that was the end?" Eider asked. He lowered his head for a bite, never once taking his pale blue eyes from Jacob.

"No, I—"

"It won't happen that way. I have experience in these matters. It's not worth it if the donor is frightened." Eider paused to let the calming words do their work. "Do you need anything more? There is a another course, and you must save room for desert!"

Donor. Jacob couldn't bring himself to say the word, let alone laugh at it. He wondered how many Buddhist monks had thought themselves donors, or Nobel Laureates, or high school teachers—the good ones—or even the real Jacob Soule? Nor, he expected, was every zombie as urbanely considerate as Constantine Eider.

"What do you get out of it, exactly?" Jacob asked. "Brains, I mean. Is it another directive from the net, another . . . impulse?"

"No, no. A discovery, you could call it." Eider's gaze took on a thoughtful, unfocused quality. "Not an urge at all. An acquired taste, known to some. I don't believe the rest of us would care if they knew."

Putting down his utensils, he laced his fingers as if about to pray, but rubbed them together vigorously instead. "When I was young we learned in school of a creature, a microscopic flatworm, I believe. You could train some worms, grind them up, feed them to others, and thereby pass on the training. Isn't that something?"

Jacob agreed that it was, and responded with the obvious,

"You want to consume my . . . intellect in order to become a poet?"

"No, I want to be alive, Mr. Soule! I want to feel life and thought; I want the muses to speak to me, not the buzz, buzz, of the swarf! Ah, my friend, if you want the taste of life between your teeth, you don't eat a potato. That's how I think of your graveyard friends, your traitorous woman: potatoes! You, Mr. Soule, are an apple, an orange, a tangerine perhaps!"

"I was hoping to be something more expensive than fruit."

"Then it's time. Name your price."

The price had been brewing in the back of Jacob's thoughts for some time.

"Are you familiar with the story of the Old Man of the Mountain?" Jacob asked.

Eider nodded. It was no more than a movement of the eyes, but thus Jacob's fortnight of indulgence began.

The women arrived that evening—the first shift, that is. Once Jacob might have believed in love and family, but life had a way of overwhelming the beliefs he'd held. What remained was to get his. They provided sex: hot, wet, and steamy—more than Jacob could have handled at seventeen. They did the spread-eagle, the lap, the crawl, the head to toe, activities for which Latin and French words were used, and one rather endearing position called "fireside." They knew the spot named after Ernst Grafenberg, they made up spots, and nothing embarrassed them. Their physical appearance ranged uniformly around a bull's eye of supermodels and porn stars, and in the hours when Jacob's energies flagged, the women fussed over him and supplied massage, delighted to have a living client. All this went on for days.

Soft drugs Eider permitted and supplied in quantity, though nothing that might damage more than a few million synapses. And the food and the liquor came to order. Sitting down before the house's net terminal, Jacob did a quick search, giggling as he uncovered gourmet delights of unpronounceable name and impossible price. Porterhouse and coleslaw might do for starters, but why not *amuse-bouche*, a *blancmange* of sole topped with caviar? Duck and *foie gras*. *Châteauneuf-du-Pape*. Cigars and Cognac.

The Old Man of the Mountain could not have done better by his victims. In that ancient tale, a Mohammedan chief gave his young warriors a taste of paradise, of wine, women, and song amid luxuriant circumstance. Believing they had been to the afterlife, the warriors became heedless of their own mortality and loyal beyond compare.

Loyal beyond compare.

Jacob found white caviar packed in gold, modestly valued at twenty-three grand a kilo. He almost choked on his swig of single-barrel millennium tequila when Eider agreed to fly it in.

This is really going to happen, he thought. *Eider intends to eat my brain.*

That night Jacob ordered a meal of blowfish. An entire meal. After all, if prepared incorrectly, the toxins in any variation could kill, and wouldn't that be a shame? Blowfish hor d'oeuvres, *fugu sashimi,* blowfish-and-rice soup, and *fugu* stew. But Eider supplied it all. Perhaps he employed tasters to insure its safety, as did the kings of old.

In the evening, Jacob and the rich man walked a tiled esplanade, a promenade enclosed between the walls of the property and the forest beyond. Forty-five minutes precisely beneath brilliant, moth-clouded lights. Here Jacob recited volumes. Longfellow and Tennyson came to life on his lips. Shakespeare, Edwin Muir, and the incomparable works of Rabindranath Tagore rose up from a memory that could take in any sort of oddity, and be disciplined to remember whatever was required of it. Only the hum of the house's generator and the far-off drone of insects accompanied his eager voice. Sometimes he danced out the rhythms, or did a jig to celebrate his prowess with the words, or because he was stoned. He wasn't sure. His new clothes glittered in the light as he humored Eider with a selection of Jacob Soule's most famous works.

"Your instincts about the De Lorean were correct," Eider informed him on the fifth outing. "They found the problem in the drive shaft." He let the statement hang in the air, as if it were a question. They had stopped near the edge of the esplanade. Eider was careful not to set one gleaming shoe off the walkway.

"Yes, I know cars, Mr. Eider," Jacob said honestly. "I am a poet, but I make my living with my hands. It's what the world left me. It's why I'm here."

"You must have done so before the Breakdown, to know De Loreans."

Jacob laughed. He bowed. "It's not something I'm proud of. Would you make me an offer to be your personal mechanic?"

Though Eider smiled, he declined and released Jacob to his fun. Retiring to his tub, Jacob gathered his harem and began a luxuriant soap and scrub. After five days, the last rough black of auto grease was gone from his hands.

It was time to escape.

He had gotten down the routine of the house, of the hours Eider and his attendants spent grooming, the shopping on the net, the bouts of communal television where commercials were interrupted by advertisements, of the precise intervals when attention turned to the radio, or to interior decorating, or babying the De Loreans. He delighted in the few minutes set aside each day for Eider and his entourage to admire the trees. *Whose idea was that?*

Meanwhile the guards skated in circles about the house, their arms thrown wide, their faces to heaven as if receiving bliss from above.

Jacob made final plans for the seventh night. To be greedy and indulge himself any longer risked becoming a head entrée, literally.

On the walk along the esplanade that evening, Eider inquired, rather courteously, after what Jacob had been composing since the Breakdown. Jacob demurred. He attempted some Robert Frost, but Eider insisted.

"These recitations strengthen the qualities for which I am paying," Eider said. His tone lost its semblance of courtesy. "In another week, I want everything."

Jacob laughed, but the last thing he wanted to do was arouse suspicion. Closing his eyes, he relaxed into the world of details and imagination that had always served him so well. He was not the poet he pretended to be, but he had once held literary dreams, honest ambitions of his own. How hard could it be?

The rhythms moved dark and restlessly within him, and when he spoke, the words came in cadences of despair and ambitions left unfulfilled. Though he stumbled at first and sweat moistened his lips, Jacob went on for the full ten minutes left of the evening's forty-five. Then Eider dismissed him with a tip of the hat.

"I have more. . . ."

"Tomorrow then. They were quite excellent. Good night, Mr. Soule."

Strangely, Jacob trusted Eider to be a man of his word, a zombie of distinction. But even with half the fortnight left to fulfill his whims, then a painless pill taken before sleep, Jacob had no intention of playing along.

Returning to his room, Jacob sent the girls to the pool. He gathered a few valuables, a cache of drugs, and prepared to exit the scene. It was tempting to stay. He liked the sound of his own words and wanted to come up with more, perhaps even commit them to paper. The girls would miss him. Eider, too.

His pockets bulging, a makeshift pack stuffed with food across his shoulders, Jacob took an extension cord he had stripped with a kitchen knife, wrapped it about a lamp pole, and plugged it in. Blue fire jumped out at him like a mad animal. Suddenly it was pitch black. He turned, hands shaking, and felt for the window. Then he was moving, past the sill, down to the low roof and toward the veranda, all along a path he had practiced in his mind many times.

Jacob's effort had not darkened the entire house, but enough to conceal his route to the woods in shadow. Swinging down from the roof, he rolled onto the veranda, cursing at the effort. It might take a minute or two for someone to reach the circuit breaker. Was it worth it to break into the generator and disable the thing? Or should he run straight for the woods?

He had little time, but if he could make it past the range of the floodlights, Jacob expected no pursuit into the sylvan night. Zombies were the remnants of the wired elite, the mall children, the technocrats, the fastidious and the inflexible. Where he was going the worms crawled. Life was dirty and unpredictable, the road too rough for skates and De Loreans.

But as Jacob got to his feet, already winded, a light came on—a flashlight attached to the barrel of a rifle.

"You are not Jacob Soule," said Mr. Eider, standing behind the gun. "Those words . . ." He shook his head.

From deep in the house Jacob heard the click and rush of wheels, a gathering storm of skate-borne thugs.

"Who are you?" Eider demanded.

"Well. . . ," he said, canting his head innocently, a child caught in the embarrassment of a white lie. "I'm not Jacob Soule. The name *is* Jake, though." He bowed politely. "Jake Skeeler, at your service."

Mr. Eider's pale eyes held something close to astonishment. "I am afraid the name is unknown to me." His gaze narrowed, becoming fixed on a point somewhere beyond Jacob—Jake. As though lost in contemplation, he allowed the muzzle of the weapon to dip slightly. "Nevertheless, you have a remarkable talent, Mr. Skeeler."

"Why, thank you. I once had a few humble stanzas on Rhyme&Reason.com, and—Hey, is that bird shit on your shoe?" Jake moved on the question mark.

Eider's blue eyes flicked down long enough for Jacob to snatch away the rifle. Had Eider's finger been tight on the trigger, Jake might have lost, but now the gun was his. He flattened the dead man with the rifle stock, then turned the gun on the generator and emptied the clip until the electric hum choked into silence and the world went dark. Inside, the in-line skaters stumbled and fell. There was yelling, but it seemed frightened and mournful, especially from the dead.

Jake turned back once at the edge of the trees, but now there was only silence along the esplanade, up to the veranda and into the mansion itself, all of which lay black beneath the stars.

"'An' 'e guv me 'arf-a-pint o' water green. It was crawlin' and it stunk. But of all the drinks I've drunk, I'm gratefullest to one from Gunga Din.'" He smiled and waved. "Bye now."

Hours later, Jake Skeeler was still wired with nervous energy and finally laughing right along with the trees.

HOLLYWOOD FLESH

L. J. WASHBURN

"What the hell is a zombie?" asked Lucas Hallam.

Martin Larribee puffed on his pipe for a moment before answering. "One of the walking dead. One who has risen from the grave to shamble about in a grotesque, twisted mockery of life."

Hallam thought about that. If he hadn't already known that Larribee was a writer, he would have been able to tell it from the way the Englishman talked. Finally he shook his head and said, "Nothin' dead can get up and walk around again. It ain't natural."

From where she sat in a comfortable armchair near the fireplace on the other side of the crowded living room in Larribee's Hollywood apartment, Eliza Dutton laughed. "Now you understand, Mr. Hallam. It certainly isn't natural."

She and Larribee made a pretty odd pair. The Englishman was short and stocky, with sandy hair and a drooping mustache. Eliza Dutton was tall and slender and darkly beautiful. Hallam had seen her around ever since she'd arrived in town a few years earlier, in '25. Her name then had been Gertrude Something-or-other. Hallam had never heard anything else about her background. But she had gone from bit parts to ingenues to second leads in a hurry, and now she had a couple of leading roles to her credit.

Hallam rubbed his jaw, feeling the two days' worth of stubble. Since he'd known he would be working today, he hadn't bothered to shave this morning. "I just don't know if I can do you any good, Mr. Larribee."

"Because you don't believe that zombies exist? Look at yourself, Mr. Hallam. Aren't you a creature of myth?"

Hallam glanced down at his outfit. It was true that not many folks wore fringed buckskins these days, or packed a long-barreled Colt .45 in a tied-down holster, along with a sheathed Bowie knife on the other hip, or looked at the world from under the broad brim of a high-crowned brown Stetson. But there was nothing mythological about any of it. The costume department at the studio didn't have to come up with anything for him to wear when he was working on a picture. These duds were the real thing. He'd owned them for years.

"Cowboys are real," he said. "I reckon I'll have to take your word on it for zombies, Mr. Larribee, 'cause I ain't never seen one. Hope I never do."

Larribee took his pipe out of his mouth and wearily scrubbed a hand over his face. "I wish I could say the same about never seeing one, I honestly wish I could. But I have seen them, Mr. Hallam. I know they exist." The Englishman raised his head and met Hallam's eyes squarely. "I know because they want to kill me and eat my flesh."

Yep, thought Hallam, *this fella has definitely been into the loco weed.*

Larribee put out a hand. There was a hint of desperation in his manner. "Please, Mr. Hallam, hear me out. I know that you sometimes work as a . . . a private inquiry agent—"

"Private detective."

"Yes, of course. A private detective. And to put it in simple terms, someone is trying to kill me. I want you to put a stop to it."

"If somebody's been threatenin' you, go to the police."

"And tell them what?" Larribee shrugged helplessly. "I saw how you reacted a moment ago. Do you honestly believe the authorities would give any credence to my story or try to help me if I told them the same thing?"

Hallam thought about the detectives he knew on the police forces in Hollywood and Los Angeles. "They'd think you were off your nut."

"Precisely. That's why I need to hire you to act on my behalf."

Hallam was holding his hat in his left hand. He tapped it against his leg as he thought. He was tired from riding all over Bronson Canyon all day, pretending to be one of the outlaw gang that Ken Maynard was after, but he didn't suppose it would hurt anything to listen to what Larribee had to say.

"All right, you can tell me about it. I ain't promisin' I'll take the case, though."

"Fair enough. Please sit down."

Hallam lowered his rangy, powerful frame into an armchair and waited.

Larribee drew up a chair near the unlit fireplace, next to Eliza Dutton. "I'm a scenarist, as I told you when I called. Perhaps you're familiar with my work?"

Writers, thought Hallam. "Can't say as I pay much attention to the names on the scripts when I read 'em."

"Yes, well, no matter. I've published several novels in England, and I came to America several years ago to try my luck over here. Done quite well, if I say so myself. I've written features for some of the leading studios."

And been paid pretty well for it, Hallam decided as he looked around the expensively furnished apartment. Larribee had himself a good-looking actress as a ladyfriend, too, and that cost money.

Larribee puffed on his pipe. "Well, to the point of the matter. A couple of months ago, I went to Haiti to research a scenario. Geoffrey Mason planned to make a picture about the sugar cane plantations on Hispaniola, and he wanted me to write it for him."

Hallam nodded. He knew Mason, another Englishman who'd had some success as a producer and director after coming to Hollywood in the early '20s.

"Geoffrey went along on the trip to search for suitable locations, and so did Eliza here, who was scheduled to play the female lead."

That jogged something in Hallam's brain. As a rule, he didn't pay much attention to the gossip columns in the trades, but he recalled seeing some mention of Eliza Dutton and Geoffrey Mason being engaged. Now Eliza was in Martin Larribee's apartment, and seeing as how she was wearing a silk dressing gown and not a hell of a lot else, she obviously wasn't planning on going home tonight. Larribee had done more in Haiti than research.

Larribee took a deep breath. "While we were there, Eliza and I . . . well, we fell in love, Mr. Hallam. I'll not deny it."

"Neither will I," Eliza said softly.

"Naturally, Geoffrey wasn't pleased with this, but we're all professionals, after all. We continued with the work that had taken us to that lovely but haunted island. Geoffrey told me that he had found a perfect spot to film the picture, an old deserted plantation house out in the forest northeast of Port-au-Prince. He suggested that I go out and take a look at it, that it might . . . inspire me in my writing. I agreed to do so."

"But it was some sort of double-cross," said Hallam.

"He told me to go at dusk." Larribee seemed not to have heard Hallam's comment. "He said the light was spectacular then. That much was true. With the sun setting over the sea to the west, and the golden light washing over that old, moss-draped plantation house, surrounded by trees and with the green mountains and the darkening eastern sky behind it . . . it truly was a beautiful scene."

Hallam could see it clearly. Larribee was a pretty fair word wrangler.

"But that wasn't all that was there. I walked right in on the . . . the most ghastly thing. . . ."

Larribee stopped, and Eliza Dutton leaned forward in her chair, reaching over to him to rest a hand on his arm. After a moment, the Englishman was able to go on.

"I had walked into a voodoo ritual. Do you know what voodoo is, Mr. Hallam?"

"I ain't rightly sure."

"The actual name is voudon. It's the old religion of the former slaves and their descendants, brought with them from Africa. A dark religion, Mr. Hallam, full of vengeful gods and bloody sacrifices."

"And dead fellers who get up and walk around when they take a notion to," Hallam guessed.

Larribee nodded. "That's right. The voodoo priests, called houngans, can recall the dead to life as zombies. They rise from the grave, unthinking monsters who obey only the will of the houngan, filled with an unholy craving for . . . for human flesh."

Hallam leaned forward. "You saw this?"

"God help me, I did. The ritual I interrupted involved the raising of a new zombie. And just as I came along, the . . . the thing was given a young Haitian woman—" Larribee's pipe rattled on the floor as he dropped it and pressed his hands over his face. "My God, I wish I could get that awful sight out of my mind! That woman's screams still echo in my ears. I screamed, too. I couldn't help it. But that drew the attention of the voodoo worshipers to me. An outsider. A white man. Having witnessed their blasphemous practices, I couldn't be allowed to live. They pursued me."

Larribee lowered his hands and looked across the room at Hallam again. "I ran faster than I ever have in my life, Mr. Hallam. Thank God the car I had rented started quickly and easily. I was able to drive away from there before they caught me. I returned to Port-au-Prince and told Geoffrey and Eliza that I had to leave right away and come back here to California. I pleaded a sudden illness. Eliza agreed to come with me."

"What about Mason?"

"He was angry, of course. He said it was because I was running out on his picture. But he was really angry because his attempt to murder me had failed."

"Murder?"

"Of course. Somehow, Geoffrey found out about the ritual that would be going on at that plantation, and he sent me out there so I would stumble on it and be killed. That was his way of eliminating me so that he could try to win back Eliza's affections."

Hallam looked at Eliza Dutton. "When did he tell you about all this?"

"On the airplane back here."

"And you believe him?"

Eliza took Larribee's hand. "Of course. Martin wouldn't lie."

Hallam thought about it. Maybe Eliza Dutton was just being loyal to Larribee, or maybe she was as loco as he was.

"Where's Mason now?"

"Back here in Hollywood," Larribee said. "He took a later flight. He's abandoned the Haitian picture, at least for now."

Hallam put his hands on his knees, ready to push himself to his feet and get out of there. "I reckon what you'd best do is not go to any of the same parties as Mason does until he gets over bein' mad at you. No charge for the advice."

Quickly, Larribee put out his hands. "No, Mr. Hallam, you don't understand. Geoffrey's not the only one who came back here from Haiti. He brought the houngan—and a zombie—with him. You see, once an interloper has witnessed one of their rituals, these voodoo worshipers will track him down to the ends of the earth to kill him. That's the only way to satisfy what they see as an affront to their gods."

Hallam leaned back in his chair. "You mean there's one o' these voodoos—I mean, zombies—chasin' you around Hollywood tryin' to kill you and eat you?"

"I know it sounds insane! But I swear it's the truth. I swear it on all that's still holy in a world grown ever darker and more evil."

Eliza Dutton said, "It is the truth, Mr. Hallam. I've seen the Haitian man—the priest—and his . . . *creature* stalking Martin. One night he barely escaped from them. You have to help us."

Hallam sighed. He had never been good at turning down folks who were in trouble. While he didn't believe everything Larribee had told him, it was possible that as a jilted lover, Geoffrey Mason was doing something to scare the bejabbers out of his fellow Englishman.

"I reckon I can look into it, but I ain't makin' no promises."

Instantly, Larribee was out of his chair and across the room, shaking Hallam's hand. "Thank you, Mr. Hallam, thank you. I've spoken to quite a few people in the motion picture community, and they assure me that you're quite a competent fellow. And discreet as well. That's very important."

Sure it is, thought Hallam, *because if word gets out that you're crazy as a loon, you might have trouble getting work. On the other hand, this is Hollywood.*

✛ ✛ ✛

Lucas Hallam had been a lot of things in his time: Texas Ranger, Pinkerton operative, deputy United States marshal. Now in his fifties, he spent most of his days working as a riding extra and occasional stuntman in the countless Western pictures the studios cranked out. He liked the cowboys who worked in the movies with him. Most of them were the genuine article, fellas who had drifted to Hollywood because there wasn't enough real ranch work to go around in these modern times.

But Hallam was also a licensed private investigator and supplemented his picture income by taking a case now and then, usually one that had some connection to the studios or movie folks. Like Martin Larribee's. The next morning, as Hallam drove his battered old flivver through the main gate of the studio where Geoffrey Mason worked, he thought with a grin that maybe once this case was over, he could add zombie-wrangler to his list of jobs.

The guard at the gate waved him through; Hallam knew every studio guard in Hollywood. He drove past several huge soundstage buildings to park in front of a row of neat little bungalows that served as production offices.

A secretary at a desk in the front room of one of the bungalows looked up as Hallam came in. "I'd like to see Mr. Mason," Hallam said.

He wasn't wearing buckskins and a Stetson today. Instead he wore a dark brown suit and a cream-colored Panama hat. He still carried the same .45, however, tucked into a holster under his left arm. The sheath that held the Bowie knife hung between his shoulderblades from a thong around his neck.

"I don't believe you have an appointment, Mr. . . ?"

"Hallam. Tell him it's about Haiti."

Hallam had noticed that the door into the other room was open. He spoke loudly enough to be heard in there, and sure enough, a second later, a man poked his head out. "Haiti? What the devil?"

Hallam recognized Geoffrey Mason. They had never been introduced, but Hallam had seen him around town. Ignoring the disapproving look the secretary gave him, he stepped toward the door and extended his hand. "Lucas Hallam, Mr. Mason."

"How do you do." Mason shook Hallam's hand. "What's this about Haiti?"

"I hear you had some trouble with a picture you wanted to make down there. I'd like to talk to you about it."

Mason hesitated, then jerked his head toward the inner office. "Come in. No calls, Doris."

The secretary sniffed and nodded. Hallam stepped into the office, and Mason closed the door behind him.

The place wasn't fancy, just functional. The only touch of luxury was a small bar where bootleg booze could be dispensed. Successful producer-directors like Geoffrey Mason didn't have to go to a speakeasy to get their hooch.

Mason was slender and handsome, with sleek dark hair. He looked a lot more like the type to date beautiful actresses than Martin Larribee did. But Eliza Dutton was lounging around in silk dressing gowns in Larribee's apartment these days, not in Mason's Beverly Hills mansion.

Mason walked behind his desk. "What can I do for you, Mr. . . . Hallam, was it?"

"Martin Larribee says you sicced some voodoo priest on him down yonder in Haiti, and that now there's a zombie here in Hollywood that's tryin' to kill him." Sometimes when you slapped all your cards face-up on the table right away, it startled a gent into saying something he didn't want to.

Mason's eyes widened. "I say! That's mad!"

Hallam stayed on his feet but dropped his Panama on a chair in front of the desk. "Maybe so, but somethin's got him spooked, and since he took your gal away from you, I reckon you might have somethin' to do with it."

Mason's face darkened with anger. "So that's it. It's not enough that that miserable little scribbler stole Eliza away from me, now he's started spreading ugly rumors about me as well. Well, I won't stand for it, Mr. Hallam. I simply won't stand for it." His hand started toward a button on the desk. "I see this for what it is. You and Larribee intend to blackmail me. Go ahead and try. You'll be laughed out of Hollywood, and I'll sue both of you. But right now, if you don't leave immediately, I'll have you arrested for trespassing—"

Hallam leaned over the desk. His big hand covered the button without pressing it. "I ain't a blackmailer, Mason, and neither is Larribee. He just wants whatever's been goin' on to stop."

"The only thing going on is that Larribee has lost his mind!"

Hallam's eyes narrowed as he looked across the desk at

Mason. He had survived a lot of years in an assortment of dangerous professions by being able to know when people were telling the truth. He had a feeling that Mason wasn't lying.

Hallam straightened and took his hand off the button. "You want to push that, go ahead. But it'll be ugly for you, too."

Abruptly, Mason sank into the leather chair behind the desk. "Just go away, Mr. Hallam. I don't want any trouble. I've had enough problems recently, what with having to postpone a picture because my leading lady and my scenarist walked out on me. I can replace them both, but the delay has cost a great deal of money."

"I reckon it's easier to replace a writer than a fiancée."

Mason laughed hollowly. "Not at all. This is Hollywood, after all. There's no shortage of beautiful young women eager to have a career in motion pictures. If not for those blasted morals clauses, think what a hotbed of debauchery this town would be."

"I reckon I'd rather not." Hallam picked up his hat. "Larribee better not have any more trouble, or I'll be back to see you, Mason."

Mason waved a hand. "Threaten me to your heart's content. I've done nothing to Larribee, nor do I intend to. That's a closed chapter in my life." He chuckled. "Larribee certainly has come up with a colorful story, though. Just imagine . . . zombies in Hollywood. The living dead stalking through the hills of Bel-Air. . . ." Mason began to frown in thought. "Hmmm . . . there might be a picture in that."

Hallam tried not to grimace as he turned and walked out.

✛ ✛ ✛

The only thing Hallam's visit to the studio had accomplished was to convince him that Geoffrey Mason wasn't responsible for whatever was happening to Martin Larribee. Mason hadn't seemed all that broken up about losing Eliza Dutton, either, so the idea that he had sent Larribee out to that plantation knowing he would interrupt a voodoo ritual and be marked for death was pretty far-fetched, too. Hallam supposed it could have happened that way, but he sensed that something else was going on here.

He still didn't believe in zombies, but something sure had Larribee spooked. Maybe the thing to do was keep an eye on the little Englishman for a few days and see if somebody tried to murder him.

Hallam figured zombies wouldn't wander around in broad

daylight, not even in Hollywood, so he waited until that evening to go back over to Larribee's apartment. He had just parked the flivver and gotten out when he saw a figure running through the shadows toward him. Hallam's hand started under his coat toward the butt of his gun, but he paused as he heard Larribee's voice.

"Mr. Hallam! Thank God you're here! Eliza is in trouble."

"Hold on there," Hallam said as Larribee came up to him, panting from fear or exertion or both. "What are you talkin' about?"

"E-Eliza just called me. She said she saw the zombie when she was on her way over here earlier tonight. She tried to run it down with her car, but it escaped. But she followed the creature! She trailed it back to its lair!"

Hallam frowned. The story bubbling out of Larribee's mouth sounded like something a writer would come up with, not an actress. But whether Eliza Dutton was chasing a zombie or something else around town, she could still wind up in trouble.

"Did she say where she was?"

Larribee swallowed and nodded. "At an old house up off of Mulholland, near the Hollywoodland sign. Actually, she was calling from a drugstore at the bottom of the hill, but she said that was where the zombie went!"

Hallam tugged at his earlobe. "Wait a minute. I got the feelin' these zombies ain't supposed to be very fast on their feet. How'd the thing get all the way up there?"

"The houngan has a car. The creature got back to the vehicle, and it sped away. Eliza was able to follow it."

So now voodoo priests and zombies are driving around Hollywood, thought Hallam. *Well, California does have a way of changing folks. . . .*

He nodded abruptly, suddenly anxious to see just what Eliza Dutton had followed up into the hills. "Let's go."

"Really? You'll go with me?"

"Damn right. Pile into my flivver."

Larribee climbed eagerly into Hallam's car. Hallam drove through the streets of Hollywood, then started the climb up Mulholland onto the long, rugged ridge that overlooked the city. One of his cases had ended in a shootout up there near the Hollywoodland sign. He hoped that wouldn't happen tonight, but if it did, his Colt had five rounds in the cylinder and the hammer resting on an empty chamber.

Five was usually plenty when Lucas Hallam slapped leather.

Eliza Dutton had given Larribee good directions. "Right there!" he said excitedly when the flivver's headlights picked out a small dirt road turning off to the left. Hallam swung onto the winding road and followed it for about a quarter of a mile before they came to a large clearing where an old house stood. Beyond the house, the ground fell away and the lights of Los Angeles spread out across the valley in a glittering carpet.

Larribee let out a moan when he saw the old house. "It's like the one in Haiti!"

Hallam had never been to Haiti, but he figured the plantation houses there didn't look much like deserted old mansions in the Hollywood Hills. Still, the resemblance was close enough to put a scare into Larribee. The Englishman pressed back against the car seat.

"I don't know if I can do this."

"There's a car parked over there." Hallam pointed through the windshield. "Is it Miss Dutton's?"

"Oh, my God. Yes, that's Eliza's car. I have to find her. You don't think she went . . . in there?"

Hallam opened the door beside him. "Reckon we'd better find out."

He stepped out of the flivver. Larribee emerged tentatively from the other door. No sooner had they started walking toward the house than a scream rang out.

"Eliza!" Larribee shouted. He broke into a run, his fear momentarily forgotten.

Hallam went after him, the bad knee he had suffered years earlier when a horse fell on him slowing him slightly. Larribee reached the rotting old steps first and started up onto the porch.

A huge, slow-moving figure loomed out of the darkness and lurched into Larribee's path. Larribee's shriek of terror was cut short when a hand closed around his throat. As Hallam started up the steps, he saw moonlight shining on the gaunt, gray, hideous face of the thing that had hold of Larribee. The Englishman's wildly kicking feet came up off the porch as the creature lifted him by the neck.

"Drop him, you son of a bitch!"

Hallam didn't draw his gun. He went up the steps two at a time and lunged onto the porch. The zombie said, "Shit!" and swung Larribee around so that the Englishman was between it and Hallam. A hard shove sent Larribee reeling into the detective.

Hallam batted Larribee out of the way, figuring he could apologize to his client later for knocking him down, and caught hold of the zombie's shoulder as the creature turned to run. Hallam hauled the thing around and swung a hard right fist, landing the punch squarely on the zombie's jaw. The creature sailed back into the porch rail, broke through the rotten wood, and crashed down into what had once been a flowerbed.

"Be careful!" Larribee cried from where he lay on the porch. "The walking dead cannot feel pain! The only way to stop one is to cut off its head!"

The zombie groaned.

"Oh, I don't reckon we'll have to go cuttin' off any heads tonight," said Hallam. He reached for his gun. "But I do plan to keep this fella covered until we find out what's goin' on here."

Eliza Dutton spoke from the shadows at the other end of the porch. "Don't, Mr. Hallam." She came forward into the moonlight. It shone on the pistol in her hand.

The zombie in the flowerbed rolled onto its side and started cursing. It sat up and rubbed its jaw, then asked angrily, "What the hell did you hit me with, a two-by-four?"

Hallam ignored the creature and kept his eyes on Eliza Dutton, figuring she was the greater threat at the moment. "Where's the houngan?" he asked as he took his hand away from his gun.

Another figure came scurrying around the corner of the house and hurried over to the zombie. "Casey, you all right?" the newcomer asked worriedly.

"Yeah, Al," replied the zombie. "That big son of a bitch walloped me, that's all. Hey, lady, you said all we had to do was kill one little guy. Where'd this other jazzbo come from?"

"Will you two shut up?" Eliza grated. "Obviously, things didn't work out as planned."

Martin Larribee was still sitting on the porch. "E-Eliza?" He sounded stunned. "What are you doing?"

Eliza Dutton sighed. "Getting rid of you, Martin. And don't act so surprised. You blackmailed me into your bed, after all. My God, I was engaged to Geoffrey Mason! I would have played the lead in all of his pictures from now on!"

"But I . . . I thought you'd come to love me."

"A writer? Please, Martin, be reasonable."

Hallam had pieced some of it together on the drive up here, and now he thought he had the rest of it figured out. "You got Mason to suggest that Larribee go out to the old plantation house, didn't you, ma'am? Did you pay some fellas to pretend to put on a voodoo ritual?"

"No, that was real," Eliza said as she came a step closer.

The gun in her hand never wavered. "I heard about it from one of the maids in the hotel who was as impressed by the gods of Hollywood as she was by the gods of voodoo. I had learned enough about how seriously they take all that nonsense that I thought there was a good chance Martin wouldn't come back alive."

"But when he did, you got the idea to get rid of him once the two of you came back here."

"Imaginative people are easily frightened. I toyed with the idea of trying to actually scare him to death." Eliza shrugged. "But that was going to take too long."

Hallam jerked a thumb at the fake zombie and houngan. "So you decided to just have these two knock him off. You must not have liked it much when he called me."

"You were an annoyance, Mr. Hallam. But if you hadn't happened to come along tonight, everything would have been fine. Martin would have been dead—after having been made to suffer like I've suffered—and his death would have been blamed on zombies . . . or on Geoffrey."

"Would've made it hard for you to go back to Mason if he was under suspicion of murder."

"There are other producers in Hollywood."

Hallam knew she was right about that. Everything was easily replaceable in Hollywood, especially when you didn't have to worry about morals or honor or anything of the sort.

"What did Larribee have on you, anyway? I reckon it must've been something pretty bad if the studio could use it to break your contract."

"The little bastard found out somehow that Gertrude Singleton is still wanted on prostitution and narcotics charges back in Illinois."

The only reason she's telling me this, thought Hallam, *is that she doesn't plan on me leaving here alive. And those two fools she hired to help her will die, too, more than likely. A clean sweep, and she's in the clear, ready to move on to the next important man who can help her career, now that her detour into Larribee's bed is over.*

"You know, as cool as you are about this, ma'am, I'd bet you've pulled the trigger a few times before."

"The less said about that, the better," Eliza noted.

The barrel of the gun in her hand came up slightly, and Hallam knew she was going to fire. He tensed, ready to try a leap to one side and a desperate grab for his own gun.

"Damn!" exclaimed the zombie. "What the hell is that?"

Eliza hesitated and turned her head. Hallam knew he

ought to reach for his gun, but instead something made him look, too, and he saw the same thing the others had. Martin Larribee pushed himself back against the wall of the house and screamed.

Things were coming out of the woods around the clearing where the old house sat. Things that walked slowly and awkwardly, not like men but like creatures that had once been men.

The night breeze carried a foul scent to Hallam's nose. It smelled for all the world like rotten meat. He heard something that sounded like the beating of a drum, but it might have been the pounding of his own heart.

"What the hell?" said Eliza Dutton.

Hallam counted six of the things spread out in a half-circle. At first he had thought this might be another of Eliza's vicious tricks, but she sounded just as startled and frightened as Larribee was.

"Let's get out of here!"

That was Casey, the fake zombie. He and the other man, who had masqueraded as a houngan to frighten Larribee, ran toward the woods, trying to dart past the shambling figures. With shocking swiftness, two of the creatures lurched into their path and intercepted them. Casey was a big man, bigger than the thing that had hold of him, but it jerked him into the air as if he were a child. Casey screamed as bones began to crack in his body.

The other man didn't cry out at all. He couldn't. Bony fingers were locked around his throat, stifling any sound.

Hallam wasn't worried about Eliza Dutton anymore. He palmed out the Colt and brought it up. He'd seen gents who were hopped up before, and he figured that's what he was looking at now. But he'd never seen anything that couldn't be brought down with enough lead. There was plenty of moonlight for him to aim by as he squeezed off two shots.

Both slugs went through the right knee of the nearest creature. It fell as that leg collapsed underneath it.

But then it got back up again, seemingly without feeling any pain. Balancing awkwardly on its one good leg, it started toward the house again.

Hallam's jaw tightened, and he muttered, "Damn." He shot the other leg out from under the thing.

"The head!" screamed Martin Larribee. "You have to cut off the head!"

Sure enough, the creature Hallam had wounded kept coming, pulling itself along the ground with its arms.

Hallam reached into his coat pocket with one hand while he flipped open the Colt's cylinder with the other and dumped the empty shells. He thumbed fresh cartridges into the gun, loading all six chambers this time.

He had faced down owlhoots all over the West. This was no different, he told himself. A fella just had to keep a cool head. . . .

Hallam brought up the Colt and blasted six slugs through the skull of the closest creature. That pretty much took its whole head off. It managed another step or two, then pitched to the ground and scrabbled around a little before finally growing still.

Hallam was already reloading again, trying to calculate mentally how many shells he had and how many it was going to take to fight off the . . . the . . .

Oh, hell, he thought, *might as well call the critters zombies.*

Eliza was firing at another of the creatures, but her aim wasn't as good as Hallam's. She hit it in the head a couple of times, but that didn't slow it down. The zombie reached the edge of the porch and threw itself toward her, breaking through the rotten railing and getting its hands on her. She shrieked and fought frantically, but the zombie was too strong for her by far.

"Let go of her!" howled Martin Larribee. Suddenly he was on his feet, throwing himself at Eliza and the creature that had hold of her. He battered it with his fists, but it swatted him aside. The zombie jerked Eliza's forearm upward and clamped his mouth on it, tearing out a ragged chunk of flesh as she screamed and spasmed.

Hallam tossed the Colt from his right hand to his left—the old border shift—then yanked the Bowie knife from the sheath at the back of his neck. He swung it with all his strength at the zombie. The razor-sharp blade sliced through rotting flesh, grated on bone, and then the zombie's head toppled off its shoulders. The thing collapsed, and so did Eliza.

Hallam swung around, saw that Martin Larribee was lying huddled against the house, either dead or unconscious. The detective drove the point of the Bowie into the wall so that it stayed there, quivering, within easy reach if he needed it. He pivoted, saw that another of the creatures was almost at the porch, and fired left-handed. The thing's head exploded, making the stink in the air even worse, and it went down.

Three of them were done for. The one with the legs shot out from under it finally made it to the porch and started pulling itself up the steps. Hallam took a step and swung his leg, and the toe of his boot caught the zombie under the chin. He hoped the thing's bones were brittle. The kick drove the zombie's head back. There was a sharp cracking and ripping sound, and the head came completely off its shoulders to fly through the air like a football that Jim Thorpe had just punted.

Hallam put his back against the wall of the house and reloaded the Colt yet again. Only two of the zombies were left, the ones that had been occupied with Casey and Al until now, hunched over the bodies of the hired killers, shredding and tearing with fingers and teeth. Hallam snapped the Colt's cylinder closed, took aim, and blew the head off one of them. That finally got the attention of the other. It stood up and lurched toward the house, its face smeared black with blood in the moonlight.

Hallam reached in his pocket and closed his fingers around his last four cartridges.

He felt fear rising in him as he thumbed the shells into the gun. He was operating mostly on instinct now; that was the only thing that kept him from giving in to hysteria. He closed the cylinder. If four shots weren't enough, there was still the Bowie. He told himself he would carve that damned zombie from gizzard to gullet before he'd let it chomp on him.

The Colt bucked against his palm—one, two, three, four times. Shards of bone and the slime of decayed brains flew through the air. The last zombie fell forward on the steps, twitched a few times, then lay still.

Hallam heard a faint whimpering and looked down to see Martin Larribee sitting up again, his back propped against the wall of the house.

A faint rustling sounded from the trees. Hallam's eyes jerked in that direction. If anything else came after him tonight, he'd have to rely on the Bowie to fight it off.

The rustling died away. Breathing shallowly because of the stench in the air, Hallam watched the woods, and after a few moments, his instincts told him that whatever had been out there was gone. The houngan, more than likely. But without the zombies to do his bidding, there was a limit to how much the voodoo priest could do.

Hallam blinked and rubbed the back of his left hand across his eyes. He was starting to think crazy, too. He believed that folks could get so caught up in their religion that they'd follow somebody clear across the country for vengeance, but that didn't mean the gents he'd shot—and decapitated with his Bowie—and flat-out kicked the head off one of them—that didn't mean they were really the walking dead.

A moan of pain came from Eliza Dutton. Hallam holstered the empty Colt, slid the Bowie back into its sheath, and reached down to grab Larribee's collar. He hauled the Englishman to his feet and shook him.

"Can you drive?"

"Wh-what?"

"Can you drive the gal's car?"

Larribee shuddered. "I . . . I think so."

"Good. I'll put her in it, and you take her to the hospital. She's lost some blood from that arm, but she might still be all right."

"I can't do that! What will I tell them?"

"There's wolves and coyotes in these hills, even now. Tell 'em you were attacked by one or the other. Hell, you're the writer, Larribee. Make something up."

Larribee gestured shakily at the carnage around the front of the house. "But . . . what about all this?"

"I don't reckon I feel much like tryin' to explain it to the cops. Do you?"

A moment of silence, then, "No. No, I don't. But Eliza. . . . She tried to kill me."

Hallam lifted Eliza Dutton's unconscious form and started toward her car. Over his shoulder, he said, "Next time see if you can get a gal without makin' her so mad she wants to sic a zombie on you."

✜　✜　✜

Hallam saw Martin Larribee only one more time. The Englishman stopped by his place to give Hallam a check and announced that he was going back to England.

"As you might expect, Hollywood holds few charms for me these days."

"What about Miss Dutton?" asked Hallam.

"I've made arrangements with a sanitarium to have her cared for. The doctors say there's a faint chance she might someday emerge from the catatonic state she's in, but they don't hold out much real hope."

Hallam shook his head. It bothered him that Eliza Dutton wouldn't face the legal consequences of what she had done. On the other hand, he didn't want to have to testify in court about the things he had seen up there off Mulholland Drive.

There was no real evidence, anyway. The cops, tipped off by the anonymous call Hallam had made to them, had found the bodies of Casey and Al, but the corpses had been so torn up their deaths had been put down to an animal attack.

There had been no sign of the zombies.

The houngan had disposed of them somehow, or maybe after a while the destroyed creatures had turned to dust or something. Hallam didn't know, didn't want to know. All that mattered was that it was over.

"Taking care of Miss Dutton in a place like that is goin' to be expensive."

"Yes, well, you see . . . I really do love her. I forced her to break off her engagement to Geoffrey and stay with me because I love her so much."

Hallam didn't say anything to that. Nothing he could say would mean anything to Larribee anyway.

"I'm on my way to catch a train now," Larribee went on. "When I get to New York, I'll be taking a boat for Liverpool. No offense, Mr. Hallam, but if I never see your fair country again, that will be fine with me."

Hallam grunted. "Don't reckon we'll miss you, either."

Larribee shrugged and turned to go down the walk from the foyer of Hallam's apartment building to the cab waiting at the curb. His head twitched nervously from side to side. He got into the vehicle and it drove away.

Hallam stood there long enough to see another cab go by, as if it were following the one Larribee was in. A dark face in the back seat turned toward the detective for a moment as the second cab went past. Then it was gone, too.

Martin Larribee will spend the rest of his life—however long that might be—looking over his shoulder, and probably for good cause, thought Hallam.

And for a while, Lucas Hallam might be checking his own back trail, watching the shadows, listening for the soft, shuffling tred of inhuman footsteps in the night. . . .

It's a good thing I'm just a hard-headed old cowboy and don't believe in such nonsense, he told himself as he went inside and shut the door.

Scenes from a Foreign Horror Video, with Zombies and Tasteful Nudity

MARK McLAUGHLIN

Grainy, sweeping shots of skyscrapers, crowded metro sidewalks, hectic traffic, and a pale young woman entering an office building. The Daughter. Her thick black hair is piled high, and held in place with several large silver clasps.

Suddenly the camera sweeps up, up to a blazing sun, and shimmering blood-red letters appear: *Nightmare of the Watching Dead.* The words fade away, and then names, names, and more names appear, shimmer, and disappear. Then the camera sweeps down, down to a crow picking at a glowing eyeball on the hood of a black limousine.

The Reporter gasps as the bird flies away with its juicy prize. "Did you see that?" he whispers. "A terrible omen." He has deep, sullen eyes and gray streaks at the temples.

A passerby—a fortyish woman with maroon lipstick—laughs, though it sounds more like a bark. She is The Nurse. "I have seen worse," she says, matter-of-factly.

✛ ✛ ✛

The Heavyset Man cruises the Internet, clicking here, clicking there. He is wearing a stained bathrobe and is sitting at his desk in the middle of his cluttered apartment. A crow watches him from the sill of an open window.

"What is this?" the man says to no one. "A website about witches?" The screen is filled with images of pale women with long, straight red hair. "They are pretty, these witches."

The image of an eyeball pops up in the corner of the screen. The eyeball begins to pulse with a greenish light. Intrigued, The Heavyset Man clicks on this link.

Instantly, a beam of green energy shoots out of the monitor. It splits in midair and hits the man in both eyes. He leans to one side, then falls out of his chair and hits the floor, dead.

The crow flutters into the room, settling on the man's neck. The bird leans forward, gently slides its beak around one of his eyeballs, then gives the orb a sharp tug, pulling it free.

The crow flies out the window, and the camera watches it disappear, up into the roiling clouds. When the camera turns to view the room again, the body is gone.

✝ ✝ ✝

A tropical island at night. Too many animal cries—growls, hoots, monkey-shrieks, and crow-caws—echo at the same time.

In a pavilion swathed in mosquito netting, The Fat Witch hands a goblet to The Young Witch. Both are pale with red hair.

"Soon," says the fat one, "everyone will be screaming. No one can withstand the dead when they are instilled with the nuclear life-force." Occasionally, the movements of her lips match her words.

"Yes, it is a perfect plan." The young one drinks deep from the goblet, leaving a smear of red, too thick and shiny for wine, on her top lip. "But how shall we begin?" She wipes at the stain with the back of her hand, but only succeeds in spreading it along her cheek.

"The answer is easy. I have already begun the process. How the fools love their Internet computers." The fat one turns suddenly, pointing, and the camera zooms in the direction of her finger. A computer monitor sits on a makeshift altar of bloody bones and broken keyboards. The screen of the monitor is broken, and a decayed hand is pinned on some of the larger shards of glass. The hand softly glows with green energy.

"The Internet, yes." The Young Witch nods. "They do not know it is controlled by witches and nuclear power."

"We set sail in the morning," hisses The Fat Witch.

The hand twitches, fingers churning like the legs of an eager spider.

✝ ✝ ✝

The morning sun shines down on The Businessman's patio.

Here, practically everything is white—the metal furniture, the tiles, the marble rim of the pool. The water is blue, but it is a pale, oddly milky sky blue.

The Daughter has finished swimming and is drying herself with a fluffy white towel. She is the pale woman who had entered the office building earlier. She looks up at the sky, lost in thought.

(*I've done this before. I know it. A hundred, a thousand times before.*)

She walks to a table where The Businessman, her father, is having breakfast with The Scientist, her boyfriend.

"Father," she says, "I saw a news program last night. They were saying terrible things about the Internet."

"Ridiculous. An outrage." The Businessman spears a sausage with his fork. "The Internet is good. My best investment yet. What lies were they saying on the television?"

"Pay them no mind—they are jealous," The Scientist says. He is very handsome, with boyish good looks.

The Daughter picks up and eats a sausage from The Scientist's plate. "They say the Internet has too many websites about witches on it, and that people are disappearing. And, there have been many terrible omens. In fact, last night I had a dream." She takes another sausage. "I dreamed that mother was not dead. I dreamed that she was a witch on an island, and that she was very fat and evil."

The Businessman turns to The Scientist. "These liars on the television are upsetting Miracula. Take her into the house and look at the Internet with her. See all the good things it has to show."

"I will do so immediately," says The Scientist.

"I do not like it when you two gang up on me," The girl says, pouting. "And I do not like it that you will not tell me about mother. You say she is dead, but even if that is so, I still have a right to know more about her."

The Businessman takes her hand. "Someday I will tell you everything." He then nods to The Scientist, and the young man leads her into the house.

✛ ✛ ✛

Scenes of the young couple looking at the Internet, taking turns clicking on this and that.

Scenes of The Nurse examining ancient, leatherbound books in cobwebbed chambers.

Scenes of zombies stumbling through dark, filthy alleys, tipping over trash cans.

Scenes of birds and bats flying out of shadowed church entrances.

Scenes of crows, always crows, with eyeballs in their beaks.

A close-up of one of the glowing eyeballs. The voice of The Fat Witch is heard: "How much they see, my pretty pets."

✛ ✛ ✛

Midnight. An enormous room filled with computers, monitors, cables. The very walls are lined with computers. Tiny lights of blue and white twinkle like stars.

This room is the mighty heart of the Internet. Over the door is a framed portrait of The Businessman.

A fly lands on the portrait. The camera zooms in tight on the insect, cherishing the repulsive details of its filthy, squirming mouth. The fly zips off and the camera follows it, up and down, all over the room.

The fly darts through a disk slot in one of the computers. The camera continues to follow it on and on, through a mad eternity of flashing lights, shifting geometric patterns, clouds of blue lightning, and everywhere, eyeballs attached to sparking cables. The eyeballs glow green with radioactivity. Crows fly in to add new eyeballs, popping them onto free cables, or to take away old ones that have lost their glow.

✛ ✛ ✛

A cemetery under a full moon. Tombstones, dead trees, statues of angels with broken wings.

A young couple embrace, sitting on top of a large granite tombstone. A twig-snap echoes.

"What was that sound?" the woman says, startled.

"A stray dog. A cat. Nothing at all. Kiss me." The man has a gentle face and full lips.

"I tell you, I heard something." The woman looks around, then sees a faintly glowing figure, partially hidden by a tree, about thirty feet away. "My God. What is that?"

"You," the young man shouts to the intruder. "We see you. What are you doing there?"

Slowly the shape moves forward. It is The Heavyset Man, still in his robe, which is now even filthier. His body glows a faint, sickly green. He stares at them with his single eye as he advances. A thin line of green slime drips from the empty eye socket.

"Hideous," the man whispers.

"We must get out of here," the woman cries, tugging at her lover's arm.

"No. I want to see this. I have heard of these zombies." He moves a few feet toward the creature. "He is very slow. I can escape him easily."

"You are insane," the woman says.

"They say on the television that the Internet is responsible." The young man moves closer, even as the zombie inches toward him. "There may be a reward for finding one."

"Madness," the woman hisses.

The man turns to his sweetheart. "If I had a rope, then I—" While he is looking away, the zombie rushes forward and leaps upon him, digging his meaty hands into the man's belly.

The zombie then looks up to stare at the screaming

woman. A green bolt of energy blazes forth from his eye, and splits to strike both of her eyes.

She falls to the ground.

A crow lands on her neck.

✣   ✣   ✣

The press conference.

The Businessman and his associates are seated behind a long table. Each has his own microphone and glass of water.

Facing them, in rows of metal chairs, sit The Reporter and his colleagues from various television stations and newspapers.

"More and more witch websites are appearing," The Reporter suddenly shouts, standing up. "Plus, more zombies are being spotted. They have attacked many innocent people. You cannot deny there is a connection."

"That is not a question," The Businessman says smugly. "Are you deciding the news for yourself? Is that how it works? And you call yourselves reporters."

This enrages the media people, and many begin angrily shouting questions:

"What about the crows of death?"

"Do you realize that radioactivity is involved?"

"Can you explain the missing eyes?"

Suddenly The Fat Witch enters the room through a door behind the reporters, and The Businessman stands up. "What are you doing here?" he says. "Are you again trying to destroy my life?"

She smiles and nods, and steps aside as glowing zombies shamble into the room. They dig their strong hands into the throats and bellies of the media people. Green bolts fire from their eyes. Crows flutter gracefully into the room.

In the confusion, The Businessman slips away through a door behind some large potted ferns. The Fat Witch sees this and follows him.

Once she is through the door, she finds herself at the top of a metal framework staircase. She sees The Businessman on the landing below. The two regard each other.

"So you are behind all of this. I suspected as much. You and your witches, making my life into an insane delusion." The Businessman's face is beaded with sweat. "Why can't you leave me alone?"

"Fool," she cries. "Can you not see that together, we are unstoppable?"

"I once loved you," he says, "but I cannot live in a world of misery and death. You want to control everything."

"Admit it. My power excites you." The fat one moves a step closer to him. "I love you. I am your destiny. Together, we can rule the planet. Without me, you will be dead. Your corpse will provide food for my zombies and the crows. You will be nothing. Do you hear me? Nothing."

"You talk of love. What do you know of such a thing? To you, it is just another word." He turns and scrambles down the stairs.

The Fat Witch does not follow. "There is no escape," she whispers. "No escape." A tear glides down the powdered roundness of her cheek.

At the base of the stairs, The Businessman opens the door to the parking garage. Glowing hands seize his arms, his shoulders, his throat.

✛ ✛ ✛

Scenes of The Nurse, rushing through busy offices, smashing computers with a hammer.

Scenes of zombies staggering down busy streets, into department stores and restaurants and hospitals.

Scenes of merciless hands tearing into soft flesh.

Scenes of glowing teeth ripping into gleaming innards.

A close-up of a beak, lovingly ripping an eye from its socket.

✛ ✛ ✛

Twilight. A parking lot outside of a church.

"It is all so impossible," The Daughter says, wrapping her arms around The Scientist, crying on his shoulder.

(*Why am I doing this? I do not love him. He is boring. He babbles like a fool.*)

"I have learned the truth, Miracula," the handsome man says. "Witches have seized control of the Internet through the power of nuclear reactions. They are using radioactivity to reconfigure the brainwaves of crows, and to re-energize deceased human tissue. They can even download images through the eyes of the living dead. Their power is horrifying."

The Daughter points to the church. "Then why doesn't God help us?"

He shakes his head. "I am afraid even God cannot defeat the science of the witches."

The Nurse walks up to the couple. She is tired and breathing heavily. In the fading light, her maroon lipstick looks black. "Excuse me. We have not met, but I know much about you from an old acquaintance. I used to be a friend of your mother."

"My mother? Tell me about her." The Daughter grabs The Nurse by the wrist. "I have waited so long to learn her identity."

"You will wish you did not know," the older woman says. "The truth will break your heart."

"And what is the truth?" The Scientist asks. "Tell us now."

"Very well." The Nurse takes a deep breath and stares into the girl's eyes. "Your mother is The Queen of the Witches. She is the most evil creature to ever walk the earth. I was once her handmaiden, but then I learned I was going to have a baby, so I escaped and hid myself from her. I did not want my child exposed to her vileness." She strokes the girl's cheek. "A few years later, when you were born, your father had the same thought. He stole you away from your mother while she was asleep. I helped him to hide from her. Your mother has been waiting for the day when she can at least reclaim you. Our only hope now is to destroy all the Internet computers."

"I want to meet my mother," The Daughter says. "My love will make her good."

(*I do not believe that. Why did I even say it? Why am I inviting doom into my life?*)

"Impossible. You must hide," the older woman says. "I have looked in all the old books. You cannot win." Suddenly she sees The Young Witch at the far end of the parking lot. "There. That woman is spying on us. She is your half-sister. Her father was one of the living dead."

"The living dead? Then she is a demon." The Daughter looks with fright—and curiosity, too—at the slender red-haired woman. "But running away cannot solve the problem." She turns and walks toward her half-sister.

"We must stop her," says The Nurse.

"Let her go. She has goodness in her heart," The Scientist replies. "She will speak to the witches on behalf of humanity, and God." He looks from the older woman to the church.

A moment later, The Daughter and The Young Witch enter a black limousine, which drives off into the gloom.

✛ ✛ ✛

Scenes of zombies ripping the clothes off of attractive men and women.

In some scenes, they simply devour the living. But in others, they drag their prey into the shadows, subjecting them to horrible pleasures of the flesh.

Close-up of a television screen.

"The situation is a catastrophe without end," says The Reporter. He is badly bruised, with scratches on his forehead and jaw. "The hungry dead continue to infect the world with their horror and radioactivity. The streets are filled with the torn bodies of the innocent. Plus, it has been revealed that the zombies are now forcing their victims to succumb to foul carnal acts. Authorities fear that these acts of abomination will result in grotesque cross-breed births. It is rumored that some of the resultant infants may grow to become Internet witches. Stay tuned to this television channel for further developments."

✢ ✢ ✢

An enormous cave lit by blazing torches.

The Daughter's clothes are torn, and she is wrapped in chains. She has been placed on a bloodstained stone altar.

"So," The Fat Witch says. "We meet again, Miracula. I am your mother, The Queen of the Witches. Does that make you happy, my child? That means you are a Witch Princess."

"That does not matter," The Daughter says. "All I have ever wanted is your love. Forget your evil and be a good and kind mother to be."

(*This old whore is repulsive. I wish that she was dead. But I am trapped.*)

"I could not do so even if I tried," the fat one says. "I could never forget the thrill of my great and terrible vices. A simple life means nothing to me. You are the one in the chains, but mine is the greater prison. Join me in the exquisite hell of ultimate power."

The Fat Witch touches a finger to The Daughter's forehead. Her black hair slowly begins to turn red.

"I do not want your madness," The Daughter cries.

The Young Witch enters the cave, followed by a male zombie. It is The Scientist. Both of them are naked except for loose strips of cloth wrapped around their hips. The Young Witch fondles the zombie's face and well-muscled shoulders, and then leads him into the shadows.

The fat one touches the chest of The Daughter. Her plump finger is just a few inches from the captive's heart. A red glow spreads through the girl's body, and she screams.

"There is no escape, my sweet," The Fat Witch says. "Soon the world will be a radioactive wasteland inhabited by witches and the living dead."

The Young Witch, satisfied, emerges from the shadows. She takes the knife from beside the altar and, laughing wildly, thrusts it repeatedly into the chest of The Scientist. Then she jabs it into his empty eye socket.

The fat one smirks as the zombie falls to the cave floor.

Then she turns back to The Daughter. "Waves of my energy are surging through you. Soon you will feel the power of my vast knowledge. And knowledge is simply another word for evil."

The Daughter begins to look around, and see—

(*Now I see why I cannot remember my childhood. Why sometimes words appear in the sky. Why there is a toilet in the bathroom, but I never need to use it. This is not life—it is a twisted fantasy, a nightmare born in some diseased brain. No matter what I want, what I wish, it will never change. Why doesn't my God help me? Why—?*)

"Why does God allow this to happen?" the girl screams.

The fat one throws back her head and laughs. "Perhaps your God finds this all very amusing. Yes, no doubt He is watching right now, enjoying this quaint little drama: the end of the world."

The Young Witch laughs as well. "Dear Miracula's hair is now red and her eyes—see how they glow with fire," she cries.

"But I do not want to be a monster," The Daughter screams.

(*But I do. I want to destroy this filthy world of lies.*)

She begins to cry. "I want to go back to my old life. I was happy then."

(*Inside, I have always been miserable. I want to die.*)

Suddenly a figure looms before them all. It is the zombie that had once been The Scientist. He pulls the knife out of his eye socket. With a roar of triumph, he lashes out, cutting through the pale throat of The Young Witch. He plunges the knife into the heart of The Fat Witch, releasing a torrent of black blood. He then begins to unwrap the chains that bind The Daughter.

"I—I love you," he croaks through his dead, dry lips.

"And I love you," she says, her smile suddenly hard and twisted.

(*You disgust me. But that is a small matter. I am just a puppet hanging from unseen strings, dancing for a God who does not care.*)

She takes the hand of the creature and leads him out of the cave, through winding passageways, into a world that they now rule. An endless domain of chaos, agony, and tears.

Names, names, and more names. Darkness. Static.

Rewind.

La Carrera de la Muerte

JOE MURPHY

The skeletons stopped running; they dangled from the roofs, papier-mâché legs growing still as the breeze from the ancient bus melted into the afternoon heat. At least six radios, all tuned to different stations, babbled over the excited crowd inside the bus. Vincent stood and tried to stretch without jamming an elbow into the matronly woman beside him. In spite of the heat he shivered, hunched his shoulders, and followed the passengers out.

Ladera looked the same as last year. Grinning skeletons hung from the eaves of the shops and the hotel. Garlands of white yucca blossoms, already yellowed from dust, adorned the doorways. Up the street by the fountain, a mariachi band brayed a passionate *cumbia*, accompanied by a dozen hammers as shopkeepers boarded up their store windows.

The driver brought Vincent's small bag with his running gear. Vincent tipped him. The driver stared at him, then tucked the bill into a shirt pocket. Only a trickle of passengers made their way toward the hotel, a two-storied white plaster building, and the largest in tiny Ladera. Vincent followed, eager for the shady darkness promised by the hotel doorway.

An old woman, already in a white festival dress, stepped from the darkness. Her eyes instantly fixed on his and she scowled, clenching small, bony fists that looked like leather knots in the sun.

"Greetings, Señora Del Castillo," he said, forcing a smile. "How are—?"

"She'll kill you." The señora's jaw worked harshly, her English sharp and quick. She marched in front of him, barring his way, and jammed her fists against her hips. "She ruined everything she ever touched."

"I don't know what you're talking about." Vincent set down his suitcase, wincing as his spine crackled, still kinked by the long trip from Matamoros. His hands spread innocently.

"My husband made a mistake," the woman shrilled. "Neither of you can change that."

Some nearby shopkeepers turned their way. Customers looking over the merchandise spread on bright blankets in front of the shops stared at Vincent. A young man in baggy

American jeans and a sleeveless undershirt stopped boarding up the hotel windows and moved to the señora's side.

What little Spanish Vincent knew deserted him when the young man spoke. Señora Del Castillo answered in a gentler, but no less rapid burst, and the young man glared at him, the hammer lifting slightly.

"My grandmother just told you, hombre." The young man stepped in front of Señora Del Castillo. A cruel grin spread across his face and he lifted the hammer to point at the bus. "There's no place for you. Go now."

"Look, please." Vincent clenched his hands, hoping to keep them from trembling. He hadn't come for a fight. What he had come for frightened him more than enough. "I have a reservation. Your grandfather said so. If you'll just check—"

"Are you deaf, gringo?" The man stepped in close. "Or just stupid?" He shoved the American in the chest with his free hand. Stumbling back, Vincent tripped over his running bag to sprawl in the dirt. He glanced back at the bus driver's expressionless face. Vincent caught hold of the bag and hauled himself up, ready to fling it at the young man.

"Ernesto!" A reedy voice crackled. Instantly the young man turned. Vincent's gaze followed. An elderly man in an immaculate white suit had come around the corner of the hotel.

"Señor Del Castillo!" Vincent found his own voice too shrill, almost like a teenager's, and heat rose to his cheeks. "It's good to—"

The old man's voice cracked and his wife flinched, stepping back. The young man—Ernesto, no doubt—retreated with his grandmother as Señor Del Castillo limped closer. Voices rose, the bursts of Spanish so quick Vincent couldn't catch a word.

Señora Del Castillo whirled abruptly and marched into the hotel, her husband shouting, lifting his arms and cane toward the mountains as if appealing to a higher power.

"Ernesto." The old man turned and leveled at the younger another burst. Ernesto's fingers clenched, and the look he gave Vincent could have skinned paint off the bus. Then, returning to his work at the window, Ernesto pounded in nails with such fury the hotel shuddered.

"Ah, Señor Walterson." Del Castillo's voice dropped to a gentler tone. "It is good to see you again."

"And you, sir." Vincent hurried to grip the elder man's offered hand. He leaned forward and carefully kissed Del Castillo's cheek. According to the guidebook, this was the appropriate greeting between two good friends, yet his own cheeks burned.

Del Castillo's polite smile broadened as Vincent pulled away. Vincent released his hand and fought not to wipe his own on his jeans; his palm still stung from the fall.

"I'm sorry you received such a rude greeting." Del Castillo picked up Vincent's bag and nodded toward the hotel. "My wife is a good woman, but age hasn't softened her feelings."

"Perhaps it's my fault." Vincent studied the old man's face. "I didn't realize I made such a bad impression last year."

"My wife quite enjoyed both you and your family." Del Castillo placed a hand on Vincent's shoulder and guided him inside. "You do not bring Señora Walterson and the *niños*?"

"No, sir." Vincent blinked, eyes adjusting to the dimness. Sweat beaded on his skin; it was too damn hot to talk about the divorce. "My wife felt other obligations were . . . more important."

"Such obligations lead us to our fate." Del Castillo opened a narrow door and gestured Vincent inside. The room was tiny, a single bed, a small table with a blue pitcher and basin. Vincent wondered when the pitcher's water would boil; with the windows boarded up, the place seemed stifling. "The room is to your liking?"

"Perfect." Vincent turned to the old man. "I very much appreciate you fitting me in. You were so busy this time last year."

"Ahh, festival time." Del Castillo set down the running bag and lifted his hands with pride. "People are dying to get in, no?" He laughed loudly and started to leave.

"Thank you." Vincent reached out, not quite daring to touch the man's elbow.

Del Castillo turned, eyes like black pits as they studied him. "I will see you tonight on the rooftop?"

Vincent's breath choked in his lungs. Now, in the darkness, he couldn't keep the trembling from his hands. "Uh . . . I was hoping for something more."

"You don't return as a spectator?"

"Is such a thing permitted?"

"This is a local festival." Del Castillo shook his head. "Even those from other villages don't join in, unless they have relatives here."

"Then it isn't possible." Vincent's knees gave out and he sank down on the bed. Relief, such a blessed thing.

"I didn't say that." Del Castillo rubbed a cleanly shaven jaw.

"I'm in the best shape I've ever been in," Vincent said. Del Castillo reached out abruptly, pulled a cord, and a weak glow yellowed the room. The elder man settled down beside Vincent and sighed. He looked at Vincent again.

"I mean . . ." Vincent searched for the words, something the old man would understand that didn't quite admit his reasons for returning. "I mean that I can go the distance. I would like to do so in honor of you and Ladera."

Del Castillo shook his head and studied the floor. "You haven't come for sport."

Vincent's fingers gripped the mattress. Ernesto couldn't have hit him harder with the hammer. How easily the old man had demolished the façade he'd hoped to build. Without doubt, Del Castillo knew why Vincent had returned.

"Even my wife has figured that out." Del Castillo clutched his cane and rose. "You intrude on more than a simple festival. This is a family matter."

"I tried to stay away." Vincent looked up at him. "I really did."

Del Castillo limped to the doorway. He turned, glaring at Vincent. "If you will be part of it, then you'll be part of everything. You must place yourself in my hands and accept whatever is meant to happen." His voice grew louder as he spoke, until Vincent was certain the whole hotel must have heard. "Do you agree?"

"All of it." Vincent stood and looked the old man in the eye. "Whatever happens."

"There's still much to be done." Del Castillo nodded. "Come on."

Vincent swallowed; his stomach twisted into a dozen knots. He swiped at the light cord and stumbled after Del Castillo. He'd never been so frightened his whole life—or so elated.

✝ ✝ ✝

A group of men milled in front of the hotel as they emerged. Ernesto stood with them and came forward, fists balled when he saw Vincent.

"Wait here. I must talk to my grandson." Del Castillo limped over and put his arm around the younger man.

"No!" Ernesto's voice rang loud with anger. Del Castillo made a curt gesture and continued softly. Ernesto looked back at Vincent, shaking his head, eyes wide with disbelief.

Hoping not to make things worse, Vincent stared down at his shoes, refusing eye contact. Del Castillo reached up to turn

Ernesto's chin back to him and continued talking. After a moment, Ernesto grinned.

"Come along now," the old man called and the two started down the road. "Everyone!" Vincent hurried after them; the others, staring at him, followed.

Ladera, which meant "hillside," perched on a broadly sloping mound with higher-thrusting mountains, part of the Sierra Madre Orientals, overpowering the eastern sky. The road to Ladera wound up the hillside, crooking a right angle to become the village's only street.

As they walked down the road, more men joined them. Most still wore work clothes, a few carried pry bars. Their voices grew louder, more excited as they reached the village edge.

"Señor Vincent, come help me down." Del Castillo pointed toward a steep path, hidden by gnarled mesquite and sage; it led down the hillside a good three hundred yards to disappear under a stony outcropping.

Vincent took the old man's arm and helped him over a sharp ridge. "What's down there?"

"Ladera's wisdom." Del Castillo winced and clutched at Vincent's sleeve, nearly stumbling. Vincent steadied the older man. The others followed.

Sweat burned Vincent's eyes, sopping his shirt by the time they swerved beneath the outcropping's shadow. Stone blocks formed a broad wall under the ledge. It crumbled in places, and though the squared-off columns every three feet or so hinted of colonial architecture, the overall impression reminded Vincent more of the Aztec ruins he'd visited last year with his family.

He halted at the thought of Karen and the kids. The hurt in Ashley's and Heather's eyes when they realized he was leaving. The desperation in Karen's voice when she begged him to get professional help. Dark bruises had appeared on her arms and legs; he'd woken them both too many nights, breathless, drenched in sweat, arms and legs pumping as he ran Ladera's only street again and again.

Ladera. He'd known he would come back and the year had simply been a blur of bad times. Unable to focus on something so mundane as tax records, he'd lost his job. Even his running, something that had always kept him sane, deteriorated; he'd placed a lowly twentieth in the Pittsburgh Marathon. Karen had given up and finally filed for divorce.

But how could he tell her the truth? A truth that sickened even him. Until Ladera, his life had always revolved around his family. Now he had no life.

A loud burst of Spanish brought him back and Señor Del Castillo clasped his shoulder, then pointed to the stone wall. "It's time to take it down. You must help with this."

The other men had already moved forward. Some pried out the rough-cut blocks, while others stacked them nearby. They didn't look at Vincent, flowing around him as if he were a ghost. But when he stepped up to the wall someone handed him a block. A dark opening had already appeared, the cool breeze wafting through, ripe with the smell of earth.

Vincent carried his block down to the others. Another man, glancing only at the distant opening, added it to a stack. Soon the blocks were gone. A rusting grate of iron bars, pitted with age but locked by a new copper-colored padlock with a shiny steel chain, formed a barrier between them and a dark passage.

"Ah, here comes Father Hildago." Del Castillo slapped Vincent on the back. "He's just in time, eh?"

Hildago was the only man in Ladera older than Del Castillo. A gaunt Franciscan, sweating profusely in his brown cassock, Hildago moved slowly down the path, leaning heavily on the shoulder of a boy about thirteen.

The father sank down on the blocks, fanning his face with a weathered hand, and breathing heavily. His eyes met Vincent's. Frowning, the priest called Del Castillo over.

The two spoke softly, glancing the American's way while the other men lounged in the shade, smoking cigarettes. The smoke burned Vincent's throat. He was about to back off from the group, though doing so would bring him out of the shade, when Del Castillo motioned him.

"Father Hildago says you have no place in this." Del Castillo patted the space beside him, and Vincent sank down gratefully.

"Rufino here pleads a fine case." The gray-haired priest cocked his head at Del Castillo. "He tells me you helped his grandson immigrate to Pennsylvania and enter the college there. He says you're a good man. But you are an outsider. I don't know. . . ."

"I never meant to intrude. Our car broke down last year; I left my family and walked into Ladera hoping for a mechanic. I saw the festival, everything."

"True enough," Del Castillo prompted. "Be honest with the padre now. Why have you returned?"

Vincent clasped his hands and stared down again at his dusty running shoes. The bottom threatened to drop out of his stomach. To say what he felt, speak it aloud—if he admitted such a thing the priest might curse him on the spot, perhaps even set the others on him.

He'd never dared admit it, even to himself. But Karen had sensed it in the way he'd wandered, dreamlike, through their world. He'd lost the ability to focus on his work, his family. Even his children's faces eluded him when he shut his eyes. His dreams bore the same mesmerizing image, while his life swirled into an ever-shrinking vortex whose apex was this very moment.

"A girl," he began, looking up to meet the priest's expressionless eyes. "A woman, I mean. She was running and . . . and I just can't get her out of my head."

"I think he means he's infatuated," Del Castillo said, and chuckled at the shocked expression that crossed the priest's face.

"Or possessed." Father Hildago jumped to his feet and glared at them. "My English is not so good as Rufino's. I'm not sure if the correct word is *blasphemy* or *abomination!*" Whispering prayers, the priest started away.

"It's necrophilia," Del Castillo called out. "But, Padre, he speaks of Inez."

Hildago turned back to them. The priest gazed at Vincent, then at Del Castillo. Hildago returned, brushed absently at the stone, sat back down, and clasped his hands. "I will listen."

"That's her name?" Vincent resisted the urge to clutch Del Castillo's hand.

"Inez Maria Pachecho." Del Castillo nodded. "My wife's sister."

"So, Rufino—" the priest studied Del Castillo's face "—I'm to allow this because it's your wish?"

"I failed her." Del Castillo looked away, his gaze aimed at the high mountains. "You know that; you were there. Perhaps in this matter I might give her now what I couldn't give then."

"You're mad as your gringo friend." The priest rose.

"Father," Del Castillo lowered his voice. "Your sister's family, they're already here?"

The old priest turned and scowled. "Of course, they always come."

"How many of her grandchildren will participate?"

"Only one. Asdru has just come of age." The priest glanced at the thirteen-year-old who'd helped him down and grew slightly pale. "Very well," he said at last. "Señor Walterson, you must join us now."

"It's up to you." Del Castillo gestured for Vincent to precede him. "I've done my part."

Swallowing, Vincent nodded, still unsure exactly what had transpired.

Father Hildago moved to the iron gate. He lifted a key tied to a red ribbon from around his neck. The other men rose and drew into a tight knot around the priest. Bowing his head, the father began a prayer in Spanish.

Vincent understood nothing, but found himself caught up in the rhythm of the words. From time to time Hildago would glance at the mountains. Their shady patch had grown larger, darker. The vast, welling slope of the mountains glowed, bare stone crags reddening with the sun's last rays.

When twilight replaced the shade, Father Hildago's voice rose to a singsong crescendo and stopped. He turned and unlocked the gate. Young Asdru lugged the heavy chain and lock over to the masonry stacks.

"What do we do now?" Vincent whispered to Del Castillo.

"We run, of course." Del Castillo grinned and cocked his head at the others, already filing up the path.

✣ ✣ ✣

Mariachi music blared from the hotel rooftop as they entered the village. People cheered, clustered on the roofs until Vincent wondered if the smaller buildings would collapse. Children dangled papier-mâché skeletons from long sticks.

"Hurry and change your clothes." Del Castillo gripped his arm and dragged him toward the hotel door.

"My clothes?"

"You're not going to run like that, are you?" Del Castillo looked him up and down, frowning. "That's no way to make a good impression. Did you bring that jogging suit you wore last year? My wife laughed about it for days."

"But—"

"No time." The old man pushed him inside. Vincent hurried to his room and spilled his bag onto the bed. It wasn't really a jogging suit, but a running suit, the fluorescent yellow Gore-Tex windbreaker and tights he usually wore for marathons.

A gift from Karen two Christmases ago. Karen, would he ever see her again? He stared at the track shoes he'd brought, their neon streaks glittering in the weak light. He didn't have to do this.

Three distinct gunshots sounded from the roof. The crowd roared and the music blared louder. It was starting, he realized. Maybe he could get it out of his system. Maybe that's all it would take, and he could hurry home to see the counselor Karen had suggested. Quickly he dressed and jerked on his shoes. A moment later he was out the door, taking the stairs to the roof three at a time.

Vincent shouldered through the mariachi band, past a family of twelve, to the roof's edge where the old man stood, a pistol in hand.

"Ah, there you are." Del Castillo beamed at him. "And just in time. I've fired the warning shots. It begins." He pointed down the street toward the trail. The darkness wrinkled with movement.

Del Castillo levered himself down until he sat on the roof's edge, feet dangling. "This is as close as an old man comes, no?" He patted the spot next to him. "Come. Sit by me. I've no one to share the moment with."

"Where's Señora Del Castillo?" Vincent asked, squatting down and then swinging his legs over the edge.

"Apparently she's angry with me." Del Castillo smiled happily. "She's with the padre at the fountain."

Vincent squinted up the street just as someone fired off a Roman candle. The flash of brightness left flickering purple images of the chapel. Father Hildago, in an ornate robe, stood before the fountain in the churchyard. Several others clustered in a small group behind him. The old priest lifted his hands.

"Ah the padre begins the blessing early." Del Castillo chuckled. "He started too late three years ago and they almost got him. Fortunately, he can still move quickly when he has to." A rocket exploded overhead, showering the village with fizzling balls of crimson light.

"Here they come!" Del Castillo gripped his shoulder and shook him. "Now the fun begins!"

A gaunt, misshapen shadow staggered onto the road, reaching the first shops at the village edge. Children on the roof squealed with delightful terror as it pounded on the door. Some lowered their skeletons on sticks, and the shadow swiped at them. A young man, dressed in festival white, leaped from the roof and pranced toward the creature.

Another shadow came out of the darkness, then another. The young man danced before them and those on the roofs roared. A string of flashes blossomed in the night sky.

"Rhapeal, Imanuel, and Carlos Pachecho," Del Castillo told Vincent pointing at each of the lumbering figures in turn.

"Brothers?" Vincent asked as more shadows staggered from the darkness.

"Ernesto's cousins." Del Castillo began clapping when a smaller white-dressed figure leaped from the roof of the stall across the street. "There goes the padre's grandnephew."

The kid wiggled his fanny at the nearest of the approaching dead. Shrilling laughter, he dashed in a circle around a dead one as it reached for him with a strangely crooked arm.

"Asdru . . . Asdru . . . Asdru," those on the roof chanted.

"He's a brave boy," Del Castillo called proudly. "And quick, as well."

More dead lumbered into view, staggering, crawling, flopping along with missing limbs. Other white-suited men dropped from the roofs to run before them, taunting the dead, dashing round to touch their backs or ducking under their clutching hands.

"Ahh, the Remoras boy has gotten really brave!" Del Castillo aimed a finger at a teenager who stood with his back to the cluster of approaching dead. Not until their knobby fingers touched his back did the young man leap forward. One of the dead tumbled down, still clutching the kid's shirt.

The boy fell, and the dead dropped on top of him. Two runners rushed to their comrade, dragging him by his feet from the lifeless hands. Before the slower creatures could converge, they hauled the Remoras boy up and, laughing, pranced away.

"Show-off. They'll get him one of these days." Del Castillo shook his head.

"Guess I'd better get down there." Vincent stared at the ever-growing throng of dead clustering around the shops, their taloned fingers reaching for those on the roofs. "You know, I never realized you had so many."

"We are rich with death." Del Castillo's chest puffed out. "The secrets they'll share this night will make us even richer. The dead save their deepest wisdom for the bravest, you know." He put a hand on Vincent's shoulder. "But wait, I don't want you down there yet."

Swallowing, Vincent nodded, surprised at the sudden gust of relief blowing through him.

"There's Inez." Del Castillo pointed into the night as another string of rockets went off. But Vincent already knew. He'd recognized her even before the rocket flashes revealed her desiccated features. The sublime symmetry in the swing of her sticklike arms. The sultry smoothness as each leg lifted, knee poised in eager anticipation before the climactic thrust of her heel strike.

She sped up the road with a grace divine, a surety of motion that held his eyes and pulled his soul until it stretched taut, caught only upon the rough edges of his bones. Here was his dream made real.

Fascination. Obsession. Her running form was perfect, immaculate in its beauty.

Inez zipped around a knot of dead ones with an ease that left him breathless. She rounded on one of the white-dressed runners, scooped him bodily from the ground and, with a wrestler's bravado, broke his back over her knee. Before the body stilled, she buried her face in his neck.

Her eyes and cheeks shimmered red in the fireworks, her grinning teeth obscenely bright. Tossing the body away, she charged another runner. He swerved, but her speed caught him anyway. With the haughty disdain of a matador, she lashed out, catching the youngster beneath the chin. He slammed heavily into the packed earth.

Inez's pointed fingers drove into his gut, deeper than Vincent thought possible. The boy shrieked as she jerked a writhing, wet mass from his insides up to her mouth.

"She's the finest runner Ladera has ever known," Del Castillo said proudly. "But we can't go on losing our best young men." His hand slammed into Vincent's back, forcing him off the edge.

Something alarmingly brittle broke his fall, then gripped his leg. Vincent blinked at the empty sockets of the dead man staring at him, jerked his leg from his grip even as jaws opened. Vincent found a strength that would have won the Boston Marathon, or even the Peachtree. Rolling to his feet, he searched for Inez but she'd already seen him.

Her stride lengthened as she bore down on him, her arms piston pumping with no rise and fall to her chest. She too wore white, the dress in tattered streaks flailing behind her. Her eyes had been plucked from a steel furnace.

Vincent dashed to the side; her fingers hissed along his right sleeve. She swerved easily, the beauty of her form so mesmerizing it hurt to look away.

Vincent fled, the whisper of her footfalls louder in his mind than the flaring fireworks. He darted back down the street, shrugging through the clawing hands of nameless, faceless shadows. His breath roared in his ears and his heart fought to hammer its way out of his chest.

A prickling along his spine, like the way his groin felt a heartbeat before an erection, told him she was right on his heels. Vincent sprinted, turning at the last minute to avoid another living runner, and dashed up the street.

"Eyaah!" the young man screamed behind him.

Whirling, he realized it was Ernesto, now in festival garb, pushing with both hands against Inez's face. Vincent pivoted, for the first time daring to touch her. Gripping her arm, he spun her to the side and she released Ernesto.

"Gringo." Ernesto glared at him.

Vincent gazed back and grinned. "Slowpoke."

"Perhaps my grandmother is wrong about you." Ernesto raced away. Inez wiped an earth-stained sleeve across her bloody mouth and charged.

Vincent had never run so fast, not even during his personal best at New York. His feet hurtled down, lifting in the same instant; the street skimmed beneath him.

She followed.

"To the fountain!" Del Castillo's shouted as they passed the hotel. "Quickly now!"

He'd almost forgotten. Vincent wove through the clusters of dead, dashing around other runners, focusing his gaze on Father Hildago and the fountain waters, now strangely dark in the moonlight. All he had to do was get her to the fountain.

A hundred yards away and all uphill. Vincent's legs burned now, his hands growing numb as they pumped, and there wasn't enough air in all Mexico to fill his lungs. Red swirls hazed his vision, but her hand grazed his shoulder. He thrust his torso forward, knees lifting higher, and poured it on.

Fifty yards. . . . Thirty. . . .

Something white flashed to Vincent's right. Unwilling to lose focus, it wasn't until Señora Del Castillo caught the corner of his eye that his head turned.

"This time you'll run no more," the old woman screeched; something dark swung in her hands. It thwacked into his gut—a baseball bat. His stomach wrapped around it, tying him in a knot. He tried to puke and breathe at the same time while toppling face forward to smack the road.

Inez tripped over his leg and sprawled. Rising, she glared at him, thick welts of black hair falling across her mummified cheeks. Then her eyes found the señora.

"*Madre de Dios*," the old woman muttered, the baseball bat clutched like a talisman. "Don't let me miss this time."

She strode forward and swung again, the bat tip so close to Inez's head that it swept the dead woman's hair into a long shadowy slash.

Inez shrieked, a keening that shot spikes through Vincent's ears. She charged the old woman headlong, sinking down on her, pinning the señora's arms with her knees.

Clutching his stomach, Vincent stumbled up. As Inez

lifted her fingers toward the old woman's face, he could do nothing more than fall on her. Somehow, that knocked her off the señora.

A low growl rattled from Inez's throat. Grabbing a handful of his hair, she jerked him close. He clutched her arm, but her strength nearly broke his fingers. Opening her mouth, she pushed back on his head, exposing his throat.

"Hold on, my boy!" Father Hildago appeared over the top of her head. Something splashed across Vincent's face, stinging his eyes. A salty, iron taste filled his mouth; redness dripped down Inez's pinched cheeks.

The dead woman blinked and licked her lips.

"Here." Father Hildago thrust a white cup into her hands. "You must be thirsty, Señora."

Inez brought the cup to her lips; blood sloshed down her chin as she gulped. Emptying the cup, she looked up at the padre, the crimson glare gone from her eyes, replaced by a haunting, dark brown.

"*¡Buenas tardes!*" she said, her voice an exotically low contralto.

Vincent flinched when she reached for his arm, but all she did was help him up. They stood next to the fountain. He had made it, thanks to the padre.

Other dead had reached the fountain, as well. One stumbled down to push his face into the water—except it wasn't water, Vincent realized, but blood. When the creature's head lifted, Vincent watched, open-mouthed, as life came into the dead man's features.

"You're a foreigner, no?" Inez pulled Vincent's gaze back to her. Raven hair swirled around her shoulders; slightly sunken, her cheeks took on a delicate beauty.

"And he's not for you." Señora Del Castillo came closer. "Go back to your crypt, whore." From beneath her shawl an ancient revolver appeared.

Lifting the gun in her tiny hands, Juana Del Castillo let loose a burst of Spanish so loudly intense that it brought Father Hildago between the two women.

Vincent stood transfixed; he'd understood every word. He licked his lips, the taste of blood still in his mouth. Had the fountain's blood changed him in some way?

"You can't, Juana." The elderly priest shook his head. "You can't kill the dead and you can't kill fate. It's time for this feud to end."

"Feud?" Vincent asked, and grinned when it came out, "*Enemistad?*"

"But I can kill you, Padre." Señora Del Castillo cocked the revolver. "You and my husband keep the festival going. If no one transmutes the fountain, the dead will stay dead, and my bitch of a sister can take her rightful place in Hell."

"Juana, don't you dare." Señor Del Castillo limped toward them.

"My betrothed!" Inez wrapped her arms around Señor Del Castillo. She kissed his cheek and rested her head upon the old man's shoulder. "If only you'd left with me when I begged you to."

"My heart has always been in this place." Del Castillo shook his head, chest swelling as he glanced around at the village. "You knew that, Inez."

Juana Del Castillo pointed the gun at the dead woman. "God served you well for your blatant ways."

Señor Del Castillo gently disengaged himself from Inez and faced his wife. "Not God, but Fate, Juana. I loved you both." His hands spread. "Sometimes one cannot help such things."

"Liar!" Juana shrilled. "You make excuses for your lust. And the padre absolves you of such things simply because you're men. You think I don't know? The secrets the dead bring me, the secrets from all those Inez has killed, tell me this is so." The revolver cracked, the sound lost beneath the fireworks and music.

Father Hildago lifted his hands. Señor Del Castillo flinched away. Vincent was never certain who the shot was meant for. Someone pushed him forward.

Like a million baseball bats at once, the force of the bullet launched him backward. Vincent slammed into Inez. He careened off Father Hildago, tumbling over the low stone edge into the fountain. He flailed, hands fumbling before he sank beneath the crimson ripples.

Ungodly deep, his hands and feet found nothing, the agony in his chest blotting everything but the sensation of depth. Abruptly stone took form beneath him. He wanted to cough but couldn't. Mouth full of blood, he staggered up. Miraculously his chest didn't hurt, but his head did. Secrets tumbled through his mind, secrets that weren't there before.

Señor Del Castillo struggled with his wife. A pallid-faced padre sat on the ground holding his leg, watching. Inez stood nearby, gaze rapt upon the Del Castillos, grinning in ecstasy as the two fought. The revolver lay on the ground.

Vincent staggered out of the fountain and picked up the gun. Drenched in blood as he was, it was impossible to tell how badly he was hurt. He lifted the revolver overhead and fired. The Del Castillos leaped away from each other to face him. Inez whirled, and he pointed the weapon at her.

"You pushed me," Vincent said.

"So what if I did?" Inez shrugged, still smiling. "You're a gringo. You had no business butting in."

"He couldn't help it," Señor Del Castillo said while gasping for breath. "His fate drew him here."

"Not his fate." Juana placed her hands on her hips. "You bewitched him, Inez. It was all your evil doing."

"No." Vincent swung the gun toward Señor Del Castillo. "I remember now, seeing you in Matamoros with Ernesto last year. You had him tamper with my car. You used the tricks learned from the dead over the years to lure me here."

"That's . . . that's absurd." Del Castillo stepped back. "There's no way you could know that."

"Fool!" Father Hildago climbed to his feet. "It's the wisdom of the dead turned back upon us. Can't you see? Señor Walterson is dead!"

The shocking truth of the padre's words rattled through Vincent. His finger twitched, levering back the revolver's hammer.

"Get some jugs," he ordered the padre. "As many as you can find." The old priest nodded hastily and hurried toward the chapel. Vincent turned to Del Castillo. "Find me a car, a fast one."

"But there are no cars in Ladera," the old man said.

"Liar. Ernesto owns one. Bring it here."

"What if I don't?" Del Castillo asked.

"I'll lock you both in the crypt with only a jug of blood. You can learn the secrets of the dead firsthand." Vincent laughed. "You and your wife will spend eternity at each other's throats."

The old man grew pale. Eyes downcast, he hurried away.

"I tried to warn you." Señora Del Castillo hobbled over to sit heavily on the fountain's edge. "If only you'd listened. . . ."

"If only you were a better shot," Vincent replied. The padre came out of the chapel, arms laden with plastic jugs. "Now, everyone," the American said, "fill the jugs from the fountain."

Three sets of dark eyes bored into him, but they obeyed. Vincent grinned. He would end this mess. By the time the jugs were filled, Señor Del Castillo rumbled up in a black and red Chevy so ancient it still had fins.

"That's the best I can do." Del Castillo eyed the blood pooling around Vincent's running shoes.

"Load up the jugs," Vincent ordered.

"The blood won't last." Father Hildago stared at him. "When dawn comes it will turn back to water."

"Then put them in the trunk." Vincent turned to the priest. "In the dark it will last as long as it lasts. Besides, there are other sources."

Hildago's eyes grew wide.

"He's right." Inez nodded, slamming the trunk closed. "Even Rufino knows this. That was part of your plan, no? To have the gringo lure me away?"

Señor Del Castillo refused to look at them.

"He could only hope." Vincent turned to the woman who'd haunted his dreams. "But no power that he could command, no old man's scheming, could have forged the feelings I have for you. Come with me, *Magnífica Criatura*. We'll run the nights until the blood is gone. And you'll achieve the fate meant for you, not die in this stupid little town."

"Perhaps you're not such a bad sort." Inez smiled back at him; her cheeks glowed as she climbed into the car. Vincent slid in beside her and gestured to the others with a sweep of the gun. "There's no need for us to return. Unless, of course, you continue the festival. Father Hildago, should you ever transmute the fountain again, we will know and we will come back. Ask the others, ask the dead. Their answer will be the last secret they give up to you."

Somewhere the mariachi band broke into "*Himno Nacional Mexicani.*" Fireworks lit the village; the dead sipped transmuted blood from white Styrofoam cups, whispering their wisdom to the living. A rocket's bursting blossoms reflected the ghostly flickering of something that should have been mountains but weren't quite.

"*Mucho gracias,*" Vincent murmured, staring up at a great face of stone and shadow that only those who drank from the fountain might see. In the running of the dead, in his own death, he'd found something worthwhile. Not his old life, but surely a fate wilder than anything but his dreams.

Grinning at Inez, Vincent gunned the engine. Both the living and the dead sprang from the road as he roared out into the darkness.

ELECTRIC JESUS
AND THE LIVING DEAD
JEREMY ZOSS

Staring at the soft blue glow of Electric Jesus, Lawrence Schwarzenbach wondered how much longer he had to live. The windows and doors of his small house were all boarded up and barricaded, but he knew that the living dead would smash through those defenses eventually. He could hear them banging on the walls, scratching at the windows with their ragged fingernails. They moaned, and chewed at the siding. It wouldn't be long until they found a way in.

Three days ago, zombies were one of the few problems Lawrence didn't have. Now, none of his other troubles even mattered. He would gladly trade his zombie problem for all the previous crises in his lonely teenage life. An acne-scarred, overweight sixteen-year-old, he spent most of his time alone in his room, listening to bad metal music and thumbing through *Hustler*. When he tired of staring at the airbrushed, silicon-enhanced beauties and touching himself, he moved his two hundred pound frame over to his computer desk and focused on his collection of ultra-violent video games. He'd sit for hours, the pale blue light of his monitor washing over his pasty complexion and reflecting off his short, greasy hair as he blasted computerized foes into oblivion.

Now, with a horde of the living dead trying to pound their way into the shabby one-story house he shared with his mother, Lawrence wished he could smite his real-life foes as easily. Yet, he had none of the elaborate weaponry his digital counterparts carried. He had nothing special to strike out with, nothing special to protect him. The only object that offered him any hope at all was Electric Jesus.

Electric Jesus was his mother's favorite knickknack. He stood on top of their ancient console television, radiating a gentle blue light. His foot-tall, plastic-molded form froze Him in a welcoming pose, arms against His tawny brown robes and outstretched, palms upward. His head tilted slightly to His right, and a gentle smile brightened His face. Where the front and back plastic pieces met and formed a seam, a series of small slots allowed light to escape from within—a soft azure glow that emanated from the single neon-blue lightbulb housed inside the plastic Savior.

Lawrence had seen his mother praying to Electric Jesus many times since she first brought Him home from the flea market, years ago. She would get down on her knees, her elephantine belly resting on her thick thighs, and beg for Jesus to help her with her Godless son. Now Lawrence imitated the posture that he had secretly mocked for so long, hoping the statue could provide—something. Anything. He was desperate, and ready to admit it.

He buried his knees deep in the brown shag carpet in front of the TV, the drone of the automated radar weather map seeping from the tinny speakers. He folded his hands together and, with a stained, black Cradle of Filth T-shirt pulled tight across his large belly, Lawrence lifted his voice to heaven.

"Lord," Lawrence said, "I know I never go to church or read the *Bible* or anything, but I could really use your help. I know I told Mom that I didn't even believe in you, but I always sorta did, and I don't really know what else to do. There are zombies outside, and they're trying to get in. And my Mom went out to the store three days ago, and she hasn't come back. I'm afraid they got her."

Lawrence stared at Electric Jesus, waiting for a sign. Tears welled up in his eyes and rolled down his round cheeks.

"Help me, Lord," Lawrence begged, voice wavering. "I ran out of food two days ago. The phones are dead, and the TV and the radio don't have anything on except static and the Weather Channel. I took all the furniture and used it to seal off the doors and the windows, but they're going to get in!"

"And just what do you expect me to do about it?" Lawrence heard a smooth, silky voice say, and he practically fell on his ass.

"Jesus!" Lawrence exclaimed.

"That's my name, tubby, don't wear it out," the voice called back. Lawrence got up off the floor, waddled over to the TV, and stared at the glowing blue figure.

"You can talk?" he asked incredulously, wiping his eyes on the back of his hand.

"I am the son of God, genius," Electric Jesus answered.

"But you're plastic," Lawrence stammered. "You aren't *the* Jesus, are you?"

"You tell me, porky," the voice said, seemingly from somewhere inside the statue, since the lips didn't move.

Lawrence frowned at the figure. "I didn't think Jesus would be so mean."

"Yeah, and I didn't think the next person I appeared to would have every Cannibal Corpse album," Electric Jesus answered.

"Hey!" Lawrence yelled. "I prayed to you for help, and you aren't doing anything but calling me names!"

"You called me, I came. What more do you want?"

"I want some help, goddammit!"

"Watch the blasphemy, piglet."

Lawrence grabbed the plastic statue from atop the TV. Electric Jesus' long cord jerked from the wall and his blue light went dead. The set's console shook and a framed picture on top tumbled to the floor.

"I could smash you to pieces, you know," Lawrence said.

"Who's gonna help you then?" Electric Jesus asked.

"Some help you've been so far."

"Okay," Electric Jesus said. "Make you a deal. Plug me back in, and I'll see what we can do."

"Deal," Lawrence said, and set the statue back down on to the TV. He took the cord and reached down behind the console, plugging Jesus back into the outlet. Electric Jesus' ghostly blue aura returned immediately.

"Aaaaaah. Thanks, kid," Electric Jesus said. "I do love the juice. Have a seat."

Lawrence plopped himself down, cross-legged, in front of the TV just as he had done so many times before. He stared up at Electric Jesus, awaiting instructions.

"So do you need electricity?" Lawrence asked. "'Cause you kept talking when you were unplugged,"

"Naw, I don't really need the juice," Electric Jesus said. "It just . . . relaxes me."

"Well, I don't want you to be *relaxed*!" Lawrence struggled to rise, reaching toward the cord again as he rolled to his protesting knees. "I want you to be alert, 'cause—"

"No!" Electric Jesus shouted. "Don't you unplug me again!"

"You do need it, don't you?" Lawrence asked, shaking his head. "You're not really Jesus. You're . . . something else."

"I don't need it," Electric Jesus protested. "I can quit anytime I want. But it helps me think, so just leave my cord alone!"

"Whatever," Lawrence grumbled.

"And I am really Jesus."

"Fine. Whatever you say."

"All right then. So, what did you say your name was, kid?" Electric Jesus asked.

"Lawrence."

"Hi, Larry. I'm Electric Jesus. Can I call you Larry?"

"I don't really like that much. The kids at school always call me Larry, even though I ask them—"

"That's just swell, Larry," Electric Jesus interrupted. "You got bigger problems right now than what kids call you at school, am I right?"

"Yeah, I guess so."

"Well, Larry, what's going on? What's the situation? Where are we?"

"You're Jesus. Don't you know?"

"Hey, I just got here. Fill me in."

"OK, here's what's going on," Lawrence said, wiping his sweaty palms on his chest. "A few days ago, I was sitting in my room playing video games, and my Mom comes in and says that we were all out of food, so she was gonna go down the street to the store to get some donuts. I told her to get me some jelly ones and I went back to playing my game. A few hours went by, and I noticed she wasn't back yet. So I went and looked outside, and I noticed that there wasn't a single person around. I thought it was weird, but no big deal. So I came inside and turned on the TV."

"I'm gonna guess that you do that a lot," Electric Jesus snorted.

Lawrence ignored the comment and resumed his story. "Every channel had on a news report about how people were being attacked by maniacs, and everyone should stay inside. I figured my Mom might be holed up at the store, so I got out the phone book and called. Nobody answered. I waited and tried again. More than once. No answer, and she never came back."

Lawrence's story was interrupted by a loud crash from outside. He froze, and waited for some further indication of the zombie hoard's status. After a few moments of relative calm, he continued.

"So, the next day, I turned on the news again. This time, all the different stations were saying that the maniacs were actually zombies, that dead people were coming back to life and attacking the living."

"Hmm. People coming back from the grave," Electric Jesus mumbled. "Never heard of that one happening before."

"Huh?" Lawrence asked.

"Oh, nothing. Continue with your fascinating story."

"All right. So on TV they were saying people were coming back to life. I wouldn't have really believed it, except they had footage of these dead people walking around. They looked just like they did in all the zombie movies I've seen. They moved around all slow, and looked all rotted and gross. But they looked real. A few hours later, a couple of the channels went dead, so did the phones. I got real scared, and so I started to board up the windows. While I was nailing a shelf to the big window that looks out over the street, I saw my first zombie close up. He was some old guy who used to live up the street. He was all yellow looking. His eyes were really black, and he wandered around like he was lost, dragging one leg behind him. I saw him, and I knew he was one of them. I boarded up the window before he could see me."

"You sure he wasn't just some guy whacked out on crack?" Electric Jesus asked.

"I doubt it. When I was boarding up the rest of the windows, I saw more and more of them. They started to gather into groups and now they're moving around together, like a pack of animals. I got the whole house sealed off, and even planned an escape route. If they get in, I'll run through the door to the garage and get into my Mom's car. Hopefully, the automatic garage door opener still works, and I'll back out and drive away." Lawrence bowed his head and muttered into the shag, "Too bad I don't know where I'll go."

"Where are we now?"

"Las Vegas," Lawrence said.

"Great," Electric Jesus groaned. "I'm in the one place on the planet where a zombie infestation is an improvement."

"It's not that bad," Lawrence offered weakly.

"Yeah, and crucifixion is just a little uncomfortable."

"Can I get back to my story now?" Lawrence asked, furrowing his brow.

"Whatever works for you, pal," Electric Jesus said, though not at all facetiously. If Lawrence hadn't been so preoccupied, he might have caught the significance of that.

"Now, where were we?" the young man mused, a bit pompously; it wasn't every day he had Jesus for an audience. "Oh, yeah. So today the zombies started crowding around the house, trying to get in—you can still hear them pounding on the walls—but I didn't know what to do. I mean, I don't have a gun or anything. And none of the TV stations except for the Weather Channel were coming in, and for some reason they aren't even saying anything about the zombies. So I prayed. Just like Mom would have done."

"And this is where I come in," said Electric Jesus brightly.

"Yeah. So are you gonna help me or not?"

"I guess I'll try—although I'm not all that happy about it," Electric Jesus grumbled.

"Why?" Larry snapped, fat face red with anger. "Aren't I good enough to help?"

"Well, your Mom prayed to me a lot, and she always asked for me to help you find religion. There are a lot of people out there that need my help, Larry. People who go to church. You didn't even believe in me until this whole zombie thing started, but you want me to ignore all my faithful flock and help you?"

Lawrence looked down at his stumpy fingers as he picked absently at the fraying shag of the carpet. "Then why did you come here?"

"Because I promised your Mom I would," Electric Jesus sighed. "You might have had your problems with her, but she was a good Christian woman at heart, and only wanted the best for you."

"Yeah, well then why did she leave me here at home with nothing but Twinkies to eat so many times, huh?" Lawrence asked, looking up at the statue. "How come she let me get so fat? How come I turned out to be such a loser, if she's such a great Mom?"

"I didn't say she was mother of the year, or anything," Electric Jesus said. "But she did love you."

"Well, I don't love her," Lawrence hissed.

"Honor thy Father and Mother, Larry," Electric Jesus scolded. "Besides, you said you were worried when she never came home from the store."

"Shut up," Lawrence said, wiping his nose on his bare arm. "I don't want to talk about this. Like you said, I have other things to worry about."

"Yeah, you do," Electric Jesus said. "Hear that?"

The pounding outside the house was growing louder.

"So what should we do?"

Electric Jesus yawned. "I don't have a clue."

"What?" Lawrence yelped, on his feet faster than he—or anyone else—would have though possible. "You said you'd help me!"

"Before we go on with this, Larry," Electric Jesus said calmly, "you really should think for a moment about the con-versation you're having. Have you considered the possibility that you are hallucinating right now?"

"You mean . . . you're not really talking to me?"

"You tell me. You said yourself that you have no food left. I can't imagine you've been sleeping well. You're scared and freaked out. . . . Your mind may be playing tricks on you."

Lawrence slouched as a fresh wave of despair washed over him. "So . . . you're not real."

"Does it really matter?"

The quick, calm answer made Lawrence square his shoulders again, as much as they ever were squared, anyway. "I guess it doesn't matter." A sly smile went creeping across his face. "In fact, that would explain why you were such a prick. The real Jesus wouldn't act like that."

"If I am a hallucination, then everything I'm saying comes from you. Low self-esteem, Larry?"

"Any reason I should have *high* self-esteem? Look at me!" Larry tilted his head down toward his protruding belly.

"Well, you survived this long. That's more than a lot of people have done."

"That's true," he admitted. "I guess I have that going for me."

"Right on, big boy!" Electric Jesus exclaimed.

"So what should we do?" Lawrence asked.

"Well, partner," Electric Jesus said. "I think we should amscray on out of here. You must smell like a pig sweating gravy to those things out there. And let's face it, there's a lot of you to go around. As soon as they break in, you're a full-course Thanksgiving dinner"

"Where should we go?"

"Anywhere but here. We'll go find us some nice gals and repopulate the world."

"Even if I was the last guy on earth, I doubt I could score."

"There's that self-esteem issue again," chided Electric Jesus, this time more kindly. "But let's focus on the problem at hand. How does one survive an attack by the living dead when your only ally is a talking statue?"

"I was hoping you'd have an answer for that question," Lawrence said.

"Never fear. We'll figure something out. Now let's—"

A loud, nearby crash interrupted Electric Jesus. At the sound, Lawrence turned a shade paler and his eyes widened. "It's them!" he exclaimed. "They're going to get in!"

"They smell bacon, piglet," Electric Jesus said.

"Shut up and help me!" Lawrence yelled.

A second crash followed the first. The sound of wood groaning rolled in from one of the bedrooms.

"What do you want me to do? I'm plugged into the wall here!"

"Do something!"

"Abracadabra," Electric Jesus bellowed, "zombies go away!"

Yet the pounding continued. The sound of glass shattering filled the air, followed by the crack of splintering wood.

"They're coming through the kitchen window!" Lawrence shrieked.

"Time to get out of here, Larry," Electric Jesus said. As if to prove his point, there was a dull thud in the kitchen, followed by a series of hungry moans.

"One of them is inside!" Lawrence said, trembling at the shadow moving closer to the kitchen door.

"You gotta make your way to the garage, Larry," Electric Jesus said. "You got the car keys?"

"Y-Yeah," Lawrence stammered as he patted his pockets. "I got 'em, but where will I go?"

"I don't know, but you'd better decide quick," Electric Jesus said. "Look."

Lawrence turned to see a rotten-looking thing shamble into the TV room. Its head was cocked to one side and it held a limp left hand close to its chest. The creature's dark eyes widened as soon as they took in Lawrence, and it staggered toward him, moaning.

Lawrence backpedaled until his butt pressed against the old TV. The zombie continued forward, and soon was upon him. The young man screamed as the zombie's clammy hands pawed at him. The dead man leaned in, jaws working furiously, trying to take a chunk out of the fat face before it. Lawrence jammed his forearm across the zombie's neck to hold it off. The creature snapped at the air in front of Lawrence's nose, and the hot smell of rotting meat escaped from its throat.

"Hit it with something!" Electric Jesus shouted.

Lawrence's left hand shot out behind him and groped at the top of the television. As soon as he connected with an object, he grabbed it and pulled it to him.

He raised Electric Jesus high above his head and brought Him crashing down on the zombie's skull. The statue's hand pierced the dead man's head and stuck. Electric Jesus let out a disgusted cry. The zombie moaned louder as Lawrence pulled the statute free and clubbed the creature again. It groaned and released its grip, falling to its knees. As the creature kneeled before him, Lawrence battered it with Electric Jesus until its skull opened wide, spilling the dark mess inside onto the dingy brown carpet.

The zombie had no sooner hit the floor than Lawrence shot out off the room, Electric Jesus still in hand. As fast as his thick legs could carry him, he ran down the hallway toward the garage. He hustled through the door and slammed it behind him. His mother's car was waiting for him as he had planned. The huge, early-eighties Oldsmobile seemed like a steel savior, come to take Lawrence away from the swarming dead.

"Think you could find the time to wipe the zombie brains off my face?" Electric Jesus said.

"Once we're on the road." Lawrence replied as he opened the driver's side door and got behind the wheel. He flung Electric Jesus on the seat next to him and started the car.

"Got your driver's license, Larry?" Electric Jesus asked.

"Does it matter?" Lawrence hit the electric garage door opener clipped to the sun visor.

"I guess not," Electric Jesus sighed.

The garage door opened and Lawrence began backing out the mammoth car. As he rolled down the driveway, Lawrence saw the swarm of zombies clawing and pounding their way into his house. Somehow they hadn't noticed the huge Oldsmobile pulling slowly away.

"Seatbelts save lives," Electric Jesus noted, and Lawrence dutifully pulled his shoulder strap across his round belly and clicked it in place.

"I meant me," said Electric Jesus.

Lawrence set Him upright on the seat and pulled the lap belt tight across His plastic torso.

"And plug me into the cigarette lighter while you're at it," Electric Jesus added.

"God, you are the pickiest talking statue I ever met," Lawrence grumbled as he attempted to fit the power cord into the socket. The prongs of the cord scraped along the inside of the metal cylinder, but kept slipping out. He gave up trying and angled the car onto the street. Electric Jesus mumbled something in disgust, but Lawrence ignored him.

"Goodbye, Mom," he whispered as he shifted into drive.

"If it wasn't for her, you wouldn't have this car," Electric Jesus said. "Or me." Lawrence nodded solemnly. "So where are we going, Larry?"

"Anywhere but here."

"Then let's get this wagon rolling!"

The car crept down the road in the direction of the setting sun. As they made their way cautiously down the street, Lawrence took in the overturned cars and ransacked houses that had once been his neighborhood.

"I bet this street has seen better days," Electric Jesus commented as the car rolled past a fire hydrant spewing water into the air.

"Yeah," Lawrence said as he brought the car up to speed. "You know, I've never been outside of this town. Too bad it took something like this to get me out."

"Think of it as an important turning point in your life," Electric Jesus offered.

"I think that's the first helpful thing you've said," Lawrence smirked.

"Well, don't get all mushy on me," Electric Jesus scoffed. "We don't exactly have time for male bonding. We still need a place to go."

"The Weather Channel was still broadcasting," Lawrence said. "We'll find out where they're at, and head that way."

"Nice to see you take charge here, Larry," Electric Jesus said. "So, why do you think they're still on the air?"

"I don't know. I'm hoping the zombies haven't gotten that far yet. I mean, they can't be everywhere yet."

"Yeah, I'm really tired of this Lazarus crap. Coming back to life used to be something special. These days, it seems like everybody's doing it."

Lawrence smiled. "But you did it before it was popular."

"Was that a joke?" Electric Jesus asked. "Good one, Larry. I'm glad to see you can get your mind off all this."

"Thanks, but call me Lawrence."

"You got it, pardner," Electric Jesus said as Lawrence guided the car around an overturned Jeep in the middle of the road.

Finally confident that he was at last far enough away from the house that the zombies wouldn't hear the engine revving, Lawrence put his sneaker-clad foot to the floor. He headed toward the highway entrance and away from the only home he had ever known.

"What do you think is out there, Lawrence?" Electric Jesus asked solemnly.

"I don't know," Lawrence said. "Let's find out."

Live People Don't Understand

SCOTT EDELMAN

Everybody knows in their bones that something *is eternal, and that something has to do with humans.*
—*Our Town*, Act III

Emily remembered what it was like to be alive.

In fact, at first, she had forgotten that she was dead. She lay in a coffin, the confines of which she could not yet bring herself to see, and thought herself newly risen from a nap. Gazing upward, she wondered why the familiar ceiling above, the one under which she had shared a marriage bed with her beloved George, had been replaced by stars.

Adding to her puzzle, she sensed other sleepers stretched out nearby. Their presence made her uncomfortable. It had been difficult enough for her to grow accustomed to being a wife, to sleeping with another beside her—she remembered her nervousness on her wedding night and smiled—but to have strangers nearby her as well was more than should be asked of her. Their closeness here did not make sense, but then, dreams on waking often lost their sense, and so she did not let herself worry much about her confusion. She trusted that she would understand soon enough. But then she remembered those who should have been nearby, and all those feelings faded, to be replaced by a greater loneliness than she had ever felt in her life.

If she asked, perhaps these strangers would tell her why George was not at her side—the two of them had yet to spend a night apart, which is exactly as it was supposed to be—and where her newborn baby had gone. She had just had the baby, hadn't she? George, Jr. was four by now, and could cope without her there every moment, but the little one . . . it must be hungry without her there to share her milk. Emily couldn't even remember whether she'd had a boy or a girl—how could that be?—but she knew that she had to find her baby.

She had to find her George.

"Wake up," she shouted. It rattled her to do so, because she was not a person accustomed to shouting. "Oh, you must wake up and talk to me. Where am I? What is this place? Help me, won't you? Help me understand. One moment I was at home in my bed in Grover's Corners, and the next I'm waking from a nap . . . where? Hello? You can't fool me. You're out there, you can hear me, I know it. Stop trying to pretend that you're still asleep. It just won't work, not when I need you so badly."

"Hush," came an old woman's voice to her left. Or at least Emily thought her to be old. The voice sounded vaguely familiar, but Emily could not place it, because the woman's throat was drier and raspier than she remembered it.

"I can't," said Emily. "I won't. Really now, I don't see how you can ask me to be still, not when there are so many unanswered questions."

"Nonetheless, just hush," insisted the woman, and as she continued to speak, Emily realized who she was. "You'll get used to unanswered questions. Soon enough, they'll no longer bother you so much."

"Really now, you shouldn't be talking that way, Mrs. Soames," said Emily, ill at ease at talking so sternly to an elder. "It *is* Mrs. Soames, isn't it? Forgive me for saying so, but there's no need for you to be so rude."

"There's no need to be anything any longer," said Mrs. Soames. "Which is precisely my point. Just settle down and let me be."

"How can you sleep away the day that way?" said Emily. She did not pause to consider what forces could have possibly brought them together at this time. "It's Emily, Mrs. Soames. Remember how much you enjoyed my wedding? You always loved a good party. I remember that about you. How can you just lie there when there is so much out there to live for?"

A rich burst of laughter came from somewhere off to Emily's right. The sound startled her, but gave her no offense. She did not feel that her emotions were being mocked, and remembering back to another who would chuckle with a wisdom Emily had not yet earned, she realized who it was who lay so close beside her, and felt loved and embraced.

"Mrs. Gibbs?" she whispered, stunned to see her mother-in-law there, and yet pleased by her presence.

"Can't you get her to keep quiet?" said Mrs. Soames.

"Don't be so hard on Emily," said Mrs. Gibbs, as the woman's laughter died down. "She's only a child. The two of us had plenty of time to make our peace with what would come here. But she was at the beginning of things. Besides, don't you remember how you felt when you first got here, even with all that preparation? Don't you remember what it was like when you first took your place?"

Emily listened, and listened hard, for the answer meant everything, but there was only a long silence, as if Mrs. Soames was having difficulty remembering how to speak, let alone the moments of her arrival in this place, whatever this place was.

"Vaguely," Mrs. Soames finally said. "Yes. Yes, I *do* remember. Only . . . I don't think I want to remember."

"Well, there you go," said Mrs. Gibbs. "But you weren't always like that, let me tell you. She's young yet, in more ways than one. She can't help but remember."

Emily waited for Mrs. Soames and Mrs. Gibbs to address her again, instead of just bantering amongst themselves, but instead, their conversation petered out, and they fell to silence. Emily called out to them again.

"I think I know where I am," said Emily, astonished. "I'm still dreaming, aren't I?"

"No, dear," said Mrs. Gibbs, her voice sleepy. "All that happened before, up until the time you found yourself here, that was the dream, dear. Let it go."

"I can't." Anguished, she began to cry, but no tears came. She thought to touch her face to find out how it could possibly be that the weeping failed to dampen her cheeks, but her arms would not move, no matter how hard she tried. Struggling like that, the truth of her situation came upon her with a suddenness that was sickening. "I'm dead, aren't I?"

"No need to say it that way," said Mrs. Gibbs. "It's really not so bad. The experience can become quite pleasant after a while, actually. Now you rest, girl."

"Please," said Mrs. Soames.

"I can't!" Emily said, feeling herself grow hysterical. How ridiculous was that, to be dead and hysterical? She refused to be either. George wouldn't want her to be either. "Don't you see? I'll never be able to let go!"

"Enough," said Mrs. Soames. "Someone's coming! Behave!"

"What if it's a thief?" said Emily, made fearful by the sound of unsteady footsteps trudging up the hill. George was supposed to protect her from such things, but now her only comfort was in two old women, and what could they do? "What if he's here to rob us?"

"Don't be silly, girl," said Mrs. Gibbs. "You have nothing more which anyone would wish to steal."

There was so much more that Emily needed to say right

then, but before she could respond further, she sensed her poor dear husband above. George was there, right at the edges of the newly turned dirt of her grave. She was shocked by how much death had distracted her, for until that moment, she had not been aware of his approach. He seemed different to her, though, than when she had seen him last.

"Mrs. Gibbs," she said. "What's happened to your son? He's so . . . old."

"*Tempus fugit*, dear," she said. "You'll learn that soon enough."

"Could I really have been asleep so long?" said Emily. "It must have been years. But he's here! He still remembers us, Mrs. Gibbs."

"That isn't always a good thing, dear. No, not at all. And he's here to see you, not me. Listen."

"Emily," George moaned. He dropped to his knees directly above Emily's head. As he sobbed, she wished she could touch his lined cheek to comfort him, but she could do nothing. "I'm sorry, I'm so sorry."

"You needn't apologize, George. Not you."

She could feel a wrenching in his heart, could feel his essence seeking her out but not being able to find her. Their two hearts had once beat as one, destined for each other from the very start, but now, his lone heart was barely a heart at all. She pleaded for a way to break the barrier that kept them apart, but it was useless. Though he was alive to her, she was dead in all ways to him. His fingers bunched in the wet dirt, pawing it like a soggy blanket that he hoped to pull from across her face.

"No one should have to die in such a horrible way," he said, gasping. "I cannot change that, so I will myself to forget it. But I can't do that either, Emily, no matter how hard I try. Do you forgive me after all these years, Emily? Could you?"

He wanted an answer from her, one that she, in turn, wanted to give, and he listened for words she could not make him hear. But she would forgive him anything, could not recall having ever wavered from such a thought, in part because she knew that he could not possibly do anything that it would actually be necessary for her to forgive, not in a thousand life-times. Not George.

The urgency of his yearning was overpowering, though, and it came back to her then, not all of it, not the details, just enough to know what had delivered her to her final resting place. Her mother had told her during those few times when she'd tried to impart the lesson of womanhood to her, that some women were not built for childbirth. How unfortunate for Emily to have to learn that first hand. But at least . . . at least their baby lived. She had that much to be thankful for. At least she had seen that much before she vanished from her first world and was forced to take her place in the next one.

"Don't blame yourself, George," said Emily. "You need to be strong for our child."

Emily wondered how old their littlest one would be, considering the sprinkling of gray in George's hair, and wanted to ask him, but he would not have heard, had heard none of it up until then. Feeling his pleas unanswered, he fell forward, and sobbed into the dirt, his cheek pressed so close to her that she could almost feel his breath.

"I shouldn't have done it," he said. "I know that. I even knew it then. But I was a coward. And I'll keep paying for that until the day I die."

George stood suddenly, and shook off his raw emotions as easily as he slapped the dirt off his knees. She felt her window on him closing down to be replaced by the face that he let the world see.

"I'll try to forget you," he said, a coldness to his voice. "With enough time, perhaps I could do that. But I doubt I'll ever be able to forget what I did. Goodbye, Emily."

He ran off too quickly, stumbling as he had when he'd arrived. Emily could not hold on to him, so she held on to his words.

"What did he mean?" asked Emily. "He was your son, Mrs. Gibbs. Is your son. Help me understand."

"Better not to know," said Mrs. Gibbs. "Let him just go. Let it all go."

"Should I?" said Emily. "Really? But you know. I can tell. You've figured it out. Why won't you tell me?"

"Because I care about you, dear. You'll be much happier that way."

"Then I'll have to ask Mrs. Soames to help. Mrs. Soames!"

No matter how Emily whined, she could not rouse the woman. She had slipped off to her final sleep. Only Mrs. Gibbs was left, perhaps invigorated by the visit from her son. Emily had no choice but to badger her mother-in-law further.

"But you must tell me what he was talking about," said Emily. "You must! Why was he asking for my forgiveness? He's your son, you know him best. I don't remember him ever doing anything I'd need to forgive! Do you?"

There was a sudden silence, and in that space, months seemed to pass.

"Mrs. Gibbs!"

"Dear?"

"George, Mrs. Gibbs. Tell me about George."

Mrs. Gibbs sighed.

"It's much better that way," said Mrs. Gibbs, "to not remember. I'd rather not think about my son, if you don't mind. And you should do the same."

"No! I could never do that. This is my life—"

"*Was* your life, dear."

"—and I can't let it go as if none of it happened. I need to remember. How sad he was up there! What could have happened to make him so sad? Don't you care? You're his mother!"

With no seeming provocation, Mrs. Soames spoke up.

"If you really must know—" she began.

"Hush!" said Mrs. Gibbs. "Now I'll say it. Hush! Don't tell her any more! It will only bring more pain. She's here to learn to put the pain away, not to pick it up again."

"Tell me what?" said Emily. "I have to know."

"You *can* go back, you know," said Mrs. Soames. "You can go back and see how it was. How it used to be. Others have done it before."

"It isn't a good idea, though," said Mrs. Gibbs softly.

"I'm going to do it anyway!" shouted Emily. "I have to do it! I have to know again, to feel."

"Feelings are overrated, dear," said Mrs. Gibbs. "You'll learn that soon enough, whatever you do. So you might as well take the easy way. Walk around the pain, don't walk through it. That's always the better way."

"I don't care!"

"Oh, give up," said Mrs. Soames. "You're not going to talk her out of it. She's a tough one, all right. The sooner she gets it out of her system, the sooner we'll all manage to get some rest."

"I can see that you're right, Mrs. Soames," said Mrs. Gibbs. "I guess you knew better all along. So go, dear. You won't be able to change anything, you know. That much will always be true. But you'll be able to see. And it will hurt, dear, it will hurt a great deal. Knowing what you know now, how you'll end up, how there's no permanent way back, well, it won't be pretty. Are you sure you want to do this?"

"As long as I can see my Georgie again, see what it's like to be alive, that's all that matters."

"You're braver than I ever was," said Mrs. Gibbs. "And a great deal more foolish. But I knew that when you became a

Gibbs, Emily. No matter. I suspect that you'll feel quite differently when you come back."

"If I can see my George, I'm not coming back. I'm never—"

Before another syllable could pass through her stiff lips, the stars above Emily were replaced by her husband's eyes. There was no strength in them as he looked down at her. She saw only fear.

"What's wrong?" she asked. He was young again, his hair dark, his face smooth. And she was young again herself. She could feel her baby struggling within her to be born. All seemed well with the child—her experience with George, Jr. had taught her so—and there should have been no reason for her husband to be afraid.

"I don't know," he said.

She remembered having done this all before, remembered herself asking, and him answering, just that way the last time, but now, there was a difference. This time, the surface of things revealed the truth beneath. When, in response to her questions about his demeanor, he'd said, "I don't know," she could tell that he was lying. She *knew*.

Emily was stunned by this revelation. George had never lied to her before. But then, shifting her head on the sweat-soaked pillow, she corrected herself. Her worldview was not the same as it had been mere moments before. She now knew that she had only *believed* that George had never lied to her before. Mrs. Gibbs had been right in telling her that she would see things she did not wish to see. And what was worse, though she could watch events unfold, she found that she could not change her words, could not respond using the new information she had earned.

"But everything will be all right, won't it, George?" she said. "The baby—our baby will be all right, won't it? Tell me that the baby will be all right, George."

She already knew what he would say, but still, Emily was distressed when George could find no other words than the words he had spoken before.

"I don't know," he repeated.

Emily lay in the bedroom in which she'd expected to be when she instead woke to find herself in her grave. She could see all the possessions that once were hers, and the happiness at seeing them brought tears welling up, but because she could change nothing about this scene, they were tears from the pain of childbirth that her new self only interpreted as joyous. She was happy to feel them wet her cheeks as they could not do before, to know life again, but that joy did not stay long, for she could also see the bedroom as if from above, as if she'd lifted the top off a doll's house to peer down. And so when George turned his back on her in her pain, Emily could see that his action was not entirely motivated because he was overcome with grief, though that is what her earthly self would have thought, *had* thought years before. With the eyes in her body, she could see George reaching to the end table for a glass of water, but with God's eyes, with the sight she had been given, she could see through him and around him and beyond him to the other side, watch helplessly as he slipped a small vial from his shirt pocket and tilted its clear contents into her drink.

"Here," he said, his voice leaden, and this time she knew that it was not so in a tone of concern. "This should make you feel better."

He held the glass to her lips, and as the liquid touched her tongue, the emotions that barreled through her grew even more grotesquely twin. Her living self, the one that knew of nothing but the living, and thought the dead were impossibly far away, was relieved to feel George's left hand at the back of her head, comforting her, urging her to drink deeply. She was loved. She was protected. Her new self, the one with the blinders of life burned away, saw things with sudden clarity as they really were, saw into George, and could see the panic there in him. She knew him then as a wife should never know her husband. He did not want this child, had not even wanted their first child, was not entirely sure that he had ever really wanted her at all. He had always felt himself trapped by his snap decision to stay in Grover's Corners. It had all become too much for him.

And so with trembling fingers he held the poison to her lips. He planned to tell his family and friends that she had died in childbirth. They would be surprised, but would not disbelieve. After all, such things were not so unusual. It was known to happen from time to time, just as her mother had warned her.

But Emily had never figured it would happen to her.

And truth to tell, it hadn't happened. But only he would ever know. George, and now, most unexpectedly, Emily as well.

She drank deeply, and soon felt the movements of her baby slow, and realized that she had been wrong, that it, too, had died, and as she began to sleep for what was meant to be the final time, she looked into her husband's eyes and thought, with knowledge of the grave and with complete sincerity, *Poor, poor George.*

And then her husband was gone, her baby was gone, and she was back on the hill under an open sky, where she was meant to be boiled down to her essence in preparation for the world to come.

"I'm going back," she said, to no one in particular. The stars had no answer, but at least one of her neighbors did.

"Is that you, Emily? Still worrying away at the world, I see. Don't you remember? You've already been back."

"Not the way I plan to go back now. You don't know about George, what he's done. I've got to go back for real."

"You can't do that, dear."

"Don't patronize me, Mrs. Gibbs."

"I'm not, dear. It's only that no one has ever gone back that way before."

"I'll do it. Just watch me."

"You know it will only mean more pain. You've learned that much already, haven't you?"

"It doesn't matter," said Emily. "I've got to see my George, see him now, see him and say more to him than the shallow things I said before. After what he's done, I've got to tell him something. Live people don't understand."

"They never will, dear," said Mrs. Gibbs.

"I can't let myself believe that. George will be different. George will understand. I'll make him understand."

"You can't *make* the living do anything."

"It doesn't matter. George will listen to me. I know he will."

"Oh, my boy will listen all right. But you're not the pretty girl you once were. If you go before him as you are now, and he sees you again, like this, he'll have to listen. You'll certainly get his attention. The true question is, will he *hear*?"

"I'll make him hear," said Emily, with the confidence possessed only by the newly dead. "You watch."

"I don't believe I will, dear. It's terribly tiring staying awake like this for you. I believe I'll rest for a while. And don't worry about the likes of us, dear. We'll still be here when you get back."

Emily listened for the sound of her mother-in-law sleeping, and the sounds of all the others around her who made up the history of Grover's Corners, but there was nothing—no breathing, no snoring, no hint that there was any life there. And in truth, there was not. But Emily refused to sleep the sleep of the dead, not when George was out there, his double crime still a fresh wound in her mind.

All of the strength that had been missing before, when George had wailed above her, coursed through her explosively now. Her hands, which had been tied by invisible bonds, now pushed against and through the flimsy wooden roof of her coffin. Carrying her will before her like a torch, she pierced the dirt above like a swimmer surfacing after a dive, and found herself on the hillside, looking down at the few distant lights of the town she so loved. She wished she could feel the wind against her face, but could not. Her torn and leathery skin was beyond that now. She looked down at her headstone, looked beneath her name at the dates that insulted her with their brevity.

"I was so young," she said.

"We all were," said Mrs. Gibbs with a final yawn, before turning back to sleep. "Now go do whatever it is you think you have to do."

Emily walked down the gravel roadway up which she had been carried. She remembered that now, remembered it all, though when it had occurred she had still been taking her first brief nap. Along the way she passed so many sleepers, and as she saw them, she felt their presence in a way she never had when as a child she played hide-and-seek among the tombstones. How could she have missed them? She wanted to call out to them all to join her, to return to their loved ones as she was doing, but she knew they would not listen. Unlike Mrs. Gibbs and Mrs. Soames, they were long gone, and would not have responded no matter how loudly Emily called. The part that belonged to the living had been completely burned away, so that all that remained was the eternal.

What she and George had was eternal, too. She would never forget that. And once she reminded George of that fact, he would be unable to forget it either.

She thudded noisily through the home that she and George had once lived in together. Her heart sank to see the clutter that he had allowed to overgrow the place she used to keep so clean. The piles were high and the dust was thick. It was late, and he was surely to bed, and that is where she found him. She sensed no others in the house. Her baby was dead, but where was George, Jr.? Perhaps he was spending the night with a cousin, which was just as well. She wouldn't have wanted him to hear what was to come.

Their half-full marriage bed looked bleak, and even though George was in the bed alone, he was curled as far away as possible from the side Emily had once occupied. He teetered at the edge of the mattress. Emily could not help but pause before the site where she had died. George, as if in his sleep sensing her there, turned fitfully. She spoke his name, but words were not enough to wake him. Her lungs did not seem to house the strength of her limbs, and so her words were but a whisper.

She leaned over to touch a shoulder, and his eyes snapped open.

"Emily," he said. His eyes were still full of fear, but it was not solely of Emily. It was of everything, as if there was no longer a part of the world that did not torment him. And he looked so old! Even older than when she had last seen him. Now his hair was completely white, and his skin was so wrinkled as to match the face she remembered on his grandfather. No wonder George, Jr. was not here; he was long gone to a life of his own.

How much time had passed in slumber? How much life had been lost?

"I'm so sorry, Emily," he said.

"I know that, George," she said, leaving her fingers pressed against him. He did not move, just lay there and studied her with eyes near tears.

"I cannot stop dreaming of you," he said. "Even when I'm awake, I dream of you. How can I ever make you understand, Emily? I can barely understand myself. I was so afraid. I thought I knew how to make my fear go away. But after what I did to you, after what I did to the baby, it only became worse."

"I know that all already, George. I've been given that gift. And that's why I'm here. That's why I've come back. To tell you that there's no reason to be afraid. No reason at all."

He smiled then, and sighed. From the strength of that sigh, it seemed to have been the first one he had allowed himself in a long while.

"Do you really mean that?" he said.

"Yes. Yes, I do, George. Life is wonderful, you see. I want to make sure you understand that."

"I do. I know that now, Emily."

"I'm glad," she said. "I love you, George."

"And I love you, too, Emily," he said, lapsing into sobs. "I'm sorry I never realized that until it was too late."

"It's never too late," said Emily.

And then she killed him.

✛ ✛ ✛

George remembered what it was like to be alive, but the stars above did not surprise him. He was not for a moment fooled that he still remained in such a state. There was no more life in him, and he knew how, and he knew why. He shuddered there in the grave beside his wife.

"It was all so terrible, wasn't it?" he said. "And silly. And pointless. How did we ever bear it, Emily? Emily?"

She was sleeping more deeply now, having done what she needed to do. There was no George out there whose presence in the world of the living kept calling her back.

His cry beside her woke her from her slumber.

"But it was wonderful, too, at times," she said, her voice still soft with the dreams of what would come. "Only we hardly ever knew it."

"If only we could have."

"I don't think that's possible, George, not for live people. That peace and that beauty was beyond us. I love you, George. Now you go back to sleep. Go back to sleep until we are made ready to meet again."

"I can't, Emily. There's something . . . I sense that there's still something out there."

"Don't be silly, George. It's time to wean yourself of all that."

"Wait! Listen!"

There was a shuffling on the rough road coming up the hill toward them, the hill beyond which the town of Grover's Corners had grown nearer to the graveyard. A middle-aged man stood over them, stooped with sorrow, his face achingly familiar to George.

"Why, it's like looking in a mirror," said George. "It's George, Jr., come to visit us. And look at him. How long have I been here?"

"He's far too old to be called junior any more, George. And he's not here to visit us, darling. He's here to visit himself."

"He seems so sad."

"That's because he still thinks of us from time to time. He thinks he lost us both too soon. How sweet."

George looked up at his son and felt the guilt that only the newly dead know.

"I don't want anyone to feel such sadness because of me, Emily. It reminds me of the way I couldn't help but feel about you. Couldn't we—shouldn't we—do something?"

"No, George. It's not the same with children. At least not with our child. His pain is different. It's not our place."

"Are you sure?" said George. "I feel it. I feel it right now. I have that choice. I could come back and free him from that burden. I know I could."

George's fingers twitched as his son shed tears by the

tombstone above them. But before he could lift his arm toward the surface, Emily roused herself from her great slumber and snaked her hand through the mud to lace her fingers through his.

"No, George," she whispered with a yawn. "Let him be. He may be blind, but soon enough, he'll see. Soon enough, one by one, all of them will."

While George was focused on his wife's eternal touch, he realized that his son had stolen away. He did not know how much time had passed. He realized that he had been sleeping. By now, George might even have joined them through the natural coursing of time, though he did not sense his son in the ground nearby.

He called once more to Emily, but this time she did not answer. She had already been weaned of this world for once and always, as he would soon be, too. He looked forward to that moment.

As he felt himself drift back to sleep, maybe for the last time, he studied the swimming stars above. Someone had once told him about stars, how it took the light from them millions of years to get to Earth. It didn't seem possible, even with the promise of what was to come, that time could stretch on that long.

He could no longer feel Emily's fingers wrapped in his own, but he knew in his heart that they were still there. Millions of years. They were hurtling toward him. As the light raced above and the living raced below, George was ready to spend that time exactly where he was.

CONTRIBUTORS' NOTES

C. Dean Andersson's published works of horror include *I Am Dracula, I Am Frankenstein, Buried Screams, Torture Tomb, Raw Pain Max, Fiend, Crimson Kisses*, and *The Lair of Ancient Dreams*. His heroic dark fantasy trilogy about a resurrected Viking warrior woman named Bloodsong—*Warrior Witch, Warrior Rebel*, and *Warrior Beast*—predated *Xena* by ten years, prompting some to call Bloodsong "the original Warrior Princess." Back in print for their fifteenth anniversary, the new editions feature cover paintings by Boris Vallejo. Dean is at work on a continuation of Dracula's autobiography and the new adventures of Bloodsong.

Lana Brown is a middle school teacher in Oklahoma. Her previous jobs include librarian, bookstore manager, and motor home assembler. She has an M.L.I.S. and an M.A. in U.S. History. She has written for college literary magazines and the OSFW newsletter, as well as collaborating on a movie script, as yet unsold. This is her first story published in a professional market.

Warren Brown lives with his wife and daughter in Oklahoma. He has published stories in *Omni, The Best of Omni Fiction, The Magazine of Fantasy and Science Fiction, After Hours, Amazing Stories*, and *Tomorrow*. Two of his stories—"What We Did That Night in the Ruins" and "Mayfly Night"—received honorable mentions in anthologies of the year's best science fiction and best horror. His e-novel, *What Happened in Fool the Eye*, is available at www.ebookomatic.com/brown/. Warren has an M.A. in Modern Letters and an M.L.I.S. He works in telecommunications.

Tobias S. Buckell is a "born Caribbean" SF writer hailing from Grenada (spending some time in the United States and British Virgin Islands) who now lives in Ohio. Some of his often island-flavored work has appeared in such places as *Science Fiction Age, Writers of The Future XVI*, and *Whispers from the Cotton Tree Root* (an anthology of Caribbean Fabulist Fiction edited by Nalo Hopkinson). Tobias is the webmaster for TangentOnline.com, and also maintains a homepage at www.torhyth.com.

Scott Edelman has been the editor-in-chief of *Science Fiction Weekly* (www.scifi.com/sfw), the Internet magazine of news, reviews, and interviews, since October 2000. Prior to this, Edelman was also the creator and only editor of the award-winning *Science Fiction Age* magazine. He was also the editor of *Sci-Fi Entertainment*, the official magazine of the Sci Fi Channel, for four years, and has edited other SF media magazines such as *Sci-Fi Universe* and *Sci-Fi Flix*. He has been published in *The Twilight Zone*, *Asimov's*, *Amazing Stories*, and numerous anthologies, including two appearances in *Best New Horror*. He was a Stoker Awards finalist for "A Plague on Both Your Houses." He has been a Hugo Award finalist for Best New Editor on four occasions.

Steve Eller might live in northern Ohio. He's moved so many times he's not certain exactly where he is anymore. His stories have appeared in a variety of magazines and anthologies. He is the editor of the Stoker Award-nominated anthology *Brainbox: The Real Horror*. He is also fiction editor at the Stoker Award-winning *ChiZine*, the electronic magazine of The Chiaroscuro horror community. He is an active member of HWA. Steve resides in a house with other living things, where he plays guitar, consumes spicy food, and cowers before Maynard.

Matt Forbeck has been a full-time writer, editor, and game designer for over twelve years and has around two hundred credits. He co-founded Pinnacle Entertainment with Shane Hensley in 1996 and was president until 1999. His work has been published by Wizards of the Coast, Games Workshop, White Wolf, Image Comics, and many others. Projects Matt has worked on have been nominated for fourteen Origins Awards and won nine. He lives in Beloit, Wisconsin, with his wife, Ann, and their son, Martin. For more information, visit www.fullmoonent.com.

Award-winning writer, game designer, and columnist **Ed Greenwood** has been called the "Canadian author of the great American novel" and "an industry legend." The creator of the Forgotten Realms fantasy world, Ed has published over one hundred books (which have sold millions of copies worldwide, in over a dozen languages) and some six hundred articles and short stories, and co-designed several bestselling computer games. His novels include *Spellfire* and its sequels, the Elminster saga, and the Band of Four series. In real life, Ed is a large, jolly, bearded guy who lives in Ontario, Canada, and likes reading books, books, and more books (which more than fill his farmhouse).

John C. Hay, if asked, will claim he is trying to be a "renaissance man" as opposed to "Jack-of-all-trades, and master of none." He has, in his thirty years, been an anatomist, a nude model, a professional chef, a web designer, and a computer technician. An avid gamer, he was also a contributing writer for Biohazard Games' *Blue Planet*, and helped with *Apocrypha* from Frontiers Design Group. He lives in Columbia, Missouri, with his girlfriend and his iguana. Despite his infatuation with zombies and rumors to the contrary, he has never tasted human flesh.

Jim C. Hines' history is a common one: He started experimenting with science fiction and fantasy during college. Though his habit appeared harmless at first, writing quickly began to occupy more and more of his time. SASE's, old story notes, battered writing guides, and other writing paraphernalia began to appear in his home. The problem grew worse, and his work appeared in *Writers of the Future XV*, *Marion Zimmer Bradley's Fantasy Magazine*, and *Speculations*, among others. Jim lives in Michigan, where he's currently working on an urban fantasy novel and a rape awareness script for TV. Friends and family have given up hope.

Daniel Ksenych is the assistant manager of Putting It Together Productions, a community arts studio. He has written short fiction for a number of online magazines including *PlanetMag*, *QuantumMuse*, *EOTU Magazine*, *The Online Reader*, and *Opi8*, as well as contributing to various supplements for Atlas Games' Unknown Armies. Daniel has recently completed his first novel, *Mana-Junkies*.

Gregory G. Kurczynski lives in southwest Florida, where he spends his spare time writing dark fiction, reading, watching old horror movies, and frightening himself with his atrocious golf skills. He has several short stories to his credit, including "Mark836," recently published online at www.tailtellers.com. Gregory can be contacted by e-mail through his website, which can be found at www.gravethoughts.com.

Michael Laimo's first novel, *Atmosphere*, is forthcoming in paperback from Leisure in August 2002. He's published a hardcover collection, *Demons, Freaks, and Other Abnormalities*, with Delirium Books, and two chapbooks, *Within the Darkness, Golden Eyes* from Flesh and Blood Press, and *The Twilight Garden* from Miranda-Jahya. His work can be found in many anthologies and magazines, including *The Best of Horrorfind*, *The Dead Inn*, *Dark Whispers*, and *The Edge*, with stories soon to appear in *The Year's Best Dark Fantasy*, *Redsine*, and *Screams and Shadows*. October 2001 will see the publication of his second collection, *Dregs of Society*, in limited edition hardcover, from PRIME. He serves as associate editor for *Space & Time*, and fiction editor for *Bloodtype*, a hardcore horror anthology from Lone Wolf Publications. His website is at www.laimo.com. E-mail: Michael@Laimo.com.

Robin D. Laws' novels are *Pierced Heart* and *The Rough and the Smooth,* both from Trident, Inc. A third novel, tentatively titled *A Promise of Thunder,* is on its way from Issaries, Inc. Robin designs games for a living. No, not those computer-type games—the old fashioned roleplaying kind. His designs include *Feng Shui, Pantheon and Other Roleplaying Games*, and *The Dying Earth*, a game based on the classic fantasy stories of Jack Vance. He is also a contributing editor to *Dragon Magazine*. Robin lives in the beautiful city of Toronto, where he attends movies, visits galleries, and videotapes squirrels.

Kenneth Lightner is a partner and the last remaining original founder of Holistic Design. Along with co-writing a couple of the Fading Suns books, he was the lead designer and programmer of *Final Liberation*, *Epic Warhammer 40K*, and is the co-designer of the *Noble Armada* miniature game. Ken has programmed and co-designed seven successful computer strategy games, including *Emperor of the Fading Suns*, *Hammer of the Gods*, *Battles of Destiny*, and strategy game of the year, *Machiavelli the Prince*.

James Lowder has worked extensively in fantasy and horror fiction on both sides of the editorial blotter. He's authored several bestselling dark fantasy novels, including *Prince of Lies* and *Spectre of the Black Rose* (the latter with Voronica Whitney-Robinson), and short fiction for such diverse anthologies as *Historical Hauntings*, *Truth Until Paradox*, and *Realms of Mystery*. His credits as anthologist include *Realms of Valor*, *The Doom of Camelot*, and *Legends of the Pendragon*. He also serves as executive editor for Green Knight Publishing's line of Arthurian fiction.

Pete D. Manison is a forty-one-year-old native of Houston, Texas. He began writing at the age of fifteen and got his first taste of publication as a finalist in the Writers of the Future Contest in 1989. Since then he has gone on to write stories for *Analog*, *Science Fiction Age*, and many other genre publications. He's recently taken a year off from writing to recharge his batteries and earn money, not necessarily in that order, but plans to return to writing in the near future. "It's been a crazy year," he says. "I should have plenty of new material."

L. H. Maynard & **M. P. N. Sims** have had more than one hundred and fifty stories published, details of which can be found at the website www.maynard-sims.com. They've released two collections, *Shadows At Midnight* (1979, 1999) and *Echoes Of Darkness* (2000). A third, *Incantations*, has been accepted. "Moths," a new novella, is due out in United States in 2001, as are two additional collections, *The Secret Geography of Nightmare* and *Selling Dark Miracles*. They edit *Darkness Rising* and, as publishers, run Enigmatic Press in the UK, which produced *Enigmatic Tales* and related titles. A new collection, *The Business Of Barbarians*, is currently in the works, as is a novel, *Falling into Heaven*.

Mark McLaughlin's fiction and poetry have appeared in more than three hundred magazines, anthologies, and websites. These include *Galaxy*, *Talebones*, *Ghosts & Scholars*, *Masters of Terror*,

Terror Tales, 100 Wicked Little Witch Stories, The Last Continent: New Tales Of Zothique, Bending The Landscape, The Best of Palace Corbie, and *The Year's Best Horror Stories* (DAW Books). His currently available fiction collections include *ZOM BEE MOO VEE, I Gave At The Orifice,* and *Shoggoth Cacciatore.* Mark also serves as the editor of *The Urbanite: Surreal & Lively & Bizarre.*

Christine Morgan is a long-time gamer who divides her writing time between fantasy and horror. As a result, she and her husband are raising a daughter who knows more monster-lore than any grade-schooler should. Christine's current projects include the ElfLore books (follow-up to her self-published MageLore trilogy) and a series of novels set in northern California. She works as a counselor in the mental health field and has grown accustomed to the well-meaning foibles of social service that gave her the inspiration for "Dawn of the Living-Impaired," her first published short story.

Having published over thirty short stories in the science fiction, fantasy, and horror genres, **Joe Murphy** feels he has finally achieved his goal of becoming a professional writer. His work has appeared in *Age of Wonders, Altair, Cthulhu's Heirs, Demon Sex, Electric Wine, Legends of the Pendragon, Marion Zimmer Bradley's Fantasy Magazine, Outside, Silver Web, Space and Time, Strange Horizons, Talebones, TransVersions,* and many others. Twelve of his previously published stories are now on the Internet at Alexandria Digital Literature (www.alexlit.com). Joe is a member of SFWA and HWA, as well as a graduate of Clarion West 1995 and Clarion East 2000.

Scott Nicholson's first novel *The Red Church* will be released as a mass market paperback by Pinnacle Books in June 2002. Other books include the story collection *Thank You for the Flowers* and the novella "Transparent Lovers." He has sold more than thirty stories in six countries and won the grand prize in the 1999 Writers of the Future contest. Nicholson's virtual home is www.hauntedcomputer.com.

Scot Noel spent seven years working as a producer of computer games with DreamForge Intertainment, Inc. Among his projects were *Sanitarium* and *Anvil of Dawn,* two Game of the Year award winners. These days he works with his wife, Jane Yeager Noel, at their family business: Computers Made Easy, a training and consulting company. Scot's other fiction includes publication in *Writers of the Future, Tomorrow Magazine,* and numerous small press magazines and computer games. The idea for "On-Line Zombies and Dry-Land Skates" came while playing with Jane's nephew, Tim. Confidently poised on his in-line skates and blessed with his own active imagination, eleven-year-old Tim raised his arms straight out in the classic pose and announced, "Look, I'm a zombie!" Scot immediately headed for the house and anything that would write.

Aaron T. Solomon was born in Kilgore, Texas and is a newcomer to horror fiction. He believes the modern zombie, as social metaphor, has at least the same amount of staying power as Frankenstein or Dracula. "The mindless, flesh-eating monsters of the American zombie story are as powerful as the consumer society they are often used to lampoon," he holds. "Zombies were big with the underground punk scene in which I grew up, where we saw more and more artists ripped apart by the mainstream, and then gobbled up by consumers until nothing remained." Mr. Solomon lives in central Arizona, where he is currently drafting his first novel.

Robert E. Vardeman is the author of forty fantasy novels and eighteen science fiction novels, in addition to another sixty titles ranging from Westerns to action-adventure and mystery novels. Titles include the fantasy *Dark Legacy*, set in the Magic: The Gathering "Dark" era, and the recently published SF novel *Hell Heart*. Recent short fiction includes "Spectral Line" in the *Gothic Ghosts* anthology and, forthcoming this fall, "Feedback" in Al Sarrantonio's Redshift anthology. Vardeman was born in Texas and is a longtime resident of Albuquerque, NM, graduating from the University of New Mexico with B. S. in physics and a M.S. in Materials Engineering. For more information, please surf on over to members.home.net/rvardeman451/

L. J. Washburn, a lifelong Texan and professional author of twenty years standing, has produced many novels and short stories including sagas of the American West and mysteries. Washburn's debut mystery novel, *Wild Night*, which introduced her popular character Lucas Hallam, won both the Private Eye Writers of America Award and the American Mystery Award as Best Paperback Original of 1987. L. J. Washburn lives in Azle, Texas, with her husband, writer James M. Reasoner, and their two daughters.

Jeremy Zoss has been into horror ever since he watched *Psycho* when he was eight, and has worked at his craft as a writer since he was in his early teens. "Electric Jesus and the Living Dead" is his first published story, but it won't be the last. He is a firm believer that horror and humor can coexist, and tries to mingle the two in much of his work. While his tale for this collection is more funny than scary, he hopes it brings a wicked grin to your face.

GOT FLESH?

A New Horror RPG from Eden Studios using CJ Carella's UNISYSTEM

Compatible with the WitchCraft and Armageddon Roleplaying Games

Enter the world of Zombie Survival Horror

NOW AVAILABLE
Ask your local game store retailer
EDN8000 $30.00 (US)

www.allflesh.com